Pr

"Assured, expertly paced, and terribly moving . . . [Simon's] prose is often shimmering, acidly comic and clever. . . . *Pretty Birds* is a pitiless, moving account of people maintaining their dignity, grace and humanity in the face of almost certain destruction." —*The Atlanta Journal-Constitution*

"Powerful . . . intense . . . *Pretty Birds* is a finely crafted, disturbing novel." —*Rocky Mountain News*

"Full of evocative and persuasive detail . . . *Pretty Birds* . . . crackles with the black humor of everyday Sarajevans forced to endure the most absurd—and deadly—of conditions. . . . Reading it, you feel you might begin to understand what it was like to be in Sarajevo, dodging bullets, subsisting on cigarettes and deflecting fate with artful wisecracks." —*Newsday*

"Extraordinary . . . A magnificent tribute, not just to the Sarajevans whose siege Simon reported, but to the indestructible human spirit." —*Kirkus Reviews*

"Accomplished . . . Simon's deeper questions . . . echo Orwell's critique of Gandhi's passivity in the face of Nazi mass murder. When, and on what terms, is it right to wage war?" —*Chicago Tribune*

"Compelling . . . Simon vividly details this heartless siege . . . [with] an ending whose poignance rivals all of Sarajevo's difficult times." —*The Seattle Times*

"Simon launches another brilliant career with his stunning debut novel. . . . [*Pretty Birds*] is rich with details—about the lives of these threatened individuals, their participation in the struggles taking place in this war-torn land. . . . A real page turner." —*The Sanford Herald*

"Fascinating . . . impressive . . . remarkable." —*The Virginian-Pilot*

"Simon . . . puts the events in a war-torn land into human perspective with memorable characters struggling with issues of ethnicity, survival, friendship, and betrayal."
—*Booklist*

"A deeply felt, boldly told story and clean, forceful prose distinguish this striking first novel." —*Publishers Weekly*

"Captures the ugliness and desperation of a bitter war . . . vivid . . . disturbing." —*The Free Lance-Star*

"Authentic, gritty . . . [an] outstanding debut." —*Library Journal*

"Powerful and riveting, Scott Simon's *Pretty Birds* is the best kind of war novel: about the reality of war, day by day, about what it does to the human heart, and about who wins, and what that costs." —Alan Furst

"*Pretty Birds* captures the impossible—the humanity of a teenage girl caught up in the madness and inhumanity of war. Scott Simon is a writer of great power." —Anchee Min, author of *Red Azalea*

PRETTY BIRDS

ALSO BY SCOTT SIMON

Home and Away: Memoir of a Fan
Jackie Robinson and the Integration of Baseball

SCOTT SIMON

PRETTY BIRDS

A Novel

RANDOM HOUSE TRADE PAPERBACKS

NEW YORK

This is a work of fiction. All incidents and dialogue, and all characters with the exception of some well-known historical and public figures, are products of the author's imagination and are not to be construed as real. Where real-life historical or public figures appear, the situations, incidents, and dialogues concerning those persons are entirely fictional and are not intended to depict actual events or to change the entirely fictional nature of the work. In all other respects, any resemblance to persons living or dead is entirely coincidental.

2006 Random House Trade Paperback Edition

Published in the United States by Random House Trade Paperbacks, an imprint of The Random House Publishing Group, a division of Random House, Inc., New York.

RANDOM HOUSE TRADE PAPERBACKS and colophon are trademarks of Random House, Inc.

Originally published in hardcover in the United States by Random House, an imprint of The Random House Publishing Group, a division of Random House, Inc., in 2005.

LIBRARY OF CONGRESS CATALOGING-IN-PUBLICATION DATA

Simon, Scott.

Pretty birds : a novel / Scott Simon.

p. cm.

ISBN 0-8129-7330-5

1. Sarajevo (Bosnia and Hercegovina)—Fiction. 2. Yugoslav War, 1991–1995—Fiction. 3. Women soldiers—Fiction. 4. Teenage girls—Fiction. 5. Muslim girls—Fiction. 6. Snipers—Fiction. I. Title.

PS3619.I5626P74 2005

813'.6—dc22 2004061432

Printed in the United States of America

www.atrandom.com

9 8 7 6 5 4 3 2 1

Title page image by Marcie Jan Bronstein/nonstøck

Book design by Barbara M. Bachman

TO SARAJEVO

THOSE WHO FELL IN HER DEFENSE, AND DEFENDED HER IDEALS

AND TO THE REAL IRENA, AMELA, AND MIRO

AUTHOR'S NOTE

During the siege of Sarajevo, Serbian and Bosnian forces deployed snipers to shoot down into their separate halves of the divided city. Occasionally, these snipers were agile teenage women. It was considered desirable to recruit young women for such service, because this freed up young boys to go into frontline fighting units. Besides, the girls were good. They tended to be slender, lighter, and easier to conceal as they prowled around mountains and the skeletons of bombed-out buildings, looking for positions from which to fire. They were conscientious, careful, and meticulous in ways in which boys of a similar age do not always excel.

I once interviewed a young woman who was a Serbian army sniper. She had blue eyes, and said she preferred to shoot first at people with brown eyes. While I have borrowed a few features of the sniper's work from her, this is not her story. I have also given the names of a few old friends in Sarajevo to some characters in this story. I do this to honor those people who opened their lives to us. But this is a work of fiction, and they should not be confused with the characters who bear similar names.

Our army has surrounded Sarajevo. Our boys and girls and tanks are so thick, not even a bird can get past them!

RADOVAN KARADZIC
BOSNIAN SERB LEADER
INDICTED FOR WAR CRIMES

PRETTY BIRDS

1.
NOVEMBER

1992

IRENA ZARIC PUT HER LAST STICK OF GUM IN HER MOUTH, WINKED at a bird, and wondered where to put her last bullet before going home. Sometimes she conferred with the pigeons that flocked along her arms. "What have you seen, boy? What's going on over there?" The birds were cohorts; they roosted together.

The grim sky was beginning to open into a briny blue. The first winds of the day from the hills blew in with a bite of sun and a smell of snow. It was the time of day when sharp sounds—the scorch of a shot, a scream, a humdrum thud—could be heard best in the hollow streets. After a long night alone in the city's rafters, Irena was consoled by the swish of the pigeons. They reassured her: she wasn't the only one left in town.

The birds were tired and, she imagined, cranky from hunting for tree limbs to settle on. Their feathers clapped in the stillness. People with hatchets and kitchen knives had hacked down most of the city's trees to burn them for heat and cooking fuel. The park across from the old Olympic Stadium, where Irena used to go with boys, now sprouted only grave markers scored with sharp, blunt letters: SLAVICA JANKOVIC 1956–1992. Or BLOND GIRL ON KARLOVACKA AND PROLETARIAT BRIGADE BOULEVARD 27-5 (those who had slashed the graves into the ground last spring never imagined they would have to specify the year, but already a new one was approaching).

The planks offered no leaves or bugs to the birds; no shade or shelter to people. At dawn, the pigeons became like any other hungry citizen of Sarajevo. They settled in the exposed bones of bombed-out buildings, perching on bent and blackened iron rails.

...

WHILE IRENA CROUCHED soundlessly on a scarred concrete landing behind a smashed wall, she could hear the tinny blast of a loudspeaker begin to blare the Knight from just across the line. He was the morning voice the Bosnian Serbs broadcast from Pale, the old mountain resort a dozen miles away, where they had wheeled artillery pieces in among the ski jumps and hot tubs, and declared a capital. Irena heard the first chords of the Clash song the Knight often used to begin his show after a night of pouring mortar fire. *London's burning,* she could make out as the words battered her ears, *all across the town, all across the night.* The Knight's voice crept in over the last lines as the band sang about wind howling through empty blocks and stone.

"That was some night, wasn't it?" he said with a show of wonder. "Over in Novo Sarajevo, Hrasno, and Bistrik. Sexy motherfucker fireworks!" he declared in English. "It looked like *The Terminator*! I don't mean to be ungallant—but my lady and I actually got it on by the blasting lights. Each boom—another boom. I almost cannot keep up with those cannons! Boom, boom. Boom, boom. My lady said to me, 'Is that you, Knight, or the bombs making the earth rumble? Whatever it is, do it again! My ass is yours!' " The Knight seemed to chuckle at unseen companions nearby.

Forty years of turgid state pronouncements had dulled citizens on all sides of the old Yugoslavia to the kind of dreary propaganda that broke into phony, breathless bulletins—"Truly astounding, comrades! A new record for cucumber production!"—between tuneless socialist anthems. Outlandishness had become a new state language, audible in the decrees of Milosevic and Karadzic, Serbian turboprop nationalist rock, and the Knight's morning monologues.

"Are you preparing your breakfasts over there?" the Knight asked solicitously. "We are. I'm getting ready for toast, sausages, and coffee. Fresh eggs and milk. What do you get? Oh yes, I've seen them—those hard beans in plastic sacks from the United Nations. They look like bird turds. Do they taste like bird turds? We've seen you trying to claw each other for bags of those turds in the food lines. Do even birds do that? Besides, you have to soak these bird turds first, which I don't know how you do with all your water turned off. We've seen you guys standing in lines. You have to fill empty plastic detergent bottles with water and run home, just to make a cup of coffee. I'll bet the Frenchies don't have to do that! Ask to take a look inside those cute little white tanks they have. I'll bet they have espresso makers inside."

The Knight sounded disconcertingly tender, almost candied. Irena and other women she knew, including her mother, had tried to imagine what he might look like.

"A sexy voice usually means an old mole," Mrs. Zaric had advised. "It's all they have."

But Irena envisioned a round-shouldered man with curly black hair damp from the shower, a curly-lipped grin studded with a cigarette, and sleepy-lidded cobalt eyes behind curls of smoke—the blue-eyed bad boy who flattered with insolence.

"And what," the Knight continued, "do you make out of that canned American army meat the Yanks have left over from Vietnam? The Yanks send you food that Americans wouldn't give to their dogs. Look at those pictures in American magazines of Americans fluffing up juicy food into their dogs' bowls. Doesn't it look delicious? Wouldn't you just about die for a bowl of American dog food?"

The Knight paused to share another indulgent chuckle.

"Americans love their dogs. Love them more than Muslims, Jews, and Gypsies. Pray to Muhammad that you come back in your next life as an American dog. Leap into their laps! Lick their faces! That's the life!"

One of the first U.N. commanders to come to the city was Indian. He was aghast when he read the English translation of the Knight's routines. The general had gained most of his soldierly experience in his country trying to quell riots that had been inflamed by flowery ethnic harangues.

"Oh, the kid is just a comedian," said Radovan Karadzic, the Bosnian Serb leader with great Chrysler-like swells of silvering hair. "I know him a little. You would enjoy him. Perhaps we'll have a drink sometime, if that doesn't offend Krishna. The Knight—Necko is his real name—is a nervous little wisp. He wears thick black glasses to cover a nervous twitch. Kids like to shock, you know? I am a psychiatrist. I have insight that other political leaders lack.

"Besides, Commander"—and here Dr. Karadzic leaned in, as if confiding something personal—"he doesn't mean *your* Muslims. He means ours. *Turks.* Yours have an ancient, noble history. Ours are descendants of turncoats, who have professed their faith for only a few hundred years, then expect to be treated like the ancient Greeks. I am the only man who should take offense at the Knight. Each of his little monologues takes up time that could be used to read my poetry!"

The commander rather expected a smile to follow. But Karadzic's face stayed stony. The commander was replaced in Sarajevo within a few weeks. The Knight continued his morning recital.

"And what do you do with those slim tubes of condensed French army milk left over from Algeria?" he asked. "They look like toothpaste. Oh, wait—why would you need toothpaste when you have no food, and no water? Civilized people use toothpaste. But all these Muslims swarming into town from the hills squat on the floor to go to the toilet. Hand them a tube of toothpaste and they would probably just squirt it up their ass."

The Knight then took his voice down a notch until it was low and slow.

"Well, Muslims, savor your crumbs. Our boys are coming over to party tonight. While you're in bed, unable to sleep, they will sneak around those young boys and girls and all the old men who are your sentries. Do you think the Frenchies will stop us? They will turn their blue helmets around and face the other way. The United Nations are united in being scared. Serbs are warriors, not faggots. We will track down all the rag-heads, Jew-lovers, and Gypsy whores. We will shake them out of their beds and then take them from behind. Oooh-aaah! Oooh-aaah! They like that! People who squat on their heels to shit must like it up the ass. Our boys will wring your necks like fragile birds. We'll pour your blood into a silver Jew's cup and drink it like plum wine. Tonight, we Serbs will eat roast duck, golden potatoes, and rich red beets," and here, underneath the Knight's voice, she could hear Phil Collins beginning to sing. *She calls out to the man in the street. . . .*

"But we will leave room in our gullets," the Knight went on over the music, drawing out each syllable almost dreamily. "We will leave room for your homes, your jewels, your televisions and cars. Your wives and daughters. Oh, think twice!" he joined in imprecisely with Phil Collins's rasp. "It's just another day in paradise. . . ."

SOMETIMES, IRENA THOUGHT, you have to listen to an awful lot of crap just to get to the music.

A PIGEON FLAPPED onto Irena's head, flexing its claws in the chain stitch of her black ski mask, one-two, one-two, like a disco step. The matchstick-thin pink toenails that she found so exquisitely petite and endearing cut sharply into her scalp, one-two, one-two. Irena cursed the sociability of pigeons as another flapped in.

"Damn birds," she muttered. "Damn pretty birds. Do you think I'm hiding a pile of breadcrumbs?" Beneath her ski mask, a slick of sweat began to sting.

The sky continued to lighten. Irena began to pick out small, inadvertent glints in the dim landscape across the way. She saw a cat drowsing in front of a shade drawn down on a windowsill. A man had lit a candle without realizing the board he had pressed over his doorframe had a crack that let through a splinter of light.

The Miljacka River, which used to tie the city together like a ribbon, now divided it like the edge of a serrated knife. Grbavica apartments looked north over the wiry green river, into the Ottoman-age monuments and minarets on what had become the Bosnian slice of the city: the ruins of the National Library, the old synagogue, the main Serbian church, and the city's central mosque. Apartment buildings in Grbavica had been posh addresses just a few months ago. Officers of the Yugoslav National Army had appropriated many of them (for only Communism, not favoritism, had fallen in Yugoslavia).

But now the national army had been converted—guns, tanks, and officers—into the Bosnian Serb army, which had quickly captured two-thirds of Bosnia. Most army officers and their families saw no need to live like the people they were shooting across the way, crouching below shattered windows in shot-out rooms. Many Serb military families had moved out of range, to country places in the resort towns nearby. But scavengers, thieves, and Serb refugees had come to squat in Grbavica apartment blocks, alongside Serb snipers.

Across the way, Irena observed certain rules. She had been taught a few, and kept a few more for herself. Tedic, her chief, had told her not to shoot at children. The morals were dubious and the publicity devastating. On her own, Irena had determined that she would not shoot at pets. Tedic had instructed her not to shoot at grandmothers, and when she'd wondered if grandfathers were included by the same logic, he had reminded her that Milosevic and Karadzic could have grandchildren.

Tedic had also directed Irena not to shoot at squatters. He said they weren't worth the waste of a bullet, or the risk of revealing herself. Serbs reviled squatters as bothersome bumpkins and pests; their loss would cause no inconvenience or remorse.

"Why should *we* clean out *their* rats' nests?" he asked.

Irena decided that she would not shoot at someone who looked like Sting, the Princess of Wales, or Katarina Witt. She wanted to be able to enjoy looking at their pictures without seeing ghosts. She would not shoot at someone who was already wounded, though she would judge if someone limped because he had truly been wounded or because he had jammed his toe kicking a plugged-up toilet.

Irena knew that Tedic would have a score of sensible objections to each of her rules. What if Serb snipers started tucking puppies under their arms? What if a Serb mortar team carried a little ginger cat as their mascot? Would she shrink from firing at a Serb setting off an artillery piece if he had eyebrows like Katarina Witt? Irena kept her rules in confidence so that she could not be reasoned out of them. She already knew that when the bullets she fired singed the air, they sailed under their own authority.

"TWO FACTS TO keep in mind," Tedic had told Irena when she began work. "*They* are always up. *We* are always down." The Serbs and their heavy guns inhabited the hills. The Bosnians of Sarajevo looked up into those guns from the valley into which their city was tucked—or trapped—along the river.

When Irena looked across into the landscape of windows and balconies where she had once lived, she imagined that she could make out bowls of glistening hard-boiled eggs, glossy brass pots of strong black coffee, and stout platters of fat brown sausages, passed between the dirty hands of brutes.

Sometimes she could steady her sight and see little curlicues of pink or blue petals dappling the family pottery. She imagined what it would be like for a Serb family to sit at their table listening to the Knight. She liked to picture their surprise when a loud snap smacked through their window and punctured their coffeepot. She saw a brown downpour splash against the wall, runny as blood, while the family scrambled under the table. The sausages would go down like blasted ships, the lacy ivory tablecloth would tear as the young son dived, grasping at the scalloped stitching for covering. Irena imagined delicately tapping out their telephone number. The family's phone would quiver slightly as it trilled in the window (most phones in Serb territory worked), a trembling hand scrambling up for the receiver.

"Good morning. Are we enjoying our breakfast? Please let us rag-heads, Jew-lovers, and Gypsy whores know if there is anything we can do to make you more comfortable."

Every few days Irena would see a coffeepot in a window and be tempted. But she knew she should not waste a bullet to kill kitchenware.

IRENA RARELY SAW Serb soldiers. They were sealed into tanks, armored cars, and blockhouses across the way. They parked their tanks in blind alleys between garages. She knew their snipers were obscured in the opposing cityscape and the mountains beyond. She had been told to look for threads of cigarette smoke during this last morning hour, curling from behind a half-smashed wall or a dangling beam. Smoking for snipers was presumably proscribed. But telling Sarajevans on any side that smoking could get them shot was as convincing as telling them that smoking could give them cancer.

Irena saw no smoke. She could not see any black sweaters, truck headlights, or burly men with somebody else's shirt pulled improbably tight across their shoulders to cloak bulletproof vests. The bird had ceased its two-step.

Irena saw a glint of yellow gleaming against a gray street. At first she thought it was a tennis ball, fallen away from a child's game, abandoned in an alley. But when she sharpened her gaze through her scope she could see that it was a lemon, then another, then a whole crate of fifty, opened like a pirate's hoard of doubloons. Lemons from Crete, she guessed. Lemons that used to be so plentifully and casually squeezed into drinks and dressings, sliced and strewn to wreathe lamb roasts. She guessed that a black-market trader had bought them in Montenegro, and trucked them up to be sold to Serb soldiers in their posts who had not seen lemons for months.

Irena would not want to shoot at a man standing in line to buy a lemon. But she would not mind trying to hit a man who would sell lemons for the price of beefsteak. If she hit the man trying to buy a lemon, she could live with the consequences; he had more money than was suitable. Lemons were for seasoning and adornment, not nourishment. If he was standing in line to buy a lemon, it was probably because he didn't need to stand in line to buy milk or meat. If he didn't need to stand in line for food, it must be because he was a bully who was eating off the plates of Muslims who used to be his neighbors.

So if a shoulder should come into Irena's scope, a pair of flashing hands, she would not worry too much about who was selling lemons and who was buying them. She would pull in her breath and let it out slowly. When the air in her lungs had rolled out, she would squeeze the trigger just under her chin and wait for the jolt against her shoulder.

For long minutes, though, she saw only lemons. She raised herself a couple of inches, carefully, by squeezing her buttocks against the floor, trying to sight more. But the man selling lemons had opened the crate in an alley behind Dinarska Street that was guarded from view by a two-story garage. She could fire through the wire-screen sides of the structure. But her bullet would likely strike only an abandoned, burned-out car, or smash against an unseen wall or floor.

The sun was beginning to get higher and brighter. The lemons seemed almost to hiss with the morning's first low light. Irena trained her sight on the top of the mound, then counted one, two, three lemons to the right, because she felt a mild wind blowing down from the mountains in the east. She stopped breathing. The Knight was playing *The further on I go, the less I know, friend or foe, there's only us. . . .*

She squeezed her breath out gently, as if she wanted to make a candle flame tremble. She tickled the trigger almost tenderly, as if she were rubbing the underside of a kitten's chin, and then squeezed it just as gently, until there was a jerk against her jaw that jolted clear into her shoulder. She kept her gaze focused through her sight, as if she could guide the shot. Within a second, she saw lemons jumping and quaking in their crate like minced garlic on a scalding skillet. They tumbled as the overturned trash can on which they had been set whined and tipped over into the alley. Lemons spilled past people scrambling over the street for a place to hide.

Irena's pigeon skipped a step and strutted with involuntary alarm. But over the past few months pigeons, too, had learned to snap back quickly on alert.

"Pretty bird," Irena said softly. "I'm sorry to disturb you."

TEDIC WAS WAITING in the back of the truck on Mount Igman Street. Irena had pocketed her last brass shell and made a final notation in her small orange notebook before clambering down a shattered stairwell and walking a block into a covered alley. Tedic's truck was as large as a tram, and tented in an unwashed white canvas top. The sides bore an old green-and-gold crest: SARAJEVO BEER, then in smaller letters below, SINCE 1864.

Irena scratched her short nails against the back flap of the canvas. The flap began to fall back as the zipper that held it in place rose, disclosing a small bald man in a black leather coat.

"What was that last one?" he asked as he helped her into the truck.

"I saw someone selling lemons," she said. "Behind Dinarska Street. But I couldn't see a man. So before it got too light, I put it in the lemons."

"Mist?" asked Tedic.

"Yellow," she said with a smile. "Just lemons."

"WE HEARD SOME commotion," Tedic said. He shook a cigarette rolled in old telephone-book paper (a local factory still turned out cigarettes; it had tobacco, but had run out of paper) from a fold of his coat. He pressed it into her hand and took the rifle from over her shoulder. Irena noticed that the names on her cigarette were *G*'s from the directory. She wondered if she was about to smoke through Svjetlana Garasanin's family.

"We're out of Marlboros?" she asked.

"You are developing expensive tastes," said Tedic. "These are supposed to be getting better. The factory proposed a trade and we couldn't say no."

"But do we actually have to smoke them?" Irena had a red plastic lighter zipped into the chest pocket of her gray garage mechanic's smock, next to the embroidered DRAGAN. She lit her cigarette.

"Not Marlboro for sure," she said through a cloak of smoke.

"Apparently the bastards have been forced to use the Bulgarian tobacco that they used to export," said Tedic.

"Export. Are they in the same business we're in?" Irena asked.

"Everyone in town," said Tedic, "is caught up in the same business right now."

IRENA HAD ALREADY rolled her ski mask into her pocket. She took down her gray smock and stepped out of it, leaving her red basketball jersey over a black T-shirt and her old yellow schoolgirl's athletic shorts. She unlaced her boots while Tedic continued to talk, consulting the notepad that she kept against the crinkles of a map folded into a black vinyl book.

"You put a couple into Spomen Park shortly after two? By the monument?"

"I saw a couple of uniforms around a truck. But they were unloading something and moving in and out of the shot."

"You slowed them down."

"I moved down a floor about five minutes later and just threw a round into the back of the truck. I could see a tear in the canvas. But no mist, no scrambling."

"A nice little ping to wake up the boys sleeping off their slivovitz," Tedic noted. "Five-eighteen—the clock in the coffee bar?"

"On Lenin Street. A light snapped on. Mr. Popovic, the man who used to catch us sneaking looks at dirty magazines, was probably just setting up. I waited until the red second hand went by and tried to put the shot down in the center of the clock face. But I couldn't follow it."

A pause fell between them while Irena pulled on the jeans she had taken off six hours ago. They sat on the slats of empty beer bins. Nine crates near the front of the truck were kept conspicuously filled at all times, on the chance that a U.N. inspector might demand proof that the truck actually delivered beer.

Irena unscrewed the flash suppressor on the front of her rifle. It was still warm from her last bullet; she liked to roll it in her hands. She laid it out to cool. She put a scrap of tatty burgundy cloth (Irena suspected it had been cut from the napkin of an old Chinese restaurant in town) over a bottle of canola cooking oil. She turned the bottle over until it had soaked through the scrap. She then wrapped the patch around a slim steel rod and clipped it into place. She raised the metal rod, as she imagined a cellist picks up a bow, and rammed it in one deliberate motion clear to the end of the barrel, back and forth, counting off ten times.

By the time she extracted the rod, Tedic had another scrap of the old napkin in his fingers. She pulled the blackened burgundy patch away and put it into Tedic's palm. She fixed the new, dry patch onto the end of the rod and then put that one through, one, three, five times, before pulling it out and seeing, with some satisfaction, a rusty light residue.

Tedic held out a plastic canister of squares saturated with rose-scented lotion. People in the West used them to wipe babies' bottoms. She rubbed a sheet in her hands until it was smudged with the same rusty residue and peppery flecks of grime.

"Full breakdown and cleaning this Saturday," said Tedic. "You don't want me to do it all by myself."

"Oh God, oh shit, Tedic," said Irena. "I hate it when I'm all wet with tushy wipes and you make it sound like we're some old married couple."

...

THE DRIVE TO the Zarics' apartment block was brief and clear. Sarajevans joked that, while their city was starving and bleeding, local traffic congestion had been greatly relieved. Before Irena turned to lower herself out of the delivery door, Tedic waved two cans of beer at her. "For your mother and father," he said. She took them into her hands like small barbells.

Irena walked heavily up the three flights of stairs to her grandmother's apartment and joggled the smashed lock of the door. Her mother could not take herself away from the two cups of water she was bringing to a boil in one of her mother-in-law's kettles. She had kindled a tiny fire in a tin stove out of one of the stubby wooden feet of the Mandos' living-room sofa and the edge of the frame of their wedding portrait (Mr. Mando had smashed the glass before they left, and rolled the photo over his shin, like a bandage). Mrs. Zaric called out to her daughter. "You're home."

"Tedic dropped me off behind the barrier on Irbina."

"It sounded bad last night over in Dobrinja," said Mrs. Zaric.

Sometime during the summer Irena had helped her mother clip her hair close to her skull, closer even than Irena's. She'd then scoured the remains with kitchen bleach. It had the effect of an electric charge, making Mrs. Zaric's hair bright, spiky, and a little shocking.

Many Sarajevans were dismayed at how the war had spoiled their appearance: matted hair and mottled skin, whitening gums and graying teeth. But nothing about the past few months made Mrs. Zaric want to hold on to the way she had looked. She was delighted to turn her hair into something pug and purposeful.

"I'm trying to save the batteries," said Mrs. Zaric. "Haven't heard the news."

"I think I can get more at work," said Irena. "I heard the Knight say it was Novo Sarajevo and Bistrik. Tedic has the BBC in the truck. They said maybe six people made it to the hospital. There's some kind of trial making people angry in Los Angeles. The radio says a hundred-some men in Prijedor were locked up in a tire factory and forced to sing Serbian songs before they were shot and thrown into a dump."

She set the two beer cans down on the floor by her mother.

"Tedic sent these."

"I'm trying to make tea. We can use that beer later to buy coffee," said Mrs. Zaric. She remembered to smile at her daughter. "Oh, forgive me. And you are all right, my darling?"

"Fine," said Irena. "I worked a little in the basement."

The voice of Irena's father jangled against the tiles from the bathroom. "Is the match between Bobby Fischer and Boris Spassky going on yet?"

"Didn't hear," Irena answered.

Mr. Zaric now spent most of his time in the apartment, wearing a pale jade robe he had brought out of his mother's closet the morning after she died. He had taken to beholding his reflection in a tin cooking sheet propped over a hole where a piece of shell had crashed into the kitchen.

"Okay," he'd say, squaring his shoulders and pointing at his own bleary likeness. "Ziggy Stardust, right? Raves in London."

"There was a new *Q* magazine in the basement," said Irena. "From May. Cher is on the cover. She's a redhead with blue eyes now, and says she likes it. Annie Lennox is going to give up her music to help the homeless. They say she's going to give hope 'to those who sleep tonight in a home made of cardboard.' The Troggs—remember how you used to sing 'Wild Thing' at us?—made an album with R.E.M. Bruce Springsteen says, 'It's a sad man who's living in his own skin and can't stand the company.' Isn't that an amazing line? Somebody tore out the k. d. lang interview, but there's still a picture. She has hair like mine. Michael Jackson is crazy about EuroDisney. They have a quiz—twenty-five questions about American southern music. I only knew one. Didn't Eric Clapton learn guitar from Muddy Waters? But if we can answer the questions and figure out a way to send them in, *Q* will fly the winner and his family to Tennessee and give them six hundred pounds."

"Muddy Waters or B. B. King," said Mrs. Zaric from over the first spits from her small fire. "Nadira Sotra says everybody in town is pretending to be Jewish so they can get out of town on the bus the Serbs are letting leave from the synagogue."

"It's about bloody time that somebody got a break for being a Jew," Mr. Zaric declared.

"Well, *sha-lom*!" said Irena, speaking into the babble of laughter that followed. "Work was"—she drew out the word in English—*"oh-kay."*

2.

SPRING

1992

MOST PEOPLE IN TOWN DIDN'T HAVE A SEPTEMBER 1ST OR A DECEMber 7th in their minds—a day they could say the war began. Sarajevo had a plaque at the spot where, on a June 28th, the assassination of Archduke Ferdinand had lit the fuse to world war. Grotesque men, strutting in jackboots and gingerbread uniforms, struck up wars. Wars weren't begun by people who wore soft French jeans and stylish running shoes.

There were blood wars in the hinterlands—feuds, really, among country people who clung to their father's work, their grandfather's lands, and the primitive bigotry of their forebears. But Sarajevans considered themselves refined. They didn't live in the woods but along a crossroads. People intermingled, intertwined, and intermarried. Few families couldn't trace at least a drop of all bloodlines into their own. People might be Muslims or Serbs (or even Catholics or Jews) at birth. They became city people by custom. They found more faith in coffeehouses and movie theaters than in churches or mosques. They were obeisant to Billie Holiday, Beckett, and basketball, not ministers or imams. The rest of what had been Yugoslavia might be broken up by blood grudges. But Sarajevans were convinced that they could find sly ways to maneuver around tribalism, as they had around Communism. Sarajevans could be stupid, brutish, and blinkered between the river and the valley. They could be irrational, indolent, and self-indulgent in their cafés; they joked about it themselves. But the sheer, blunt dumbness of war—it didn't fit. (The plaque marking the shooting of the Archduke extolled the assassination as a blow for Serbian nationalism. But Sarajevans usually strolled past the brass tablet without giving it as much notice as a soft-drink ad.)

So each Sarajevan had a different date for the start of the war. It began in that moment they said to themselves, "This will not be over by morning."

FOR IRENA ZARIC, the war began on a greening weekend in early April. Young Sarajevans who wanted Bosnia to stay peacefully together were marching downtown; many people at her school were going. Eddy Vrdoljak had asked her to go. But Irena knew that Eddy's interest in the endurance of a multiethnic democracy was his hope to impress girls of varied backgrounds with old myths.

"You know what they say about Croat men, don't you?" he would say with a toss of his dark, disheveled head. "You know why, all kinds, all over the world, they're crazy for us, don't you? I could help you find out."

Eddy was harmless in small doses, and dependably amusing. But Irena had basketball practice at eleven in the morning. She couldn't miss a workout so close to their sectional championships.

Irena and her teammates were often teased about being jocks; mocked for having no concern for history, culture, or politics. But they knew that basketball now competed with political assemblies on Friday nights. The city bristled with national fronts, liberation movements, and people's assemblies, all making raucous vows in smoky basements. It could even be risky to drive across the river for a basketball game—or to buy a string of sausage.

They knew that some Serb police had taken off their uniforms and badges and overturned a garden-store delivery truck along the Brotherhood and Unity Bridge. The defrocked police (now anointed "paramilitaries") swept aside the tulips and sunflowers and set up a barrier. No other police would dare to remove it. Men in black sweaters with rifles on their hips barked at people to show identity cards before passing into what they called Serb Sarajevo.

Just a week earlier, the school principal, Miss Ferenc, had introduced the men's and women's basketball teams at a school assembly in the gym. She presented the players by position and declared, "There you hear it—Serb names, Croat names, Muslim names." She turned slightly toward Miriam Isakovic, but kept her lips above the microphone, so her stage whisper would not be lost. "Even a Jewish name," she said to a satisfying chime of laughter. Miriam blushed at being singled out—she was a sweet, studious girl who rarely made it into games of consequence.

The principal continued in a soft tone. "Serbs, Croats, Muslims, Jews—they are all *our* family names here in Number Three High School in Grbavica. Different names, different histories. Today," Miss Ferenc fairly thundered, "we all play for the same team. *Our* team. *Just like every citizen of Sarajevo!*"

The students rose to their feet, folding chairs scraping, clapping their hands above their heads. The speech gave them a new stake in winning. Grbavica couldn't lose to a team like Number One High School, over in Bistrik, where only Muslims lived; it would let down all Sarajevo.

"Let's show all Bosnia!" Miss Ferenc churned her right arm above her head, as if she were ringing a bell. Her glasses slipped down her nose. "Muslims, Serbs, Croats, Jews! Rastas, Hindus, Buddhists! Jains, Shintoists, Scientologists!" Miss Ferenc ran out of religions just in time for the laughter to overtake her.

THERE WAS AN awkward moment at that Saturday's practice; at the time, it seemed only that. Emina Sefic, the team's center, and Danica Tomic, a guard, had fallen to the floor in a scramble for the basketball. The girls heard squeaks, shouts, and swearing of no particular affront among athletes—"Bitch!" "Idiot!" "Whore!" Then they heard Emina snarl, "Greasy Serb slut!" Danica's face reddened like an electric coil. She barked back, "Raghead whore!" Irena could remember other times when the girls would shout such insults at one another for laughs. But when Coach Dino sensed that the two girls seemed more intent on slapping each other than on grabbing the basketball, he lowered his shoulders into the snarl of legs and arms, shoving them aside with his tattooed arms.

"You are teammates, dammit," he hollered for all in the gym to hear. "You are *teammates*!"

Conversation in the locker room was muted and brittle. No one knew what to say; no one wanted to say the wrong thing. Even playful conversations could turn a dangerous corner. All the girls had heard terrifying stories over the past few days. A man in Kovacici had come home after a round of beer and schnapps and thrown a stone wrapped in a burning towel into his neighbor's bedroom. A woman had been found dead on the Ali Pasha Bridge, her tongue cut out (actually, a newspaper noted drily, cut *in half*). Such butchery was clearly the work of amateurs and, therefore, more worrying.

...

IRENA CAME TO the mirror at the same time as Amela Divacs, the team's other forward. They did not know what to say, but they did not swerve away from each other. Amela smiled slightly as she combed through her long, pale, damp hair, and finally said, "They are both stupid sows."

"I didn't know which to root for," said Irena, whose short chestnut hair had already dried in place.

"Danica is sinking her free throws," said Amela, who smiled and turned back to her locker before she caught herself. "But I wouldn't, you know, choose her for any other reason."

IRENA AND AMELA were partners on the court, and lived in the same housing block in Grbavica. They had played together for two years, after Amela's family had moved from the older area of Skenderija. Amela could pick out the top of Irena's head above a thicket of players, and loft a pass at just the best height for Irena to pluck it away from those around her. Irena could see Amela's long whip of yellow hair lash between two players' shoulders, and she would bounce the ball where Amela could jab out with an arm and take it in her stride. They were comrades, to be sure, and friends in most of the important ways: the foremost was basketball. Their camaraderie was rarely tested by envy.

Irena was a better shooter, that was for sure. This didn't bother Amela, who was shorter and prettier, at least in the swelling assessment of teenage boys. Yet the older boys in their housing block who had gone off to the army or university regarded Irena as sexier.

When the boys came home on weekend passes, they played basketball with Irena, Amela, and sometimes another teammate, Nermina Suljevic. Irena's pet parrot, Pretty Bird, was the game's unofficial official-in-charge; the gray bird said, "Bbb-oing!" in imitation of the sound a ball would make ringing against the court's orange iron hoop. The young men liked to play just under that hoop, hoping for Amela to leap up for a rebound and come down jiggling. They liked to watch Irena from behind as she dribbled the ball downcourt. They would try to press against her backside when they faced the basket. Irena had come close to slapping a couple of boys for their brazenness. Instead, she exploited their distraction to steal the ball.

Both girls had been stamped as athletes from an early age. They had won badges, ribbons, and medallions, which their parents had long ago piled in drawers as so much clutter. Both girls were used to being watched by strangers, and used to looking at each other as competitors and teammates.

Amela was smart—the more serious student of the two—but she wasn't an intellectual. Away from class, she mostly read captions under the pictures in Western fashion and pop magazines.

Irena was blasé about schoolwork. She would wait until the morning of a test to learn what she needed and nothing more, which was hardly the way she trained for basketball. Yet few of Irena's teachers were disappointed. Her mind had depth. She would give herself over completely to a book, a song, or a magazine, absorbing a sports or music monthly from the letters in front to the personal ads on the last pages.

Irena and Amela knew they were the best two players on their team, and two of the three prettiest (the third, Jagoda Marinkovic-Cerovic, was a redhead, and beyond comparison—some boys were simply fools about redheads). Amela wore lipstick. Irena tended not to. Both sprayed jots of cologne on the soft undersides of their forearms after showering, tucking small gift spritzers back into their gym bags.

SOME LESBIANS ASSUMED that Irena, with her Martina Navratilova bearing, was gay, but loath to accept it. In fact, Irena had no dread of being gay. She just wasn't. Amela, who had more of the blond, billowy look of a girl in a Coca-Cola ad, was never taken to be gay. But she had enjoyed a couple of gentle kissing and hand-holding encounters with other women. She thought her sexual register was still settling.

Irena could seethe and flash. Amela was considered almost tiresomely sweet. Yet Irena remembered the time Anica Dordic, the center for their rivals at Veterans, was throwing elbows at Miriam Isakovic's nose when she came down the court. The referees were watching the ball, not Miriam; or, at any rate, they weren't inclined to call a foul committed against a player of no particular consequence. Irena didn't whimper to the officials. She challenged Anica for a rebound and launched a jab into her chin while ostensibly stretching for the ball. Anica, who'd played her ruse enough to know her next move, staggered back, looking confused and wounded. Irena was ejected. She was slipping the orange Number Three jersey over her head in the locker room when Amela took a pass from Nermina Suljevic and took a layup, hard, into the wincing chin of Anica Dordic. Anica got flagged for the foul when she called Amela a bleach-haired whore.

...

AMELA WAS KNOWN as a Serb, Irena as a Muslim. It would be sentimental to say that the difference was undetectable or insignificant. Insults and nasty jokes about the differences were traded. Bar fights broke out. People could hear the difference in names; some were convinced they could see it in a person's nose, eyes, or jawline. Some neighborhoods in the city were considered Serb, others Muslim. But family trees, flecked with intermarriage and conversions, had been entwining in Sarajevo for most of the century.

The girls and their friends were more intense about basketball than about any of the city's array of religions. No one on their team wore a religious medallion. Almost every day, Amela Divacs wore a yellow No. 32 Los Angeles Lakers jersey that an unnamed older boy had gotten for her. Amela tucked the jersey over blouses when she went to class, and often pulled it over a T-shirt at practice. The jersey was an amulet for Amela. It announced that she was both an outstanding basketball player and unavailable to the boys in her school. They were kids, not like the man who had given her a Magic Johnson jersey.

Irena was not certain that she knew anyone who went to a church, mosque, or synagogue regularly. Whenever her friends became briefly fascinated by a faith, it would be Baha'i or Buddhism, in the same way they were captivated by vegetarianism or yoga.

"THAT'S IT, YOU'RE home for the night. We all are," Irena's father told her when she arrived at their apartment after practice. Before she could object, he raised a hand and tipped his head toward the television set. "You've been at school. The march today. Some people opened fire from inside the Holiday Inn. People were hurt."

Names of friends who might have been there flashed into Irena's mind: Azra, Dina, Jelena, Eddy, Hamel, Morana.

"Do you know who?"

"Serbs, of course. That's Serb headquarters. They dragged a couple of gunmen out of their offices."

"No. *No!*" said Irena. She could hear her voice hardening. "Who was *hurt*."

"No," her father said quietly. "I know they didn't have enough ambulances. Twenty people are in the hospital."

Irena had her keys in her hand, and conspicuously began to stuff them into the pocket of her jeans. "I'm going to check on my friends," she announced.

Before her father could respond, Mrs. Zaric stepped into the hallway. "It's getting worse," she said. "We've heard a few shots today."

"They were just from the television set," said Irena.

"Some Serbs have put burning barrels in the streets in Ilidza," Mrs. Zaric went on. "Serb army officers are staying at home. Serbs on the police force aren't showing up for work. They're staying at home—with their weapons."

"Like they were forming their own army," said her father.

IRENA COULD CALL no one. The panic in the city—that's how people on television were beginning to put it—had overwhelmed the system: people dialed, there were clicks, then a thunk. Irena didn't join her parents before the drone of the television. She looked down from the dining-room window to the small park below and saw no one, not even the grade-school kids who usually flocked there on Saturday nights. On Saturdays, the high-school girls would pull on tight jeans and stretchy Western tops to prowl and parade past the snack shacks and coffee bars in the narrow streets of Old Town. Irena and Amela liked to stop by the park's basketball court on their way out. They would take off their weekend rings and give their hoop earrings to a little girl to hold while they showed the kids how to change hands on a dribble, then turn away with a hook shot and walk off to their tiny-handed applause.

Irena stayed in her room, listening to Madonna: *Tears on my pillow, what kind of life is this, if God exists* . . . The lyrics bounced through her head amid the sounds of the city, as cars backfired—or guns were shot—and sirens yowled. She took Pretty Bird out of his cage and perched him on her stomach, his rust-red tail feathers splayed out on her hips.

"Do you like this music, Pretty Bird?" she asked in the small, child's voice she used for conversations with her parrot. "Does it remind you of home?"

Pretty Bird was a Timneh African gray. But Irena and her family had invented a storybook life for their bird: he had flapped into Sarajevo from Copacabana Beach across the ocean, because he was tired of rubbing suntan lotion into his feathers. Pretty Bird could not manage to speak much more than his name. Congo Grays were considered better orators, and were commensurately more costly. But Pretty Bird's bargain price did not account for his outstanding talents as a mimic. Sometimes he trilled like their telephone, jingled like their doorbell, or creaked like the chipped yellow-steel kitchen cabinet next to his cage. Their veterinarian said Irena ought to write up Pretty Bird's talents for a professional journal. His vocabulary of sounds made him a particularly amusing companion, sending the Zarics scampering to answer phantom phone calls, or wake up wondering who was vacuuming in the middle of the night.

Shortly after nine o'clock, Pretty Bird began to chirrup like their new Danish telephone and do a kind of rumba—one step forward, two steps back—along the belt line of Irena's blue jeans. Her mother rapped quietly on her closed door. "It's Coach, dear," she called.

Irena took Pretty Bird onto her shoulder and sat up with some alarm as the doorknob turned and she saw Coach Dino standing beside her mother.

"Hi, chickie," he said lightly. "I told your mother, the phones seem to be out, and this was important. Sorry to interrupt your fun."

Irena had begun to notice that even at their games Mrs. Zaric often seemed flustered and shy around Coach Dino; she couldn't seem to say three words without taking one back. The coach was a rangy, rugged man in his early thirties, with stabbing dark eyes and wiry muscles, which were often exposed by sleeveless shirts.

"Tea? Coffee?" asked her mother. "Oh, I'm sorry. Perhaps a beer? Wait, no, we have some nice Danish vodka. Well, actually not vodka, but something made from seeds. Well, not birdseed, of course, but like rye-bread seed. . . ." Mrs. Zaric's voice trailed off as the coach shook his head.

"Thank you, no. I am always in training."

After Mrs. Zaric had closed the door, Coach Dino sat on the cedar trunk at the end of Irena's bed. Pretty Bird waddled down her right arm and settled himself on the bedstead. Coach Dino smiled tentatively.

"Hey, chickie," he said with exaggerated lightness. "Look, I'm sure this is no big thing. But there will be no practice tomorrow. Or Monday. If you and your family wanted to go off for the holiday"—Monday was the anniversary of the victory of Tito's Partisans over the Germans—"there's no reason not to."

"That's not going to get us ready for the tournament," Irena said. "Why don't a few of us just shoot around in the gym?" Back on her shoulder, Pretty Bird whirred like her mother's bread mixer.

"They have to close the school," said Coach Dino. "All the schools, in fact. Under the circumstances." His voice dropped. "Maybe for a while."

"What's 'for a while'?" Irena could hear her voice flutter with anxiety.

"That's not up to us," the coach said gently. "There's a lot of people acting stupid right now."

"The championships begin in two weeks."

"I'm sure this will all be over soon," he said. "People just have to get it out of their systems. Listen," the coach continued, "this other thing I had to tell you. I've been called back into the army."

Irena felt a prickling in her scalp. When she reached up for Pretty Bird, she noticed that her fingers didn't respond immediately, as if the signal she had sent to them had to go around a barricade.

"There's no war," she said finally. "You said it: just stupid people."

"But there is an emergency," said Coach Dino. "They're calling everyone. I'm sure they just want me for another competition." He had been a biathlon champion his first time around in the national army, and still won occasional local tournaments, firing rifle shots while skiing.

"There won't be snow for months," Irena pointed out.

"There are shooting matches all the time."

"Oh, for fuck's sake," said Irena, "you could hold those in our parking lot this weekend."

THE COACH SAID he had to go. He had to find Amela and Nermina to tell them, too, that school was closed and he was leaving. As Coach Dino got up, Irena reached up and put her arms clumsily around his shoulders. For the first time in the confusion of the past few weeks, she began to cry. She blotted her tears against the coach's right biceps, just above his mermaid tattoo.

"I am sorry," she said in a small, choked voice, "to rain on your mermaid."

"Shh," he said gently. "Shh. Shh. Shh. It will be over."

"This is so much worse than I thought," said Irena.

"The mermaid is waterproof."

Irena nestled her nose and chin into the coach's shoulder. She stood nimbly on her toes to turn her lips against his ear. "She is an ignorant, titty blonde," she whispered, and then licked the inside of his ear softly, as she knew he liked.

"Oh, shit," said Coach Dino. He ran his right hand slowly down Irena's back, squeezing gently every few inches. "Your parents."

"Watching television," she whispered slow and deep into his ear. Irena went on slowly, so that each syllable would be a small, boiling breath playing over the small hairs in his ears. "I won't talk if you won't."

The coach lowered his hand to the crack in Irena's ass, pressing his palm across her buttocks and squeezing. Irena shivered against his neck; it smelled of smoke, coffee, and his lavender splash. She felt Coach Dino swell and press against her. (Irena loved the obviousness of boners. They were one of the few ways in which boys were utterly reliable.)

The Madonna tape had stopped and rewound. Irena breathed into the coach's ear, *"I'm down on my knees, I want to take you there."* She felt for the drawstring of Coach Dino's blue warm-up pants and tugged out the knot. She put both of her hands on his thighs and pulled down his pants with her thumbs. Because she was an athlete, and knew about the fragility of ligaments, Irena sank into a crouch instead of getting on her knees. She kissed him through his white cotton shorts. The top of his cock looked like a purple serpent. He held Irena lightly behind her ears as she licked once, twice, five times, until she tasted several salty, soapy drops. She made a comic smacking sound. Her joke panicked the coach. She could taste it. He stopped churning his hips. Gently, Coach Dino pushed back her chin and tugged up his pants. He brought her face against his and began to kiss her wet brown eyes. He ran a thumb down over her crotch until he found the top button of her jeans and unlatched it, then slipped his thumb between her legs.

Irena sang under her breath, *"I close my eyes. . . ."*

Pretty Bird clacked his pink feet a few inches over on the bedstead and buzzed like Mr. Zaric's electric shaver. "*Zzz-zzha, zzz-zzha,* Pretty Bird," he said. "Pretty Bird!"

3.

AS COACH DINO LEFT, HE DREW A RED BASKETBALL JERSEY FROM THE front pocket of his gym jacket and laid it across Irena's bedstead. "Guard this while I'm gone," he said. "Sleep in it. Keep it in your bed. That's the place"—he ducked his chin toward her—"where I want to be."

In fact, Irena and Coach Dino had never been to bed. Their couplings were staged in stairwells, equipment closets, and—most challengingly—in a crawl space between the gymnasium bleachers and a wall of the women's shower room. The verticality of their sex was a joke between them. Fucking on her feet, he counseled, was good for her quadriceps. "You can run fifty laps around the gym," he would say, raising his eyebrows like exclamation points. "Or—"

"Anything," Irena would say, "to avoid running laps."

It wasn't until Irena had opened up the shirt that she saw JORDAN across the back, CHICAGO on the front. The gift, along with the gunshots and emptiness outside, alarmed her. Irena was cunning. She knew that Coach Dino enjoyed having sex with her, but she assumed that one day he would approach her with his sad hound's face and announce that he was returning to his wife (or, at least, to their bedroom from the couch on which he professed to sleep) or moving in with Julija Mitric, the hazel-eyed women's soccer coach. Irena enjoyed her moments with Coach Dino, but she spent more time dreaming about Toni Kukoc, the great Croatian player, or Johnny Depp than about the coach. She hid their relationship like a shoplifted lipstick.

Irena would never wear the red jersey to school or practice. But her parents would see it on the bed, in her closet, under her pillow. No lie would be convincing; accepted, perhaps, for the sake of peace, but never believed. The red jersey was like an indiscreet letter left in a drawer. Coach Dino must have known that the jersey would lead Irena to proclaim her adulthood by flinging his name into her parents' astonished faces. He must have known that he wouldn't be coming back to Sarajevo anytime soon.

MR. ZARIC CLEARED his throat, smoothed his hair, and told his small family that he had to declare what he had been thinking. It was shortly after eight o'clock on a Sunday, and coffee was dripping down into the electric glass pot. Pretty Bird made bubbling, popping, and sizzling sounds as the coffee crackled against the hot plate. Mrs. Zaric sat next to the bird, at the far corner of the kitchen table, her eyes shining and rimmed in pink.

"I've been thinking," he began. "All night, really. Your brother even mentioned this a few days ago. When our phone was working." Irena's brother, Tomaslav, was traveling with friends in Vienna, and would call every couple of days as he heard increasingly harrowing news from home. "I'm thinking it's maybe a good time to visit your grandmother." Irena's only living grandmother, her father's mother, lived in the apartment she had shared with her husband near the synagogue in Old Town.

"I am thinking that it is not good to leave her alone. Under the circumstances. Especially at night."

Irena was baffled. Her grandmother lived about ten blocks away. Visits to her flat were casual and unceremonious. "Shouldn't Grandma come here?" she asked. "Our place is larger. She likes Pretty Bird, too."

Mrs. Zaric's eyes began to brim with water once again.

Irena's father clenched his right hand tightly on his daughter's forearm, then loosened his grasp as he felt her shrink back. "The idea is for us to stay with Grandma," he said. He let the idea stare at his daughter for a moment. "If we stay here—I don't know. Mr. Kemal downstairs—their car was burned. He said the phone rang, and someone said, 'Your wife and son and dog are in the trunk.' They weren't, thank God. But now they've all left for Vitez. There's something spray-painted on a side of your basketball court now—"

"Kids," said Irena.

"—about 'This is Serb country.' "

"Kids, kids, kids," Irena insisted. "Kids and their crayons."

"I don't recognize this planet," Mr. Zaric said with slow ferocity. "I can't walk across the bridge to get the tram, because thugs in black sweaters want to see my identity card. They warn me that I'm living in 'stolen Serb territory.' I should say, 'Listen, you goons, we are both living in Bosnia, a free country where everyone is equal. I will go where I like.' But they have

guns. They make their point. I went into the bank on Friday. Mr. Djordic said he hoped I wouldn't mind a sign he had to put up on instructions from Belgrade. You know what it said? 'No money handled by Muslims.' Can you imagine? Signs like South Africa. Mr. Djordic got all flustered. 'Oh, Mr. Zaric,' he said, 'I just have to humor the assholes.' Some fucking sense of humor. I should have said, 'Why don't you show them a Woody Allen movie?' But some people have guns, and the bank has our money. One day it's a rude call, a lewd note, something lurid scrawled in the parking lot. The next? What do you think you've been hearing at night—champagne corks?"

"Jerks shooting guns into the sky," said Irena. "Coach said that last night. They don't want to hurt anyone. They're worried about being outnumbered."

"Well, they are changing the numbers," said Mr. Zaric evenly. "Sending Muslims and Croats packing from Vukovar, Nadin, and Skabrinj, with only what they could carry on their shoulders. Bombing those beautiful old stones of Dubrovnik back into biblical dust. 'Ethnic cleansing,' they call it. A little light housekeeping. You know what happened, don't you, when the people in Vukovar had to give in after all that shelling and shooting? While you've been listening to Madonna, I've been tuned to the BBC. But late, to keep it from you and your mother. But I can't anymore. They hauled all the non-Serbs out of their houses. Marched them out into the cold streets and bare fields. Then they'd pick a man here, a woman there. Who knows on what whim? They'd line them up and shoot them. The rest took the hint. They were 'deported for their protection.' Like 'sanitized for your protection' across the strip of a toilet seat."

Mrs. Zaric stirred now, and rose as if to protest.

Mr. Zaric raised his voice to stop her. "She has to hear this!" he shouted. "In Bijeljina, a Serb leader named Arkan set fleeing Muslims on fire. They treat him like Napoleon."

"For fucking Christ's sake, Daddy!" Irena exploded in fear and fury. "Who is *they*? *We* are half Serb! At least, I am!"

"Half isn't half enough for them," her father bellowed back. "Yes, *them*. Or too much. Don't you see? They want 'purity.' My father was a Serb married to a Jew. I married a Muslim whose mother was a Croat. Serb, Croat, Muslim, Jew—what does that make you and your brother? We have no name. And now we have no place."

"Those weren't *our* Serbs," Irena insisted. "They're peasants. The kind of people who squat in fields, for fuck's sake."

"And those weren't *our* Muslims in Vukovar or Bijeljina?" asked Mrs. Zaric softly. She had tried to shrink into the wall behind her husband and daughter, keeping pointedly unaligned. "Just country people in black dresses and rag scarves—not city folks like us? Maybe we should see Grandma today, anyway. Have her tell you about when the Nazis came here, and dragged away the Jews and the Gypsies. Has your life been so kind," she asked her daughter, "that you thought Nazis were only in the movies? Like Godzilla and the Terminator?"

At some point, as Mrs. Zaric spoke, they had all sat back down in individual surrender. Irena's chair thumped, and Pretty Bird began to whir again like Mrs. Zaric's mixer. They all fought a smile, then gave in.

Mrs. Zaric went on in her softest voice. "We've seen the bonfires in the streets. Someone threw a bomb into the synagogue. Somebody threw a match into the library. Someone set a fire in the post office, and snipers shot at the firemen. You run out of accidents. This is how it starts."

"How will we be safer just a few blocks away?" asked Irena. She began to cry into her mother's shoulder as her father hovered, speaking gently.

"Safer across the river. We'll each pack a bag. A week's worth of clothes. No, three days—Grandma has a washing machine. Let's bring a little cheese, some coffee, the things Grandma forgets." Mr. Zaric smiled down at his daughter. "And, of course, Pretty Bird. I'll carry his cage. We'll stay here today. There's a march headed from Dobrinja. The streets are crazy. Tomorrow is a holiday. We'll lock up and leave, like we're going to the mountains."

Irena fixed a hopeful look on her father. "And if it's quiet tonight?"

"I'll go anyway, to check on Grandma, if the phones are still out. If it's calm outside, I'll come right back."

"Maybe we won't have to go?"

Mr. Zaric hesitated. "Maybe. *Maybe*. But get packed. Start now. If something breaks out at that march, we might leave earlier."

Irena wiped her eyes and stood up. "This is fucking insane," she said.

"Yes," said her father. He spoke gently, and laid a palm against his daughter's cheek. "It sure fucking is."

Pretty Bird made a boiling noise, like the rumble of Mrs. Zaric's electric kettle.

"Get packed," Mr. Zaric reminded Irena from the hallway. "No more scenes. I don't want to give another history lesson to someone who's so young she thinks Yuri Gagarin was one of the Beatles before Ringo."

"That was Pete Best, you clod. You clod, *dear,*" Mrs. Zaric called out from the kitchen.

"You taught me that," said Irena. "Who in the hell is Yuri Gagarin?"

IRENA ZIPPED OPEN the shiny black nylon Adidas bag she had gotten when the team went to Zagreb for a tournament. It seemed to yawn. She laid out three American polo shirts (red, blue, and black, each of them HECHO EN HONDURAS—perhaps Pretty Bird had flown over the factory on his way to find their family), two pairs of Esprit jeans (one blue and one black), three pairs of white socks, three panties (two pink, one white), two white cotton bras, and a pair of scuffed brown loafers. Irena lowered each bundle into the bag and pressed down. Then she laid out the clothes she had decided she should wear to walk over to her grandmother's apartment: her favorite black cotton shell with the lacy neck, a short Esprit denim dress, her gray West German army jacket, and the red-and-black Air Jordan shoes Aunt Senada had sent from Cleveland. She rooted around in the box under her bed for some of her favorite magazines. Grandma didn't have a television set, and Irena doubted that her parents would let her walk into Old Town.

Irena had *Q* magazine from June 1991, with Madonna on the cover in a snug white swimsuit, saying, "Everyone thinks I'm a nymphomaniac, but I'd rather read a book." (Mr. Zaric had brought that one home from the news kiosk, saying to his daughter, "If she can read a book, so can you.") She chose *The Face* from July '91, with Johnny Depp on the cover. Inside, Irena recalled, he insisted that he and Winona did the dishes together, at least once. She found another *Face* from May '91 with a sensational shot of Wendy James on the cover: she had strung strands of white beads around her breasts and nipples, turning them into Christmas trees. She selected a *Sky* from August '91. Vanessa Paradis was on the cover, but Irena had saved it for the interview with Madonna ("Her Again!" it squealed on the front) and a feature on teenage sex kittens through movie history, including old pictures of Brooke Shields, Jodie Foster, Milla Jovovich, and really old shots of Brigitte Bardot that Irena had been meaning to show to her grandmother. She thumbed through the article briefly before packing the magazine away, and thought she rather resembled the shot of Nastassja Kinski wearing a man's shirt. It reminded her to pack her Michael Jordan jersey, but to squeeze it below the magazines, into a corner.

Irena placed a copy of *The Little Prince* on top of the magazines (that, at least, was a book she had read and enjoyed), and a copy of *SportNews* from Zagreb, with Toni Kukoc on the cover, his jazzman's goatee glistening. Finally, she reached back to her bed table and plucked up a bottle of Honey Almond makeup, a roll of Fire & Ice lipstick, and a small glass bottle of Deeply Purple nail polish. As she pressed down these last, small items, she remembered one more. She rolled back the drawer of her bedside table and picked up a row of three foil-wrapped condoms, which she pressed a little more carefully into the crinkles of the magazine. She had begun to zip the bag closed when she caught sight of the threadbare old brown Pokey Bear who had shared her bed since she was three. She zipped the bag as far as it would go before nipping the red bow on Pokey's neck. He would be borne like a pasha to her grandmother's house. Irena used a toe to push her bag into the hallway, under the Degas blue dancer print hanging by the front door.

"Done," she called out, and Pretty Bird began to trill like an unanswered telephone.

THE ZARICS WERE packing when the noontime march began from Dobrinja. Legions of short-haired students and long-haired academics, a delegation of hard-hatted coal miners and woolly-shirted farmworkers linked arms and surged down Proletariat Brigade Boulevard, chanting, "Bosnia! We are Bosnia!"

Perhaps a third of the marchers were Serbs. They did not want to live in some Greater Serbia, pruned and purged of all other peoples. Many of them hoisted peace symbols, an emblem pointedly imported from the West. They wanted the Bosnia they had just invented to be an unarmed Lennonist state, blameless and beloved.

Just before one in the afternoon, marchers began to stream into the flat plaza surrounding the Bosnian Parliament building. Some people thought they heard lightning crackle overhead; then hornets zapping around their shoulders and feet, smacking off the concrete, and biting into legs and foreheads. Two or three seconds later, almost timidly, pops of blood plumed. Men and women began to flop down hard, like birds that had flown over a hunter's blind. The Zarics could hear something like paper bags being popped overhead, knew they were not, and turned on their television. Some of the marchers in the square stayed down, as if they could hide. Some got up on their knees and lurched, then staggered, and tried to run for the shelter of trees in the plaza. Bullets clipped the leaves and gouged the tree trunks, then smacked into the bones of men and women. There were screams, screeches, sirens, and sobs. But the sounds that stayed with people in the plaza were the thuds of steel spanking flesh, and the splash of blood against the hard pavement. In the fantastic silence that survivors remember more clearly than a noise, the splash sounded like water spilling from a hose into the street.

Somebody got a brave and absurd idea: surge over the Vrbanja Bridge into Grbavica, and dare the snipers to lay down their guns. Chants rose from the streets. "Stop the war! Peace for Bosnia! Put down your guns!" In their high roosts, the snipers paused for a moment, disbelieving the marchers' audacity. Two young women, Suada Dilberovic and Olga Sucic, ran ahead of the rest, cheering, waving, and skipping into a squall of bullets.

4.

THE ZARICS STARED AT THE TELEVISION SCREEN, AND KEPT STARING as it blinked and went blank. Pretty Bird gurgled like the bubbling from the kitchen sink. Mr. Zaric crossed over to the telephone, and Irena waited for him to sum up to someone what they had seen and heard. But he slammed the receiver down angrily. "Dead," he said. "Dead, fucking dead!"

He opened the closet and reached for a blue windbreaker hanging on a peg. "I've got to go find her," he said. His car keys clanged on the wooden floor.

Mrs. Zaric stiffened as if she had heard glass being shattered. "We're going with you," she announced simply. And as Irena began to lace up her Air Jordans, her mother called out, "We're bringing our bags. I'll get Pretty Bird."

Cabinet doors squeaked, dresser drawers squealed, feet stamped up and down hallways, and within ten minutes the Zarics had turned the lock on ten years in Grbavica.

"I'll keep the keys," said Mrs. Zaric as she bolted the door.

"I have the ones to the car," her husband said. They stood for a moment to look at each other in the murk and gray of the hallway.

IRENA HAD GROWN up seeing pictures of people being expelled from the ghettos of Europe. Many of them looked fat, her grandmother had explained, because they had put as many coats and shirts on their backs as possible. By then they knew they would not be back, although most had not figured—or refused to accept—that they were going to die. Irena remembered pictures she had glimpsed while flipping through newspapers to get to the sports—Salvadorans, Ethiopians, Koreans, carrying only what they could squeeze into a wicker hamper, a paper box, or a length of cloth.

Now she was carrying the contents of her life, so incompletely accounted for, in a gym bag. Her father, so careful about his appearance, hadn't shaved that morning and wore the brown tweed jacket that her mother was always trying to hide. Her mother hadn't made up her face for the day; her hair had been pulled back from her forehead with a green scarf. She would rather die, Irena imagined her mother saying, than be seen that way outside the apartment. A poor choice of words today.

OUT IN THE hallway, the Zarics saw that some of their neighbors had the same idea. Mr. Hadrovic had his hands in the pockets of the worn burgundy sweater he pulled on in any weather to watch television.

"There are Serbs in black sweaters headed this way," he reported breathlessly. "With rifles and those long tubes."

Mr. Zaric was puzzled. "Bows and arrows?" he asked.

"Oh, for Christ's sake, no," snapped Mr. Hadrovic. "You know, the things we used to see in World War Two movies."

"We're going to see my mother," Mr. Zaric told him as they walked to the elevator. "We will see you in a couple of days." Then he stopped. Mr. Hadrovic, he remembered, was a widower who was alone in his apartment, his son at school in Sweden. "Can we do anything for you before we leave?" he asked. More grave offers seemed to form in each sentence, with the rising din of emergency car alarms and pistol pops outside. "Leave you with food, so you don't have to go out? Would you like to come with us?"

"Oh, good Christ, no," Mr. Hadrovic said. "There are enough idiots out there already. They will have to come get me right here."

Irena had already pressed the button for the elevator, and it was like pressing the knob on a tree trunk. "I don't even hear the car moving," she told her father. Her mother had been tapping one of the bare lightbulbs in the hall. "I think maybe the power is off," she said glumly. "Too many people doing their wash on Sunday afternoon." Sunlight still swept through the hallway from the slatted windows, but when the Zarics opened the steel door into the stairwell, they stepped into darkness.

OUTSIDE, THE HOUSING block looked empty and still. Irena's friends were not perched on the flower boxes and benches, sneaking smokes and gossiping. No one had gotten up a game on the basketball court. There were a couple of cars in parking spaces—Mr. Rusmir's saucy new red

Volkswagen, and the Aljics' old blue matchbox Lada—but they seemed abandoned. The Lada listed from a tire that had been blown so far off the wheelbase that the orange iron inner ring scraped against the pavement at a slant. The Volkswagen's windshield had been shattered, and it looked as if the car's paint had somehow been smeared across the Lada's hood. Irena looked to see if the car was still serviceable. She leaned in to open the door and saw that Mr. Aljic's hair, brains, and a wedge of his head had been spilled above the steering wheel.

"Maybe we should get out of here and down to the basement," Mr. Zaric said.

THERE WAS A small window high on the wall of the basement laundry room that looked out on the parking lot, four swings, and the basketball court. The Zarics and people from several other apartments (the Zarics were embarrassed again to realize how few of their neighbors they knew) sat or knelt along the baseboard of the cinder-block wall, jostling for comfort on a grit of old soap powder and dust.

Franjo Kasic, a waiter at the Bristol Hotel, and Branko Filipovic, an automotive teacher whom Irena couldn't recall seeing before, stood on their toes for a few seconds at a time to report on what they could glimpse: flashes of white whizzing through the sky, and shadows streaking against the dingy yellow panels of the building across the way. Every minute, it seemed, they heard the sound of glass cracking and falling. Mr. Kasic said that he saw a whole sheet of concrete peel away from the side of the ten-story building across the street. They waited for a thud, but Mr. Kasic said it broke apart on the way down.

He and Mr. Filipovic went back and forth.

"That's a mortar."

"Thank you, Mr. BBC."

"Well, some kind of fucking bomb."

"Very perceptive."

Pretty Bird began to pick up the sounds. His red tail flared out behind him like the flame on a rocket: *"Shhh-ruumph! Shh-ruumph!"*

"I cannot believe you brought that fucking bird," Mr. Filipovic said, but then softened. "I guess he's a member of your family."

Nenad Hadzic, a willowy blond woman from the second floor who had shown Irena how to apply lipstick on her way to school so that her mother wouldn't see it, called out encouragingly. "Pretty Bird is a delightful neighbor—I'm glad he's here," she said. She wondered if she ought to go back for her cat. "I left Pedro upstairs because I thought it would be just a few minutes. Now I'm thinking maybe he shouldn't be alone."

"Muris and the children?" Mrs. Zaric began.

"In Srebrenica, to see his mother," said Mrs. Hadzic. "I would be there myself, except I have a presentation at the school this week."

"My basketball coach said there is no school," Irena volunteered.

"Really?" another voice called out.

"I wonder if they will have trouble getting back," said Mrs. Hadzic cautiously. "Holiday traffic. And now . . ."

"Mr. Hadrovic is still upstairs," Irena pointed out.

"Should we go get him?" asked her mother.

"Wait," said Mr. Zaric.

"Men are coming," Mr. Filipovic announced suddenly. Mr. Kasic bounced up for a better look.

"Yes. A few." He jumped once more. "Shit, maybe a dozen."

"And more behind," said Mr. Filipovic after another bound up toward the slim window.

"Who are they?" Several voices rang out at the same time.

"Not a girls' football club," said Mr. Kasic.

Mr. Zaric motioned for Branko Filipovic to boost him up to the ledge of the window. He clutched the window frame for a few seconds, then dropped down heavily. "They're walking by that first soccer goal when you come out of the trees across the way," he said. "Black sweaters, black jackets. Black guns. Each of them has a gun."

"Serbs?"

"How do I know?"

"Do they have beards?"

"Lots of Muslims have beards."

"I don't mean like the Ayatollah Khomeini. Blunt, black beards. Serb beards."

"They swagger like policemen," said Mr. Zaric. "They are wearing what look like policemen's boots."

"Do all policemen have boots?"

"You know what the radio said."

"Did anyone think to bring a radio?" asked Mr. Kasic. "Shit, I forgot. And there's a big game, too," he added. "Between Mostar Central and

Vitez." The laughter in the laundry room sounded like the cracking of glass. Voices skidded off the cinder-block walls, as people bounced up and down for a look through the window.

"Are they shooting?"

"Not that I see." The sound of gunfire ended further speculation.

"The radio was saying that Serb police—"

"I heard that." It was Voja Bobic, who ran the La Terrasse café along the Miljacka. He worked long hours, Mrs. Zaric was convinced, trying to keep company with two or more girlfriends on opposite sides of the river.

"Mr. Zaric," he suggested, "why don't you and I go out and say something to them."

"Because we are part Serb?"

"Because we are sensible, diplomatic persons who happen to have a little Serb, yes."

Mr. Zaric stood up, the blood rushing back into his legs as he stamped his feet in the dark and damp. "I think you may be right, Mr. Bobic," he said. "At least we should try."

Mrs. Zaric looked up from the floor, opening her mouth like a fish gasping, only to say, "Milan!"

IRENA COULD NOT easily imagine her parents when they were her age. She had seen pictures, of course. A young man with flaxen hair piled on his head like hay, a red corduroy jacket with lapels like the wings of a comic-strip space rocket, and John Lennon glasses. A young woman with hair curly as copper rings, who wore tube tops as tight as sausage casing, and sunglasses that she had to slip down onto her nose in order to actually see.

Mrs. Zaric—whose first name was Dalila—sang in a rock band at Number Four High School. They called themselves Band Sixty-nine. They told school officials that their name was to venerate the worldwide student revolution led by the likes of Daniel Cohn-Bendit. When a skeptical assistant principal pointed out that 1968 was generally considered the year of upheaval, they dropped their voices. "We are trying," they said, "to avoid all mention of Prague." The assistant principal did not believe them, but he thought that, at any rate, their trick reasoning had reached the safest conclusion.

The group's specialty was slipping unsanctioned English lyrics into Beatles songs. "Lovely Tito" was inevitably the best remembered, though hardly the cleverest. (*Lovely Tito, Brezhnev's maid, may I ask the Marshal discreetly. Will we be free to take a pee on thee?*) Mrs. Zaric naturally favored her own featured song, in which she got to vocalize: *So we sail up to the sun, till we hit the sea at night. 'Cause we live behind the Wall, in our Russian satellite!* A crowd of any size joining in with her on the refrain—*We all live in a Russian satellite! A Russian satellite!*—had given her a feeling of elation that she could still summon. She might not always understand her daughter's devotion to sports, but she recognized—and remembered—the allure of an audience.

Milan was a fan of Band Sixty-nine. Dalila began to recognize his Lennon-lensed face peering up from the crowds. When the band performed at the class graduation party, he was there. "Does this mean that we won't see you again?" she asked. She had included the *we* pointedly—to afford him, if he chose, an escape. He was astonished, and stammered. He patted a big flapped pocket on the right side of his corduroy jacket. He wrote poems himself, he explained, and had often tried to send a few to her. But they felt light once they were in the envelope. And, as for any accompanying letter—what would he say?

"I don't demand Shakespeare," she told him, and on that note, more or less, they had grown up together ever since.

A BOLT OF light darted through the room as Mr. Zaric and Mr. Bobic unlatched the door leading up to the stairs that opened into the parking lot.

"If this is our last whiff of life," said Mr. Bobic, "it smells like laundry soap."

A CLUSTER OF four men in black sweaters moved into their path, holding rifles across their chests. Mr. Zaric hailed them with a good show of friendliness. "Hello. How are you?" he said. "We are Serb brothers. Welcome to Grbavica."

The men muttered and halted. One man, who had red-rimmed eyes and prominent incisors, appeared to be in command. "Are there Muslims here?" he asked with agitation.

"There are Muslim neighbors here," Mr. Bobic said a little tensely. "With whom we live side by side in peace."

"Oh, crap," said the leader sharply. "You are fucking rag-heads. I can see that now." His men lifted their rifles. "Hit your knees for Allah, assholes." The instant of shock that froze Mr. Zaric and Mr. Bobic on their feet, the men chose to take as defiance. They began to poke at their chins with the rifle barrels.

"Lie down. Put your fucking faces on the ground!"

The people in the basement couldn't see, but Irena could hear a rasp of small stones as her father and Mr. Bobic scrambled onto the pavement, headfirst. Mr. Zaric spread his palms and fingers under his chin over the pitted concrete. One of the men slammed the butt of a rifle into the nape of his neck. Mr. Zaric's head snapped up like a hooked fish before it thudded back onto the pavement. The man kicked his head into the ground. His glasses broke and pebbles ground against his forehead. Mr. Zaric could hear the toes of Mr. Bobic's feet thrashing the ground, tapping terribly, as another man banged the back of his head with a rifle and cracked his chin against the concrete.

"Down, rag-head, fucking keep down."

Mr. Bobic blubbered. "My mouth. It's gone."

"Do you think I fucking care? Stay down."

Mr. Zaric felt the spiny steel nose of a rifle barrel being forced into the crack of his buttocks.

"Stay down and answer my questions or I'll fire a bullet up your ass. Where are your families?"

"Gone!"

Irena had leaped up to the window on her own. The old stone ledge ground into the palms of her hands. When she peered outside, she could see that her father's glasses had been smashed against his eyes. Blood bubbled in his eye sockets. She tasted blood herself at the back of her throat, and let her fingers slip from the ledge so that she could fall back down. No one asked what she had seen.

Mrs. Zaric held her daughter's head against her breast as Irena began to gag, dribbling a sour sap of that morning's coffee and tomato juice on her mother's pale blue top. "Just turn away," she said softly into Irena's hair. "Stay down and pray. Hope and think."

Outside, other men in black sweaters had rushed up and now stood around Mr. Zaric and Mr. Bobic. "Where is your family, Mustafa? Your fucking family?"

Incredibly, Mr. Zaric answered. "All of our families are hidden away," he said. "No trouble to you, sir."

Irena clambered up once more to see that Mr. Bobic was trying to lift himself to his knees, so that he would not choke on the blood filling his throat. Several of the men with rifles began to laugh.

"He moves like a wounded bird."

"He squirms like a burning worm."

One of the men swung his black-booted right foot into Mr. Bobic's crotch. The force of the blow turned him over, like a speared fish. "Oh, this one cannot even fucking talk with those teeth," the man said.

"Rag-heads who cannot talk," scoffed another, "cannot venerate Allah." He jabbed the barrel of his rifle into the raw sore of Mr. Bobic's face. The sound of the shot was almost swallowed: a disarmingly flat, final splat of brains against the ground.

Irena let go of the ledge and fell forward on her knees. "Mr. Bobic. Dead. I'm sure." She mouthed the words; her breath was trapped in her ribs.

Mrs. Zaric raised her right hand to rest it on her daughter's shoulder and stood up slowly. "I'm going to tell them we're in here," she said. Irena couldn't hear a budge of protest. Mrs. Zaric was not nearly as tall as her daughter. She stood back toward the rear of the darkened room and shouted, "*Stop! Stop!* We are the families who live here, and we're coming out." She paused while her neighbors stirred slowly around her. "Please. We are coming out."

5.

THEY STAGGERED AND BLINKED UNDER A PREPOSTEROUSLY BRIGHT sky. Irena had taken charge of Pretty Bird, who had stopped pacing in his cage and crumpled to a posture on his claws. About twenty people came up from the basement, wearing spotted old slacks, scuffed shoes, and rumpled shirts, the casual clothing of an afternoon at home. The man who seemed to be in charge left Mr. Zaric twisting on the ground and waved his rifle like a ringmaster as he motioned for the basement-dwellers to stand together.

"I am Commander Raskovic," he announced. "We are taking control of this area so that it can be made safe for Serb people. We cannot let you leave until we have recovered what you have stolen. Open your bags, please. Open them now!"

But before the group could unzip their scuffed athletic bags and scratched luggage, the men in black sweaters bent down and helped themselves. They pulled out American blue jeans and rolled them under their arms, holding them like logs. They threw down men's underwear with a laugh, and stamped on the crotch pouches; they put women's panties over their heads, licking and breathing through them as if they were pink and red surgical masks.

One man found a burgundy-bound family album. He moved through the statuary ranks of stunned people, asking, "Yours? Yours?" When no one answered, he tried to wrench the book apart with his hands, but it held: superior German bookbinding technology. So he flung it down in loathing, unzipped his pants, waved his penis over the book, and began to piss on it. Another man ran over and kicked the book open with the edge of his boot, lowered his pants to his thighs, and began to piss on the book, too. Irena could see the black pages fizzing and turning maroon. She could see the edges of pictures curling, like bugs dying on their backs.

The men turned around and saw Irena watching. She could hear Pretty

Bird flapping against the wires of his cage. One of them charged into her face. "Bitch! You're smiling."

"No, I'm not."

"You are!"

"Why would I smile?" said Irena, with more wrath than she wanted to display. "What the fuck is there to smile about?"

"I will make you smile."

The man walked over to Irena with his pants sliding down his thighs, his gun and the head of his penis snapping up. She tried to move, but her feet felt like a statue's. She heard bullets crackling and, just as she looked up to see pigeons winging, the man pinched her buttocks and pushed up her small bleached-denim skirt. He wrenched her panties down to her thighs, put his heel between her legs, and dragged them down to her ankles. Then he forced himself into her—hard—once, twice, several times before slipping out limply. Irena did not fall. Crazily—the man had a gun, after all—she took a step in his direction. She raised her arms, as if to wring his neck. He staggered back in stunted little-boy steps, his pants sagging around his knees. Irena saw an opening. She kicked him hard with the toe of her shoe.

The man crashed back onto his bare ass in a rubble of shattered glass. The sling on his rifle rose around his neck. His accomplices began to laugh—he had been kicked in the nuts by a girl, and choked with his own rifle sling. For an instant, they seemed to cheer Irena. One of them laughed, and pointed at her feet. "American basketball shoes." The downed man scrambled up with lunatic quickness, aghast at the blood cascading down his legs. He tried to aim his rifle in Irena's direction, but some of the others stepped in front of him; one actually took his gun out of his arms. Irena's mother took a quick step toward her daughter, but the men stopped her. They let the wounded man run at Mrs. Zaric and try to ram himself inside her skirt. He bellowed, "Bitch! Bitch!" into her face. But then his own face began to crumple. His jaw plunged, his top teeth cut into his tongue, his eyes rolled about in his head, and he tottered before flopping to the ground. Mrs. Zaric had slipped a hand into her dress to find her house keys and stabbed them into the man's testicles.

"You are not a man, cocksucker," she shouted from inside a circle of restraining arms. "You have to grab ass from baby girls like my daughter because you can't get your cock up for a real woman. My son had bigger balls when I bathed him in the sink as a baby."

The thugs restrained her, but they didn't try to keep her quiet. She had become the crazy lady in the story they would tell later.

"I've seen bigger balls on French poodles," she went on. "Get up. Come back here. I'll still slice your balls off and feed them to a goat. Nobody else would have the stomach to swallow—"

The man who called himself Commander Raskovic loomed over Mrs. Zaric, holding his left arm out toward Irena, as if he were about to ask the mother for permission to dance with her child.

"This is your daughter?"

Mrs. Zaric was silent.

"Okay, yes? Is your husband with you?"

Mrs. Zaric managed to point toward the ground, where Mr. Zaric was still stretched out, his feet twitching.

"Okay, anyone else in your family? A son?" She shook her head. "No young sons?" She shook her head again. "I'll take your word."

"Our bird," said Mrs. Zaric. "Pretty Bird."

"Okay. You take your daughter and you help your husband up and pick up your bird. The four of you can leave, okay? Leave your luggage and run off to wherever you were going."

Mrs. Zaric and Irena moved wordlessly over to where Mr. Zaric lay smashed on the ground. They lifted his shoulders lightly. Mr. Zaric pressed his hands against the ground and lifted himself to his knees, blood dripping from his eyes and mouth. He carefully touched the red wounds around his eyes, as if trying them on for size. He stiffened slightly as his wife and daughter took him by his elbows and helped him to his feet. He began to speak—he wanted to. But only blood ran out of his mouth.

They walked toward the riverside. Mrs. Zaric figured that Commander Raskovic's remarkable act—it couldn't be called kind, but surely it had saved their lives for a moment—would not give them more than a few minutes of opportunity.

"Don't worry, my darlings," she said, speaking softly into her husband's shoulder. "We will never, ever talk about this."

But Mr. Zaric had swallowed the blood in his mouth and was determined to say something. "Leave it," he gurgled in the direction of his wife, "for Shakespeare."

COMMANDER RASKOVIC CAUGHT their eyes—and waved. A big, bearded man in a dark sweater toting a gun waved. *Waved!* God dammit to hell. *Where have you been? Glad you could join us! Be back soon!* Mrs. Zaric stopped and steadied her husband's left leg before turning and walking back toward Commander Raskovic. Worse than waving—he was smiling.

"Do you think this makes everything all right?" she roared.

Commander Raskovic stared at her in disbelief. He thought they had become friends through troublesome times. "Please, go on," he said. "Get out of here. I am sorry to be friendly. You have this one chance I am giving you."

"You're giving us? Like you're Mother Teresa?"

"I don't think I'm Mother Teresa. Please, don't shout at me in front of my men. You may regret it."

"Regret shouting at you?" she screeched. "You *fuck-face*! What's one more regret? Your gangsters have just raped, beaten, and pissed on my family."

"Don't use such words. Just get going," Commander Raskovic said almost plaintively. "Please. *Please.* My men will obey me for only a moment more." But Mrs. Zaric only moved closer, so close that she imagined plugging the barrel of his rifle with her finger to turn back the bullets so they would blow up into his bearded face.

"We're going to meet again, you son of a bitch," said Mrs. Zaric. "All of you!" she shouted.

"Call the police!" someone cried out. "Call Butter-Ass Butter-Ass Ghali!" someone else shouted in English.

"I don't need the police," said Mrs. Zaric in a cold, jagged dagger of a voice. "I don't need the United Nations. And I certainly don't need your crumbs of favors. All I need is this *anger*"—she positioned her fist above her heart and bellowed the word in his face—"to stay alive to track you down."

IRENA FOUND THAT she could not place the face of the man who had forced himself on her. She remembered that he had a beard. But then so did most of them, and she had used all of her strength to shut her eyes. She remembered more clearly the faces of cute boys who had smiled at her on the tram.

She could feel a sore spot on her right cheek where the man must have scorched her with his chin. She could feel wetness in her panties. As she walked on, she felt sore.

But Irena knew that she healed quickly. She didn't nurse an injury. She played on the old jammed ankle or broken toe as hard as before. God, Allah, or the stars assigned us our talents to be used, not doubted or denied. The game needs every player. Irena, who believed in nothing absolutely, believed in that. She had just seen people killed, and walked away with a limp. She told herself—*consoled* was not a word that occurred to her—that she could make any memory disappear, along with the sore spot on her cheek.

6.

THE ZARICS HAD BEEN HEARING BOMBS ALL DAY: THUDS, POPS, AND crackling. Now, as they moved along Lenin Street and onto the riverbank, they saw them. There was a hiss above their heads, something that looked like a tin pail with a fiery tail. Then it became a harebrained hawk that smacked straight into somebody's third-floor window. An orange bloom burst out of the window, blistering into black gashes and boiling gray clouds.

The Zarics' sense of personal geography had changed with unexpected speed. That morning, a bomb striking just a block away would have seemed like the peril of a lifetime. This afternoon, a bomb a block away may as well have exploded on the other side of the Adriatic Sea. The Zarics kept moving.

They did not break stride when another group of men in black sweaters with rifles asked where they were going.

"To our grandmother's house," Mrs. Zaric said forcefully. "Commander Raskovic told us we could go."

Amazingly, the men accepted that, and let the family go on. Mr. Zaric kept blinking blood from his eyes. Finally, he unbuttoned his shirt and pressed a shirttail over his sockets to stanch the bleeding. Within a few blocks, his staggering grew worse. Another group of men approached them and demanded of Mr. Zaric, "Your watch! Give us your watch!" They stopped for only a moment as Mr. Zaric carefully took his arms from around the shoulders of his wife and daughter to undo his Swiss army watch. He glanced at the time—6:04 P.M.—before tossing it over to the men as mechanically as someone flinging a coin to a porter. One of the men flaunted his rifle in the direction of Irena's feet.

"Air Jordans?"

"Yes," Irena told him boldly, "and I need them to walk."

The Zarics walked on, and the men in black sweaters continued picking through their collection of sweaters, slacks, Adidas, Nikes, and amber-beaded necklaces. TV sets, brass coffee mills, and ice-white German juicers were arrayed on the sidewalk, almost like a marketplace.

Flashes sizzled through the air. Their noses clenched at the stinging smell of fire. A ginger-haired woman in a flowered pink skirt lay on her back, as if sunning herself. She had no face. It must have been eaten by one of the plundered irons or radios whose unplugged cords gave them the look of sated rats. Beside the woman was a small sandy-haired girl in cute blue jeans with kittens on the cuffs. She was either napping or dead; the Zarics chose to leave her in peace. The ground around them sometimes opened up as they walked, spouting rows of flame and sprays of mortar rounds. The Zarics said nothing to one another as they went on. Why would they want to reassure one another that they had seen this?

MR. ZARIC'S MOTHER lived on Volunteer Street in a gray cement apartment building with small balconies and—a curious design feature, given Sarajevo's harsh winters—an outdoor wooden staircase that did not quite disguise the six-story building as some kind of chalet. As the Zarics approached, they could see a man curled up next to a trash bin on the ground floor; perhaps he had been trying to hide. In any case, a bullet had found him—a neat, purpling hole above his right ear. His unblinking eyes were two blue mosaic stones. Mrs. Zaric remembered him.

"Mr. Kovac," she said softly. Then, rather uselessly, "He was a Serb."

"It's hard to tell at the moment," said Irena. Or maybe what she said was "Not that it did him any good," or "I guess they didn't notice." She meant to say all that, but she wasn't listening to herself.

The Zarics skidded on a slick of blood that had gushed from the hole in Mr. Kovac's head. Irena's grandmother was on the landing between the second floor and her apartment on the third, as if she had been headed downstairs. The blood on her blue smock was already hardening into burgundy spatters, like chocolate or strawberry cream.

Mrs. Zaric bent down. Irena and her father could not see her face. "You go on up," she said gently. "I will take care of Grandma."

Mr. Zaric opened his mother's apartment door into the first silence they had heard for hours. A shade flapped lightly at a window. Moving into the kitchen by instinct, he sat in a straight-backed chair. Irena followed and picked up a kitchen towel, held it under hot water, wrung it out, and placed it carefully against her father's eyes. He pressed his forehead against her hand. Mrs. Zaric came in quietly.

"I have taken care of Grandma," she said. "With that pretty Irish throw we gave her. Later, we will take better care of her. But now, I think we need a cup of tea."

Irena ran water into her grandmother's electric kettle and plugged it in while her mother poked in a cabinet for some tea.

"Damn, damn, damn," Mrs. Zaric said. "I cannot figure out where Grandma keeps her tea things."

Mr. Zaric looked up suddenly with a new concern.

"You took care of Grandma with that fluffy green blanket we brought her back from England?"

"Yes," said Mrs. Zaric.

"Take care how?"

"I wrapped her in it. It's soft and warm."

"We may need that blanket," said Mr. Zaric. "Let's be practical."

"Soft and warm may mean more to us," Irena agreed.

When they had finished their tea and rinsed out the cups, they took two tattered old sheets to where Mrs. Zaric had wrapped her mother-in-law. Irena thought the blanket did look a little pointlessly luxurious for a shroud. They whisked the blanket off Grandma, without paying much attention to her face, tucking the sheets under her head and over the plastic flip-flops she was wearing. Mrs. Zaric motioned for Mr. Zaric and Irena to stop, uncovered her mother-in-law's feet, and took off the flip-flops.

"Stupid shoes," said Mr. Zaric. "Not the way to spend eternity."

Irena left her parents alone with her grandmother and took another sheet down to Mr. Kovac by the trash bin. The blood around him had thickened into a kind of burgundy mud. His shoes were the old black Soviet kind, bought before Italian and Spanish shoes could be so freely imported. Soviet shoes were laughably flimsy. The leather was about as durable as paper and the stitching unraveled like string. Many Yugoslavians had lost faith in Communism because of Soviet shoes. How could you believe in a workers' paradise if the workers made shoddy shoes? And *had* to wear them? Mr. Zaric told Irena that he always knew America would reach the moon before Russia, because any cosmonaut would be scared to step onto the moon in a Soviet shoe.

Irena was certain that her father would never wear Mr. Kovac's shoes.

But someone might. Or might trade them for something else. Even old Soviet shoes shouldn't be wasted on the feet of a man who would no longer be going anywhere. She pulled on the laces and slipped the shoes off carefully, then stretched the sheet above him.

"Thank you, Mr. Kovac," she said out loud. Carrying the shoes in her right hand as she went back up the stairs, Irena had to step over her grandmother.

"When Grandma Melic died we called a funeral home," her father was saying. "Funeral homes handle all aspects."

"Even tea cakes," his wife remembered. "But that would be expecting a lot on a day like this."

Irena took charge of the directory and the telephone. After several calls went blank, she got a response from a man at a Muslim funeral home on Sandzacka Street.

"I'm sorry, but we're really too busy to take any more bodies," he told Irena. "Our hearse is getting shot at, and for what? Picking up dead people."

Irena's father motioned her to hand over the telephone.

"We can pay," Mr. Zaric assured the undertaker, one businessman to another.

"Money?" The man laughed as if he had never heard anything so ludicrous. Irena and her mother could hear him chortle clearly through the earpiece until the line went dead.

"We just can't leave Grandma and Mr. Kovac like this," said Mr. Zaric. "It's not right. They deserve to rest."

So as darkness fell on the blackening city, blinking with fires but no light, and booming with explosions and cries, Irena Zaric and her father inched carefully downstairs, smashed the window of the shed in the backyard, and took a shovel. Irena lay down for her father in the small backyard so that he could mark the dimensions around her. For about ten minutes, Mr. Zaric struggled with the shovel, wrenching up loads of soil.

"Shit," he said to Irena. "Now I remember why I work in a store."

Mr. Zaric had just handed the shovel to his daughter when a middle-aged woman with blond hair caught their attention by leaning out of her first-floor window.

"Excuse me—what are you doing here?"

"We are the Zaric family," said Irena's father. "I am Milan. My daughter, Irena. My wife is upstairs. Perhaps you know my mother, Gita?"

"Of course. I am Aleksandra Julianovic."

"Yes, I've heard your name. Well, my mother is dead."

"I am sorry. A lot of people are. We might be soon."

"Yes. Well, Mother is dead already. And Mr. Kovac too."

"Him I didn't know."

"Second floor, I think. Well, we are digging graves to get them into the ground quickly."

"Omigod, are you religious fanatics?" Aleksandra Julianovic said. "We are European in this neighborhood."

"Not at all," said Mr. Zaric.

"They are already dead," Aleksandra Julianovic pointed out. "What more can happen to them?"

Irena stepped in, because she sensed that Mrs. Julianovic was trying her father's civility. "Things can get messy. Think of a piece of fruit."

But Mrs. Julianovic still directed her inquiries to Mr. Zaric. "Are you an undertaker?" she asked.

"No. I sell clothes in a men's store."

"Which one?"

"The International Playboy clothing store on Vase Miskina Street."

"I don't know it. I have never had to buy clothes for a man."

"We have a small women's section," said Mr. Zaric. Irena thought that while the conversation might grate, her father welcomed the respite from digging. "You have to, now that men and women are equal."

"If they are equal," asked Mrs. Julianovic, "why is the women's section smaller?"

"You are too smart for me," said Mr. Zaric. "I just manage the store and sell shirts."

"Do shirt sellers dig graves these days?" she asked.

"We all have to do different things right now. The funeral homes are busy."

"I go to Number Three High School," said Irena. "We learned that Muslims, Jews, and Hindus bury their dead within twenty-four hours. It's a ritual. But holy men made it a ritual because it was a necessity."

"Well, I live here," said Mrs. Julianovic. "It's been a rough day. I liked your mother, and I have nothing against Mr. Kovac. But they're not rose-bushes."

Mrs. Julianovic had a request. "One hole, please," she said.

"There are two bodies," said Mr. Zaric.

"I know that," she said. "But if you dig a separate hole for each person we might have to bury here, we won't have room to plant flowers. Or tomatoes or squash. Why not the same space?"

"It sounds like something Grandma might think of herself," said Irena. Mr. Zaric's face broke into a small smile.

Together, Mr. Zaric and his daughter dug out a space that was a little over six feet long and three feet deep, so that when Irena stood up in it the sides of the hole almost reached her elbows.

Mr. Zaric carried his mother alone, in his arms. "Grandma is heavier than I thought" was all he said.

"We can help," said Mrs. Zaric.

"Mama carried me," said her husband.

They carefully laid Mr. Kovac in first and smoothed the yellow sheet over his body. Then they lifted Mr. Zaric's mother and lowered her down over Mr. Kovac and stood back.

"I'm going to go up and get Pretty Bird," Irena said.

Mr. Zaric waited for his daughter to return with his wrist held over his eyes. When she did, he said, "We are sorry, Mama, for what happened and that we have to leave you here like this. *Put* you here like this," he amended. "In some ways, we are closer than ever."

"And she is closer yet to Mr. Kovac," said Irena, which made Mr. Zaric smile again.

"Wait," said Irena. "The blond lady. I think we should invite her."

Irena rapped on the window just above their shoulders. Aleksandra Julianovic, it seemed, was never far from there.

"Of course, I will be out," she said, and in a moment she was. "We should be quick and careful," she hissed. "Shit is blowing up all around."

They waited for Mr. Zaric to speak. "Thank you, Mama," he said after a moment. "For . . . so much."

It was hard for them to see Mr. Zaric's face in the dark, but they could hear Mr. Zaric holding his mouth open to breathe, and as if to speak.

"Maybe we could sing something," said Mrs. Zaric finally.

"I wouldn't mind hearing 'Penny Lane,' " said Mr. Zaric. "It makes me happy."

"Shouldn't we sing something religious?" asked Aleksandra Julianovic. "It's kind of that occasion."

"What about this?" said Mrs. Zaric, placing her right hand at her throat and gently singing: "*Here comes the sun, doo-doo-doo-doo. Here comes the sun, and I say*— Oh wait, I'm not sure how the rest of the lyrics go. Let's just do the chorus."

Mr. and Mrs. Zaric, Irena, and Aleksandra Julianovic all sang, softly and slowly. Irena was close enough to see her father's face straining. She worried that if he cried the cuts around his eyes would open and blood would wash into his tears. Then he sank to his knees so abruptly that she thought he had been shot. Mrs. Zaric rushed to him. She held the palm of her hand over his ear and cradled his head against her hip.

"Shh, darling, shh, baby," she said. "Be strong, baby, I'm here."

Mr. Zaric fell forward onto the heels of his hands and began to rock back and forth on his head—not so much crying as bleeding with tears. Mrs. Zaric sank to her knees in the coarse ground around her husband, and as he rocked she held her face against the small of his back.

"Give it to me, baby," she said gently. "Give it all to me, baby. I can take it, baby. Give me everything, everything, baby."

A mortar wrinkled across the sky, leaving a crease of light. Something crashed seconds later, clapping against concrete several blocks away. Pretty Bird was silent. Gunfire kept up a low boil.

Irena knew that there was no place for her in this embrace of her parents. Certainly they would have opened their arms for her. But she sensed that what she had seen ran deeper than any experience she had ever had, even after today. She permitted herself a brief flash of jealousy—not because her mother loved her father more, or had loved him longer or differently than she loved her. Irena just couldn't imagine that she would ever love anyone so much.

AGAINST THEIR EXPECTATION, the Zarics managed to eat and sleep. The electricity had been cut off, and there was no water. Aleksandra Julianovic joined them for food, bringing six slices of soft white bread on which to spread the liver sausage they had found in the refrigerator. But it had already hardened too much to eat—or so it seemed on that first night of the war.

So they sat in Grandma's lightless living room, below the windows, and tried to make a meal of small pickles rolled into bread. The Zarics told Aleksandra Julianovic only that they had been expelled from Grbavica. They shared no particulars. Details about that day, and the fine points of their concerns for the future, were unnecessary in any case.

Mrs. Julianovic (she accepted the honorific but had made no mention of a husband, present, former, or deceased) had already analyzed the calamity. "I am sorry for your troubles," she said, tamping her Coca-Cola lighter against a knee. "But, believe me, this is the worst day. You'll be back home in Grbavica soon. I can't promise that your car will still be there. A four-year-old Honda? Pray they go for Volvos first. You took your jewelry? When I traveled through France—I am a retired art teacher—they warned me about thieves in railway stations. So I turned round the stones in my rings and stored my pearl necklace inside my brassiere. I recommend the sensation, incidentally, especially if you're traveling alone. And perspiration and skin oils are supposed to be good for pearls, although they gradually deteriorate lingerie fabric. As no doubt you have observed, Mr. Zaric."

"Ah, yes," he said.

"The West won't permit a war to last more than a few weeks these days," she continued without an audible change of direction. "They put a stop to wars these days before bankers and brokers start hurling themselves through windows. The United Nations already has soldiers here. For Croatia, of course. But they will have to get their hands dirty in Sarajevo, too. Vietnam, Afghanistan. Capitalism, Communism—the big *ism*s learned their lessons in those petite shit holes. They'll let the little brats of the world make their point, then clean up their mess. That's why Kuwait, Panama, Haiti were short wars. War burns money. For each bomb you see, imagine a million dollars in cinders. For each body you see—and, I beg your pardon, I am thinking of your mother, too—imagine someone who can't buy a thousand more Cokes. Losses add up. The West might let killing creep on in Ethiopia or Somalia. People there don't have two rubles to rub together for a Coke." Mrs. Julianovic slapped her hands against her wrists for emphasis. "But *they're* in the Dark Ages. *We* are in *Europe*. We have Benettons here on Vase Miskina Street. Richard Branson sells music next door. Forget that human life is priceless. Consumers' lives have *market value*. In the end, it's a better guarantee. My motto: you can't sell Volvos to dead people."

Mr. Zaric was a moment realizing that it was his turn. "Still," he said. "Milosevic, Karadzic. They seem explicit about wanting this Greater Serbia. There wouldn't seem to be room for good old mixed-up Bosnia in there."

"Ah, the bastards," Mrs. Julianovic said. "Please pardon my French. Slobodan Milosevic's game is Kosovo. I suppose he has promised it to his teenage Russian mistress. She would probably prefer another platinum

Cartier, although I am told there is display room remaining only on her right ankle. The Holy Grail of the Serb nation resides in Kosovo. He who reverses the disgrace of that defeat, so many centuries ago, lays claim to the Serb kingdom. Milosevic is content to keep Bosnia in his basement. But he doesn't want Karadzic's self-proclaimed Bosnian Serb kingdom in his gut. Karadzic, that overweight silver worm, wants to brandish the jewel of Sarajevo in his navel, to rival Milosevic. How can Slobo sit easy on his throne if Karadzic is looking for a chance to steal his velvet slippers? So in the end," said Aleksandra Julianovic, as if presenting the final course of a holiday dinner, "we won't have to lift a finger. I am old and have seen a lot here, as did Gita. The Blue Helmets and the Iron Chump will shut this mess down and we can pick up our lives. I am wondering," she said, "if I want to chance it downstairs in the dark to see if I can find some candy."

GRANDMA'S APARTMENT HAD two bedrooms. But the Zarics chose to spend the night on the floor of the living room. Each took a space along the wall, just below the front windows. They reasoned, on the basis of recent experience that was incomplete but compelling, that any sniper shots or mortars fired through the glass would zing past their heads. Irena lay under her German army jacket, her spine flat against the floor, Pretty Bird quiet by her head. They said good night. Whatever they said to one another, it was at least one thing more than what Irena could remember of the day.

AND SHE SLEPT. Irena was an athlete. Just as she knew that she could rely on her training to bestow speed and strength on demand, she knew that she could now count on her body to grant her sleep.

7.

IT WAS SEVERAL WEEKS BEFORE MOST OF THE REST OF THE CITY decided that the war had begun. It seemed safer to believe that some kind of madness was moving through, like a sudden, blinding snowstorm. No one could stop it; no one could be blamed for it. But at some point it would melt away. You could come up out of the cellar and find all the comforting artifacts of your life set up in your living room.

Yet within just a few days Irena and her family had made critical adjustments. Some of them were more or less instantaneous and, once done, more obvious than amazing. Irena was surprised to hear that Bruce Springsteen had left Julianne Phillips, or that Mick Jones had left the Clash to begin BAD II, or that Magic Johnson had gotten sick and could no longer play basketball. But sleeping through the pops of mortars and the rattle of machine guns; taking care not to sit above the line of the windowsill; opening old canned goods and dividing a few ounces of waxed beans into four cold meals; keeping all spigots open so that when the Serbs teasingly turned on the water for an hour they could spring up to capture it in tubs, cups, and bottles—all of that became their daily custom.

"Hell must also have its routines," Aleksandra Julianovic said to Irena.

THE SERBS WOULD turn on the water only to keep Bosnians up all night, anxious and itchy, hoping to hear a splash. Turning on the water in a Sarajevo apartment building was like strewing bread crumbs around trees to attract famished pigeons. Serb snipers knew that if they turned on the water briefly, they could shoot into almost any bathroom window and hit or scare a Bosnian concentrating on an old milk jug under the bathtub spigot.

. . .

THE ZARICS HAD to decide what to do about the windows. The windows in each bedroom of Grandma's apartment faced the mountains and the snipers. They could leave those windows alone, and go into the rooms only when they had to forage for possessions to sell or burn.

The window in the bathroom also faced the mountains. It was small, high, frosted, and risky. They could only hope that it would not be noticed across the way. To compress any profile he might offer a sniper through that window, Mr. Zaric decided always to sit on the toilet when relieving himself.

The center of their puzzle was the three large windows in the living room on a side of the building that faced away from the mountains at an angle. Mr. Zaric made a drawing on the inside flap of one of his mother's old romance novels. He sketched out lines and arrows, and concluded that the plane was still broad enough to tempt a sniper. People in surrounding buildings, and in apartments on other floors, could be heard hammering doors, crates, and tabletops across their windows.

"Ah, but that must be so gloomy inside," said Mrs. Zaric. "Like living in a cave."

Mr. Zaric agreed. "So unlike our glamorous present surroundings." This earned him the laugh he had sought from his wife.

"Snipers have a city full of targets to choose from," said Irena. "Why would our windows be looked at in particular?"

"Because they're there," said Mr. Zaric. "Still there."

"Pretty Bird would always be asleep," said Irena. "I think darkness turns on some kind of sleep channel in his brain."

"Well, if we don't cover the windows," said Mr. Zaric, "I don't know how long I can scuttle over the floors like a crab." He hunched up his shoulders and let his arms dangle to make his point.

"That's a baboon," said Irena. "They go from tree to tree." Pretty Bird obliged with a trill.

"We can stand up in the hallways when we need to," said Mrs. Zaric. "In shifts. You love schedules." It was her turn to win a laugh. "Sing. Dance. There's room enough for Toni Kukoc to stand up in our hallways."

Mr. Zaric began to rock back on his heels in the hallway, as if he were about to deliver a judgment from on high. "You've convinced me," he said finally. "In the end, it all pivots on advertising. Covering the windows with a door is like putting up a billboard for those bastards across the way. We might as well install a bloody blinking sign that says, 'Hello, mate! Someone is living in here. Fire away!' I think," he went on, "that the windows ought to stay. At least for as long as they last."

"I give you my word," said Mrs. Zaric. "You will never catch me cleaning them."

GRANDMA'S BUILDING WAS six stories tall, and each floor had six apartments—basic, boxy, late-Tito-era housing crates, with cold concrete floors and painted white cinder-block walls. The Zarics had been pleased when Grandma moved in. The building was well situated for an elderly person who was energetic and wanted to be independent. The apartments were just below Old Town's picturesque twisting streets, coffee bars, and kebab stands, a block away from the central synagogue, which offered many cultural programs (*Tuesday Night Rabbi Zemel will show full-color slides of his spring trip to historic Orlando USA*) and served hot lunches at noon (although Mr. Zaric's mother had preferred to have her lunch at a kebab stand, where she could have a beer).

War depreciated these assets. Mountain and river views now meant exposure to mortar and sniper shots. Early on, a mortar round had pierced one of the yellow panels, one of the building's few gestures toward charm. The explosion gouged deep into a fourth-floor hallway, where people were snoozing in rows.

The Zarics heard crashing and screaming above them. They sprang out of their own sleep to rush upstairs. But, just as quickly, they heard snipers shooting through the hole. The Serbs had fired a mortar to shed blood that would draw more people to be killed.

"Wait," said Mr. Zaric, holding up his arms. "Not just yet. Wait."

"We have to do *something*," said Irena.

"What?" snapped Mrs. Zaric. "Hurry just to fill their gun sights? Give them more targets?"

For a few long minutes, the Zarics faced one another across a dark room again, trading words heavily.

"Maybe it's stopped."

"Maybe. Wait."

"For what?"

"For it to stop."

"Stop? When?"

"Oh, fuck, it's a war," said Mrs. Zaric finally. "It never stops."

They went upstairs and found that three people had died. A man flashed a beam of light from a torch over each set of eyes.

"Recognize them?" he asked Mr. Zaric.

"We're new here ourselves," Mr. Zaric answered, a touch defensively. "From Grbavica. We had to move into my mother's apartment."

"Yes, Gita," said the man with the torch. "I heard. Aleksandra brings the word. She is our Columbus these days, sailing between worlds. Each floor is a continent."

"Can we . . ." Mr. Zaric's thought drifted off.

"Oh, hell," said the man. "I don't know these people. I know the Ciganovic family was living up here. But they may have gone across the other way. I don't know if it's forever or just for a while, though I can't see that they have much reason to return. These folks might have come in from the country." He flashed the light along their shoes, which were heavy-toed and mud-brown. "Bijeljina and Zvornik. Walked here with what they had on their backs and just kept turning doorknobs until they found a place left open. Made themselves at home. Even this place might seem like bloody Paris after Vukovar. And then, poor devils, they run into the same damn bastards here."

The man scoured the cold faces with his torch: two men and a boy. Their blood had spilled out quickly, leaving their skin white and glistening under the light, almost like ice. God forgive me, Irena thought to herself, for seeing anything beautiful right now. She imagined the two men and the boy sleeping for centuries in some arctic gorge, safely awakened long after the men who killed them had gone.

SHE WALKED OVER to the hole in the wall and reached out to touch the rough bottom where concrete and plaster had been punched through. It was still a little warm, and gritty under her fingers. More of the wall gave way at her touch. It was the middle of the night, and the sides of the hole felt like stones and sand in a hot sun.

"That's a stupid thing to do," Mr. Zaric said from behind.

"It's dark," she said. "They can't see me."

"Infrared sights," said Mr. Zaric. "Night goggles. *Star Trek* glasses. Even the old Yugoslav Army has them."

"They'd have to be looking," said Irena, as she drew back.

"You can see all these lights out there, you know," she said. "The other side, I mean. Over here, it's like someone just rolled a blanket over everything. Over there, in the hills, back home, close enough to touch. You can see porch lights, car lights, streetlights. You can see the little lights between floors in staircases, and fizzing little yellow display lights in windows for beer. I can see the light on the orange roof of the old Serb church, and the light over the loading dock at school. It's amazing. It's normal. I'm sure they even have ice cream."

"Don't they know that there's a war going on?" Mr. Zaric took his daughter smoothly by the shoulders to steer her away from the hole.

"I could kill them," said Irena softly.

"Don't say that," said her father.

"All right," said Irena. "I won't. All the same"—she turned toward the hole again, and saw another maddening sprinkle of pretty lights—"I could."

JUST BEFORE DAWN, a dozen more families from Grandma's building took their own ten minutes to fill gym bags and garbage sacks with as much of their lives as they could carry on their backs. A few had places in mind, and were welcomed into the apartments of relatives or friends. Others begged shelter from strangers, and a few, they heard, simply threw out other people at gunpoint.

The city was being reshuffled. The relocations began as a temporary inconvenience that each party vowed to bear cheerfully, as a human and a patriotic duty. As the weeks went by, though, cheerfulness and courtesy began to wear thin. Inside the apartments, people who had been relative strangers suddenly had to share the same small supply of food, water, and breathing space.

THE ZARICS FORCED open Mr. Kovac's door to find anything he might have to help them get by. There was a little money and jewelry. They kept the money and hid a gray-stoned ring and a silver money clip in one of Grandma's market bags.

"To save them from thieves," said Mr. Zaric. He had ventured into Mr. Kovac's closet and found that he could fit into the other man's coats, shirts, and sweaters. The slacks pinched somewhat—he had to strain to button them. But the scarcity of food in the city was already working to tailor his waist to the garment. A green felt vest, a couple of pink oxford shirts, and four pairs of red Dutch socks were unexpectedly jaunty, and Mr. Zaric quickly got over his initial discomfort with wearing the undershorts of a dead man whom he had barely known.

"Plain white briefs," he emphasized to Aleksandra Julianovic. "No pink silk panties, per your suspicions."

Irena and her mother helped themselves to Grandma's clothes. They hung loosely, but Irena found two pairs of blue jeans—one left by her, another apparently by her brother—that were a better fit.

THE INTERNATIONAL PLAYBOY clothing store ("No relation to Playboy International Inc. claimed or implied" had to run below the title ever since the fall of the Berlin Wall had given copyright lawyers more standing in local courts), which Mr. Zaric managed, was closed.

Mr. Zaric himself glumly brought back the news one morning after walking over to Vase Miskina Street in Old Town. He had promised to stay near people who looked as if they were streetwise and shrewd. He had been following a vigorous young man in a leather motorcycle jacket when a bullet snipped between them and slammed into the bricks of a water fountain.

The young man rolled into a drainage channel. Someone must have taught him that maneuver, thought Mr. Zaric admiringly. He could only scramble behind a green trash bin. There was a tinny sound as he thumped it gently, and he realized that the bin probably afforded him as much fortification as an olive oil can.

"I wouldn't grip the thing with my fingers like that," the young man called out.

"Oh, shit, you're right," said Mr. Zaric. "Fingers showing." He drew in his hands and tucked his elbows into his sides. Knees, ankles, and now his elbows—every joint was straining to keep Mr. Zaric tucked behind his olive oil can. "A real Houdini pose I'm holding here," he called back.

"Now would be the time to make yourself disappear!" said the man.

They heard their laughs falling on the empty streets.

"You seem to know how to handle yourself out here," said Mr. Zaric. "Are you a soldier?"

"Oh, shit no!" the man called up from the drainage ditch. "A priest at St. Francis."

"You seem streetwise," said Mr. Zaric.

"I am Irish," said the priest.

"Belfast?" asked Mr. Zaric.

"Sorry to disappoint. Donegal."

"Where did you learn to duck like that?"

"Where does anybody learn anything? Television."

"I wish we were having this conversation in a pub," said Mr. Zaric. He could hold that posture comfortably for only about three minutes, and painfully for only another two. "I've got to turn round," he shouted over to the priest. "Can't do this anymore. I'll just tumble over and look like a goose on a platter to him."

"Turn carefully," said the priest.

"My name's Milan Zaric, and we used to live in Grbavica," he said without moving. "My wife's name is Dalila. I have a son, Tomaslav, who is in Vienna now, and a daughter, Irena."

"She plays basketball," said the priest.

"You know her?"

"She's good. Number Three beat our girls' asses at St. Francis in the Tito youth group games."

"Well, if this turn isn't so triumphant," said Mr. Zaric, "we're living on the third floor of a building right over on Volunteer Street. With an outdoor staircase."

"The chalet, I'll find them," said the man. "I'm Father Chuck. I'll pray for you to turn like Katarina Witt."

And, indeed, the mere intonation of the name seemed to inspire Mr. Zaric to spin his shoulders and knees around to bring his back against the trash bin. He settled in more easily.

"Bra-vo!" Father Chuck called over. "I heard that. Nine-point-eight, say the judges."

Mr. Zaric could feel a crease from the bin pressing into his forehead, and kept his right elbow in at his waist as he raised his arm to touch it; he felt no blood. He had not been able to read well since his glasses were smashed in Grbavica. But he could make out a message that a hand had scored in large black letters on the side of the fountain: FUAD IS OK TELL HIS MOTHER. Mr. Zaric didn't know the name.

"How long do we wait here, Padre?"

"Until dark wouldn't be bad. But I have to go to the bathroom, and I'm sure we both wouldn't be out here if we didn't have things to do."

"Maybe our friend in the hills figures he's got us pinned down and has turned his attentions elsewhere," suggested Mr. Zaric.

"Or he's waiting."

"Or bored. I am."

Within ten minutes, they heard the sound of shots ringing elsewhere.

"Oh, that's downtown," said Mr. Zaric. "Blocks away."

"They have more than one gun, I'm sure," said Father Chuck. "Let's get up at the same time," he suggested. "Confuse the bastard."

"Count to three. One."

"Two."

"Two and a half?"

"Yes, keep going."

"Three!"

The two men scampered under the eaves of an old lunch shop that was known for its *cevapcici,* the small lamb-sausage sandwich of Sarajevo, and shook hands.

"You must come to our church for a meal sometime," said Father Chuck. "During a lull or a cease-fire. Better yet, when this nonsense is over. We don't want a family of three running through these streets for the canned soup we're going through at the rectory."

Later, Mr. Zaric didn't tell his family about his ten minutes behind the trash can on General Stepa Stepanovic Quay. He simply said, "I met the most delightful young man in Old Town today."

WHEN MR. ZARIC turned the corner onto Vase Miskina Street, there was a gaunt gray dog eating a carcass. Looters got greedy. They would run off with their arms overstuffed, and shed a trail of running shoes, cigarettes, soap bars, and cologne bottles. Mr. Zaric supposed that the looter of a *cevapcici* shop probably took more carcasses than he could carry. Then he saw that there were bits of blue cloth clinging to the underside of the lamb's hulk. There was nothing to do except to keep walking, which is what Mr. Zaric did. "I have seen more sickening things," he told himself. "I'm almost glad that the man and the dog could be useful to each other."

THE INTERNATIONAL PLAYBOY store was now a shell. The windows had been smashed, and all the goods on the shelves had been stolen, down to the last pair of ankle socks. Someone had even ripped the toilet bowl away from the bathroom wall, leaving a bare pipe and angry black letters on the tile: MUSLIMS EAT SHIT.

"Like, 'Katarina Witt Drinks Pepsi,' " Mr. Zaric told his family. But there was no concealing the depression behind his rueful jokes. "No work means no money," he told his wife and daughter. "Our savings are locked up in Greater Serbia. I don't know how we're going to live. Did I just say that?" he asked them. " 'I don't know how we're going to live'?"

IRENA WAS BEWILDERED when her father told her that he didn't want her going into the streets to pick up some of the aid supplies that U.N. troops had begun to hand out in the city. She had begun to feel cramped in the confinement. Spring was usually a pivotal time for her in basketball. She missed the challenge of being useful.

"I can carry more than anyone," she argued. "And run faster besides."

"That's just the point," said Mr. Zaric. "You can run faster than your mother or me. You might even run faster than a bloody gazelle. But not faster than a bullet."

"You were fine," she pointed out.

"I was fortunate," he said. "That's different. Michael Jordan couldn't move fast enough to avoid a sniper if his aim is good. His or her, I suppose you have to say for everything nowadays."

Mrs. Zaric, who thought that her husband had seemed blithe about his afternoon out, said, "I'll go with her. We'll be together."

"So you both get in trouble?"

"You can't expect us to stay cooped up in here forever."

"No. Only as long as necessary," he said.

"Like what?" asked Mrs. Zaric. "The Frank family?"

"I was hoping for a happier ending," said Mr. Zaric.

"Look, we could use the food," Mrs. Zaric said in the low tone of voice she had always used to keep Irena from hearing them (Irena heard them anyway). "If she doesn't get out, Milan, she will be intolerable company in here. Besides, she's right: she can be useful. And," she added more urgently, "Milan, Irena has a right to see."

THE RADIO SAID that a water tap had been opened on a small street off General Radomir Putnik Boulevard. They rinsed out a large plastic soft-drink bottle and an old roasting pan.

Irena sang, *"Good, good, good, good vibrations!"* as she drummed her fingers over the bottom of the pan she was carrying under her arm. Her mother carried the empty soft-drink bottle under one arm and a yellow pail in the other.

Mr. Zaric's eyes softened as he saw them to the door. "Oh, my God," he said. "You two look as if you were going to spend the day at the beach in Dubrovnik."

MRS. ZARIC AND IRENA walked down Proletariat Brigade Boulevard without incident. But the silence of the main street was unnerving. Irena loved losing herself in the hum of the city—the clink of coffee cups and human commotion, the purposeful clatter of heels along the boulevard. She loved stepping in and out of knots of people and absorbing their conversations. Now she could hear only her voice against the stones. It sounded lonely when it came back to her.

"The temperature is better than I expected" was all she could think to say to her mother.

They joined a line of about twenty people, standing behind a bus that had been overturned in the street so that its undercarriage could block sniper fire. A Bosnian policeman in a blue shirt had opened a water spigot on the side of a red-brick building, and people took turns holding their soda bottles under the stream. The crowd was conspicuously quiet. People kept their eyes down. No one said, "How happy I am to run into you, hungry, unwashed, wearing borrowed clothes, and standing in line for water."

Mrs. Zaric and Irena had been waiting for perhaps five minutes when a man came up behind them. He had three young children in tow, two boys and a girl, barely old enough to manage the jugs each carried.

A woman wrapped in a brown blanket turned around. "Those kids won't get you any extra water," she told him. "It's two bottles for everyone, no more."

"But I have three children," he explained.

"It's a rule. You shouldn't drag those children out here anyway."

"Their mother is dead," said the man.

"So will they be if you don't get them out of here." Now she was upset, red-faced, and sputtering.

"I'm to leave them alone in our apartment, where they can crawl up to a window and be shot?" the father asked.

Mrs. Zaric moved closer to the woman in the blanket.

"I think everyone has made a good point," she said.

When Mrs. Zaric and Irena got to the spigot, the policeman confirmed that they could fill only two containers—any two.

"So we can fill this old roasting pan?"

"Of course," he said.

"And the pail?"

"Yes," he said. "No matter."

"But we could also fill just the bottle and the pail. Or two roasting pans? I'm not sure I understand the sense of this limit."

People behind Irena and her mother were beginning to stir and snort as as if to say that they didn't have all day. But although Irena wasn't about to remind them, all of them probably did.

"Filling two containers—or ten—is not the problem," said the policeman. He motioned them to place the first of their containers below the spigot.

Mrs. Zaric felt the pail get heavier as it filled with water, and enjoyed the cold splash over her knuckles. As she braced the full pail against her hip, Irena positioned the roasting pan below the spigot.

"That's too much!" someone complained, but the policeman held up a hand. "We are fed by a spring here," he told them. "Plenty for everyone." The spigot made a rusty screech as he turned it open again to fill the pan.

Irena bent over to lift it and realized that it wouldn't budge.

"Serves you right for being greedy," someone called out.

With the pail in her left hand, Mrs. Zaric used her right hand to take hold of a handle on the roasting pan while Irena lifted it with both arms. Water splashed out of both the pail and the pan with their first steps. The more they walked, the more water splashed. Small waves rolled in the roasting pan and crested over the sides, spilling water over Irena's chest. They had not taken ten steps before they had to stop and set down the pail and the pan heavily. They were losing the water, and losing strength from their laughter.

"I'm glad we didn't bring a bathtub," said Mrs. Zaric. "We'll have empty pans and wet shoes."

They waddled past the overturned bus and back down Proletariat Brigade, looking a little like tottering ducks to anyone who might have been watching.

MR. ZARIC HAD found a sheaf of postcards in his store that he used to send out to customers; he put them in his jacket pocket. He was a methodical man who believed in orderliness. He could see using the cards to prepare lists of things the family should bear in mind: the bottles they had available to bring to public taps, the number of cans of beans and meatballs that were still in the kitchen, the number of bandages they had left. He put the cards aside when his wife reached across the kitchen table for one and wrote "Tuesday: Stay Alive" in the center.

MR. ZARIC HAD worked every day of his life since the age of eighteen, including most Saturday afternoons. This had occasionally conflicted with Irena's basketball games, and he had asked for his daughter's understanding: they both served the public. She couldn't play a league game on, say, Wednesday at ten in the morning, when it would not conflict with social plans for her and her teammates. Games were scheduled for fans. Games had to be played when their work was done, dinner was done, and the dishes had been put away. So it was in selling, he said. What they did served others; that made it worth doing.

Mr. Zaric had no job to go to now. Mrs. Zaric asked Irena to understand that this was another loss for her father, like the sudden disappearance of a longtime friend. Mr. Zaric missed the companionship and sense of purpose that his work had afforded him.

They were running short on candles. The electricity had flickered and then died when Serb paramilitaries severed the power lines. Stores selling candles had stocked only enough for birthdays and romantic dinners, and had already been looted, in any case. So Mr. Zaric went to work. He took the residue of wax left by each candle that burned down and put it into an empty bean can. While his wife was heating water for tea over a fire in the kitchen one morning, Mr. Zaric lowered the bottom of the can into the water. In time, the water began to sputter. So did Mr. Zaric.

"It—it—look! I'm on to something!"

Irena and her mother sat bleary-eyed, wanting only their tea.

"Look!" he cried, brandishing the bean can in an oven mitt like one of Irena's basketball trophies. "Do you see? Do you see?" They didn't, quite.

"Look here," he said, presenting the can for consideration as if it were a prop in a magic act. "Observe that the wax has begun to melt. Had we heated a little more water," he went on with obvious excitement, "more of the wax would have melted."

Irena and her mother smiled—amenable, if still uncomprehending.

"So. A candle burns out. But, as philosopher John Lennon once observed, we all shine on. The candle merely waits—and under the circumstances I don't avoid the spiritual connotation—for resurrection. *Voilà!*" he said, irresistibly. "When we heat water for tea or coffee, for washing, we remember to add the previous day's candle droppings into the bean can. I'll make out a schedule. No, I'll take charge of it myself. I have laid a length of string vertically inside the can. We suspend the bean can in the simmering liquid. The old wax melts into the bottom. Each day, another inch or so accumulates. Until—" He motioned for Irena to give him a match, and she slipped one into his hand.

"Until," he intoned while striking a match and lighting the string, "a new candle is born. This spent bean canister becomes a *cauldron* for new light." A small flame burned over the lip of the can.

"We won't be able to see the flame in a few minutes," Mrs. Zaric pointed out. "It will dip below the side of the can as your precious candle burns down."

"I thought of that," her husband said, pinching out the flame with his fingers. "We cut away the can and let the candle stand free."

"Cut with what?" she asked. "I didn't see a steel cutter among Grandma's kitchen things. She didn't build cars in here."

"With my teeth, if need be," said her husband, undaunted and somewhat touchy.

"Let me point out," he went on, "how this system renews resources. I truly think—I am being serious here—we should tell the United Nations Earth Summit. Sarajevo shows the world! We do not build an extra fire to melt the wax. No extra precious kindling. We use heat from water that is already boiling. All candles burn. Ours will burn over and over. We have invented the self-perpetuating taper!" he said.

Irena had never seen her father in such a state, and thought he had gone mad. Mrs. Zaric, standing with her hands on her hips, said, "Sometimes catastrophes unveil the true geniuses among us."

ONE MORNING, POLICEMEN from the new Bosnian government came to the apartment building on Volunteer Street and announced that all men over the age of eighteen had to report for army duty. Irena's father received them grandly.

"I have been expecting you," he said. "I would have enlisted myself, except that I hadn't heard where to go. I have Serb heritage, you know, and I am proud to defend Bosnia. I am ready now."

The police were a bit taken aback by his ardor, but they didn't want to dampen it. "Noncombat duties are important, too," they said in Mrs. Zaric's direction.

"Who among us in Sarajevo has a noncombat life right now?" he replied. The officers chuckled into their buttons and said that if Mr. Zaric came with them they would find something for him to do; he could return for home leave in a few days.

At an officer's suggestion, Mrs. Zaric packed a change of Mr. Kovac's clothes for her husband, wrapping them inside a pair of slacks that he could carry under his arm.

"It's a new army," a policeman had explained with some embarrassment. "We have no uniforms per se. Everyone kind of wears what he can find."

Mr. Zaric kissed his wife and daughter goodbye. They held themselves back a bit, so as not to spoil Mr. Zaric's delight in his new sense of purpose. He pressed his face against Pretty Bird's cage to blow a kiss. "Keep our family laughing, Pretty Bird," he said. "I will keep the nation safe and be back before you know!"

Mr. Zaric was back in the apartment that night.

"THEY DIDN'T QUITE know what to do with a forty-four-year-old nearsighted clothes salesman," he said. "I volunteered to be a general. They said they didn't need to dip that far down into the barrel yet.

"They asked me if I had ever done anything besides sell shirts. 'Well,' I said, 'I wrote poems in school. I know about a hundred words of Chinese. I know every lyric ever written by the Beatles and Leonard Cohen.' The captain in charge—a capable young man from the country, I think—just rolled his eyes and said, 'Fucking Sarajevo.' I told him that I've been digging graves recently. He said, 'Well, maybe you're not totally useless.' "

THE ARMY WANTED to dig up some graves along the front lines on Kosevo Hill. The captain said that some Serbs in the Yugoslav National Army had stolen weapons from their arsenals and buried them in coffins in the Bare Cemetery. They were heard to declare, as they turned the earth, "Serb history is no longer in the grave. These coffins hold the Serbs' future!"

The captain said that a strike team from the Bosnian Army (a phrase that still rang so strangely—so foreign—as to sound hilarious to Mr. Zaric) was going to make a sudden thrust into no-man's-land that would draw fire. Mr. Zaric and three other men would run in with shovels to dig up the freshest grave there, and bring out weapons for Bosnia's new army.

"The Blue Helmets are here to enforce an arms embargo," said the young captain. "Which means that Serbs keep the weapons they have from the old national army. We have to have old men dig our guns out of graves."

"I'm not offended," said Mr. Zaric, who was, a bit.

"And I'm not incorrect," said the captain. "I hope you understand: I am not going to risk soldiers to do a grave digger's job."

SO THREE HOURS after his morning coffee Mr. Zaric met three other men of his approximate vintage: a schoolteacher, a dishwasher, and a prisoner who had just been released to lend a hand to Bosnia's war effort.

The prisoner said he had been arrested with hashish in his pocket, and avowed that he had no violent traits. The schoolteacher told Mr. Zaric that he had heard of Irena. The dishwasher said that he used to work at Fontana restaurant, and would sometimes see Mr. Zaric behind the counter of his store.

"Don't get to be best pals," the captain barked. "You may have to see one another die today!"

The captain had parked his four grave digger-uppers in a blue van partway up the hill along Jukic Street. They heard someone shout; rifle shots crackling from somewhere not far ahead of them; and then the slap of feet in front of them, to the side of the van, and finally, behind them. The captain leaped into the driver's seat.

"We opened up with guns," he gasped, "and they've just rolled out a tank."

"Maybe we should leave the van and just run down the hill," said Mr. Zaric.

The captain grunted. "No time. I'm trying to save this fucking van." He drove it down into a small dip in the road, below the tank's line of fire—or so they all fervently hoped. He ordered the others out of the van and into a sprint while shots from the Serb lines snapped in the air over their heads. Mr. Zaric felt a hot orange ball growing in his lungs as he ran. Four sets of running shoes made desperate little rubber yelps until they reached an embankment at one end of the cemetery. They rolled to a stop against one another, panting like tired dogs behind a chiseled stone wall.

"I think," said the schoolteacher, panting. "Our little raid. A mistake."

"Yes," said the dishwasher. "Intelligence. They should have. Intelligence. That tank."

"Intelligence?" the old prisoner said. Their breathing was beginning to return. "The tank is across the street. You don't need James Bond to tell you there's a tank across the street."

"That young captain is no Rommel," said the schoolteacher.

"Yes," said Mr. Zaric. "He lacks our experience."

THE MEN'S LAUGHTER was cut short by their breathlessness. The prisoner—who, Mr. Zaric thought, ought to be the most at ease behind a gray stone wall—began to squirm. "Oh, shit," he said. "We left our shovels. Back in that damn van."

"They're gone now," said Mr. Zaric. "From the sound of it, I think the Serbs have taken back a few feet of ground."

"Not that they need another van and a bunch of shovels," said the schoolteacher. "What with guns and tanks."

"Tomorrow young Napoleon will order us to break into a gun warehouse," said the schoolteacher. "To get back some shovels."

The men hunched behind the wall for more than an hour, even as the battle sounds subsided. They didn't know where else to go. In time their young captain pulled up in an old red matchbox Lada and they all squeezed in. Mr. Zaric thought of high-school science films showing packs of zebras standing head to rump, head to rump.

"I was wondering, Captain," said Mr. Zaric, "as we were all thrown into this rather suddenly. Where would you like us to stay tonight? Are we assigned to specific units? I was also wondering if, at some point, we might qualify for a small amount of food."

Captain Kesic—his name was visible for the first time on a creased plastic identity card snapped to his shirt—turned to fix Mr. Zaric with a look that could have shot down a bird.

"Do you think this is the American army? Air-conditioned barracks, beefsteak on the table, and cold beer in the dining hall? Do you want red tunics and bearskin hats like the Buckingham Palace guards? You will stay at home. You will feed your own faces at home. The Bosnian Army will not spend one worthless red Russian ruble on you. Until, God forbid, we have to call on you again. Maybe to dig a shit hole."

His sense of accomplishment restored, the captain had the men back to their families within the hour.

...

WHAT HAD BEEN Grandmother Zaric's telephone would twitch and twitter with a shrill, unbroken ring every few nights when Serb militia, tapping into some of the lines they had cut, wanted to chat. The calls commonly came in the middle of the night. Daylight would have dispelled much of the intended effect. Mrs. Zaric would leap for the phone, hoping it was Tomaslav, who might think to call his grandmother when their old number did not ring.

"Yes, please, who is this?"

"Who is this?" a male voice echoed back. "Lady, we are your worst nightmare."

"Oh, please," said Mrs. Zaric. Or sometimes, "Oh, fuck off. Call someone who cares. Just let us get some sleep."

"Sleep? We're coming over to kill you."

"Then let us sleep until you do," she said.

"What's your name? You sound cute."

"I am. What's your name? You sound pretty pathetic if you have to call women you don't know in the middle of the night."

Then the line went dead.

"I think the boys are passing out our number over there," Mr. Zaric whispered heavily.

"They call to scare us, and I scold them," said Mrs. Zaric. "We're even."

"Not so," said her husband. "Not close."

MRS. ZARIC LOOKED over in the dark to see if Irena, who had stirred at the sound of the phone, had fallen back to sleep. She was breathing deeply. But the curve of her backside was tense.

"Pimply, horny boys, that's all," he continued hoarsely. "Calling to hear a cute girl say dirty words."

"One of those boys . . ." Mrs. Zaric's voice trailed off. She and her husband looked over at their daughter and saw that her toes were clenched, almost like Pretty Bird's. It was as if Irena, too, were asleep on a slender perch.

8.

IRENA HEARD AN INSISTENT KNOCK ON THEIR DOOR ONE AFTERnoon and called out to the other side, "Yes, please. Who is it?"

"Someone who thinks it's charming that you still observe social conventions," answered a woman's husky voice.

"Aleksandra."

Mr. and Mrs. Zaric looked up with a smile as Irena opened the door.

"Thank you, dear," said Aleksandra. "Some of the old social niceties have taken a terrific cuffing these days. Like not shooting your neighbor." She was carrying a rolled-up magazine under one arm, and appeared to be wearing Mr. Kovac's green rain slicker as a housecoat.

"A little something I found under Mr. Kovac's bathroom sink," she said, offering the magazine to Irena. It was British *Vogue*, June 1991, the magazine's seventy-fifth-anniversary issue. There were three bare-shouldered women on the cover—blond, auburn, and brunette. "Special Collector's Edition," it said across the cover.

"Linda Evangelista is the blonde," said Irena. "I didn't know she was so tall."

"Cindy Crawford is on the right, I think," said Mrs. Zaric. "The beauty mark over her mouth—it's like the stamp on gold."

"I have such a mark," said Aleksandra. "But it takes some work to find." She sat down at the kitchen table and opened the magazine while Mr. Zaric crawled over to the living-room windowsill to fetch the old pickle jar in which he was steeping a tea bag in water warmed by the sun.

He poured the brew into three small glasses and clinked the jar against one as they gathered around the magazine. There was a model with hair as short as Irena's. Her shoulders were bare and, Mrs. Zaric thought, bonier and less appealing than her daughter's. She said so.

"Ah, but that girl is beautiful," said Irena.

"She's not much older than you," said Aleksandra. "Perhaps not even."

Mrs. Zaric had found a page of society pictures. Women in jeweled dresses had organized an event at the Café Pelican that raised thirty thousand pounds for homeless people. "The cost of just one of their necklaces, I'm sure," tut-tutted Mrs. Zaric. A few pages on, there was a whole spread showing a dark-haired woman in a red raincoat leaning dreamily against an old Greek column, her lips made creamily red by a new lipstick. "Your lips are continuously protected from damage," the ad said.

"We should cover ourselves with this lip gloss," said Aleksandra.

Irena lingered over the picture of a red-haired woman in a series of yellow velvet dresses, hugging a wolfhound on a snowy estate. The caption said, "Keep trim this summer by eschewing the elevator and bounding up stairs."

"We will be *soooo* trim," said Mrs. Zaric. "We are *soooo Vogue!*"

They were not even halfway through the magazine before they came upon a picture of the Princess of Wales in blue jeans, holding her two boys by the hand.

"She is so beautiful," said Irena. "A princess in blue jeans."

"She is famously unhappy," said Aleksandra Julianovic. "You marry a prince who's really a frog. With all she has, I still feel sorry for her."

Irena was awarded possession of the *Vogue,* on condition that she keep it available. But she did tear out the page with Princess Diana and her two boys, and smoothed it into a corner of Pretty Bird's cage, where she hoped she might be charmed by his clowning.

IRENA WANTED TO go out and bring back food and water for her family and Aleksandra, and maybe others in the building, too. Her parents were adamantly opposed, but she was persuasive. She could see that she had grown thinner and weaker over the weeks—they all felt more frail. She would stand in the hallway and pull at the slack skin over her stomach and hips, convincing her parents that she needed the exercise and challenge as much as they all needed the food and water.

Irena was also impatient to get out and see the streets on her own. She blamed only the Serbs in the surrounding hills. But she was beginning to resent her parents for keeping her curbed in the apartment like a disobedient eight-year-old. She was burning up inside. She wanted to run, find friends, and see people she didn't know. She wanted to be alone.

Mr. Zaric invented a harness that would make it easier for Irena to carry bottles of water. He laced together four belts from Mr. Kovac's closet, tongue to buckle, in two sets that Irena could sling over her shoulders. He cut four lengths from his mother's plastic clothesline and looped them through the belts to hold four water bottles, leaving her hands free for more bottles, or bags of rice, flour, and beans.

"This rig minimizes the carrying apparatus to maximize the weight that can be toted," said Mr. Zaric. "So simple, if I may say so. A few belts and a few strings. Perhaps we can even help others make them." He moved a buckle up one notch so that it came up more comfortably under Irena's arm.

"Or sell them," suggested Aleksandra Julianovic.

Mrs. Zaric stood back to appraise Irena, the belts crossed like bandoliers across her chest. "Our Rambo," she said. "I do see one deficiency, Milan. When the bottles are slung over her shoulders, she can't just drop them and run."

Mr. Zaric began to pace around his daughter; he put his hands lightly on her shoulders. "She would have to slip the belts with the bottles over her neck and shoulders," he said finally. "Or try to run with them. Either would slow her down. She could even fall over."

"I'm pretty fast, remember," said Irena, who thought it was wrong for a player to envision even the chance of ever falling. "If I could carry more, maybe I wouldn't have to go out so much."

But Mr. Zaric was already unhooking the belt under her left shoulder. "Stupid fucking idea," he said.

THERE WERE ALREADY a few hundred blue-helmeted soldiers in town as part of a small U.N. mission. There were Canadians, many with French names, French soldiers, and French Foreign Legionnaires, most of whom seemed to be from anywhere but France—they were Cambodians, South Africans, and Ukrainians. Britons, Indians, Egyptians, and other troops set up their own checkpoints.

At first, Sarajevans were flattered by their presence. It seemed to signify that the world had heard of their troubles. But they were soon baffled. The U.N. soldiers were armed, but they did not—and could not, they said—draw their weapons. They traveled in armored personnel carriers and small tanks, but if a group of Serb soldiers raised their rifles and shouted, "Fuck you, prepare to die!" they would turn back.

Many U.N. soldiers were embarrassed. They didn't want to die in what they considered to be somebody else's war, in a place of which they had scarcely heard. But they hadn't become soldiers to be played for fools by bullies, either. They were doing a job for which unarmed Benedictine monks might have been better prepared. When French and Canadian soldiers tried to escort two aid convoys into the city, Serb units let them pass, then shot rockets into the sides of the trucks and ran off with the food and medicine inside. When a U.N. commander told Bosnian Serb officials that he sternly disapproved, they blandly replied that the aid convoy had been ferrying weapons. Since the Serbs possessed almost all such weapons, they had enough to prove any claim.

Some U.N. soldiers would park their armored cars, white with U.N. emblazoned in blue on the sides, on certain corners to impart an impression of protection. They hoped that more Sarajevans would be emboldened to leave their apartments in search of food and water. But Aleksandra Julianovic was neither reassured nor impressed.

"They have sent an Egyptian commander and French troops to protect Sarajevo," she sniffed. "When was the last time the Egyptians or the French won a battle? Ancient history. When the U.N. sends Israeli troops," she said, "I'll know they mean business."

MOST OF THE soldiers were just a few years older than Irena. Those sitting on sandbags or gun turrets looked more bored or sullen than scared, with gauzy kittenish hair on the backs of their necks and jaws raw from shaving with cold water. If their commanders weren't watchful, they would delay Irena's rounds, bantering in a kind of North Atlantic patois:

"Tom Cruise and Nicole Kidman?"

"Yes. *Days of Thunder*. Vroom-vroom!"

"Tom Cruise, Maverick! Kelly McGillis. Vroom?"

"Top Gun!"

"Where the eagles fly!" Irena and the soldiers would sing together.

"Kelly McGillis. Amish lady. *Witness*."

"Harrison Ford?"

"Oh, yes. Indiana Jones!"

"Indiana Jones. Michael Jordan!"

"Toni Kukoc?" asked Irena. This usually drew less enthusiasm.

As she struggled back with water bottles in each hand, and rice, beans, and small boxes of powdered eggs in Grandma's bag, soldiers would sometimes help adjust her load and sneak a couple of cigarettes into her pack, or a candy bar.

One afternoon a Canadian soldier sitting on an armored personnel carrier held up a pack of Players cigarettes, pointed to his groin, then opened his mouth and moved his head up and down. The gesture was impossible to misconstrue as some subtle cultural difference, but Irena wasn't tempted, frightened, or appalled. The boy was coarse, not dangerous. If he had pointed to fresh apples or pears, he might have won at least the start of a conversation. He even had a vaguely cute smile. Irena just laughed and walked on.

"We're not that desperate," she shouted. "Girls like flowers and candy!" The soldier looked astonished.

"Come back tomorrow!" he called down. "I'll get them! At least the candy!"

"No! Flowers, too!" She kept walking.

"Where did you learn English?" he wanted to know, hoping she would turn back. "In school?"

"In songs. In movies."

"Wait! Please, wait!" The soldier was standing now. "I'm a nice guy. I don't usually do that to girls. I'm just going a little crazy here. I am Yves from Lachine! Who are you?"

Irena kept walking away from the small tank, aware that the soldiers inside would be watching her backside. She didn't return that way the next day. Sniper fire had peppered the route. She imagined that while Sarajevans scrambled over the streets from the hail of bullets, Yves and his fellow soldiers were battened down in the steel tub of their tank. Keeping safe—and holding their fire. Besides, Irena could already tell that it wasn't difficult to meet soldiers.

MR. ZARIC REMEMBERED the names and addresses of three of his old customers (they lived on the other side of the car park from their building in Grbavica) and decided to write notes to them. There was no mail delivery on the Bosnian side of Sarajevo. Mail carriers would not be sent into sniper fire, especially when so many Sarajevans, like the Zarics, were living in unexpected and untraceable places.

But some of the U.N. soldiers could be persuaded to put a letter in their pocket and post it. Aleksandra Julianovic had pressed six letters into a soldier's hand, including one from the Zarics to a cousin in London, who might be able to find Tomaslav. "He took the letters and gave me a cigarette for each one. I might," she added, "write out a few more envelopes to total strangers, just to be treated so considerately."

So Mr. Zaric wrote out three postcards:

> Dearest Friend:
>
> I regret that the recent emergency in our city has prevented me from offering you the traditional fine service for which I trust our store has earned your patronage. Please know that as soon as this crisis is resolved it will be my pleasure to serve you again. Please present this card for a 25% discount on a new suit. It will be my pleasure to personally tailor our fine garment for you and to stick straight pins into your balls.
>
> Sincerely,
> Milan Zaric
> General Manager

"I DON'T WANT you to get in trouble," Irena told a young African French soldier who was guarding a water line. "They are just messages from my father to friends on the other side. It is the only way they have of knowing we are alive."

The soldier seemed touched. "Well, they are but postcards," he said in slow, thoughtful English. Irena saw her chance to cinch her play.

"See here," she said, pointing to some words. "I'll translate. It says, 'It would be my pleasure to see you again.' And here, 'We must stick with each other in this madness.' Cards like these could promote peace and reconciliation in Sarajevo," she said earnestly.

The young man tucked the three cards into his breast pocket and smiled. "I can get them out tomorrow. So how does a smart young woman like you manage here?" he asked.

"Some days are better than others," Irena said. "Say, have you ever seen Eric Cantona play? I mean, in person?"

...

THE ZARICS NO longer flinched at the sound of bombs or bullets, Pretty Bird included. One morning Irena flinched on waking up—because it was quiet. Like the clack of the General Radomir Putnik Boulevard tram pulling past, shooting and shelling had become Sarajevo's pulse and heartbeat.

They were still scared, but they had found that it was impossible to keep fear always boiling inside them. A person doesn't have the strength to stay scared all the time, any more than he can endlessly keep up the first giddiness of love. Pretty Bird mimicked the sizzle of a mortar just before it fell, and the sound no longer made the Zarics laugh, much less flinch.

But one day the Zarics heard a terrific bang. It was just after ten in the morning, the hour that Irena usually went out, since it was believed, on no particular authority, that the Serb snipers on the night shift had gone to sleep while the ones coming on duty had yet to settle in. They felt a thud in their ears, throats, and bones, then a dull thump bouncing back from the street. Mr. Zaric shook his head as if a bug had flown inside his ear. Irena was holding the plastic soft-drink bottle in which they kept water; the water sloshed and shivered.

Mrs. Zaric gasped and said softly, "Close by."

The Zarics sank to the floor. They heard a second boom, and then a roar from a scattering of human voices. They could hear rifle shots crackling like fire, followed by sirens and shouts.

"They shoot the second mortar shell," Mr. Zaric reminded his family, "to hit the people who run out to help those they've hit."

There was a third shell, then the sound of sobs carrying over blocks of rubble. Once more the Zarics exchanged hard, sour smiles across the room, their shoulders hunched, their eyes widening, as if listening for an intruder on the roof.

Mr. Zaric rubbed his hands back and forth over his legs, his head bowed. "It sounds close," he said. "We can get there."

"Others will be there already," said his wife.

"No one will be there," said Mr. Zaric, "if no one goes first."

Irena leaped up from the floor to tie on her basketball shoes. She felt suddenly lighter—her fingers flicked over the laces. She felt scared, anxious, and eager, and was at the door before her parents had clambered up into a crouch.

She raced along an empty Tomas Masaryk Street. Hungry stray dogs awakened from gutters and vestibules roused themselves at the sound of her feet, as if they might try to run with her, then dropped back, too weak to keep pace. Irena had not run, really run, for months. It was good to feel blood pumping to the backs of her ears. She looked down to see her feet flashing and hear her shoes slapping the pavement. Inches of smoke, fear, and stale air seemed to drain out of her heels. No sniper, she was sure, could fire a shot that could keep up with her. She could see plumes of smoke twisting above Vase Miskina Street; she could hear sirens shout and die down below the smoke. Irena broke for the basket.

MEN AND WOMEN wearing white smocks emblazoned with red crosses pulled bodies by the one arm or leg they had left into the backseats of cars. When Irena got to Vase Miskina Street, she saw that the rusty skids on the street were streaks of blood. A man in a blue shirt with a paper badge stopped her, roughly, taking her by the shoulders.

"Who the hell—" he began.

"I ran all the way to help," heaved Irena.

"Let us get a handle first," he said.

There was a foot on the street perhaps three meters behind them, five toes intact, toenails painted pink, no fading or chipping. Blood had clotted quickly but incompletely over the stump, giving it the appearance of some improbably bloody rose.

"What happened?" Irena gasped. One of the white smocks had come over to them.

"People were standing in line to get bread," he said. "Three shells, I guess—you heard them. I don't know how many dead. Sixteen, somebody counted. Wounded—it must be over a hundred. Cars are coming and going."

Irena's parents had come up behind her, wide-eyed and huffing.

"We don't have a car to help," said Mr. Zaric. "At the moment."

"They're piling two and three people into the backseats," said the man in the smock. "They lay out others in the trunks. Children," he added with some difficulty, "fit into the trunks. Are you looking for someone in particular?" he asked, swallowing hard.

"For no one," said Mrs. Zaric. "We're just here."

"Well, maybe this is how you can help us," said the worker.

. . .

THERE WERE BODIES laid out on drab gray blankets. The first was a man who was turned onto his belly, in a blue-checked short-sleeved shirt, white socks, and black shoes that hung off his heels—they must have been borrowed or stolen. The Zarics went over him slowly, from the back of his head to his heels.

"I can't identify any part of the body," said Mr. Zaric. The man's age and appearance seemed closest to his own; he seemed to feel responsible for recognizing something. "Could I see his face?"

"Not until we can find it," the man in the smock said curtly.

Next to that man was another in dingy white jeans and a worn white T-shirt. He had a pronounced round nose and rumpled ears, almost like squash.

"I almost recognize him," said Mrs. Zaric. "Perhaps I just passed him in the street. Maybe it was the tram. Maybe we went to school together."

"I don't think so," said Mr. Zaric. "But there is something familiar." The man with the paper badge leaned over to pull up the man's eyelids. His eyes were a watery blue, but they weren't familiar to the Zarics.

"Perhaps we've just seen the nose on someone else. A cousin or someone," said Mrs. Zaric.

"Don't see too much in the nose," said the man with the badge. "I think he fell on it. God knows what it looked like half an hour ago."

Next was a young woman in a pale blue tank top who had what seemed to be only a series of slight wounds, small as strawberries, on the right side of her chest. She had dyed blond hair that had been curled around her throat, and wispy dark eyebrows. The Zarics just shook their heads. The attendant folded a blue blanket over her shoulders and chest, as if he were swaddling a kicking baby. But when she was covered her legs remained still.

"Wait," said the man in the smock. "We have another girl over here."

The man turned back a sheet to reveal a girl's face, framed by short dark hair that was just beginning to grow out, like feathers, and a length of blue ribbon around her neck, still tied tight even as her shirt and sweater had begun to pull away. She wore thin metal frames with oblong lenses. The glasses were intact and made her eyes seem huge. No one had closed her eyes; they were too startling, brown with grains of green. Irena put her right palm softly against the girl's face. It was like touching stone.

"You know her?" the man in the white smock asked, a little more gently. The sirens had stopped. The dead were already gone, and there was no need to rush.

"My teammate," said Irena.

"You remember her name?" he asked more loudly. "Dear," he added, as he turned to write in a small orange pad.

"Nermina Suljevic." Mrs. Zaric laced her right arm protectively across Irena's shoulders.

"Where does your friend live?"

"We all used to live across the way in Grbavica," Mrs. Zaric volunteered. "The girls played basketball together at Number Three. But nobody from Grbavica knows where anyone else is right now."

The man kept the sheet wound in his hands near the top of Nermina's whitening, waxen throat.

"Why is she dead?" asked Irena suddenly. "I don't see any blood. I don't see a wound. Are you sure?" She stiffened in her mother's arms.

The man took a breath before answering. "I could show you," he said. "Some shrapnel pierced her back. I could show you. Please, dear. Take my word. I want her to be alive, too." The man dropped his gaze. Irena got down on her knees and fished through folds of the sheet to take Nermina's right hand in hers.

"You know this girl's parents?" the man asked the Zarics.

"Games, school meetings. Around," said Mrs. Zaric.

"Could you find them?" he asked.

"I wouldn't know where," said Mrs. Zaric. "And they wouldn't know where to find us."

"Please. Do this," said the man. "Go to the central synagogue and put up a message for her parents. Tell them what's happened. That's where people are going to look for messages."

"Tell them about Nermina?"

"It shouldn't be a stranger," said the man.

"Like a phone message?" Mrs. Zaric permitted herself to register horror for the first time that morning. " 'While you were out, your daughter died'?"

The man in the smock looked hard at Mr. and Mrs. Zaric and tightened his voice, as if that would keep Irena from hearing.

"I doubt that they are alive," he said. "Don't you? They would be here by now."

Irena kept her hand locked in Nermina's. When the man in the smock tugged the sheet gently back over the dead girl's face, Irena leaned forward to take it down again. "Please," she said. He did not try to pull against her hand and draw the sheet back. *"Please,"* said Irena. "Let her breathe. Let it look like she can."

MRS. ZARIC WENT home and looked for sheets of writing paper. Finding none, she took three sheets of tissue paper—pink, green, and yellow—that had been packed along with the German washing machine that Mr. Zaric had hooked up for his mother three years ago and turned them over so that she could write a note to Nermina's parents. She took one of the pens that her husband had carried home so freely from the International Playboy store, and began on the green sheet; she hoped it would seem more soothing.

> 27.5.
> Dear Merima and Faris,
>
> We hope that by the time you read this letter you will already have learned what has happened to Nermina today. If that is not so, I am sorry to have to tell you something so terrible.
>
> Nermina was killed today on Vase Miskina Street. She and many others were waiting in line for bread when the Serbs fired three shells into them. Milan, Irena, and I saw Nermina among all the others. She was dead by the time we saw her. It was unmistakably she. She had that sweet face, and the delicate little flecks of green in her lovely brown eyes under her eyeglasses. We could see no wounds. A medical person told us that she had been hit suddenly, from behind. Nermina's face seemed to be at peace. She must have died quickly and without suffering. That is all I have come to wish for myself.

She picked up the pink sheet and smoothed it out to write.

> Page two
>
> The people said that Nermina would be taken to a unit in the Kosevo hospital and kept until the end of the month. I told them—

there was no one else to ask—that I did not think you had any religious beliefs about rapid burials that would be more important to you than seeing Nermina.

But if you do not receive this note by June, they will take Nermina to the cemetery on the hill just across from the hospital. She had no money, identification, or jewelry on her to pass on to you. Perhaps, like us, you were already robbed in Grbavica. Perhaps one of our fellow Bosnians told themselves they needed Nermina's things more. I have done some things myself over the past few weeks—perhaps you have, too—that have surprised me. The people promise that they will place a marker with Nermina's name on that spot so that you and all of her friends can find her.

We were also chased out of Grbavica. None of us had time to say goodbye, did we? We have been living at the apartment of Milan's mother. She is also dead. Our son, Tomaslav, is out of the country, but we have not heard from him.

Finally, Mrs. Zaric moved over to the yellow sheet.

Page three

I was always happy to see Nermina with Irena. She and Amela Divacs would go into Irena's room and close the door after the girls had played those long games in the playground on summer nights. They just as often wound up at your place. I think it depended on who had beer (and they thought we didn't know!). I would hear them play Madonna and Sting too loud, sip at their beer and draw on their cigarettes, and laugh and giggle as they talked about games, boys, music, and makeup, I suppose. God, I miss those sounds.

If you are still with us, Milan and Irena and I are in apartment 302 of the building on Volunteer Street with yellow panels and the outdoor wooden stairs. It would be a pleasure to see you.

I cringe at seeing those last words drop out of my pen. To see the word "pleasure" in this note looks outlandish—and insensitive. Yet paper is scarce. I will let you read my thoughts as they come. I think you will understand that if this note finds you alive it might give us all pleasure to hold on to each other and remember our girls giggling behind the door.

With love,
Dalila Zaric

Mrs. Zaric folded the sheets into thirds and wrote:

MERIMA AND FARIS SULJEVIC
OF GRBAVICA

in large block letters across the front.

"I hope they are even alive to read this," she said to her husband.

"They may be happier not to be," said Mr. Zaric. "Quite a few of our friends must assume we're dead. Sometimes I do. I have no other explanation for events." He tapped the top of the letter, which he had read as she slid each page over, and had to turn away.

IRENA'S PARENTS HAD left Irena to herself in her grandmother's bedroom. This meant that she was in a room with three windows and could easily be seen, especially if she persisted in lying across the bed to read an old magazine that Aleksandra Julianovic had found sticking to the inside of a mailbox downstairs. Mr. Zaric rapped gently on the door and waited for his daughter's response.

"Yes?"

He turned the knob. He was standing in front of the windows, too. Irena rolled over and gave her father a small, pursed smile. "Jon Bon Jovi says, 'I feel like shit and look like shit and I don't give a shit.' "

"Well said."

"It's in an old *Q* from last year," Irena said.

Mr. Zaric sat down beside his daughter. His mother's old bed gave a slight wheeze. "I'll bet we can get some wood out of this frame if we need to," he said. "You hadn't seen it?"

"I think we need to," said Irena. "Soon, anyway. No, I don't remember this *Q*. The cover wasn't on it." She flipped to a two-page photograph of a rectangular box wrapped in silver paper with a purple ribbon. *"Warning,"* it said below. "More than 30,000 people die in the U.K. each year from lung cancer."

"We're supposed to be horrified, right?" she asked her father. "But I want to write them and say, 'Cancer doesn't sound so bad to some of us right now.' "

"I don't think we're exactly their audience," Mr. Zaric said gently. "Smoking is still bad for you."

"Not being able to smoke is worse. Look," Irena went on. "They've got these pictures of album covers that never made it into production. One is from the Beatles, 1966. *Yesterday and Today.*"

Mr. Zaric had to put his nose close to the coaster-size image to make out the picture of John, Paul, George, and Ringo in white coats, holding cuts of raw meat and dismembered dolls' heads in their laps. "Oh, the Butcher Cover," he said. "It's famous. I've never seen it."

" 'Too barbaric for general consumption,' " Irena read from the caption. "Until they could print a new one five days later, they pasted something over this one?"

"You see?" Mr. Zaric said with some satisfaction. "The lads from Liverpool weren't always goody-goodies. That's the album with 'Yesterday' and 'We Can Work It Out.' We have it," he said, then added quietly, "we did."

"Look at this one," Irena said. "David Bowie in a dress. *The Man Who Sold the World*. He's attractive in a dress, don't you think?"

"To some tastes," said Mr. Zaric.

"But look at what they wound up using," said Irena. "A man holding a sniper rifle. Westerners are crazy. They get squeamish about a man in a dress, but not about a man carrying a rifle."

"You should remember the days of Tito," said her father. "They put thick black strips over all the breasts and butts in *Playboy* and *Penthouse*. They spared us the sight of bare tits by showing us bondage. We used to joke, 'Marshal Tito must be one kinky cat.' "

"Who shot John Lennon?" Irena asked suddenly. "The CIA? MI-5 or MI-6? I get them confused. Aleksandra says the West was worried that rock music would take over the world."

"Aleksandra forgets," said Mr. Zaric. "Rock music *is* a CIA and MI-5 plot to take over the world. Or is it MI-6? I get them confused, too."

"And Mossad," offered Irena.

"And Coke and Pepsi. Which I also get confused. Rock musicians don't want to take over the world," he added. "Just all the money." He lightly fingered the pages of *Q*, which Irena was holding almost like a bouquet. "I've got to get you some new magazines." Mr. Zaric betrayed his intention to take their conversation in another direction by clearing his throat. Irena intercepted him. "I'm fine, really," she said.

"Nermina," he began.

"Really, I'm *fine*. I just don't want to talk about it. Please, not ever. Not now. *Please*. I'm sad, okay? But I know what kind of world we're in right now."

"Not the world," said Mr. Zaric. "Here."

"Is it just here?" his daughter said with sudden defiance. "This place makes me sad. The world makes me *sick*. All the talking makes me sick. Every day they talk and talk about us in New York in all the U.N.'s languages. Every day we overhear soldiers in the street talking about us in French and Arabic. Every night people talk about us from London and Washington. There are conferences to talk about us in Lisbon and Brussels. All the fucking talk in the world"—Irena clapped her hands over her ears—"can't drown out the shots and screams. Mom is still in the next room, writing messages to put on a wall. 'Sorry to tell you that your daughter is dead. We talked about it.' Talk means nothing to clever people. It's how they pass gas."

Mr. Zaric paused for a moment as his daughter lowered her head onto a pillow. He figured—by now it was a subtle calculation that they must have made several hundred times a day—that her head was about the same height as the window, but with the sun descending the view across the way would be dark.

"Talking may help you handle your feelings," he said. "That's all I mean."

"I can handle my feelings," said Irena. She sat up to face her father. "I want to turn my feelings into a club. I want to smash—I can't believe I'm hearing this out of my own mouth—some girl on the other side. Someone like the guy we saw with the black shoes hanging off his heels. Someone like the girl with her dyed blond hair whipped around her throat. Someone like Grandma, and Mr. Bobic. Life for life."

"You know girls over there," said her father softly. "You've played with them. Your girl over there would be as innocent as you. As innocent"—Mr. Zaric's voice snagged—"as Nermina."

"But it sure would make them wonder about shooting the next girl, wouldn't it?" said Irena. "If they thought one of their own precious, innocent little girls was next. Besides," Irena announced, turning back to the pillow, "I don't want to be innocent anymore."

9.

IRENA TOOK THE LETTER THAT HER MOTHER HAD WRITTEN OVER TO the central synagogue early the next morning. There was little light in the dark interior, but Irena could see three large corkboards wheeled over in front of a wall, each stippled with sheets and envelopes. She was looking for a place to put the letter for Nermina's family when an envelope caught her eye.

THE FAMILY OF DALILA, MILAN, AND IRENA ZARIC
PRETTY BIRD TOO!
LAST KNOWN ADDRESS: LENIN STREET IN GRBAVICA

It was Tomaslav's hand, and Irena opened the envelope in the dim room, her hands quavering. The note was written on white stationery.

20–5
Dearest Mother, Father, Irena,
And dear, dear Pretty Bird!

I have sent you so many letters. I have no idea if any have reached you. I don't know where you are. I pray you are alive. The news says the central synagogue near Grandma's apartment is keeping mail for the whole city. So I went to the central synagogue here. The rabbi said he would find out how to post this letter there, where I hope you see it.

I AM FINE!!! Azra is fine. Please tell her parents, if you know where they are. We are in London, but we are no longer together. No problem—one of those things, not worth talking about now. We left Vienna a month ago, when our visas ran out and the rooming house said we had to leave. We heard that the Bosnia office in London was granting emergency visas due to war. So on the last days of our visas, we came here.

Azra and I are working as waiters in a restaurant that is near many theaters. We dress like monks. We serve mussels and fried potatoes. I wear a brown monk's hood all day, and feel very pious. Azra wears the same hood with very tight, short pants. Many customers say they want to convert to her church. The owner is an Indian Briton who says he likes Yugoslavs because they work hard and don't steal. I tell him that he doesn't know Yugoslavs. He lets us work two shifts a day, which gives me two meals. I sometimes stay late to have a beer—they have about a hundred different kinds, not even Irena would know them all—and the bartender usually sneaks us some bread and salad. So we eat well. My English is getting good. Watch this:

Can I tell you about our specials? *Marinière* means with garlic, white wine, and parsley. Can I get you another Leffe?

I AM FINE. PLEASE DO NOT WORRY. I don't know how much money I am earning, because I don't know how to figure out pounds. It is enough to pay a weekly wage to sleep on a sofa in an apartment in Blackheath, at the end of a train line. My visa is good for another eight months. I have met a man in the restaurant from Banja Luka who is trying to organize a group of us to get to Chicago, where we can get in with a group to join a Bosnian army. Why did we start a country and forget to have an army? What a supreme miscalculation! Anyway, I am saving money to make that trip.

I am not inclined to be a soldier. You raised us in a Yellow Submarine. But we see the news here each night—villages burned, Muslim men, thin as skeletons, herded into camps, our beautiful Sarajevo being brought down brick by brick and bone by bone. I cannot be happy staying away.

If you get this letter, please write to me in care of Rabbi Siegel at the Central Synagogue on Great Portland St., London W1. I love you all and miss you all. I ache to know that you are safe. I tell people from all over the world about my beautiful mother, my wise father, my talented sister, and our brilliant and amusing bird.

Love,
Tomaslav

Chirrrrp! to Pretty Bird!

IRENA SAT ON the edge of a table. By the close, she could feel wobbliness in her knees and see it in the last few lines of Tomaslav's letter. She thought he must have been exhausted from writing so many letters without knowing whether they would be read; she could see the exhaustion in the last lines of his handwriting.

A man was setting out folding chairs as more people arrived, and she asked him for paper and an envelope.

He made a face. "We're not a stationery store," he said.

"We were chased out of Grbavica," Irena had learned to explain. "My mother has just had to write old friends"—here she brandished the note about Nermina—"on some packing slips to tell them that their daughter is dead. Now I've just read a letter from my brother, and we have to write him back. He's in danger."

"Danger? Outside? The danger is here," said the man.

"That's what I mean," said Irena. She added quickly, "Please. I'm not sure I can explain. It's important." The man went back into an office and returned with two plain sheets of paper and a synagogue envelope.

"Write the address in simple block letters," he instructed. "Overseas, they cannot always read it. Don't waste space. No jokes or funny titles, just name and address, or else the Blue Helmets will throw it out and shut us down. All of the mail will get picked up this week, sent to Israel, and sent out from there. Do you have money for postage?"

Irena was caught. "Maybe at home," she said. "Maybe later."

"Okay," said the man. "Let's make the first one free. I assume you don't have a pen?" This made Irena laugh.

"Actually, I do." She fished an International Playboy pen from her jeans pocket.

"I know that place," the man said. "On Vase Miskina." He began to smile. "I always wanted one of those pens."

"In just a moment, then." She arranged the sheets on the green linoleum floor, settled onto her knees, and began to write.

Dearest Tomaslav:

I am sure that Mother and Dad will write you back, but I wanted this just between us. WE ARE FINE. WE ARE ALIVE. We had to leave Grbavica quickly in the first days of April. It was nasty, but it is also a story that is not worth talking about now. We left so quickly, we could not get any of your things. Buy many clothes along Savile Row, although I would like to see you in the monk's hood. I am sorry to hear that you and Azra are no longer together. Perhaps you will get back together. Perhaps Princess Diana will see you in a crowd and demand that you become her footman and love slave!

Grandma is dead. She was shot the first night of the war, just caught out on her staircase. So were several of her neighbors. Nermina Suljevic is dead, too. But mostly we don't know who is dead and who is alive. Someone new dies each day.

Irena flipped the first page over.

There is NO NEED for you to go to Chicago to join a Bosnian army. PLEASE DON'T. PROMISE!!! Some men came to our apartment to take Daddy into the army, then brought him right back. Sometimes he is called out to dig trenches. He is doing his part for all of us. Better, if you want to join an army, you should join the French Foreign Legion. They know what they are doing. Maybe they will send you here, but you get to train in Marseilles, which is warm and beautiful. Anyway, I am sure—we all hope—that the war will be over LONG before you need to go into anyone's army.

With all the urgent letters, this took up rather more space than Irena had expected. She went on to the second sheet.

2)

In any case, I am convinced that it was God's plan for you to be caught outside of Sarajevo when this insanity began. Your life is much more important to everyone out there. We are safe and will survive. PROMISE, PLEASE. Write me back directly, I seem to be in charge of picking up the envelopes here.

Pretty Bird says, "*Chirrrp! Whirrrr! Chugga-chugga!* Tomaslav!"

Love,
Irena

She drew an arrow pointing to the back of the second sheet, and wrote:

ONLY GO TO CHICAGO TO SEE
TONI KUKOC PLAY!
TELL HIM THAT YOUR SISTER IRENA
IS THE ONLY GIRL FOR HIM!

Her bold letters reminded her of the names she had seen slashed on some of the buildings around town.

10.
SUMMER
1992

BUT PRETTY BIRD WAS BEGINNING TO FALTER.

The seed that he ate had been taken along with their other packed possessions back in Grbavica, and Irena's grandmother had none stored away. Markets were closed, smashed, or looted, and when Irena prowled around a couple of ruins she could find no birdseed, anyway. The Zarics knocked on the doors of apartments that were still inhabited—and, in fact, knocked in the doors or windows of a couple more, looking for birdseed—but found none. They tried to induce Pretty Bird to eat cracker crumbs, gnarls of gristle from canned meats, bugs, and cookie crumbs. But he would pick around them with disinterest, eating just enough to be sociable. Surely something more delectable would turn up; it always had.

"Let us just keep trying," said Mr. Zaric. "Pretty Bird will have to eat something when he gets hungry."

But within a month Pretty Bird was no longer making siren, whistle, grinder, kettle, or doorbell noises. He had stopped impersonating rifle fire, artillery shells, tank-tread grinding, and sniper shots. Irena had accepted the sight and smell of dead friends, relatives, and strangers. But Pretty Bird had always been the one in their lives whose fantastically incongruous bleats, burrs, bells, and whistles had reminded them that the world could sometimes be added up in different ways. Irena found that looking at her suddenly silent, irrepressible gray bird cast a gloom she had not expected among all the others.

...

A NEW MARKET of sorts was operating during the morning hours on an open block behind the old central market. People raided their apartments—or somebody else's—for items they could trade. A man who had six sets of undershorts could set out two pairs and hope to barter them for ten razor blades. Or a man with twenty razor blades might decide to shave just twice a week, and trade ten of those blades for a half pound of sugar.

War had rewritten all values. Toasters, televisions, and washing machines were worthless in a place where there was no predictable electricity. Elaborate bed frames were valuable only if they could be hacked apart for firewood. But batteries could power radios and flashlights; they were more precious than brooches. Cigarettes curbed hunger and curtailed tedium. They brought more in trade than, say, cucumbers, which in a city that had no refrigeration would quickly go bad. Cucumbers were no longer produce but a perishable luxury. Cigarettes were no longer a nasty habit but hard currency.

Small-time criminals oversaw the market. Hard, blustery men in leather coats, they were as easy to spot as police officers used to be, as they prowled the ranks of people squatting on blankets, laying out razor blades, shoelaces, and sanitary napkins, like ranks of toy soldiers.

"Birdseed," said Irena, daring to tug on one of their smooth black leather sleeves. "I'm looking for birdseed. Can you get any?"

The man needed half a minute to register that her request was no joke. "Caviar would be easier," he said. "Cocaine I could point you to now. A lamb loin—maybe a day or two. But birdseed?" He turned away with disinterest.

One afternoon Irena pricked her finger with the point of a safety pin and smeared a splotch of blood over both of her cheekbones until her face had a healthy pink color. She found Yves, the Canadian soldier, sitting on the sandbags of another checkpoint; he scrambled down eagerly on seeing her.

"I am Irena."

"I remember."

"Do you have—"

"The other day, like I said, I'm sorry."

"I am not here to be mad," she said. "We have a bird who is very important to us. And he won't eat. Do you have any birdseed?" Irena could feel her eyes moistening, and wondered what would happen if the blood on her cheeks became wet.

Yves paused. “No. I haven’t seen any birdseed. I haven’t heard about any birdseed.” He called back in French to a couple of other soldiers at the checkpoint. They laughed, wonderingly.

“I can get candy bars,” said Yves. “Batteries, Tampax, shoelaces. But no birdseed.” Yves chanced to put his hand against Irena’s arm. “What a place,” he said gently. “Not enough food and water, and people ask for birdseed.”

IRENA AWOKE BEFORE her parents the next morning, disturbed, she realized within moments, by the absence of flapping from Pretty Bird, who was slumped against the side of his cage. His red feathers were curled under his feet, as if they had gotten stuck there and he didn’t have the strength to move them. His eyes looked like worn tiny brown pellets. His beak appeared to be growing soft, like an old rubber toy.

“I think our supplies will be fine today,” said Mrs. Zaric. “You must use this day to take care of Pretty Bird.”

BEFORE THE WAR, the Zarics had taken Pretty Bird to a Dr. Kee Pekar, in a stone house behind some trees on a small hill in Kosevo. Irena could remember playing a game with Pretty Bird as they skipped up the steps and counted them off, Pretty Bird riding her shoulder and making his gargling noises.

This time Irena’s parents had persuaded her not to bring Pretty Bird along to the veterinarian’s office. They were certain that the patient’s presence was not necessary for the vet to conclude that Pretty Bird was starving, and they didn’t want to worry that their daughter would risk her safety by throwing her body over their moribund bird.

Irena, for her part, insisted on going alone. She feared what the doctor’s diagnosis and advice might be, and planned to filter her recommendation. If Dr. Pekar said, “There is no birdseed, your bird must be put to sleep,” Irena was prepared to tell her parents, “She said we must keep looking for seed.”

The Knight had begun his morning broadcast. As Irena headed over the embankment at Gundulica, she could hear tinny laughter and low-voiced patter: “The self-styled leaders of Bosnia! Don’t they remind you of madmen who tell their doctors in the asylum, ‘Hey, be nice, now. I’m Napoleon! I’m Hannibal! I’m Julius Caesar! I’ll tell the authorities about you!' They run to the United Nations. They run to the United States. They wail, cry, and moan like children who've been pushed out of a soccer game. 'Ooh, ooh, help me, Mommy, help me, Daddy, the Serbs are being mean!' "

It was the first time Irena had heard the Knight's beery bad-boy chuckle. He was beguiling. He was mesmeric. His rants were crammed with tripe and nonsense, irregularly embellished with truths. Incomprehensible events had given his diatribes coherence.

"But have you heard what the United Nations says?" he asked after a hush. "The head is an Ay-rab, after all. At least he has an excuse to be a Muslim. Although he's not. Once most Ay-rabs get a little education, the first thing they are smart enough to do is stop being Muslim. Be a good Christian—drink and screw. So what's wrong with our Muslims? But even Butt-rust Butt-rust Ghali says, 'I can think of eight or nine places in the world that are worse than Bosnia right now.' From what I see in the movies, he must include New York. God *bless* America. Shut up and buy Coke—that's their policy. Their foreign minister says, 'We don't have a dog in this fight.' Bow-wooow!" the Knight howled over the river. "Bow-wooow!" He panted and slurped with impressive authenticity.

"Well, we have real leaders over here," the Knight went on. "Men and women you want to follow. Not mama's boy whiners who go crying to America. Our leader, the masterful psychologist Radovan Karadzic, says, 'Our army has surrounded Sarajevo. Our boys and girls and tanks are so thick, not even a bird can get past them!' So, Muslims, go boo-hoo-hoo on America's shoulder. They'll put you on television. Lights, cameras, action! You'll get to pose with Madonna, Robert Redford, and Sting. But don't wait for help from America! Wait for America and you take the graves next to lots of Vietnamese and Iraqis and Kurds who died waiting."

Irena was relieved when she could hear the Knight begin to ring in the Clash. *Oh I'm so boooored with the U!S!A!*

DR. PEKAR WAS IN; or, at any rate, at home, in her small apartment just above the office. Irena called up and the doctor stamped down the staircase, wearing a white coat for warmth in the chilly shadows beneath some of the last trees left standing in Sarajevo. Even scavengers were afraid to try to hack down trees on a hill that was so open to sniper fire. The doctor's windows had been blown out, and breezes moved through quickly.

She smiled and squeezed Irena's shoulders. "Of course I remember you," she said. "The charming bird who makes noises like a washing machine. Unless"—she drew back—"I have already said the wrong thing."

"No," said Irena. "Pretty Bird is why I'm here."

Dr. Pekar was wearing large hoop earrings below her frizzy ringlets of sandy hair. Irena thought that she had soft brown eyes, almost amber, like a kitten's. Irena told her about Pretty Bird's problems.

By the third sentence, the doctor was nodding vigorously. "Parrots are particular," she said. "African grays especially. As you know, it is hard to explain to them why they need to alter their diet."

Irena could feel her eyes reddening again. "We have been through so much together."

Dr. Pekar moved on quickly. "You've tried rice?"

"All the time."

"Boiled? Hard? Soft? With milk?"

"Every way. He eats a few bites, then turns away."

"Macaroni?"

"Spaghetti," said Irena. "Same story. Broken into bits. It's not easy, you know, to get the strands down to just an inch or so."

"You have to wrap them in a cloth and smash them with a bottle," the doctor explained. "Crackers?"

"Sure."

"Crumbs of whatever?"

"Always. Every time we can have a meal. A few nibbles, maybe."

Dr. Pekar's ringlets shook against the hoops in her ears. "I hate to hear this," she said. "Some birds—they are just too smart to be fooled. Maybe they outsmart themselves. You've gone on the black market?" she asked. "I've had some luck with cat food there."

"No seed."

"If I knew another family," she said with growing gloom, "who might have a bird and some seed to spare. But Pretty Bird has always been our one and only here." The two women looked at each other across the chilly room.

"LOOK, I DON'T keep a supply of seed," said Dr. Pekar. "But let me check something." She led Irena through the folds of a dark green curtain and into her office, where the wind had strewn papers and lifted up poster calendars of cats, dogs, and rabbits, winking cutely from photographic sets.

Dr. Pekar ducked her sandy head down like a searchlight into a display window, which seemed to hold a couple of dog collars and a catnip mouse toy.

"Here," she said, holding out her hand with a tone of triumph. It was a small, old, crumpled sample box of Geisler birdseed from Germany.

Irena's eyes welled. "You have saved Pretty Bird's life," she said.

"It's not so simple," the doctor said with a sigh. "This will last Pretty Bird one meal. Two, at most. He will assume there is more on the way. Which none of us can these days."

Irena thought she could detect where the doctor was trying to lead her. "I won't do anything to harm him. *Nothing!*" she said fiercely.

Dr. Pekar put out her hand. "I don't want that, either. You have to help him. Have snipers been firing into your building?" she asked.

"Of course."

"Of course. Every building. What I'm going to tell you is distasteful. But you want to do what's best for Pretty Bird, don't you?"

"More than anything," Irena said. "Anything in the world."

"Then you must do something for his own good," the doctor said simply.

"I know what you're trying to get me to do," said Irena angrily. "One hears it all the time now. That dying is kind. That it spares pain. There is nothing kind about dying, I swear. Milosevic, Arkan, and Karadzic—those are the only deaths that would be kind."

"Hear what I *mean,*" the doctor responded with almost equal force. "What I mean is, you must give him a better chance than what we have here."

Only Irena's puzzlement kept her silent.

"Take this seed. Go home to Pretty Bird. Wait until you feel there is a lull in the sniper fire—even they take breaks—and bring Pretty Bird up to the roof. Sprinkle some seeds in the palm of your hand. Not too many—you may need to try this more than once. Let Pretty Bird eat; he will be famished. Soon there will be no more, and he will look up. You must show him your empty palm. Wipe it clean in front of him. Then—this is the hard part—you must push him off your arm or hand and make him fly away. Whatever it takes—a stern tone, flapping your arm until he falls away, whatever. *Whatever.* You must make him leave you."

Irena was sobbing now. She curled her right hand up into the sleeve of her grandmother's old ivory shirt so that she could use the cuff to daub her eyes and mop her nose.

"It's his only chance," the doctor insisted, sitting down. "That he'll land over on the other side, where they still have trees and grass. Then we hope that someone over there sees him and says, 'What a beautiful bird.' "

Irena had sunk to the doctor's lap and thrown her arms around her waist.

Doctor Pekar stroked her head gently. "Maybe when the war is over, in a month, a year, you can put an ad in the paper, ask around, and find Pretty Bird," she said. "We are all being asked to make some unspeakable choices, aren't we? At least yours can keep him alive." When at last Irena sat up, the doctor tried to blot a few of her tears with the palm of her hand. "This is a rotten thing we're going through," she said.

Irena wiped her wet face with her fingers, then looked at the doctor uncertainly. "I almost forgot," she said. "How do we pay? Would you be insulted by cigarettes? My father makes candles."

Dr. Pekar smiled as she looped a tawny ringlet around an ear. "It's not necessary," she said. "But I have an idea. Do you have any free time?"

"Who doesn't?" said Irena. "I pick up food and water. Sometimes someone asks me to deliver a letter."

"Could you come here tomorrow morning?" asked Dr. Pekar. "I'm trying to stay open now and then. Word has gotten around. There are people trying to keep their pets alive. Dogs, cats, hamsters—there's not always much I can do for them. Do you like animals?"

"Very much," said Irena.

"Much experience with them?"

"We had a cat when I was a child, Puddy. She died when we were both twelve. Then we got Pretty Bird."

"Well, I could use some help," the doctor continued. "To hold the animals while they're examined or treated. Clean up when they're gone. Sometimes just to hold them. I had a nurse—Svjetlana—you may remember. I imagine she's on the other side. I hope so. I could also use some water. A little fuel for the burner in here. And I've been told there are even some hypodermic needles on the black market."

"Everything but birdseed," said Irena.

"Eight in the morning? If you aren't here, I will assume you've been delayed by shooting." Dr. Pekar rested her hands on Irena's shoulders, her ringlets jiggling. "I am sorry for what you have to do," she said. Then she added automatically, "Be careful of the snipers on your way home."

...

WHEN IRENA ARRIVED HOME, she told her mother what the doctor had said. Her mother sat down in the kitchen and cried. Mr. Zaric was in the basement, she said, cleaning it up, setting out chairs, and trying to make the space comfortable during bombings. Aleksandra Julianovic was his interior designer.

"I think that this is something you and I must do together," said Mrs. Zaric. Mother and daughter listened for gunfire, and heard several shots ringing in the distance. "Shh," said Mrs. Zaric. "Listen for a minute more." Soon there was another shot, but nothing more. Wordlessly, Mrs. Zaric took Pretty Bird from where he was crumpled against the side of his cage and cradled him in her hands. "Come on, little one," she said.

They walked to a small door that opened onto the roof, all the while listening for gunfire, and moving slowly, Irena knew, to postpone their arrival. At the top, they pressed on the rail that unlatched the steel door. They had not really seen—or, at any rate, noticed—the clouds for months. Today, the sky seemed angry, gray, and boiling.

Irena took a plastic bag out of the pocket of her blue jeans and shook a small sprinkle of seeds into her right hand. Pretty Bird looked over from his perch in Mrs. Zaric's hands, ventured an exploratory sniff, and then plunged his beak into the pile of seeds.

"Good boy, Pretty Bird," Mrs. Zaric said.

Irena added, "But eat slowly, because there is no more."

Irena and her mother had not cried together since they'd left Grbavica—no, since the night before. They had howled and beaten their hands against walls. But they hadn't shed any tears. It was as if weeping might drain away the wrath that kept them going. Blood and sobs just dried. But now they cried. They shuddered; they gasped as if they had run to the top of a hill. Then, as they doubled over to catch their breath, they began to laugh. Laughing seemed to give them back breath. Irena straightened, struggling to hold the seed for Pretty Bird as he gnawed at her palm. He left small red bites that she would study for days.

Irena said, "You love that damn bird more than you love me."

"It's close," Mrs. Zaric agreed.

Pretty Bird looked up as he finished the seeds, and began to hop, foot by foot, between Mrs. Zaric's palms. *"Bo-oing!"* he said, resounding like the basketball hoop in Grbavica. *"Bo-oing!"*

"Listen," Irena said lightly, "we have had a pretty bad time, haven't we? But we can do you a favor and get you out of here. You know what? I guess you have always been able to fly away. We are thankful that you have wanted to stay with us so long. These days would have been much worse without you." Her voice snagged. "Now here's what we want you to do," she said, brushing her mouth against the gray and green feathers on Pretty Bird's head. "You take off and fly on over to where we used to live. You look around for the prettiest spot, and then you just settle down. Make your noises. Make that sound *'Bo-oing!'* Someone will see you and say, 'What an amazing bird!' And they will ask you to come home with them. Just hop a ride on their shoulder and go home with them. Eat and rest and let them love you."

Mrs. Zaric spoke hoarsely from the other side of Pretty Bird's head. "And when this madness is over we will come find you. Even if it is just to say hello. We will walk up and down the streets and ask, 'Do you know a bird who can sing like a telephone rings and who flew here from Brazil because he didn't like all that sand? That's Pretty Bird. We have come to say hello.' "

Irena had worried that she would have to lift Pretty Bird from her mother's hands and throw him into the sky. She had steeled herself to be stern. Dire images singed her mind. She would clasp her arms behind her back, as if handcuffed, so that Pretty Bird couldn't fly back to her. He might wonder what he had done to be treated with such callousness. He might fly off only to dart back to beat his wings against Grandma's kitchen window, as if to say, "Whatever I did, I'm sorry. Let me in. I just want to be with you." But, instead, Pretty Bird cocked his head slightly to the side and took two last steps between Mrs. Zaric's palms. She lifted her hands up toward the gray sky, and Pretty Bird took a small leap from her outstretched fingers, let the wind fill his wings, and flapped once, twice, three times rapidly, then soared into the wind and circled around the back of the building. Irena and her mother stood motionless, looking up, as the fringe of Pretty Bird's red tail seemed to glow in the grayness. He took another bite of the air with his wings and flew over the tired river toward the jumbled cluster of cinder-block buildings that used to be their home.

11.

IRENA MADE HER WAY TO DR. PEKAR'S EARLY THE NEXT MORNING, and then the next. She liked being outside on the walk over. She liked the doctor, who seemed as if she might have been a little lonely for company even before the war. She liked the disarray of the office, which was still steeped in dog breath and deodorizer. She liked holding dogs and cats against her chest to brace them as Dr. Pekar sewed up cuts and gashes. She liked feeling useful.

One morning an elderly woman brought in a little dog who seemed sluggish to the point of stupor. Dr. Pekar knew her well. Marilyn was a little blond mop of a Pekingese, turning gray, who could no longer evacuate her bowels.

"This is going to be ugly," she muttered to Irena. Irena and the dog's owner steadied the little dog in place while Dr. Pekar inserted a rubber-tipped tube into her backside. Marilyn reared slightly, then settled down wearily. As Dr. Pekar sluiced water into her small body, Irena thought she could see it brim in Marilyn's eyes. She was a small dog; results were immediate. There was a cartoon splat from Marilyn's backside, and a small pudding dribbled out.

The woman wept with gratitude. She kissed Marilyn's small coconut shell of a head and took the dog onto her shoulder. Then she kissed Dr. Pekar and leaned down to kiss Irena, who had begun to swab down the steel examination table.

"Will they be back?" Irena asked.

"Three or four days, probably," said Dr. Pekar, "Ordinarily, I'd say, 'Your dog—your friend—is in pain. You have to do the one thing that would help.' But, under the circumstances . . ." The doctor's voice trailed off. "She can't last long, though."

"Marilyn or her owner?" asked Irena.

Doctor Pekar let the remark drift away as she went out to their next patient.

ANOTHER WOMAN BROUGHT in an old blue hound who was exhausted and hoarse from barking. The poor dog had been driven crazy by bombs. It was a quiet morning. But Cesar whimpered, bucked, and cringed in a corner, hearing whines from mortars and bombs that were above human register.

Mrs. Tankosic, Cesar's owner, wore a dark brown scarf over her head and kept tugging it forward just above her eyes; her eyebrows had fallen away. "None of us is getting any sleep up on the hill," she said. "They have this man, the Sniper from Slatina they call him, shooting all the time. He never takes a break, and we never sleep."

"It's probably more than one man," suggested Irena. Cesar lay crumpled in the corner like discarded wrapping paper.

Dr. Pekar laid her head against Cesar's chest. She could feel his heart shudder. She could hear his stomach slosh and churn. "I have nothing to give Cesar," she announced finally. "In places like London and Hollywood, they have tranquilizers for dogs. They have dog psychiatrists. I think what you must understand," she continued quietly, "is that life has become just hours of hurts for Cesar. He is almost—I have never seen the likes of it—barking his heart out. It may be the only way he knows to try to take himself away from here."

Mrs. Tankosic touched Cesar's back gently. His spine looked like a thin stick that was about to burst through a worn gray bag.

"You have something for that, though, don't you?"

Dr. Pekar left the room for a moment and returned with her right hand jammed into the pocket of her lab coat. "Let us all put our arms around Cesar," the doctor suggested. Irena laced one of her arms around the dog's chest. Mrs. Tankosic pressed her chest against Cesar's back, and her face against the side of his head; she cried into one of his drooping ears. "I'll see you soon, my big boy," she said. Irena heard her own breathing, Dr. Pekar's, and Mrs. Tankosic's. She grasped that Cesar's panting had stopped.

"Nothing can hurt him now," the doctor whispered. Irena had seen the bodies of friends, family, and strangers over the past few months. But she had not seen a body pass bloodlessly from life to death in a breath. The same blood and bones, the same teeth and hair, added up to life in one instant and death in the next. Irena no longer thought of the living and the dead as occupying separate provinces, merely separate timetables.

DR. PEKAR LOOKED at Cesar's stiff body in the corner of the room. A medical dilemma had become a disposal predicament. "I have an incinerator out back," she told Irena. Dr. Pekar tried to shake a cigarette out of an old pack of Drina—she had been hiding that in her pocket, too—and tapped two into Irena's hand. "I hope I'm not encouraging bad habits," she said.

"I'm not a virgin," Irena volunteered. "About smoking," she added with a snort.

"I almost am," Dr. Pekar offered. "Thirty years old and I haven't had three men."

"That's ridiculous," said Irena. "You're beautiful. You're fascinating."

"I'm covered in cat puke," said the doctor. "I stick my hands into dogs' assholes." Dr. Pekar swished out a cloud of smoke and watched it scatter. "I'm running out of pentobarbital. It's not something you stock up on for emergencies, like beans or plum jelly."

"Come with me to a soldier's checkpoint or water line," said Irena. "We'll get pentobarbital and get you Man Number Three. Dr. Oooh-lah-lah." They laughed, girl to girl, but as Irena began to help Dr. Pekar trim Cesar with twine to take him out to the incinerator, she mentioned Mrs. Tankosic. "She sounds like she wants to kill herself," said Irena. "We should tell someone and stop her."

"Why?" asked Dr. Pekar.

12.

THE VERY NEXT MORNING, A SERGEANT OOOH-LAH-LAH, AT ANY RATE, came roaring up to the concrete landing just under Dr. Pekar's office in a white U.N. vehicle. Irena and Dr. Pekar could hear the engine cut off, and the sound of booted steps. There was a knock, and a slightly breathless voice.

Sergeant Colin Lemarchand was with the U.N. forces of the French army. His pale blue beret in hand and his neat blond mustache twitching in animation, the sergeant explained that he had been cruising the streets of Kosevo just below the Sarajevo Zoo, looking for a veterinarian's sign. A Dr. Djukic had been the zoo's veterinarian, but he had not been seen since the first days of the war.

"He's a good man, I know him a little," Dr. Pekar told Sergeant Lemarchand. "You can't find him?"

"He's in Pale," said the sergeant. "He can't—they won't let him across."

"I'm a doctor for house cats, hamsters, and lap dogs," said Dr. Pekar.

"That will do," said Sergeant Lemarchand. "Until a few months ago, I was an assistant pastry chef."

THE ZOO WAS spread out on a hill in Poljine, above the Olympic Stadium and just beyond the Kosevo neighborhood. The U.N.'s field maps called it a contested zone. But there really was no contest between Serb paramilitaries and Bosnian zookeepers. Serbs had wheeled large guns into Poljine, at the top of the hill, to churn shells into the zoo. The park became a free-fire zone inhabited by trapped animals.

The lions and bears reared up at the alien roars and crashes, as if to challenge their invaders. But they were ensnared in their steel cages. Then the wolves, foxes, and monkeys began to starve. Zookeepers couldn't sprint through sniper and mortar fire to feed them, though a few tried, and died next to the animals they often had reared from the time they were young.

The pumas and jaguars went wild with hunger. The shooting and shelling made them crazy with fear. Then hungry people coming in from all over did the same. Gangs attacked cages and seized peacocks, ostriches, and alpine goats for food. Serb snipers fired into the cages, slaughtering the animals—they wanted to see their bullets draw blood, like kids smashing bugs with their shoes. People in the streets nearby swore that they saw the zoo's two lions stand on their hind legs and try to bat down bullets with their paws. They said that the lions, unlike the Blue Helmets, didn't just stand aside.

SERGEANT LEMARCHAND TOLD Dr. Pekar and Irena on the short ride over that Kolo was sick. Kolo was one of three brown bears that had sat, swatted flies, and shaken off water in a cage on a raised stone platform overlooking a slender creek. When the food ran out, the bears had turned to each other for mutual protection—and then for nourishment. Kolo was the strongest or, at least, the meanest. When a company of Canadian soldiers got to the zoo, they found a clutter of bones scattered across the cage floor. Kolo had eaten his cage mates. When he realized that he no longer had company, he played with their bones.

The sergeant left his little white truck in the parking lot, where small family cars had been smashed by shells in the first days of the war. The wind, rain, and bullets of the past few months had rusted and riddled the cars, and shattered their windows; they looked like so many flattened soup cans.

"Step carefully," said Sergeant Lemarchand. "This is what they call a contested area."

"Unlike the rest of our city," said Dr. Pekar.

SERGEANT LEMARCHAND STOPPED suddenly.

"The girl," he said, whirling around toward Irena. "You, mademoiselle"—he deployed a phrase in French to make his point—"I do not wish to bring a young girl into a contested area."

"Oh, that's *très* ridiculous," said Irena. "It's not like I'm, you know, a virgin."

As they stepped carefully up to Kolo's cage, Dr. Pekar turned to her and murmured, "Odd choice of words."

Kolo did not look like an animal who had recently eaten two bears. His brown coat was dry and gray; it hung over his spine and ribs like a sagging old rug. His penis was a small, lank worm. He had beached himself onto his side, gasping for breath through a slender, battered muzzle. He kicked his legs slowly, like a tired baby falling asleep. A Canadian doctor, a captain with a medical shield over the breastplate of his bulletproof vest, offered Dr. Pekar a reflexive salute. Irena sawed off a salute in return.

"I am not a veterinarian," said Captain Pierre Enright. "But I do not think there is much more diagnosis to be done here."

Dr. Pekar stood back from Kolo's cage. She bent down, as if trying to peer through a keyhole, to look into the bear's eyes. Mostly, they were closed. She watched for a long minute, in which Kolo finally batted them to wince away the pain. Sergeant Lemarchand wrenched open the iron gate for Dr. Pekar; it was quite pointlessly locked. The soldier knelt to steady the bear against his shoulder. Dr. Pekar passed her hand over Kolo's eyes; they did not follow her hand. She had no fear of kneeling down to place her nose against his muzzle. She held her left hand against the bear's chest; she could just about feel his heart squeeze lightly into her hand.

"He is dying for sure," said Dr. Pekar from inside the cage. "Starving to death and mad with hunger and pain."

"How much food would he need?" asked Captain Enright.

"I usually deal with house cats. But, say, six to eight pounds a day."

"Meat?" asked the captain. The two doctors circled Kolo's cage slowly.

"A little. Vegetables and fruit, mostly. And grains. But a lot."

"Is there any way we can get six pounds of food a day for this bear?" asked Captain Enright.

Sergeant Lemarchand was already shaking his head. "Captain, we can't count on six spoonfuls for the whole city."

"Perhaps an article in *Paris Match* or *The New York Times* would help," mused Captain Enright. "I'm thinking out loud. Or a television story. People love animals. Brigitte Bardot might see it."

"There isn't time," said Dr. Pekar. "This boy is already eating himself up inside. It's in his breath. Look at him. *Look at him!*" she said with sudden urgency. "And all you can do is hope that Brigitte Bardot sees him." Dr. Pekar snorted.

Derision seemed to spur Captain Enright to marshal his thinking. "I understand," he said without resentment. "How would you ordinarily end the suffering of a patient with no hope of survival? It is not a question I confront with mine," he added.

"Pentobarbital," said Dr. Pekar. "But you would need a lot for a brown bear. Even desiccated as he is. Do you have any?" she continued.

"Not a jot," said Captain Enright. "I don't know what you've heard, but we try to keep our soldiers alive."

"The right dose of morphine could work," said Dr. Pekar from behind Kolo in the cage. Sergeant Lemarchand was still holding Kolo against his shoulder. Indeed, he had put a hand behind the bear's ear, as if to protect him from the conversation. "I could never get that approved," he said. "We need it for people."

"You have another course of treatment," Dr. Pekar observed. "On your hip."

Sergeant Lemarchand's left hand dropped softly onto the handle of his service revolver, as if he had just been reminded to feel for an old sore.

"The traditional prescription for suffering creatures," the doctor went on. "One bullet applied directly to the brain. Effective and even humane. They are dead before they can hear the shot, much less feel it."

Sergeant Lemarchand tipped back onto his buttocks on the cage's cold, chipped floor. His knees had suddenly given way, and he slapped his ankles to bring them feeling. "I'm sorry," he said. "I cannot fire my weapon. Those are orders."

"You're a soldier," said Dr. Pekar. "Is your gun just for decoration? Like a bracelet and earrings?"

"I know how to use it, *madame,*" said Sergeant Lemarchand, stressing his courtesy. "But I cannot. Those orders are the specific policy of the United Nations. They are handed down from New York. You can read them in English, French, and Russian."

"Those pompous asses are a long way off," Dr. Pekar retorted with growing vehemence.

"Still, I cannot fire my gun. I must account for every bullet. *Please.* I love animals, too. That is why I brought you and the doctor here—I'd hoped you could do something for Kolo that I could not."

"This bear snapped at us," Dr. Pekar suggested. Kolo, meanwhile, seemed to be simmering in pain, his murmurs growing louder.

"He was mad. He was hungry. He was going to eat us. What lie isn't more believable than the truth right now?" she asked.

"I'll attest to whatever you say," Captain Enright volunteered.

But Sergeant Lemarchand saw instantly that the plot would have to begin with him, and he wanted no part of it. "My orders are clear," he said. "In fact, nothing is clearer. Sometimes I wonder what we are supposed to do here. Relieve the siege, but help the Serbs keep it. Assist civilians, but don't fire back at their assailants. They've sent me out here to help a sick bear. I can do everything but actually help him. One order holds firm: I *cannot* fire my gun."

Dr. Pekar sprang forward. "Give *me* your gun, then," she said.

"That's also against orders," said Sergeant Lemarchand. "Guns are not corkscrews or can openers that you lend out for chores."

"What's your problem?" Dr. Pekar shrieked at the sergeant. "I mean, what *is* your problem? Is the U.N. afraid that shooting a sick bear will infringe on the sovereignty of Serb bears? Are you really proud to stay neutral in the middle of a massacre? What kind of sick bastards are you Blue Helmets to leave your snug homes just to stand around and watch us bleed? I would rather have a spot on my conscience than nothing, like yours." Her voice was hard and cold.

Kolo's eyes seemed suddenly to lock shut. A loud crack split the sky, and reverberated through the cage; the bars buzzed softly. Kolo deflated swiftly. There was a last gasp from the big brown bear's chest as Irena watched him flatten against the floor, falling with astounding softness into a spreading, slippery red pond.

SARAJEVO CIVILIANS KNEW how to get down at the sound of a sniper shot. The soldiers were surprised and baffled, Irena noticed. Sergeant Lemarchand and Captain Enright flinched and ducked, but they turned their faces up toward the trees, looking for the shot.

"Get down!" Dr. Pekar shouted at them. "Stay down!"

A voice screamed at them through the trees from the other side. "That—animal—" he shouted in bursts, "did not—deserve—to suffer. *You*—do."

Another shot split the air; Irena could hear it clipping branches and leaves. "Run!" the voice shouted. "Get out! *Run!* Or I will give you"—he squeezed off another shot—"my autograph."

The little group in the cage stood up slowly. Sergeant Lemarchand raised his arms above his head, to show that he had no intention of reaching for his revolver; the sniper might not have heard that he couldn't fire it anyway. Captain Enright, who was a doctor and had no gun, did the same. Dr. Pekar and Irena followed, moving slowly back down the hill. Their arms felt heavy and weary after just a few feet.

"Wait," Sergeant Lemarchand said to Irena. He turned around to face the trees, keeping his arms flamboyantly upraised. With slow, exaggerated movements, the sergeant unzipped his bulletproof vest and slid his arms out of it until he held the jacket almost daintily in his hands. He motioned Irena to hold still and slipped the vest almost grandly over her shoulders. "This way, mademoiselle," he said.

As they walked back down the hill, Irena thought that she could feel a hole burning in the back of her head. When they reached flat terrain, she was both relieved and excited. She turned around, jumping on her toes, and called back through the trees, "Are you the Sniper from Slatina?" Sergeant Lemarchand helped her out of the vest, and she jumped up again, higher, shouting the question more loudly yet. "Are you the Sniper from Slatina?"

There was no response, and they headed for the sergeant's vehicle. It was a couple of blocks before they could hear one another breathing naturally, trusting that another breath would follow.

"He would have shot us by now if he was going to," Captain Enright pointed out.

"Perhaps we should have said thank you," said Dr. Pekar.

"That would have seemed—odd," said the captain.

"He might have let us come back," said the doctor.

"There is nothing left in that zoo to care for," Sergeant Lemarchand said. "Someone even shot the squirrels from their trees. Madame, am I really a sick bastard?" he asked Dr. Pekar.

MUSTAFA ABADZIC, THE zoo's director, had taken to sleeping in an old equipment shed on the grounds. It was exposed to more sniper fire than was generally desired in a residential property, but Mr. Abadzic had been turned out of his three-bedroom apartment in Grbavica. Black-whiskered men were stuffing the small carved olive-wood elephants and zebras he had brought back from Tanzania under their black sweaters when they beat him away from his own door.

"My children will love these," they said.

Mr. Abadzic had seen Kolo gorge himself on Slino and Guza, his old cage mates. "It's the law of the jungle," he told Mr. Suman, the zoo's chief custodian, who was camped in an unshattered corner of the old chimp house. "*Our* jungle, this city we have now."

The director enlisted Mr. Suman's help in digging a grave for Kolo, in the soft ground outside the bear cage. "We shouldn't just leave him there to draw flies," he said. "That would be shameful." That afternoon, the director had used a piece of burned wood to etch a message across a plank he had wrenched off a smashed storage door:

KOLO

1981–1992

WHO SAW EACH SARAJEVAN AS THE SAME

"That should stay until we can get a proper marker chiseled," he said.

"Perhaps it should stay like that," said Mr. Suman.

The men got shovels and dug a hole for Kolo. They waited until ten at night to begin, when it was seamlessly dark; they did not finish before midnight. They discovered that it was hard to dig a hole in pitch blackness. The moon shone no more than the rim of a coin in the sky. It was hard to see where to stick their shovels, and as the hole got deeper it became harder to find the ground. A couple of times, Mr. Abadzic missed and fell over into Kolo's grave. They caught their breath and had a smoke sitting on their backsides on the bottom of the hole, glad to have a place to smoke where the embers of their cigarettes could glow unseen above ground.

The men climbed out of the grave and clambered into Kolo's cage. Mr. Abadzic squinted in the darkness and found Kolo's front feet. Mr. Suman found the bear's hind legs. The men had not been friends before the war. They had done no more than nod at each other on any given day. Mr. Abadzic was a scholar and an executive who took yearly trips to Africa. He brought back slide photographs and delighted school groups and club dinners with his pictures of cheetahs lounging lazily in the Serengeti, baby chimps looking as if they were budding from tree branches in the Masai Mara. Mr. Suman had traveled only as far as some of the small beach towns of Montenegro. He had never married. Collecting restaurant menus and matches was his only pastime. But the men had been storm-tossed into a close association over the past few months, sleeping in adjacent battered buildings and struggling to help their charges. Sometimes they could only open a cage and hope that a red fox or some other survivor might spring across the creek into a home on the Serb side.

Mr. Suman learned that Mr. Abadzic worked hard. He dug holes and ran around sniper fire. Mr. Abadzic had discovered that Mr. Suman cared deeply about the zoo. He hadn't barricaded himself inside when the war began but had run to the zoo out of concern for the animals. He stayed there now, in the front line of fire, to be near them even as they perished.

Mr. Abadzic and Mr. Suman tried to lift Kolo by his legs, but the bear's great dumb brown belly left them wheezing from the strain. The men had just budged Kolo a few inches along the floor of the cage when the first bullet struck Mr. Suman in his throat. The second shot pealed through the trees and pierced Mr. Abadzic's chest.

People nearby awakened the next day to catch sight of two new bodies alongside Kolo's. They must have been humans—they were wearing shoes. Many wondered what two human beings might have been trying to do with a dead bear in the middle of the night that was worth risking death. When they saw the shovels beside the grave, they asked again.

Sergeant Lemarchand got a call to return to the zoo. He could see the bodies of Mr. Abadzic and Mr. Suman, but he was determined not to risk three or four soldiers' lives to pick up corpses—whether of men or bears. The sergeant thought that it was unavailing to override the law of the jungle, or the Sniper from Slatina, in the zoo.

13.

SERGEANT LEMARCHAND LEFT IRENA AT THE ENTRANCE TO HER building. She looked up to see Aleksandra Julianovic sitting on the outdoor staircase between the first and second floors, smoking one of her last Canadian cigarettes. Irena clumped up the stairs to sit beside her.

"You shouldn't be up here," Irena said.

"Then it is foolish of you to join me," Aleksandra pointed out.

"I'm here to save your life," Irena answered, smiling.

"Then take away my cigarettes," said Aleksandra, rolling out a Players for Irena. "But take this upstairs so your parents will only see you smoking, not endangering your life out here in the fresh air."

Irena thought that the hand Aleksandra had thrust into the pocket of her pink housecoat was fumbling for matches. But it proved to be a piece of notepaper. "I've been trying to work something out," Aleksandra said, casting her eyes over a sequence of arrows and numbers. "How many people would you guess are sitting out here like this right now in Sarajevo? Such fools as we."

"Not many," said Irena. "Aside from you and me, anyone else would be accidental."

"Can we say fifty people?"

Irena nodded her assent.

"A few scurrying across the street for water, a few caught dozing in alleys," said Aleksandra. She had plainly been preparing her case.

"There are a few people like me, just sneaking out for no larger purpose than to inhale fresh air and smoke a cigarette in the sunlight," she continued. "After a while, of course, it's the loss of such small luxuries that exasperates. It's like an irritation in your little toe that throbs. Soon you feel nothing else. You breathe, you swallow, you eat onions. You can even have sex. But all you feel is the pain in your little piggy. So here in this city we are still alive, against all odds. Still eating and breathing, if not a lot. But we are shut up in our gloomy rooms, with closet doors nailed over the windows. We are more desperate to get out than grateful to be alive." Aleksandra smiled through tinged teeth—everyone had taken to brushing with cold, unfinished tea, or stale orange soda and grains of salt—and spirals of smoke.

"So let's guess that fifty people are showing their faces and arses right now," she said. "How many snipers would you say are dug in across the way?"

"Too many."

"Let's say ten," said Aleksandra. "Let's say twenty, it doesn't matter. What are the odds that they will hit someone?"

"Who knows? Three, five, six people every day," said Irena. "When we listen to the radio, that's the number we hear. Until the next mortar, of course. Then add fifty."

"Let's say four," said Aleksandra. "It may be three one day, seven the next. But at the end of a week, sniper deaths usually add up in the high twenties. I love what you can discover in statistics," she said. "Even these. Statistics is the science of choosing the right numbers to say anything you want."

"You are surely leaving out a few factors," said Irena. "Some snipers must be better shots than others. Some people must be harder to bring down than others. Some of us are quite stealthy—we may be kidding ourselves, of course. And other people can't even hobble. There are old and injured people who fall down. Rain, wind, politics—it all must make a difference."

"The supreme, blinding beauty of statistics," Aleksandra said with a triumphal smile. "Any fifty people, and you still have more or less the same number of hobblers and speeders. Any ten snipers, and you still have better ones and worse ones. All those variables—and it still averages out that four-point-something people get shot here every day. In the universe, math prevails," she announced. "Even here."

"Nothing else does," said Irena with a grim smile.

"So, I have been figuring," Aleksandra continued. "Let's say that instead of just fifty foolish, careless, or stupid people sitting outside, that number becomes five hundred. Let's say that two weeks or two months from now people get tired of always being cooped up and cringing."

"We are tired already," Irena said.

"So let's say a thousand people just begin to spread out," said Aleksandra, painting the scene with the cigarette in her right hand. "No plan or reason. We sit on staircases, we sit on tree stumps, we stroll down Marshal Tito Boulevard. No particular purpose except to stretch our legs, fill our lungs, clear our minds. Suddenly you have snipers firing at a thousand people. The bastards won't know where to look! After the first shot, everybody scurries anyway. We are like cockroaches in the light. It will be like trying to track ants in a pile. So let's even say the figures go up slightly, because there are more of us to shoot before we scurry. Let's say it's even ten a day."

Aleksandra got to her feet, to give added weight to her conclusion. "My point, dear," she said with intensity, "is that our statistical chances of being shot go down just *because* we are out here. Isn't it better that ten out of a thousand people are hit in a day than four out of fifty? Wouldn't you rather take your chances with a thousand other people crawling the streets than with fifty? The more of us who have the nerve to stay out here, the fewer of us are likely to be shot."

Irena had been holding the cigarette Aleksandra had given her in the palm of her hand. Now she held it upright, like a teacher with a piece of chalk at the blackboard. "That sounds like the logic of a smoker," she said.

"Upstairs with you then," said Aleksandra. The two cackled like schoolgirls as Irena turned to go.

14.

TEDIC BURST INTO IRENA'S LIFE THE VERY NEXT DAY, HIS SMOOTH bald head snapping out of the folds of a glossy leather overcoat. "You are Zaric, the great basketball player," he said with a mock bow, as if Irena were the Duchess of York, and had trundled out with her empty bottles solely to see how commoners got by.

"I am Zaric, that's for sure," said Irena.

"Your game against Number Four last year," he said. "Brilliant."

"I had a good night." She remembered sixteen points, sixteen rebounds—but Irena remembered every play, score, and second of every game she had ever played.

"Much better than good," said the man. "Of course, you would not remember me." Tedic had shaved his head two years ago. He hoped it would give him a hint of predatory elegance—an intimation of Yul Brynner or Michael Jordan. But even shorn he still looked—it was the joke he had learned to tell on himself—like a man who could walk down Vase Miskina Street in a lilac tutu and people would turn only to ask, "Did a bald man just go by?"

"I am one of the gnomes who sit in the stands and acclaim the likes of you," he told Irena.

It had been months since Irena had been recognized as an athlete; she was flattered. She squinted her eyes and fixed the man with a smile that was calculated to elicit his name.

"Tedic," he offered.

"Dr. Tedic?" Irena guessed. Hearing the name had restored the face to a more familiar place in her mind.

"The assistant principal at Number Four," he reminded her. "At least, before all this. Alas, no doctor. I was also the assistant basketball coach. The man who sits at the end of the bench, hollering the utterly obvious."

"Now I remember you," said Irena, laughing. "The man on the bench shouting, 'Way to go! That's the way!' "

"Whatever it is gnomes say," Tedic agreed, laughing, too.

SHE HAD BEEN standing in line at a water tap that had been opened on a wall of the Sarajevo Brewery when a hawk-faced man in a billowing gray-checked coat approached, flashing a piece of plastic up and down the line like a talisman. The man demanded that the teenagers standing in line with rinsed milk and detergent bottles produce some scrap of identification. Most of the young people slumped, shifted, fumbled, and finally pulled out an old Yugoslav national identity card.

Irena had none, and didn't take kindly to being asked for one. "Everything was taken from our family in Grbavica," she blandly informed the man as he reached her. "Do you need to know our names before we can get water? Do you suspect that there are Serbs sneaking over the line to lap up all this water? The taps run on their side. Maybe ours tastes better."

"Take as much fucking water as you can carry," said the man wearily. "Just tell us who you are."

"I never talk to strangers," Irena said. "Particularly now."

The man had left a grain of whatever patience he had that morning with each previous teenager. He had almost none left for Irena.

"Then just tell us how fucking old you are."

"Almost eighteen."

"Are you sure?" said the man. "You have a lot of nerve for seventeen."

"And you have a lot of nerve for a man of"—she paused as she added ten years to her interrogator's appearance—"forty."

The number smacked him like an epithet, and she saw him wince. "Just tell us when you turn eighteen," he said.

"Did you want to send a present? How sweet. But, really, I need nothing."

Irena's cheek earned her a walk over to a small white van in which there were men wearing short black leather coats. They were looking down at sheaves of paper that seemed to be a printout of names.

"If you're from Grbavica," said an expressionless man in a rear seat, "did you go to Number Three?"

"Are you really some kind of officials," Irena shot back at them, "or just horny bastards trying to get young girls to give you their names?"

It was then that Tedic stepped forward.

"To spare my men," he joked later. "They were clearly overmatched."

TEDIC WALKED IRENA over to a side of the building where Bosnian police officers had driven a bus, emptied it of gas, and then overturned it to catch sniper shots. He shook out a Marlboro for her, unmistakably fragrant in its unmistakable red-and-white pack.

"I don't usually get American cigarettes from assistant principals," she said.

"For your troubles," he explained. "These men work under my direction. In theory. They should mind their manners. They should know with whom they are dealing. That was quite a team you had. Cosovic, Dino Cosovic, the coach. Strapping guy. 'You are a lucky man,' I used to tell him. 'Your girls could beat the Detroit Pistons.' I would give up my left"—he offered a quick revision—"*earlobe* to have any one of those girls, much less five. And where is the coach?"

Irena waved her right hand in the direction of the Vrbanja Bridge. "Over there," she said. "Back in the army."

"Of course," said Tedic. "An old biathlon champ."

"He came by to tell me the night before he left," said Irena. "The night before the march."

"In person? How thoughtful, given all that was going on."

Irena regretted her choice of words, and then regretted what she said to recover. "He tried to tell all of us on the team," she said, perhaps too eager to explain. "Phones were out. My mother and father were home, of course."

"Dino has always enjoyed close relationships with his players," Tedic went on smoothly. "And some of the mothers. The dark-haired girl on the team with glasses," he continued. "She set a good pick."

"Nermina," said Irena. "She was in the bread line on Vase Miskina."

"I'm sorry," said Tedic. "I have tried to find so many other ways to say that. *I'm sorry* now sounds like a hiccup. But at least its sincerity is unassailable. What are any of us, if not sorry? The blonde—terrific passer," Tedic continued in the same cadence. "Sweet-looking, like a milkmaid. I used to see her around in a Magic Johnson jersey."

"Amela Divacs. I don't know," said Irena. "Still in Grbavica, I assume."

Two misses. Tedic decided to forgo any further recitation of names. "I've heard it got ugly in Grbavica," he said.

"It did." Irena volunteered nothing.

"You are—?" he asked solicitously.

"All right." She volunteered nothing more, and shrugged as if she were shaking off a hamstring injury.

"Family? Mother, father?" It was a teacher's trick: leave the student to finish the thought. To fill the silence, she may reach for the last thing she wanted to say.

"We're here," Irena said finally. Tedic marked her coolness. "We are living in my grandmother's apartment near Old Town, behind the synagogue. Grandmother died that first day," she added. "My brother is in London. Happily for all of us."

"Yes, happily for all," said Tedic. "But we need every young Bosnian to serve his country now."

"Until there are no more left?"

"We hope it won't come to that. But yes," he added evenly. "If need be."

"IF NEED BE," Tedic repeated after a silence between them.

"My father has already been taken for the army," said Irena. She mentioned nothing of the plans that her brother had confided, and certainly nothing of her own resistance. "He is sometimes taken away to dig trenches. I would be a better digger, don't you think? Better than a man in his forties who throws his back out when he tries to imitate Keith Richards."

"There are other ways of serving," Tedic said. "For both of you."

"I scrounge food for our apartment block," said Irena. "I run around sniper fire and stand in water lines so that mothers, fathers, old ladies, and children don't have to."

Tedic reverted to the manner of a man practiced in assuring adolescents that he was their co-conspirator. "Such work is precious," he told Irena. "Irreplaceable, quite possibly. Besides, as I have told our people, 'Don't put too many girls in the army. How can you build a brave new society if your best breeding units are in the line of fire?' I apologize for my frankness."

"And who the hell are *our people*?" asked Irena. "And, if I may apologize for *my* frankness, *who the hell are you*?"

Tedic sorted through the folds of his coat for a business card. He wanted to assure Irena that he wasn't a horny bastard poring over a roster of names in a van. The card was thin and cheap—ashy black ink peeled off on Irena's thumb when she held it out to be read.

SARAJEVO BEER
SINCE 1864
ONE COUNTRY—ONE BEER
MIROSLAV TEDIC
PERSONNEL DIRECTOR
SARAJEVO BREWERY

"I thought you were an assistant principal," said Irena.

"I thought I was, too," Tedic said with a shrug. "Fourteen years from retirement. I had accepted that I would never be a principal. I had planned to serve my time at one or two other schools, rousting the odd student caught with marijuana or dangling his dick over the boiled cauliflower in the lunchroom. I was going to summer in Spain, and romance English schoolmarms along the Costa del Sol. I would finally check into one of the blockhouse retirement bins our socialist forebears planted so plentifully behind the Adriatic coast, play mah-jongg for cigarette money, and hope to worm my way into the affections of lonely old widows. The Serbs saved me from such suffocation," he said with a wry smile.

Tedic shook out two more Marlboros. It was a calculated gesture of fellowship. Contrary to the testaments of his three former wives, Tedic did have a conscience. It was just that he rarely made demands on it. But he had learned that the artful confession—inconsequential, self-effacing, and amusing—could insinuate him into someone's trust.

"I remember the night you mention," he said, pacing off puffs from his Marlboro. "That Friday before the march—such exhilaration! The halls in Number Four buzzed with youngsters making posters, flyers, and flags for the demonstration. What a weekend they had planned—give peace a chance and get laid. My principal sent me down to one of the boys' bathrooms. 'It's awful,' he said. 'Appalling.' Of course. That's why Lord Shiva made boys' bathrooms—cisterns that flush straight into hell. Boogers, boners, pranks, and turds—that's what little boys' bathrooms are made of. They are lairs for the sort of petty infractions that an experienced tutor wisely ignores. But I was bidden. So I arrived just in time to see some young Victor Hugo put the last streaks of paint on a screed across the mirror: 'Muslim girls have smelly pussies.' "

Tedic hesitated for a moment. "I apologize for my frankness again," he said.

Irena just drew on her Marlboro.

"I stood there, in front of the basins and urinals," Tedic recollected, "my head turned away, so that the authors of this lyricism might take the chance to run away behind my back. I afforded them a strategic retreat. I afforded *myself* a strategic retreat. But one of them, Ranko, stood shamelessly in front of me. Brazen, even, I would say, as if he had been waiting his chance. He had pulled on a black sweater, of course, as if it were a Bulls jersey. To look like his paragons. 'Mr. Tedic,' he said, 'you've always been okay to me. Don't stop us. Don't be here on Monday, okay? Monday, everything is different.' I wished he'd called me an asshole," said Tedic. "I wished he had told me to fuck off. Instead, he told me that the world was going to change. What was he, seventeen? The worst of all combinations. He knew nothing, and he was so certain.

"So that night I got into my car," Tedic went on. "I put two suits, six books, and another pair of shoes in the backseat. A lifetime as a teacher—and, really, only six books are important to me. That night I drove away from my mistress's apartment in Vraca. That night I came across to the police station downtown. That night I said, 'A hell's storm is coming.' Someone got the idea to take me to the Home Ministry. Someone got the idea that an assistant principal might have something to offer in parlous times. I know nothing about beer. Maybe I know a little something about people.

"Perhaps we could walk as we speak before a sniper takes an interest?" Tedic said lightly. Irena clasped the necks of the empty plastic bottles in the crooks of her fingers and they walked around the white car, into the courtyard of the brewery.

"We can fill these for you inside. We're keeping the brewery open, you know," he explained. He extended his arm as if welcoming Irena to his manor. "The United Nations is encouraging us. They know that we Sarajevans are devoted to our beer. They are convinced that the brewery is important to the preservation of our rich culture. The U.N. seems to find that more precious right now than preserving"—Tedic paused for effect here—"our mere lives."

He went on in a confidential tone. "The brewery is built over the one spring of drinking water on our side of the city. I have a few jobs open for people who might help us keep alive a vital civic resource. Would you like to take a look?"

Of course, it was not really a question. Tedic led Irena a half block down to where a brewery truck was parked, and motioned for her to open the passenger side of the cab.

"Rather uselessly grand to ferry people just a few meters, isn't it?" he observed. "But we have to drive into the garage entrance."

Irena enjoyed watching the diminutive Tedic strain to reach the truck's pedals, and wrest two hands on the stick to put the truck into reverse, then forward, like a small dog trying to push a soccer ball with its nose.

"You're not with the army or security forces?" she asked.

"Our army is an amorphous institution right now," he said. "Remember, we Bosnians declared that we wanted to be an unarmed and high-minded little state, striving to earn the plaudits of Jimmy Carter and the Dalai Lama. I'm sure they plan to drape the ribbons of their Nobel nominations graciously over our graves."

THEY PULLED INTO the ocher-brick back side of the Tito-era part of the brewery complex. The modern building had been the object of successive five-year plans; it had not quite been finished before being dented by destruction. Much of the brewery's glass siding had already shattered. The older Hapsburgian-edifice parts with gables and cupolas had never been restored. Tedic parked the truck alongside three others, and stepped like an apologetic host over a rubble of glass and scorched paper. "I'm sorry for the mess," he said. "The Serbs are finally moving along our renovations."

The brewery must have had a generator, powered by babbling springs underneath. The building buzzed with the electricity circulating in its bones. There were three old copper tubs set up on stilts in the central room. Old copper tubing nestled thickly overhead, sprouting a mossy green coating.

"Canning goes on upstairs," said Tedic as they walked across the white-tiled floor. He held up a single, empty discard from the floor, probably dented in packing. "Have you ever noticed that the diameter of a beer can suggests a hand grenade?"

Irena stopped walking and turned to look at him. "Something is going on here," she said. "You want me to see it."

"Something," said Tedic. "We make one of the best beers in middle Europe here. Or used to. They tell me that it's weaker now. I am a devout Muslim myself, and therefore drink only a good, smoky scotch." Tedic fairly strutted, hands clasped behind his back.

"This brewery sits on its own water supply," he said. "It has all manner of manufacturing machinery that talented engineers can adjust for current necessities. It receives U.N.-sanctioned shipments of ingredients, grains and syrups from Africa and Austria that friends from America and Israel can enhance with special additives," he noted with a glint in his eye. "And, just outside, there are stout-sided trucks lined up that the U.N. thoughtfully furnishes with fuel. The U.N. insists on seeing delivery manifests, of course. Orders and production figures. But, happily, the Nigerian accountant the U.N. has installed to certify our operations is more interested in seeing five American hundred-dollar bills each month, and a Ziploc bag of cocaine."

IRENA GRINNED WITH the sheer exuberance of being let in on a secret. "Do I get to hear something more?" she asked.

"Okay," said Tedic. "They're brewing beer here, on this floor. But in the brewmaster's own special cauldron they're cooking up explosives. Above us, they're canning the beer. And on another part of the same assembly they're rolling out hand grenades in exactly the same gauge. The trucks are lined up to receive the supplies of water and beer they must deliver, and stocks of other products as directed. There are also some other enterprises engaged here, a few I don't know about. A few more I do."

Tedic stopped. Irena understood—he loved that he didn't have to wink or signal to make this known—that it was her play.

"What do you want me to do?" she finally asked.

"Work here," he said, looking for the simplest beginning. "Hang around. Stamp paperwork. Help with a few deliveries. 'Other duties as assigned' is the phrase."

In the absence of something more solid, Irena guessed something wild. "You want me to be a spy."

Tedic bit back a smile. "Not really necessary," he said. "We've been one country, remember, and know each other pretty well. We hardly need to plant a Muslim girl on the Serbs when we can employ Serb girls for the same services. Unless, of course, a Serb in question plainly prefers Muslim girls. I suppose we have the occasional *Ma-ta Ha-ri*," he said with a low flourish. "But I gather that we contract with women who may have a larger field of experience than teenage boys and the coaches of girls' squads. Once again, I apologize for my frankness," Tedic said.

When Irena stopped at this, his eyes softened. "No shame, dear," he said. "It's just that you've been on better all-star teams than that one."

. . .

"WE ARE ALSO a brewery, you know," he said after a short time-out. "There are deliveries, papers to fill out, floors to sweep. 'Other duties as assigned' are impossible to predict."

"I would be paid?" Irena asked. "We are—I'm sure everyone is—running low right now."

"Of course," said Tedic. "Cigarettes. Cans of beer, all legal tender that can be traded." Then he walked a few steps to a spigot low on a wall. He turned on the tap ostentatiously. The sound of the water splashing echoed like laughter in the large brick room.

"And this, too," said Tedic above the din. "Right under our noses. Like in the old days, just a few months ago. Enough to drink, wash, and even spill. Enough for coffee, tea, brushing your teeth, and soaking your feet. We are Muslims, after all," Tedic said, laughing. "Not Bedouins."

THAT NIGHT IRENA told her parents that Dr. Tedic (she had decided that although Tedic had corrected her on this point the honorific was a useful misapprehension to pass on to her parents) had offered her the job because of her basketball career and overall promise.

"He says he's trying to give some opportunities to students he remembers," she explained.

"I'm glad you girls kicked their asses at Number Four," her father said. "Dr. Tedic sounds like he doesn't want to hire losers."

"It's a little work," Irena explained. "We get water, cigarettes, and beer. When there are overnight hours at the brewery they send a truck, so I don't have to walk. And, by taking the job before I'm eighteen, I'm less likely to wind up digging ditches on the front lines. Not that"—she glanced at her father—"that isn't honorable work."

"It is," Mr. Zaric agreed vigorously. "And better I do it than my daughter."

His daughter did not add that when Tedic had taken her bottles and run them under the splashing spigot he had put them back into her hands one by one, and loaded his words as carefully as her shoulders.

Nothing is more necessary now, he'd said. *But it would be daft to keep your talents buried in a ditch. Even an old assistant coach can see that. What we may ask you to do one day may be plenty dangerous. Don't assume that the only way to dirty your hands is with a shovel.*

. . .

MRS. ZARIC DECIDED to prepare a congratulatory dinner to mark her daughter's entry into the beer business. Tedic had given Irena four cans to take home as a kind of bonus. Mrs. Zaric had saved the water in which she had cooked some beans. If it had some flavor, she reasoned, it should have some nutrition, so she poured it into a pot.

Aleksandra Julianovic had torn off some grass from a patch outside after a rain, and had even managed to catch a couple of small snails. She drove them from their shells by holding a lighted match against their backsides. "Serb style," she called it.

Mrs. Zaric snipped the snails into halves and stirred them into the broth, along with the grass. She had a half can of tomatoes, and this she also plopped into the pot. She had stored a small burlap sack of macaroni from a humanitarian shipment in her mother-in-law's small washing machine. (Rats were becoming a problem. The Zarics could hear them scuttling behind the walls at night. The war had made them hungry, too. So Mrs. Zaric had taken to storing dry goods inside the spindle of the washing machine because no one had ever heard a rat rooting around there. "There's no need for the little bastards to eat better than we do," she had declared.) She then put the pot over a fire that she had kindled in the kitchen sink from the wooden soles of one her mother-in-law's old clogs.

Irena opened the beers. For the first time in months, they heard the liquid "Ahh" of cans being pierced. She set them on the living-room floor.

Mrs. Zaric took the pot of macaroni, grass, and snail stew in bean broth into the living room. It was the first time in several weeks that she had cooked something that was hot enough to give off steam. "Please," she said to Irena, Mr. Zaric, and Aleksandra. "While it's hot. It's hard to get things hot these days." She hoisted a Sarajevo Beer above her head, even above the windowsill, and said, "To Irena, who does so much for everyone!"

"Including be a pain in the ass!" Mr. Zaric proclaimed with a smile.

The group plinked their cans together and took long sips of the warm beer. Tedic was right; it seemed watery. The bubbles and taste were welcome, but Irena's head stayed clear. They spooned the stew into their mouths. Irena watched her father chew doggedly on a clump of grass. He kept chewing, but the grass was stubborn.

"I'm not sure nature gave us the incisors for this," he said.

"I believe that cows swallow whole shoots of grass," said Aleksandra. "But it's their stomachs that do the chewing."

Dark green leaves twitched over Mr. Zaric's lips. *"Mmm-ooo,"* he finally said through a full mouth.

"Baa," Mrs. Zaric brayed like a sheep. *"Baa!"*

"Nnn-eigh!" Irena whinnied like a horse. *"Nnn-eigh!"*

"Mmm-ooo! Baa! Nnn-eigh!" they all bleated together. *"Mmm-ooo! Baa! Nnn-eigh! Mmm-ooo! Baa! Nnn-eigh!"*

The braying and laughter of the Zaric menagerie stopped abruptly when Aleksandra plucked a macaroni from her bowl and tested it. The noodle had turned gray and rubbery. When she stretched it between her fingers, it reddened at the point of strain and finally snapped apart.

"Worms!" Irena said in the sudden silence.

No one mooed or neighed. It was Aleksandra who finally resumed the meal with a melodramatic slurp. She smacked her lips, blew a cooling breath on her spoon, and blotted her mouth with the back of her hand. "How thoughtful of the Americans to mix a few vermicelli with our macaroni," she said. She took a sip of her beer and daintily swirled her spoon through the stew, searching for vermicelli.

15.

IRENA'S FIRST DUTIES AT THE BREWERY WERE NOT DEMANDING. SHE was given a blue plastic pass that seemed to confine her to the first floor. Tedic would bustle past with a greeting and a sallow smile, then bound up to the second floor. Sometimes she encountered him in a stairwell as he descended into the basement. Once he was with a gray-suited bald man—authentically bald, not shaved, like Tedic—whose face brightened when Tedic introduced her as "Zaric, the great basketball star."

"You are a household name in Grbavica," he told her. "We are lucky to be working with you."

After the man had passed by, Tedic turned around and mouthed to Irena, "The Home Minister. *Very* important."

There was a brooding, milky-faced man in a smudged red woolen shirt who always sat by himself behind a window off the loading dock. Irena heard Tedic call him Mel. She had gathered that the man's profoundly undetectable resemblance to Mel Gibson was a standing joke. Occasionally, Mel would hold up a broom for Irena and point to a litter of dirt and wood splinters left by the boots of delivery people. Irena would make five minutes' labor last thirty, for lack of other work. "Other duties as assigned" were not yet forthcoming.

Irena was hanging a broom back on a rack near the docks one day when she saw the blue eyes of a beautiful blond woman staring up from the top of a crate. One of the woman's breasts was bared—her lacy black vest had been artfully parted. She picked up the magazine and waved it through the dispatch window at Mel.

"Can I look at this?" she mouthed.

"What the fuck?"

It had taken Irena a couple of days to decipher Mel's phrasing. He seemed to pull out of his sentences two or three words from the end, so that

"What the fuck?" could mean "What the fuck is that?" or "What the fuck are you doing with that?"

Mel stayed seated in his swivel chair, so Irena guessed it was the former. "It's Kim Basinger," she told him. "*Sky,* June '92. Maybe one of the U.N. people left it."

"What the fuck?" said Mel. "What the fuck?"

Irena translated this as "What the fuck do I care?" and so sat down with the magazine on the steps of the loading dock.

KIM TOLD *SKY* that she liked a man with good lips who had clean, bracing breath and didn't slobber when he kissed. "You have to think it's as good as what's coming later," she said, and Irena thought briefly of Coach Dino. His breath often smelled of cigarettes and beer. Sometimes he pushed his tongue so far into her mouth that his top lip would begin to slip over her nose.

She couldn't quite follow an article in English about IRA terrorists in Belfast. It showed photographs of young Catholic schoolkids hiding behind a burnt car during a shoot-out, and young IRA men in running shoes, dark sweaters, and ski masks, holding rifles. I guess that's the universal uniform for their team, Irena mused. She blinked a few times on learning that Eamonn, the young IRA terrorist who had been quoted extensively, was seventeen years old. That can't be, Irena thought for a moment. That's my age. Well, she thought after a pause, that's old enough for anything, I suppose. The author asked Eamonn why the IRA had killed more Irish Catholics than British soldiers, and Eamonn said, "Killing is the only way to get their attention." Well, Irena thought, we seventeen-year-olds are not always good at math, are we?

A few pages on was the sex-advice feature called "Confidential" (despite, obviously, appearing in a mass magazine). Susan in Birmingham worried that her vagina was too small. *Sky* told her that there was no such thing. Algie from London said his girlfriend had told him that his penis was too smooth. The magazine suggested that he take a day trip to Birmingham to meet Susan. Kim in Kent said her boyfriend insisted that she lather his cock with Nutella before they had sex. *Sky* said that seemed like an awful waste of chocolate spread, and Irena agreed. Especially here, she thought. Gobble the spread and forget the cock.

There was a gorgeous photograph of a swimmer's back in a Seiko watch ad. The young man's muscles seemed to swell and ripple like an ocean current. "He's spent 21 years getting here," said the ad. "But all that matters is the next 48.62 seconds." Seventeen years getting here, Irena said to herself, thinking of Nermina. And it's over one morning for a loaf of bread. South Korea banned Right Said Fred's song "I'm Too Sexy." But in America Sharon Stone was unveiling her crotch, like a new car design, in her latest movie. The director was a Dutchman who said, "People always criticize violence. But we humans have evolved from savage apes." Teenage gangs in New York housing projects were slicing off their legs and arms trying to ride the roofs of moving elevators; they called it elevator surfing. Well, that's one worry we don't have here, thought Irena.

Irena was immersed in the personal ads ("Handsome gay male, 17, N. Ireland. Very straight-acting. Write soon, sinking fast." Is that you, Eamonn? she thought. Better not let your brothers under their ski masks know) when Tedic turned a corner onto the dock.

"I'm glad to see you improving your mind away from the classroom," he announced.

Irena closed the magazine, but only over her thumb, so that she could keep her place.

"Do you have a jacket?" he asked. "Never mind. We'll get something. We have a 'duty as assigned.' "

Irena's Air Jordans smacked and squeaked on the loading dock as they scuttled out into a beer truck that Tedic had kept running.

"DO YOU KNOW Dobrinja?" he asked.

"We played Veterans High a couple of times."

Tedic nodded in recollection.

"That big, slow girl who couldn't be moved from the key."

"Radmila," Irena remembered. They had held her to four points.

"Out near the airport, you know, this has been the bloodiest ground. We can't even count. All those Olympic-era housing blocks out there—shooting people in their apartments has been like shooting bean cans off shelves for the valiant Serbs. But the folks in Dobrinja have been brave. They dig out of their rubble and come to greet the tanks with bricks and rocks. They hold them back. They lost three men—women, too—for every one that they killed. But they've held the bullies back. Now, we have the smallest chance to return the favor."

...

DOBRINJA'S OLYMPIAN PANORAMA of ten-story apartment buildings looked almost intact as they approached from behind. Only the accustomed old Soviet satellite corrosion was visible: shattered windows left to decompose like chipped teeth, burgundy paint peeling and retouched with the gray that alone was available.

But the faces of buildings overlooking Serb territory had been razed. The buildings just refused to accept their demolition. Artillery shells had slammed into the apartments at intimate range. They had screamed in through the windows, blazed through rooms, torn off heads and arms, and soaked the ash and powder of the burned-out walls and floors with blood. Most apartments had been turned into dark pits clinging to sheer rubble.

A Bosnian who led a defense committee from his building had once waved a handgun truculently late at night and shouted across the indiscernible line. "Why don't you just finish us off? Come on over, right now, you pussy-faces, give us your best, and get it over with."

The Serb general Ratko Mladic had bellowed back, "We have a big army, you goat-fucking fairy. If my men don't have something to do tomorrow, they'll all get the clap."

THE PARKING LOT of the apartment block had been declared no-man's-land. No Bosnian could safely inhabit it, yet the Serbs had been unable to take it for their own: fifty yards of concrete scarred with bullets and pitted with shells, some still smoldering. Six cars stranded there when the war began now looked like flattened ladybugs. There were shoes, shirts, and slats of fractured wood scattered over the old parking spaces, decaying under the autumn sun. Up close, Irena realized that they were the bones, ribs, shirts, shins, and shoes of people who had been shot and left along the front lines. A doorframe incongruously left standing in the parking lot led down to what a sign said was a bomb shelter.

Tedic remembered when the buildings had been finished for athletes' housing just before the 1984 Olympic Games. The bomb shelters had been conspicuously included to impress Western athletes with the resolve of the socialist alliance to withstand imperialist assault. But the young American skiers and sledders had grown up after *Dr. Strangelove* and were simply bemused. The bomb shelter became a rendezvous for gay men before the Olympics had even left town.

Some of the people who were putrefying into the asphalt of the parking lot may have been racing for the bomb shelter. Socialism had built bastions to survive nuclear holocaust, but not the small-arms pops and mortar bangs of ethnic cleansing.

TEDIC STOPPED THE beer truck at the side of an apartment building and took Irena by the arm over to a basement window that had been wrenched open. She backed in, feet first, a line of hands taking hold of her legs, sides, and finally shoulders before her shoes came down. None of the men or women introduced themselves. Tedic followed, slipping in with surprising agility.

"Our sewer rats," he called out to the circle of men and women.

They answered with subdued cheers, moans, and a couple of handclaps. "And we have baited the trap," said a slender, mahogany-haired woman in tight blue jeans and a baggy sweater, who seemed to be in charge of everyone but Tedic.

"I have brought you an authentic member of the Pepsi generation," Tedic said with a mock bow toward Irena.

Irena had a quick impression of young, smart people whose bodies were tapering with each week of war. Many wore glasses that looked outsized and owlish on tightening faces. A couple of flashlights shone up from the floor, cans of light splashed against the ceiling, so that the wires in various colors that had been pulled across the gray space could be traced.

"We are ready?" asked Tedic.

"Anytime," said the girl in charge. Her wrists twitched like branches from the sleeves of her baggy gray sweater. "But soon is advisable. We don't know when Romeo will be calling."

"Or coming," Tedic added.

He called the girl Jackie, and hailed a fig-shaped man in the basement as Gerry. Irena guessed it was because of their resemblance to Jacqueline Bisset and Gérard Depardieu. She had a new curiosity about Mel.

"YOU ARE A twelve-year-old girl," Tedic said to Irena. "Can you be that?"

"I was once twelve," she pointed out. "Do I have a name?"

Gerry stepped forward, and looked down at the notes he had inked on his hands and wrists.

"Vanja Draskovic," Gerry said. "Thirty-nine Hamo Cimic Street in Dobrinja."

"Parents?"

"You're a step ahead. Milica and Branimir."

"Are they real?

"They were."

"Who were they?" Irena demanded.

"Names from around here," he said.

"Where are they now?" Irena wanted to know.

"Killed when the house was taken," Tedic explained flatly. When Irena didn't register horror or disdain, he went on. He was holding a beige telephone handset of the kind repairmen hooked on their belts.

"We will put a call through to the rectory of the Orthodox Church in Dobrinja," he said. "They have installed a mortar squad on the roof of the church, so their soldiers can rain holy hot shells on the children and old people of Dobrinja who may one day advance on them with their menacing empty hands. Your parents were not members of this church. You have scarcely been there. Your parents were sophisticated urbanites who considered themselves agnostics. But everyone on the street knows the Orthodox Church."

"Who will I talk to?"

"Whoever answers. Priest, housekeeper. It could be a soldier. Improvise accordingly."

"What the hell—?"

"Here's the hell," said Tedic. "Here is the hell that has caused you to dial the church for help. You are inside your house. The house in front of you—that big stone gray one across the street—has been invaded by Muslim assholes. They are shooting into your kitchen. Your parents are away. Working, shopping. You have the kitchen phone on a long wire and are hiding in the hallway. But the Muslim bastards are so close, you can smell their greasy breath. You can practically feel the scrape of their ill-shaven chins against your soft young neck. You are a twelve-year-old girl—innocent, sweet, and unspoiled. *Unspoiled*. I hope I don't have to be too frank. Put that in your voice. You have been forsaken by everyone but God."

Jackie, who had been standing with her hands on her hips, scowled with disapproval.

"Honestly, Tedic, the only story lines men know are rape fantasies," she said.

"Jackie, love, let's try to get this job done without arguing sexual politics." Tedic turned back to Irena. "Try to sound naïve," he said. "But not stupid. Wide-eyed, not empty-headed."

"For fuck's sake, Miro." Jackie stamped her foot. "You just drag her out of the second grade and expect her to all of a sudden act like Julia Roberts."

When a chorus of kindly laughter flickered across the basement room, Tedic waited for it to die down.

"Not Julia. *Ingrid,*" he announced softly, looking at Irena. "Bergman. The maid, the maid. 'I hear voices in the bells.' " Tedic did a little singsong. "Go forth, save France," he sang, barely above a whisper.

"Whoever answers may ask you questions," Tedic continued. "Gerry over there will hear them, too, and try to give you answers. We don't have time for a tutorial. Make it up. Be specific. Let your certainty confound them. Keep your voice urgent. Make your urgency move them along."

"What the hell," Irena said, "is going on?"

"We don't have time for a tutorial," Tedic repeated, holding the phone up in his hand as if he were about to dial.

"I am a *full-court player,*" Irena reminded him. "Offense *and* defense. What the hell," she asked urgently again, "is going on?"

Tedic smiled slightly, and lowered the phone to his waist. "Look across the street at the stout gray house protruding behind that row of homes," he said. "It has a sturdy basement wine cellar. The Serbs took the house from a Serb family so they could drink the wine, and store gold, dollars, deutsche marks, and diamonds in the cellar. Their booty is installed in the basement. Some unassuming guards scratch their guns on their asses on the ground floor. The top, with its pretty oval windows, has become a sporting club for the bankers who oversee these holdings."

"Sporting club?"

"Fishing and rod club. Hunt club. Pig-sticking club. They take their girls there, to be plain. Bordeaux and pearls in the basement, creamy Swiss sheets on the beds."

"They take other people's girls, too," added Jackie.

"That's plain," said Irena.

"Ingrid," Gerry said, "about half an hour ago, one of the bankers pulled up with a young blonde. Mitar is his name. If we proceed quickly, there is a real chance of pulling off something that would disrupt the Serb cash flow. And catch a bad man with his pants down."

There was another chorus of laughter from the young people clustered around Irena in their blue jeans and baggy sweaters. Jackie had eyeglasses like Nermina's and, beneath them, pools of warm chocolate for eyes. The boys and girls all stood around Irena, looking at her, waiting for her to begin the play. She took a breath, let it go, and nodded.

Gerry punched a number into the handset and handed it to Tedic, who listened for a moment, smiled, and then held it to Irena's left ear. She heard a trilling. She heard squeals and clicks. Two rings, three rings. Gerry stood directly in front of her, an earpiece hanging from his left ear, a scratch pad at the ready. She sensed that Jackie was behind her; she smelled a rose perfume and turned around. Rosy Jackie, she thought to herself, guarding my back. When Irena looked over her shoulder, Jackie smiled as she listened to the rings, prepared to eavesdrop with her own earpiece.

"Do you hear voices in the bells, Ingrid?" she asked. " 'Go forth, kick ass.' "

Irena heard a rattling on the line, and then a rough, phlegmy man's voice. "Ah, yes." She was on.

"IS THIS THE Orthodox Church in Dobrinja?"

"Yes."

"I am Vanja Draskovic. My parents, maybe you know them, Milica and Branimir. We need help." Irena spoke in a hushed rush, as she would coming downcourt alongside Amela Divacs.

"I am Father Pavlovic. What is it, child?"

"Muslims," said Irena huskily. "They have shot their way into the house in front of ours. The Domics' house."

"Where are your parents, child?"

"Gone," said Irena. Then she added, "Work. I'm supposed to stay in the basement when they're gone. But I heard shooting and wanted to be sure that our bird was safe. I should have taken him. Oh, *hell,*" she said suddenly. Gerry's eyes widened, but relaxed when he heard the priest respond only with new concern.

"What child? What's wrong?"

"I . . . I saw one of them. In the window. Long beard, like a rabbi. A long gun."

"Can he see you?"

"I'm in the hallway. Outside of our kitchen. I have the phone on a cord."

"Stay there," said Father Pavlovic. "Stay down. Stay away from the windows. Do you know your address, dear?"

"Thirty-nine Hamo Cimic."

"How old are you, dear?"

"Twelve. I'll be thirteen next February twenty-eighth," Irena volunteered. Nermina's birthday. Gerry dashed out a note: "NOT TOO MUCH," it said in big black letters.

"Well, you're a very bright girl," the priest resumed. "Where do you go to school?" Gerry already had that on his pad, and pointed to the note for Irena.

"Number Nine."

"A very good school," said the priest. "Do you know Mrs. Ivanovic?"

"My bird," Irena said suddenly. "Miro." An inspired interjection, she thought. Tedic hovered by Gerry, who was flipping pages on his pad. "He's in the kitchen, where the Muslims can see him."

"I'm sure Miro is fine, dear," said the priest soothingly. "You say you went to Number Nine?" Irena's distraction afforded Gerry the time to find the right page and hold up one full hand of fingers and two on his second.

"Mrs. Ivanovic is a seventh-grade teacher," said Irena, then pressed ahead to close off another route. "But not mine." Gerry already had his finger on another name. "Mrs. Fejzic is my teacher. But there is no school. I miss her," Irena added. And before Gerry could groan he heard the priest brim with new tenderness.

"Of course you do, dear. This war is a terrible thing. Look, dear, I am writing something out here. I don't know your parents. Do they come here?"

"We have been to church. But not a lot."

"What church do you and your parents go to, dear?" the priest asked.

Tedic's eyes narrowed as he held his breath.

"None, really," said Irena. "My parents are still socialists. We go to Christmas Mass." She paused. "We go when we are in trouble. I'm sorry, Father. That's why we had the number in my mother's little plaid book in the kitchen." Irena imagined her mother's small plaid book of numbers, filled with listings for telephones that now could not ring.

"That's why I called," Irena continued. "All these numbers she has of friends and restaurants. I didn't know who else could help. My mother has always said, 'We go to the church in times of trouble.' "

"Oh, child," said Father Pavlovic, "your mother said the truth. Now, dear, the house in front of yours. Where the Muslims are. Can you tell me what it looks like?"

"Do you want me to take a look?"

"No, dear. Away from the window. Just what you remember."

Irena's memories of the house across the way were fresh; she softened them a little. "Gray. Nice round windows in front. Red roof."

"Are you sure?" asked the priest. "How can you see the color of the roof?"

"It is one of those old buildings. The roof isn't flat. It's like a triangle. There are red shingles."

"Does it have a chimney?"

Gerry nodded and whispered, "Kitchen fireplace."

"Yes. The Domics have a fireplace in the kitchen. Mrs. Domic loves to make *cevapcici* there."

Jackie, Gerry, and the kids beamed at Irena, almost to bursting.

"You are in the hallway, daughter?"

"Yes," said Irena. "You told me."

"Good. Good. Now I am going to have to put the phone down for a moment."

"Don't be away for long!" Irena put the crack of a command into her voice; but infused it with a child's confusion and fear.

"I won't," Father Pavlovic ardently assured her. "I won't. Just a moment, child. Bear with me."

"The Muslims," said Irena, her whisper rising. "I hear them laughing. They are over there in the Domics' house, laughing."

"Stay where you are, child. Stay down. Be quiet. Say a prayer. Think of the baby Jesus, safe in his manger."

Irena, Jackie, and Gerry were utterly still as they listened to Father Pavlovic's telephone handset settle on a hard surface. They heard a brief murmur of voices.

Jackie shook her head. "Not a thing," she whispered.

Irena whispered back, "Won't someone there know that all the money and gold is kept in that house?"

Gerry smiled. "Kept it secret," he rasped. "Else their own folks would steal it."

There was a clank and a rattle on the line as Father Pavlovic returned. "I am back, child," he said. "Now you must listen. It is important that you stay away from the windows. Are you?"

"Yes."

"Your bird, Mischa."

"Miro."

"Where is he?"

"In a corner of the kitchen."

"Well, then, he has his cage to protect him. The rest of us are not so lucky as your little bird. What I want you to do now, dear," the priest said soothingly, "is lie down on the floor. Get down, dear. I will hold on."

Irena obeyed instantly. Tedic, who was not able to listen, stared at her quizzically, but put his hands out to ease her onto the stony basement floor.

"I am on the floor, Father."

"Are you all right there?"

"Yes," said Irena. She had turned her head so that her left temple rested against the floor. The side of her skull got instantly cold against the stone. Her nose filled with the smell of smoke and stale blood. "It's not very comfortable," she said. "Is something happening, Father?"

"Soon, daughter. It will not last long. Are your eyes down against the floor?"

"No. That would put my mouth against the floor. How could I breathe? Father, Father, Father, what's going on?"

The priest began to coo into Irena's ear, as if he were soothing a lost child. Jackie appreciated his tenderness even as she admired Irena's ingenuity.

"It will not last long, child," he said. "It will be over soon. You will soon be safe. Turn your head to the floor, child. Rest on your chin. You will be able to breathe just fine. Put your hands over the back of your head. Shut your eyes. Put the phone down next to your ear. Don't worry about speaking. I will just keep talking. Can you hear me? Just grunt once, child. Softly."

Irena grunted. Softly. Once.

"Don't worry about speaking, dear. There is nothing for you to say. You reached out to God when you were troubled, and He put me nearby to hear you. Stay down, dear. Just listen to me, dear. Shut everything else out for a few seconds, dear. You are not alone. God is on that floor with you. God has His arms around you. God is with all of us who fear. His Son was fearful, too. His Son tells us that the meek are blessed. They—we—shall inherit the earth. The merciful shall have mercy. The poor shall see God. Blessed are the peacemakers, dear. They are the children of God. Anyone who has to hide on the floor, seek help from strangers, or fear men bursting through their door is blessed. The kingdom of heaven is theirs."

Irena was glad that her eyes were turned toward the floor. The tears that had inexplicably filled them could just trickle away onto the ground. Out of a corner of her eye she could see Gerry's feet turning. She looked up, and saw Jackie's chin tip upward as she looked toward the small basement windows. Irena could hear a crash from across the way, then the whine of another mortar. There was another boom, and then a spray of rock, earth, and glass falling to earth in the no-man's-land just beyond their snug little basement.

"Direct hit," said Tedic.

"Flames," said a man in a jean jacket nearby, squinting through a set of field glasses. "Nice, big orange sheets of flames."

"Dead-on shots," Tedic repeated. "Hand it to the bastards. Broke their own bank, didn't they?"

"Looks like they have a team outside, just raking the house with gunshots," said another member of Tedic's team, and Irena could hear a popcorn of retorts under the bristle of flames.

"Strike the set," Tedic ordered softly.

There was a sudden scramble of Tedic's boys and girls pulling at wires and snapping open cases. The telephone handset was turned up on the floor; people stepped back as if it were a broken glass. Irena, who had pulled herself up on her knees, picked up the handset and spoke into the receiver without listening.

"Thank you, Father Pavlovic." She let Gerry take it gently from her hand, and told him, "Really, he wanted to help me."

TEDIC SAID A quick goodbye to Gerry, Jackie, and their troupe.

Jackie slipped her glasses onto the collar of her sweater, and when she pulled a pin from her brown hair it tumbled over her shoulders. She smiled at Irena and reached a hand out to squeeze her shoulder. "Ingrid," she said. "Vanja. Masterful. Five-star. Tedic renames us all according to his screen fantasies. I will look forward to your next performance."

People began to slip out through side windows, counting to thirty to space their exits.

"We got them to break their own bank," Tedic repeated as the group thinned out. "Our banker and his pal should be in oblivion. If we're lucky, there's a funeral pyre of dollars and deutsche marks burning now. Even if we aren't, they'll have to send teams to dig out their riches. They'll be sitting ducks with shovels. We don't need the Serbs' heavy weapons," Tedic said, "as long as we can fool them into firing at themselves."

"But this was a trick shot," Jackie reminded him. She gathered a handful of her hair, then let it fall. "The spectators now know where to look for the wires."

TEDIC GAVE IRENA another four cans of beer when they got back to the brewery. He added two packs of Marlboros, and made a small ceremony of lighting one from his own pack for her.

"You were genuinely distinguished, Ingrid," he said. "Really. I don't mind telling you—sitting on the far end of the bench, as we coaches do, after all—that I wondered what you were trying to do with that bird. Miro. 'We made *cevapcici* in the fireplace.' But it was inspired. The great Zaric."

"Just trash talk," said Irena.

They were sitting in Mel's dispatch office. He had the brewery's 1992 calendar hanging on a nail over a deep green file cabinet. A new picture flapped down each month, of brisk streams, effulgent mountain flowers, and snowcapped crags, where the journey of Sarajevo Beer ostensibly began. But Mel had stopped turning the pages of the calendar in June. The months and weeks sat barren, with no appointments to keep or celebrations to schedule. It was no longer possible in Sarajevo to flip through the pages of a calendar and say, "Thank God it's Friday," "My birthday is soon," or "Our vacation starts here."

"We need to make new calendars," Irena told Tedic.

"Oh, I don't imagine we will soon put out new ones," he answered.

"But we need them," said Irena. "Not to sell beer. There's no competition—it's our beer or no beer. The kind of calendar we need now," said Irena, "would be marked differently. Not holidays or moon phases. There would be a red sign in the box for the last day of the month that said, 'If you can read this, you are still alive. Congratulations. Go on to the next month.' "

"You are a marketing genius," Tedic said finally.

IRENA WAS STILL circling Tedic's seat, prowling for scraps.

"The girl is the girl, the banker is the banker," she said. "We don't give them names, do we?"

"Terms of art," said Tedic.

"And you give us stage names. Gerry, Jackie, Ingrid."

"Sigourney, Arnold, Nicole, and Jean-Claude," he agreed.

"And the banker's girl is even just 'the blonde,' " Irena pointed out. "Brunettes can sometimes be 'the cute one.' But blondes are always 'the blonde.' "

"I suppose we don't even know if she really was blond," Tedic said.

"The banker," Irena asked suddenly. "Who was he?"

"Mitar Boskovic," answered Tedic. He flattened his hands over the packing slips on Mel's desk.

"A thief, a debaucher, a financier of mass murder," Tedic continued. "Husband, father of three, lover of many. An old Tito man who used to reassure the West that those Commies could be as greedy as any Swiss banker. I never saw him outside of a photograph. International banking buccaneers do not invite assistant school principals for ski weekends."

"Our bankers. They are so different?" Irena wondered as she rocked back on the heels of her Air Jordans.

"Ours merely steal and seduce," Tedic said. "That is practically virtuous right now. You know," he added in the admonitory tone of a teacher, "you don't look more wise and worldly by assuming that everyone is equally contemptible."

"I miss Father Pavlovic already," said Irena saucily. "He treated me nice."

"He is a message boy for a missile battery," Tedic answered more emphatically. "They shoot at civilians and hide behind the Father, the Son, and the Holy Ghost. Anyhow, I would not want to be in his cassock now, thanks to you. Fooled by a babe."

"We shoot at civilians, too," said Irena. "Today we just borrowed their bullets to get at Mr. Banker and his friend."

"He didn't run a shoe-repair shop on Rave Jankovic. He didn't drive the Marshal Tito tram. The money and riches that Boskovic and his friends plundered opened the slaughter camps in Vukovar. Not shopping centers."

"The girl?"

"His Polish girlfriend, Albinka. She was just along for the ride. Or the gold. She got caught in the wrong neighborhood when she got into banker Boskovic's bed. I wish she had stayed away. You lie down with dogs, you may not get up. But we can't let the life of an innocent trollop deter us from taking our best chance to bring down a fiend. Don't you remember? *They've been trying to kill us.* I doubt that Madame ever rested her posh nails on his arm to say, 'Give the Muslims a chance, my little pierogi.' Or whatever stage names they used. I'm sorry she got caught between bastards. It's what the Yanks call collateral damage."

Irena let the words grow between them. "That makes her only collaterally dead?" she asked finally.

Tedic swirled Marlboro smoke through his mouth until it seeped out and hung in front of his face. "It makes us less than Gandhi," he said. "We've had a few people run amok. I won't deny it. I won't pretend to be outraged. Maybe the Serbs will take us more seriously if they think we have a mad dog or two among us. But we don't shoot tank shells at people waiting for food and water. We killed a bad man and a harmless, worthless girl. All on my head, not yours. Before you feel even a twinge of remorse, let me offer you what I tell myself." Tedic stabbed the space between them with his right hand. "It was a pinprick against a bloodbath," he declared.

Death, Irena thought but kept to herself, by a thousand pinpricks.

"Maybe I will go to hell for it," Tedic continued in a strident voice. "But when they open the door, I'll see the banker and the priest there. God willing, I'll see Mladic, Milosevic, Arkan, and Karadzic there. And I'll leap into those flames the way Pelé runs toward the goal."

WHEN IRENA ARRIVED home—after a long walk, which Tedic had made only a perfunctory attempt to discourage—she told her parents that she had made a delivery in Dobrinja that morning and gotten delayed by mortar fire. That characterization was technically, if outlandishly, correct. She told them about the pockmarked apartments in the housing blocks of Dobrinja. They look like biblical ruins, Irena said, until you notice people cooking and sleeping inside. They all laughed at her description of the bomb shelter, the bastion from nuclear destruction reduced to no useful purpose between opposing front lines.

Irena was a little puzzled over her contentiousness with Tedic. The irritation that she felt was more acute and credible than any qualms she had tried to throw in his face. She decided that she had argued with Tedic mostly for the exercise. She was running out of subjects to argue about with her parents. They had learned one another's jabs and feints so well over the past few months that their arguments held no challenge or surprise.

Irena drank a beer with her parents and Aleksandra. Mrs. Zaric opened some cold beans, and they listened a little to the BBC. But after ten minutes there was nothing about Bosnia. The daily registry of blood and loss was becoming mundane, no longer news. It was just about as eventful as another bus crash in Bengal. Mr. Zaric lit one of his candles. The sun made a quick descent before seven. They had entered that time of year when the sun seemed to slip hastily into the hills. Shadows rolled up and disappeared as if they were being chased. Mortars whimpered like lonely dogs before they fell. In the quick, inky darkness, Irena sank into sleep amid the blankets on the floor. She usually slept well when she won.

16.

ONE MORNING MEL TOLD IRENA THERE WAS A STOREROOM IN THE basement that needed sweeping. She found a spare, dark room, dank with mist from the yeast simmering just above. There was a small wooden table flaking apart and listing slightly on the rough concrete floor, and two plain chairs. The back of one had been poked out, perhaps for wood to burn, with winter coming. The floor was filthy with grit, and gummy underfoot. Irena's shoes stuck when she tried to lift her feet. She thought that she must look like an astronaut trying to take steps on the moon.

The room's only window had bars, a grille, and a screen. Light from the brewery's main floor strained through, just enough for Irena to see a small pile of papers feathered out on a brick ledge. The newspaper pages had begun to brown. Irena was determined not to look at them any more than she would look at a bad old report card, but she riffled through a few pages on the top; they began to shred in her hands. A few layers below, she felt something firmer, and dug down.

It was a *VOX*. Michael Hutchence of INXS was on the cover, a gloved hand holding back his mane like a black lava flow. When she turned the page, a flow of white foam clung creamily over an amber-filled glass. "Boddingtons. The Cream of Manchester." Oh, thought Irena, so that's beer. I don't see much of that, working in a brewery.

Following the ad was a feature called "The Wit and Wisdom of Michael Jackson." In the old days, Irena would have turned past such an article, or thumbed back the page to show Amela or Nermina later and say, "Can you believe this? The *wit* and *wisdom* of a man who gets a new nose every year? Westerners!" But over the past few months she had taken to reading virtually every word of the few magazines she was able to find. In fact, she read them over and over, as monks read their missals; the way that people in Sarajevo now dived for the last dried nubbins in a bean can.

If Irena couldn't find any particular sense in what she read, she attached her own. She discovered that she could carry on entire conversations by quoting scraps of ads, articles, and captions.

"My idea of your average person," Michael Jackson told *VOX*, "is someone in a crowd trying to tear my clothes off." And mine, thought Irena, has become an average person in the hills trying to shoot me. Michael told the magazine that he had been raised on a stage and wasn't nervous there. "I feel like there are angels on all corners, protecting me," he said. "I could sleep on stage." Why not send those angels here, thought Irena, where they can really do some good?

There was an ad for INXS on tour. Michael Hutchence was spreading his arms wide, like a crucifix. The ad said, "Live Baby Live." English was eccentric, Irena decided. The same three words can be a description or an instruction. Dire Straits, Elton John, Bruce Springsteen, Michael Jackson, Paul McCartney, Peter Gabriel, and U2 were all touring. London, Liverpool, Paris, Dublin, and Berlin. *VOX* mused, *VOX* speculated, *VOX* asked aloud, "1992—The Greatest Year for Music Ever?" I guess that's another way of looking at it, Irena thought.

She read on a back page that if they ever had working telephones in Sarajevo again, she could dial a Naughty Joke line that rang somewhere in Britain. She could choose from Smutty Jokes, Loud Moans, or Saucy Confessions. She thumbed back to that page. She wanted to bring the magazine home to her mother and say, "Do you see what we're missing, cooped up in this shooting gallery?"

TEDIC ROUNDED A corner and came into the room as Irena was absently singing Phil Collins, swishing a broom over the tacky floor in time. *"Kids out there don't know how to react."* Swish. *"The streets are getting tough and that's a matter of fact."* Swish. Irena looked up at Tedic's soundless shadow. He entered rooms, and lives, as soundlessly as a stray cat.

"Please, don't stop," said Tedic. "I'd rather listen to you than to the Knight."

But Irena was discomfited. She revealed her singing reluctantly and shyly, like a mole on her breast, only to teammates and lovers.

"Bouncing off the bricks helps," she told Tedic. "Before the war, I used to sing in the basement of our building, and sing in the shower. I'd feel like—I don't know, Madonna. Now it's dangerous to sing in the bathroom.

It's like telling a sniper, 'Over here.' I don't sing. I hear myself say 'before the war' a lot," she added. "I sound like my grandmother."

"The one who died?" Tedic asked cautiously.

"The first night. I think I told you."

"I think you did."

"Dying that night made her—more interesting," said Irena. "People would say, 'Your grandmother was killed. How terrible.' Now everybody knows somebody who's been killed. Getting killed—it's boring."

"Certainly to the rest of the world," said Tedic. He crossed in front of Irena, his black leather coat creaking. When he turned around to face her, he was smiling slyly.

"I'm glad you've been able to join us," he said. "It is essential that we keep this brewery open. We Muslims of Sarajevo love our beer. Especially during the long, dry fasts of Ramadan. It helps to reassure people that some of the world we knew before the war survives. And now," Tedic declared, "I sound like *my* grandfather. We had some excitement for you the other day. I'm glad we could include you. I know that around here it's *sooo* boring." He drew the word out in friendly imitation. "At least you can keep up your studies," he added, waving his hand at the *VOX* on the ledge.

"I can quote some magazines better than I can quote Madonna lyrics, much less the Koran," said Irena, stiffening into a mock pose. "*Sky*, January 1992: Clearasil Moisturizer keeps skin soft, supple, and spot-free. Tom and Nicole are really in love. J.T. in Manchester thinks he has a tiny penis. Jodie Foster eats organic food and wants to direct. Potbellied pigs are all the rage. Luke Perry has one."

"I wish I had a potbellied pig," said Tedic. "Food for two weeks."

"Not if he were a pet," said Irena. "At least *my* pet," she added quickly.

Tedic slipped into the seat that had no slats and leaned back on its two rear legs to look up at Irena. She held on to the broom as if it were a shield.

"I wanted to have a conversation with you about your career plans," he began. "I gather that you turn eighteen early next year." Tedic chose to make it sound as if his knowledge was intuitive, not direct. "Quite a time and place for a birthday," he remarked.

"My mother says at least I will always remember it."

"I hope not," said Tedic. "Any special plans?"

"Only to see it," said Irena. She went on. Reminding herself of the plans she had once imagined was pleasant. "I used to have it all figured before this began," she said. "I'd walk into that big, circular bar of the Holiday Inn with friends and order a drink. Not beer. I've drunk beer since I was six. *A drink*. A martini, a Manhattan, a whiskey sour—names from movies. Something Sharon Stone would have. My father always said, 'I'll mix you anything at home.' But that's not like walking into the Holiday Inn and having a stranger in a red jacket call you 'madam' and mix you a drink."

It was a little after eleven in the morning. Tedic sank a hand into a recess of his coat and pulled out a gunmetal silver flask.

"Can I get you something to drink, madam?" he asked.

Irena smiled and sat down across from Tedic, bending the broom down in surrender.

TEDIC THUMPED THE flask onto the table. He produced another pack of Marlboros with a flourish, too, which Irena took as a gesture of egalitarianism, however affected.

"To your birthday," he said. "Whenever it is." He knew that it was January 21st. He unscrewed the cap; it squeaked like a baby mouse.

"Next year," she answered. She took hold of the flask, still warm from Tedic's pocket, and tilted it back for a speculative sip. The sip bit back. The smell of some smoky fruit drifted into her nose.

"Scotch whiskey," Tedic volunteered. "A blend."

"Takes some getting used to," said Irena. She reached for the cigarettes. Tedic lit both of their Marlboros from a single kitchen match.

"To Toni Kukoc," Irena proposed.

Tedic tipped the flask in salute and let the match fall to the floor. "Let me slip into an old role," he said. "Let me play teacher for a moment. What kills people in this city?"

"Is this a test?" asked Irena.

"Every day," answered Tedic.

Irena tapped a quarter inch of her cigarette ash onto the floor and squished it absently with her toe as she thought aloud for Tedic. "Bullets and bombs," she said. "Hunger and cold. How many reasons do you want?"

Tedic offered no answer. He merely looked at her through the haze of smoke that hung in the air between them.

"Boredom," she resumed. "Stupidity. Venereal disease," she went on as the words came into her head. "Caused by boredom and stupidity. People stick their dicks anywhere because they are bored. They stick their heads out the window when they're bored silly. Some Serb sniper sees them—and they're bored dead."

When Irena looked at Tedic, he held her gaze as fixedly as if he had taken her chin into his hand. "How do we stop that?" he asked. His tone was deliberately casual; he wanted a casual answer, not a philosophical one.

"If I knew that . . ." she began. Her voice trailed off as she considered another answer. "We stay down. We keep hiding," she said.

"We've been hiding," Tedic pointed out. "It doesn't stop."

"Or we could just give up," said Irena. "People do. Countries do. Or die. We can just keep hiding until we die. I suppose they'd have to stop then."

"You've never hidden or given up during a game in your life," Tedic reminded Irena.

"This isn't a game."

"Exactly. So why talk of giving up now, when the contest finally counts for something real?"

"I HAVE ANOTHER answer," said Irena. She was warming to the dialogue as she would to a scrimmage. "We can fight back. For a while, at least."

"Let's start fighting back," Tedic suggested. "Then worry about how long we can last."

"But we're surrounded," Irena pointed out. "Cooped up like pigs in a slaughter pen. We hear the Serbs sharpening their axes in the hills. We squeal. The world goes on about its business."

Tedic let a ring of smoke settle over his head like a spotlight before speaking.

"Madam, it's even worse," he said, smiling desolately. "The world rebukes us. 'Stop killing each other,' they say. Or they lecture, 'It's more awful in Africa.' As if they care about Africa."

"Europe wants to help," said Irena, but it sounded like an echo of one of the slogans she had read in a magazine.

"They just don't want us wiping our bloody feet in Europe's foyer," Tedic said.

Tedic shook out two more Marlboros. Irena gathered that the conversation was moving into another arena.

"Europeans are steeped in wisdom," he observed tartly. "They have learned over this century how to wait for the Americans and the British."

Irena finally returned his forlorn smile. She took the second cigarette as an invitation to hoist her feet up on the table between them. "My family and I," she said, "we fantasize about that. Clint Eastwood swaggering into town, shooting snipers out of windows. James Bond swooping down in his Union Jack parachute."

"They're not about to make that sequel, dear," Tedic said with a sigh. "No audience interest. Europeans say, 'Sarajevo? Isn't that where the Great War began? Those bastards have been killing each other for centuries.' The Americans ask, 'Sarajevo? Where the hell is that?' "

"The Blue Helmets are here to protect us," Irena pointed out.

"To keep us from protecting *ourselves,*" Tedic shot back softly. "To defend themselves from the dangers of beleaguered rag-heads with guns in their hands. So when the Serbs shoot us, a French commander here radios his commandant in Zagreb. He passes it on, like a phone message, to a Dutch bureaucrat in Brussels. 'Bosnians bleeding! Please return the call!' He rings up some mid-level Uruguayan in New York, who says, 'Not so fast—we have to call the Security Council.' They take their seats just as our blood is drying and the Serb guns are back in hiding. 'Give peace a chance!' they reproach us. *A chance to kill us. I swear,*" Tedic went on in the same even tone. But his words grew measured and clipped, as if he were loading them one by one into a chamber. "If the United Nations had been around when the Persians attacked Thermopylae, they would have scolded the Greeks, 'Stop throwing rocks! They blunt the spears of the Persians!' "

IRENA LIT HER second Marlboro. She sat up in her chair, like a student who had suddenly noticed the immensity of Greenland. "But why not give up? Seriously," she said. "Shouldn't we at least ask ourselves? We're outnumbered. We have no guns. We have no food. We have no water. We have no friends in the world. Why should every last one of us stay here and die? Isn't it better to hold up our hands and walk out than to be butchered?"

"Our hands up," Tedic answered. "And our heads down."

"How many people should die just to keep our heads up?" Irena retorted. "We have to crawl across the streets like scared dogs just to try to stay alive."

For a moment, Irena thought she had stopped Tedic. He turned away from her and fastened his eyes on the middle distance, as if he couldn't bear to face her. When he finally spoke, his softness had the chill of a grave.

"And what would happen when we surrender? Have you played that out in your mind? Will they greet us with figs, cheese, and bottles of Chianti? Will they escort us all to our old apartments in a fleet of Mercedeses? Flowers in the foyer, stew on the stove? 'Surprise, surprise, hope you like it.' Or will they just send us off on tour coaches with box lunches, and take us straightaway into sheds and shit holes? Why don't you ask the people of Vukovar, Visegrad, and Prijedor how the Serbs care for their guests who come out of basements, bowing and scraping, with their hands up?"

Irena pushed herself back from the table when Tedic finished. The chair legs scraped like a small howl. "Why don't you tell me what you have on your mind," she said.

WITH PANACHE, TEDIC offered Irena his right arm. They stepped down a flight of concrete stairs, past a blasé security guard in a quilted gray coat, and onto the subbasement landing. Long gray pipes, intermittently swathed in rolls of adhesive, traced the length of the room. Steam pipes, Irena guessed, but they were dry and silent now.

Near one end of the long room there was a cinder-block wall. Several mattresses had been upended and propped against the bricks; tufts of white stuffing blossomed out. She could see two, three concentric-ringed targets taped over the mattresses, at about shoulder height. Above them, someone had strung up posters of Milosevic, Karadzic, and a movie card of Isabelle Adjani. Milosevic's eyes had been shot out. The front teeth in Karadzic's smile had been blasted away, and a smattering of shots had been spattered over the dunes of his platinum pompadour. Isabelle Adjani's blue eyes, however, remained intact.

"The beautiful blue of the Adriatic," Tedic explained as he swallowed a small smile. "Times are hard enough without having to spend all day looking only at the faces of villains."

Irena sat down atop a hard bag of grain that announced in blue and gold letters across its plump chest that it was the gift of the people of Sweden. "I kind of thought that you didn't want me here just to shuffle papers and sweep floors," she said.

TEDIC LET THE silence build between them. He licked his lips. He flattened the top of an adjacent grain bag and sat down. He swung his heels from left to right, like a pendulum, and rocked his head to keep time. A slick of moisture on his turtle-smooth scalp made Irena aware that the bedding, thrumming, and yeasty aromas in the brewery had made the basement warm. But Tedic kept his leather coat cinched around his shoulders; it was his cloak of command.

"What do you want me to do?" she asked again.

This time Tedic calculated that he had to speak before the silence between them burst. "I want you to be a spear for us."

"From the look of this," she said, waving her hands at the targets, "you want me to be a bullet."

"A few bullets are all we have. I want you to go up into places where you can't be seen. Into the buildings they have bombed, burned, and left for dead. I want you to hide in those bones and strike a small blow for our city against the big guns that are trying to blow us apart. I want you to turn the corpses they have strewn across our cityscape into ghouls that will haunt *their* sleep."

"I don't know how to fire a gun," Irena told him. But Tedic had anticipated that.

"You're an exceptional athlete," he said. "Eyes, reflexes, cool. The shooting part—it's appallingly easy. Gavrilo Princip could shoot a gun. Lee Harvey Oswald. The executioners who rained shells down on Dubrovnik can shoot really big guns. Thugs all over the world can shoot guns."

For the first time, Tedic leaned forward and touched Irena's wrist. It was a token of confidence, the coach telling his star player, "Only you . . ." When Irena didn't stiffen or draw back, he went on.

"We need someone who can climb up and down into inaccessible but opportune places," he said. "We need someone who can learn new moves quickly, and perform under pressure. We need someone who can *kick ass.* Whether your shots hit or not scarcely matters. This game we score differently. Each time you shoot, the blare off the bricks lets people know that those who are trying to kill us cannot rest comfortably in the apartments they have stolen. We will not just shrivel inside these hovels, burning chairs and going hungry."

"I'm kind of a pacifist," Irena said.

"So am I," said Tedic. "When the world permits."

TEDIC DID NOT have to tell Irena not to speak of their conversation with her family that night. Irena understood—for that matter, Mr. and Mrs. Zaric would probably understand—that her life would take her through trials and events that were most agreeably kept from her parents. It was unawareness by mutual consent. Irena wouldn't discuss her emerging duties at the brewery any more than she would talk to her parents about smoking a joint or letting a boy slide a hand into her blue jeans.

Over a dinner of crumbled leaves and powdered cheese over rice, Irena did tell them about the ad in *VOX* offering Smutty Jokes, Loud Moans, or Saucy Confessions.

"I'm not sure about the difference," she said. "I notice they're all the same price."

"Smutty jokes," Aleksandra explained in a forcibly scholarly tone, "have endings that make you laugh and blush because they talk about something that polite people aren't supposed to comment on. Such as"—here Aleksandra raised her fork thoughtfully, like a mathematician's pencil—"the sailor who goes to the whore but doesn't get his money's worth, per se. 'I'm sorry,' says the sailor to the whore, 'but your whats-it is too large for my whose-it.' "

"I think I can fill that in," said Irena. "Loud Moans?"

"Let me try that," said Mr. Zaric. He carefully removed the vein of a leaf from his lower lip.

"Loud Moans jokes are funny, as when someone moans because they feel something they didn't expect. The ending of a Loud Moans joke goes, 'Yeeeow,' the sailor shouted at the whore. 'Your whats-it is too small for my whose-it.' "

Mrs. Zaric figured that Saucy Confessions fell to her. "The whore confesses to something she wants to boast about, anyway. *Saucy.* She blushes just so you can see her better. The whore says, 'You'll never believe what I once did with a sailor.' Or 'what I did *to* a sailor.' That's how it goes for a whore, I think. At least the ones in jokes."

"How much do the calls to this joke place cost?" Mr. Zaric asked.

"Three pounds fifty," said Irena. "More for long distance, I'm sure."

"I've lost track of what that is," said Mrs. Zaric. "Maybe a carton of Drina cigarettes. Marlboros or Winstons—you could probably buy only three jokes."

Mr. Zaric picked at another leaf vein that clung to the tip of his tongue. "Look at all the money we're saving by making up our own jokes," he said.

The Zarics laughed so hard and so long that they were too tired to press that night's candle scraps into the can Mr. Zaric kept for that purpose. They simply crawled down to sleep on the floor below where they had been sitting, like dogs or cats that eat and then nap next to their bowls.

17.

THE NEXT MORNING TEDIC TOOK IRENA DOWN INTO THE BASEMENT, back to the faces of Milosevic, Karadzic, and Isabelle Adjani looking down on the mattresses, pocked cinder blocks, and a lone black-snouted rifle that Tedic touched with the tip of a finger.

"You've never fired a gun," he remembered. "Father never hunted? Brother?"

"Never," said Irena. "My father has only held an electric guitar."

"Guns are beguiling, you know. All that power. Simply put your hands on it in the right way, and people scatter."

"I've never been interested."

"Not even recently?"

"Especially," Irena asserted. "I've wanted to squeeze the life out of particular people with my bare hands. But shooting someone you can barely see—someone you don't know—just because they're there? It sickens me."

"Me, too," said Tedic. "So does murder. Do me a favor, my Material Girl. Hold this for a moment. I guarantee you, it's unloaded."

Tedic was still her boss, and Irena still wanted to play. He lifted the gun as clumsily as he would a basketball and presented the weapon to her.

"No special way," he said. "Just like in American movies."

Irena was surprised by the weight, but she caught the stock of the rifle in her left arm as it began to slide toward the floor.

"How does it feel?" Tedic asked.

"Ugly. Heavy." Irena turned the rifle over so that she could see the curl of the trigger and the underside of the barrel, burned black like dried blood. She realized that she could handle the rifle's weight and held it out to Tedic.

"Ugly," she repeated.

"We'll paint one pink for you," said Tedic. "Posies on the barrel, if you like, and ribbons on the stock." He took a step back so that Irena couldn't hand the gun back to him without stepping forward.

"You see some fine old ones," he continued, like the keeper of an antique-jewelry shop. "Rich woods, superior metals, delicately engraved. That was before people could customize cars. Or athletic shoes. Their gun was an extension of themselves. The same as your Air Jordans," Tedic added with a smile and a gesture at Irena's feet. "And just about as hard to come by in Sarajevo right now."

Irena's arms were beginning to flag, but she didn't want Tedic to notice. She balanced the stock of the barrel on her left toe, as if she might actually twirl it. Tedic finally stepped forward and took the rifle from her. She gave it back without hesitation.

"Okay, what you have here," he began after a studied pause, "is an M-14 bolt-action Remington. American. Remington made the gun that tamed the West. Gary Cooper, John Wayne never used Czech or Chinese guns. Over on the other side, they use AKs. Best piece of engineering we Reds ever did. Much sturdier than our shoes or plumbing. But Communist engineering always lacked imagination. All the sick little lies that we used to hold things together instead of know-how. I say *we*—I was a Party man myself, of course. You don't become an assistant principal by being some kind of Sakharov. We were brilliant primitives, really. Tell us to get to the moon and we invented a flying oxcart. Too young to remember? The Commies got to space first. We made the Yanks look like gutless fools. But then, the Yanks beat our asses because the Russkies built these big mother ships. You can't just bonk the moon with a spaceship. You have to coax the ship down, softly. All guts and sweat, no fucking finesse. So whose gun would you want in your hands? The folks who gave us John Glenn, Al Capone, Coca-Cola, and color television? Or the folks who couldn't get to the moon, or out of Afghanistan? So what we have here is a Remington."

"How do you get them?" asked Irena.

"Little birdies from America," he told her. "Muslim brethren from Saudi Arabia. Jewish brethren from the Mossad. Anywhere we can, including greedy bastards on the other side who'll sell out their own kind for a price, Allah be praised. You know what the important part of shooting a gun is?"

"Of course not. Aiming it, I suppose."

"Partly. Calmness. Stillness. If your hands quaver by a nose hair, a shot can get thrown by ten yards. To stay calm, you need to be coordinated.

Handle the sequence the way a river handles waves. Eye, hand, breathing. Coordination, anticipation. A shot from a gun like this gives your shoulder a hell of a kick. You've got to roll with it, or you'll fall over."

Tedic turned the rifle over like a mewling child and slapped a cartridge that he'd drawn from his pocket into the stock.

"Want to try? Go ahead, put one into Slobo's nose."

"No!" Irena said emphatically. But even as she spoke she took the rifle into her arms.

"A pack of cigarettes."

"I'll be rotten," said Irena, who already could see no reason why she should miss a shot. "I can't afford a pack of cigarettes."

"You won't lose," Tedic assured her. "Keep your cheek against the stock like that, but softly."

"Kiss it. Isn't that what they say?"

"In the movies. They mean a passionless kiss. Brush your cheek against the butt as you would a lover's. Or"—Tedic revised this quickly—"maybe the cheek of a small niece."

Irena tucked the butt of the rifle against her left shoulder and brought her left eye against the viewing lens.

"Blink your right eye," Tedic instructed. "Find Milosevic's head, why don't you, then squeeze your right eye shut. Look hard at Slobo."

"Got it," said Irena almost instantly. She saw small gray circles—eyes and pouches—above Milosevic's nose.

"That ugly pig's ass of a face, grinning while Vukovar bleeds," Tedic said. "Put that small circle over his nose. See it? The nose of a pig. But none of the charm."

Milosevic's nose bobbed about in the viewfinder. "It jumps around," Irena said. "I can't keep it still."

"*It* doesn't move. *It* is your breathing," suggested Tedic. "Put the barrel down a moment. Take a breath. Exhale slightly, evenly, so you aren't holding a nervous bubble in your chest. Just when the air is done sliding out of your lungs, lift up the rifle. Tighten your finger against the trigger. As soon as you see your shot, squeeze. Waving the rifle around won't make your shot any better, and it will tire your arms."

Tedic paused for a measure, then repeated softly, "Squeeze."

Irena squeezed. For an instant, the trigger seemed to resist. But she pulled it deeper toward her chin and an abrupt clap of thunder rang down and sizzled inside her head. She felt a thump against the palms of her hands, as if a ghost were pushing back. The barrel punched her left shoulder, making her shiver. The rifle came to life like the staff turning into a serpent. The barrel rose and bucked in her hands, as if the gun wanted to dance. Irena fought the reflex to bring it down, and instead tried to coax it, point it at the wall, if not at Milosevic's nose. But the bullet had already gone. Air exploded against her ears. Spikes of wind and sound brushed back her hair and scratched the back of her head. And then the instant was over. The sound was spent; it crashed like the noise of a huge hornet landing.

Irena was still standing. On her heels, but standing, and still peering down the rifle's sight. Her shot had pulled right and punctured the pouch under Milosevic's eye. "Missed," she said finally—a little breathlessly. "Rushed it. Lifted my head too early to check and missed it."

"It would have been enough," said Tedic. "A pack of cigarettes to you. We'll show you how to get better."

Irena sat down on a pair of old flour bags—Danish, this time—overstuffed with sand and dirt. She could feel her face redden and her breath run short. She couldn't tell—she would need more experience for that—if it was the weight of the rifle or the exhilaration of getting off a shot. "What the hell do the people upstairs think we're doing down here?" she asked. She shook her head, as if trying to get a bug to fall out. "The U.N.—the beer people—don't they hear the noise?"

Tedic was already thumbing out a Marlboro for her, and acting with elaborate unconcern. "Not a problem so far," he said. "The sound of a child laughing would stand out more in Sarajevo right now, don't you think?"

MOLLY FOUND IRENA in the basement the next morning. Tedic would be there later, he explained. In the meantime, he was there. Molly was a tall, slender, pale man with a gauzy red beard that stippled his chin almost like a spill. He had a wispy reddish ponytail that he had grown, he volunteered, to confound all previous passport photos; he suggested that there had been a few other changes besides. Molly had the component parts of an M-14 laid out across the top of a trunk. He clacked improbable chunks together to show Irena that when you understood your weapon there was only one way it could fit together.

"Like your own body," he said shyly.

Molly's manner with Irena was bashful. His proficiency was visible in the lively assurance of his hands, which reminded Irena of old school films she had seen of robotic arms on a Japanese assembly line. But his speech was hesitant, as if he were measuring the words for a good fit. Irena, who thought she was good at identifying accents, couldn't place Molly's. They spoke in English. His *l*'s and *r*'s rolled like a Scotsman's. His *a*'s vaulted from his first to his last word like a German's. As gun parts clacked, she asked, "Are you from Scotland?"

"South Africa, ma'am. This is the gas port, by the way. It can be hot." Molly ran three lissome fingertips over a vented opening in the barrel.

"South African!" she said. She had grown up hearing her parents and teachers speak approvingly of the struggle against apartheid there. When students sounded as if they had discovered a correlation between capitalism and freedom, their socialist teachers usually reminded them to look at South Africa, where Communists had been in the vanguard of the struggle. Irena didn't want to assume the worst.

"Were you an antiapartheid activist?" she asked.

"This is the clip guide," Molly answered first. "Make sure there are no obstructions. No, ma'am, on all counts. I was on the other side."

Molly stood the M-14 on the back side of the stock, so that the hammer and spring, rear sight, and windage knob were all level with their eyes.

Irena tried to catch his eye through the trigger guard. "So you were one of the ones who kept Nelson Mandela in prison all those years?"

"I want you to see the bolt here, ma'am. You must be able to find it just by feeling for it, but not jam it. Never saw Mandela, ma'am. Only on the tube when he got out. Splendid presence, I thought. He could wear a candy wrapper like Armani."

"What if you had been told to shoot him?"

Molly seemed to grasp that no conversation was going to be possible until they had finished this one, so he turned the trigger guard against his wispy beard and asked his own question.

"By whom?"

"Whomever," said Irena. "Army, security, whatever your KGB was. Your boss."

Molly shrugged and almost smiled. "It's my business, ma'am," he said. "Usually, I don't miss."

Molly went back to clacking. He tried to show Irena where to pinch and turn the windage knob. But she interrupted at each sentence. Impudence was her way of exercising her independence. Molly was clever enough to throw back unapologetic answers, blunted only slightly.

"Is Molly really your name?"

"Is Ingrid really yours, ma'am?"

"Tedic's little name games." Irena snorted. "Why doesn't he hire ANC soldiers instead of you?"

"African National Congress, ma'am?" This really was new for Molly, and he rubbed exquisite fingernails over his scrub of a beard. "I guess they've got jobs now. I'm at liberty. Besides, ANC guerrillas might have a hard time fitting in here."

"They'd be treated as heroes," said Irena.

"They'd stick out like giraffes in Siberia. I've worked for plenty of blacks, miss," he added. "No problem."

"Brutal black despots," Irena snapped. "I'll bet you've rubbed a lot of blood off those pearly fingernails," she said. "They look as if you polish them constantly. What's the difference between you and the Nazis, anyway? Do you have a pat answer for that?"

Molly tilted the dull green ammunition magazine toward Irena as if it were an empty cash box. He wanted her to see the strong spring pressing the edge to the top. "Yes, I do," Molly said from behind the magazine. "Careful of that when you load bullets. Press down in the middle. Those springs have clipped many a pearly fingertip. The Nazis couldn't beat the Brits, ma'am," he added. "We did."

Irena held up one of the bullets. The body had a fine, glossy bronze color, and the hard tip was a glistening candy red. "Like lipstick," she said.

"My thought, too, ma'am," Molly told her. "A nice shade, too."

THE REST OF Irena's day with Molly was filled with the advice by which she was supposed to operate.

"Climb like a monkey into your hiding spot," he said, "but shoot like a slug. Go flat against the ground when you get there, or stay flat against a wall. Lying prone keeps you steadiest. It's the hardest for anyone to see. But it's also harder when you get up. You're most exposed when trying to get to your feet. Kneeling is good. It cuts your body in half. Keep a sock in your pocket filled with small stones. Stones, ma'am, not sand. Sand leaks. The sock can hold your barrel like a tripod, and you don't have to snap it open and shut. You can leave it behind. Standing is hardest, but best if you're hiding behind a column."

He instructed Irena to stand and fire three shots rapidly into a target. "Boom, boom, boom!" he commanded.

She squeezed the trigger three times quickly, like a pump.

When the volley subsided, Molly trotted over to get the poster and showed Irena how her three shots had trailed down, like shooting stars, away from the heart of the target. "It's not like shooting baskets, ma'am," he told her. "Your first shot is your best. The rifle gets heavier in your arms within seconds. Keep it down against your belt, pick it up when you see your shot, and shoot within a second.

"Stay calm, ma'am. That's an *order,*" he said, unable to suppress a small smile. "Any anxiety you think won't show because it's bottled inside can catch your breathing and make your hands vibrate ever so slightly. Ask a violinist. Sour notes. Don't stare where you're supposed to shoot. When you stare, things move. *Don't move.* A move could signal where you are. But also, don't play a statue. *Breathe.* Otherwise, you'll get light-headed. You won't see and you'll fall down."

Molly made his glittering fingertips twitter in the air between them. "Rain, snow, even fog will push down a shot," he explained. "Heat can make it swerve, too. But we don't have time or need for that lesson now. That's for Zambia and Lesotho. You don't get that kind of heat here. Not unless hell freezes over."

Irena returned a small smile of her own. "That happened here months ago," she told Molly.

MOLLY TOOK HER over to the serried rows of sugar sacks filled with sand, standing about a driveway's distance from the posters of Karadzic, Milosevic, and Isabelle Adjani. He had her lie down and fire ten clips—about two hundred shots—into dark blue silhouettes inked over white paper. Irena's bones thudded with her first five or six shots. She could feel a bruise begin to dampen her shirt faintly, but she felt it with satisfaction; she was playing hurt. Molly brought back a target and showed it to her: four shots were in the central oval that would have been a man's heart and lungs; three were along the edge of a T shape that would have been his eyes and nose.

"Take that last breath," he advised, "and run it up the barrel. You know?"

She did. She began to push her breath as she pinched the trigger and loosen her shoulder to clinch the kick of the rifle. After a few shots, she began to feel that her fingers had left slight indentations in the plastic stock. The gun was absorbing her touch. Molly ran ahead to fetch the next target, and came back smiling. Five holes had pierced the white T zone. The edges of each were singed a light brown; they smelled of fire.

"Do I want to know what those would have hit?" Irena asked.

"Two would be just below the left eye," said Molly.

Irena noticed that he had stopped addressing her as "ma'am."

"They would shatter the cheekbone and drive pieces into the brain. One shot would just about be in the right eye. Bull's-eye. Instant results." He poked the point of a black felt-tip pen through the last hole and wiggled it like a cartoon worm taunting a bird. "This would have shattered the teeth and jawbone," he said. "Obliterated quite a bit of brain, too. The bleeding would be most terrible. The pain would be great. I should think a man might want to rip his head off."

When Irena said nothing, Molly lay his elbow across one of the sugar sacks and spoke in a low voice behind her neck. "You don't shoot at an eye or a jaw, you know. Even I don't do that. Maybe if you saw Milosevic, Mladic, or someone who was brutal to you. Then, it's one right for the heart. But you shoot at a spot. You shoot at a target. You don't see somebody's blue or brown eyes. You don't see a smile. You see a spot in your sight. A stain, a smear, a dot. That's where you shoot."

"You don't have to make things up for me," said Irena.

"Nothing I tell you is truer," said Molly. "Hit the spot. What's behind is not your business."

Irena emptied clip after clip into the blue figures against the brick wall. She lay down on the floor, feeling the stock settle into that spot on her shoulder where Pretty Bird used to sit. The rifle began to rock against her shoulder. She began to find the trigger guard by feel. She brushed her cheek against the stock and felt for a burst of heat from the gas port. She ran her breath into the barrel with each shot, as Molly had advised her, and saw it burst and heard it bellow. She felt power bristling in her hands, breath, and bones.

"Make it happy," Molly urged at her left ear, where he was crouched on his knees. "It's just you and it. No one else. Make it hard, make it happy. Do it better than anyone does. You're alone together. No one knows, no one is looking. There is no one else."

Irena's shots screamed into the bricks, over and over, until her hands stung and sweat, or something like it, poured into her eyes.

18.

MOLLY STAYED ON HIS KNEES. BY THE END OF HER LAST CLIP, THEY could both see that Irena's bullets had blown out the largest part of the white T in the blue head of the silhouette. There was a hole the size of her fist in the center of the figure's chest. Irena turned on her ass to lean back on her elbows. She was breathless, drowsy, wound up, and unexpectedly sorrowful.

"Oh shit," she said to Molly. "It's too much."

"What?"

"I mean," she began to laugh, "I need a fucking cigarette."

Molly had none. He squirmed around on his knees and took Irena's rifle into his arms. "It's not good for you," he told her with teasing sternness.

"But this so fucking is." Irena heard herself talking in a kind of grave, astonished giggle. Her back bowed as she arched back on her shoulder blades.

"You're first-rate," Molly told her.

"Tell me I'm amazing. Tell me you've never known anyone like me."

"You're getting carried away," said Molly, but nicely.

"I'm pretty damn good," said Irena. "Admit it."

"I do. But you can still learn," Molly told her.

"Oh, fuck yes, I know," said Irena. "Show me, show me."

"Soon, soon," Molly said. He had crooked the small finger of his right hand in the trigger guard. He pressed his left palm against the heat of the barrel.

"Fuck," she snapped back. "What do you know?" Her humor had turned suddenly surly. "You could be on the other side," she said.

"Quite a few old comrades are," said Molly.

"But it's not your war. What do you care?" asked Irena.

"But I do," said Molly. "If you win, I get references."

"What does it matter?" Irena wanted to know. "You said it yourself—you could be on anyone's side."

Molly finally dipped his fingers into a shirt pocket to find a small pack of French chewing gum. The name caught Irena's attention: Hollywood.

"I could like girls, too," said Molly, upending three sticks into the palm of his hand. "I just don't."

Irena let the avowal pass without remark. She turned onto her right hip and reached her left hand down onto the stock of the rifle. "If you were on the other side," she began. "Not *that* other side. I don't care about *that*. I mean on the other side of the river. If you worked for *them*. If they paid you, you'd shoot me."

"That's too dramatic," said Molly. He rolled the foil from a stick of gum between two fingers. "If they paid me, I'd shoot anyone. Besides"—he flicked the foil like a small soccer ball over Irena's shoulder—"your side's paid up. Besides, besides, besides—if I teach you well, you'd get me first."

MOLLY DELIVERED IRENA to Tedic that afternoon just as darkness began to spread across the delivery docks. Tedic stood at an inclined gray steel shipping desk that he had appropriated as a work surface. The surrounding shadows gave his perch the look of the lair of some observant bird. Irena cinched her hands against her hips as she walked toward Tedic. "Do you have many more like Molly?" she asked.

"I knew you two would get along."

"I've heard you've got a couple of Americans," said Irena. Molly had admitted to one. Mostly, though, it was Irena's guess, and was meant to force Tedic to turn over his cards.

Tedic answered by confirming nothing. "We get volunteers," he said. "People show up from Bosnian neighborhoods in Detroit or Toronto. They weep bloody tears. 'I want to help my people.' I assume that Belgrade sends them. I tell them to dig ditches. Some of them turn out to be sincere. When they get hungry, they go home. That's why I look for professionals."

"Professional assassins," said Irena. "Molly—I've been trying to figure out his name."

"Professionals," Tedic stressed, then softened his tone. "Old French le-

gionnaires. They seem to be Ukrainians these days. South Africans who miss the good old days of guerrilla wars. Rummy old Brits who always hire themselves out to the next war going."

"They don't know the neighborhood," said Irena. She meant it as a metaphor.

"*Exactly.*" Tedic seized on the word. "They aren't neighborhood boys who get sappy about shooting into their old streets, schools, and coffeehouses, where they used to sip slivovitz. No high-school friends across the way. Most of these boys don't have neighborhoods. Most of them don't have friends. I've got a Kosovar Albanian who's eager to settle scores with Serbs. I grant him his dream. I've got a Moroccan who I'm pretty sure is really an Israeli, sent to keep an eye on armed Muslims. But he does good work for us both. A Russian or two, of course."

"Russians are pro-Serb," said Irena.

"Russians," Tedic said, smiling, "are pro-money."

"Any girls?"

"A question my wife used to ask me," said Tedic. But he went on. "Some of the best."

"And on the other side?" Irena asked. Tedic let a moment pass and twisted a paper clip in his fingers.

"Much like us, I suppose," he said.

"Who do I shoot?" Irena asked finally.

"We'll tell you. We'll go over maps, point out streets, show you where to look."

"But who, exactly?"

"It's not a matter of *who,*" said Tedic. "Often we'll just want you to shoot out the tires on a truck. Sometimes, we'll just want you to send a little love note through somebody's office window. Or put a bullet through Slobo's nose on a street poster."

"You cannot be training me," Irena told him, "just to shoot at posters."

Tedic deployed his newest world-weary smile. "Sometimes it may be a who," he said. "We look for uniforms—soldiers, police. We'll show you how to recognize the police who are too cowardly to wear uniforms, and go about dressed like you or me. Possibly in something from your very closet in Grbavica."

Irena had let a cigarette between her fingers burn down to the butt. She held out her hand in sudden surprise, and saw two smudged brown shadows between a couple of her knuckles.

"We don't shoot civilians," Tedic continued. "Let me revise that. We shoot civilians only when they are armed and mean to do us harm. The black-sweater brigades. Not exactly a boys' choir, are they? But I think you know that."

Irena said nothing.

Tedic rushed on. "Most of the work is mundane. It's waiting, being quiet, and wanting to take a piss. You almost never see anyone over there to shoot. The Serbs have figured out those areas that are blind to us. That's where they go about their business—the routine and the murderous. You make them worry. You make them restless. You make them lose sleep. You just shoot at a spot."

Irena bristled at Tedic's inventiveness. But any retort she ran through her mind sounded hollow before it could reach her throat. "Bullets aren't so predictable," she finally answered. "We've all seen that. They hit, ping, and wind up God knows where. You can hit the turret of a Serb tank and the bullet bounces a block away, into the skull of some old lady picking roses."

"An old *Serb* lady," said Tedic.

"Oh shit," said Irena. "That makes no difference."

"An old *Serb* lady," Tedic continued, unfazed, "who stood by when her Muslim neighbors were dragged away, then went into their apartment and took their teacups and television set. Some other Serb lady who cheers *Karazdic* when he says Sarajevo must be cleansed. Or one of those enchanting Serb kids spraying slogans about *rag-head girls* on their classroom walls. Could a bullet meant for a Serb general skid off and hit such a person? Past the age of twelve, I call *no one* here innocent."

THE NEXT MORNING Tedic opened the door into a small storeroom in which a bright steel light screamed down on a set of gray overalls unrolled over three sacks of grain; stubby black shoes arranged in descending order, like a family of bears in a children's storybook; a roll of paper towels standing behind on a box; and, in front of the towels, a dark blue oval shroud, slit at the center.

"I need to tell you about each and every item," Tedic insisted gently. "If you know the reason behind everything, you'll be less likely to question it."

The smudged coveralls had dark letters sewn above the left of the breastplate: DRAGAN.

"Specially made, you will notice," said Tedic.

"For someone else."

"All the same," he replied.

Irena sensed that Tedic was beginning to take pleasure in watching her discover and defuse his jokes.

"The war closes down gas stations," he continued, "and we get a bounty of uniforms. You get a gray one for camouflage among the beams and ruins. If we ever put you into a tree or on a hill, we have green and brown ones, too, depending on the season. Even quite a few blue ones we haven't figured out a use for yet. Now, I know that you know this, but please listen anyway. You have Dragan's outfit on at all times, and you keep it zipped over every part of you. We will give you this charming ski mask as well. We will give you as many as you need or want, a different one each day if it is your whim. Bosnians have lots of ski masks. What else would we use them for right now? When you aim and fire, your hands will be held in at your chest. But any inch of your precious pink flesh showing can wave like a flag to our friends on the other side. It is the first thing they look for through their binoculars.

"So, zip Dragan's sleeves down to your wrists. Tuck his pant legs into your shoes. Zip the front up under your chin, and pull the neck of the ski mask over your throat and stretch it over your collarbone. We will help you. You must think of this uniform as a spaceman's moon suit. An astronaut cannot roll up the sleeves of his moon suit a few inches without exposing his flesh to an atmosphere that would cause his body to pop. You must think of Dragan's costume as being just as essential for life."

"I'll try."

"You will!" Tedic insisted. His tongue leaped and lapsed back suddenly. "I am a sentimental man," he went on, "but it is not your safety alone that concerns us. If someone spots you in a place and shoots you, we cannot send someone back to that place for a time. I tell you the truth because I know you are a smart girl and would see through anything else. So, wear this uniform at all times. I usually have to tell girls to take care to tuck their hair inside the ski mask."

Tedic allowed himself a smile at the blunt, practical cut that Irena kept. She would be able to turn out of a pivot without signaling her direction with a flapping of curls. "Shoes, too," he said. "Not those collector's items you wear now, but something that might save your life. Size forty?"

"Usually."

"We have a pretty good selection. Before the Indian troops left town, we made them a pretty good deal on their shoes. They would have sold us their underwear. Okay, so we have you in Dragan's smock and an Alberto Tomba ski mask and Sayeed's shoes. But remember, these costumes are not armor-plated. They might obscure you among the rafters and girders, but they can't stop bullets. You can't rely on garb alone.

"There are other things you cannot take for granted. You cannot take up any water, okay? This is hard to say, because we can get water in the brewery. But you can't drink it on the job. I don't care if you're up there for two hours or eight, no water. Nothing glistens like a plastic water bottle. Hold it to your lips, you draw a target on your mouth. Even if we put water in an old goat's bladder, if you drink, you will piss. If you have to piss anyway, do it in your pants, okay? Don't hesitate. If you are nervous, and it's maybe a little cold, that will happen. You were expecting to meet Tom Cruise in one of our bombed-out buildings? He would be charmed, anyway. Piss dries. But if you unzip your gray suit to squat, you'll have to reveal your lovely pink bum to the world. I don't care if you're certain that you're hidden behind a wall. Someone sitting across the way will be looking through a telescope and see the ass of his dreams winking at him. He will thank God and then fire a bullet into the very spot on your buttocks that he wants to bite. It's basic psychology, male or female. Shoot what you cannot have."

TEDIC CROSSED OVER to the door to check for eavesdroppers. He left the door open a crack to recharge himself with air for the monologue ahead. He cleared his throat like an engine kicking in.

"*Hmmm-oookay* now. *Hhhoookay.* So, no drinking, no unzipping. No snacks. If you get hungry, well, we're all hungry, aren't we? Now, this is really important: no smoking while you're up there. This is very hard to say to a Bosnian. I have been smoking since I was six. It's especially hard to hear now, when so many people are smoking to curb hunger. But flicking a match shows a flame for miles. The end of a cigarette glows bright orange, and we're trying to keep you gray. Little white curlicues of smoke catch the light. They know they have only to follow them down a few feet to find you. If you've never believed smoking is bad for you, believe it in your working hours. Think of it this way: we want you to live long enough to get lung cancer.

"Now look, we have at least one other important diktat. Your personal life is your own. How you spend your personal time is none of our business. But don't drink booze or smoke hash for eight hours before you come to work. Drink as much beer as you can before that, if you want. Drink anything else that comes your way if you find it. But if the booze is still in your system, it throws off your dexterity and timing. Perhaps you've played the occasional basketball game while hungover."

Irena didn't fight the flush that was reddening her face.

"So you know," Tedic went on. "You need no reminder. Now listen, I know there's hashish in town. It's easier for a Ukrainian soldier to hide hash in his crotch than a veal steak. Even as a school principal, I had no problem with hash. Sometimes I've even wanted to tell some hyperactive hellion brought to my office, 'Give us all a break. Smoke a hash pipe every now and then.' When I was your age, we were proud to know that Sarajevo got the best hash in Yugoslavia. But a few hours later—I'm sure you know this—hashish makes you hungry. We don't want you fidgety and agitated.

"Now, we have to be a little more strict about something else. Don't snort cocaine—ever. This has nothing to do with morals. Morals are not exactly my area of expertise, now, are they? You're smart enough to know not to accept moral advice from someone who's showing you how to shoot people."

Irena marked this as Tedic's first admission.

He went on quickly. "My admonition is strictly practical. Your work requires calm. Cocaine makes your heart race. Then, hours later, your heart stops racing and you collapse. It's hard enough for us to be energetic now, when we're eating just a few beans, some rice, some Spam. None of us is eating what you would call a 'breakfast of champions.' Besides, in the middle of this siege no one is going to begrudge you a little grass. The police have quite enough to do without worrying about kids smoking tea leaves, but if you get caught with cocaine they'll wonder where you got the money. When they find out that you work at the brewery, they'll start asking questions—do you follow? They'll resent the fact that you have money for drugs when most Sarajevans can't buy bread or soap. Ecstasy, LSD—the same prohibition holds. They fuck with your perception. You must be clear-eyed. If anything else comes your way, ask us first. You'll find that we don't want to deprive you of fun; we're not your parents. But we need to make you the best instrument possible.

"Now then, because most of your friends and family don't have jobs, they'll be interested in yours. Make up nothing—you won't be able to remember it. Evade, distract, avoid. Tell them you've been warned not to talk because of spies.

"Boyfriends are likewise none of my business. Girlfriends, either. Just don't let yourself sacrifice a good sleep for an hour or two of recreation. What's exhausting about sex isn't sex; it's staying up, drinking beer, and trying to get laid. There's a lot of fucking going around right now. Not true romance. Just a lot of 'We might be dead tomorrow, let's fuck while we still can.' I've tried that line myself.

"Should you want to get close to someone, remember that confiding in him or her about your work is the worst way to do it. They will not be able to understand what you see or do every day, not at all. Confession will confuse or frighten the good ones, and truly fascinate only the bad ones; they'll want to use you to dispense their vengeance. Sometimes you'll hear friends—or some boy trying to impress you—talk about the war. They will assert something very positively that you know to be untrue. You must not be tempted to set them right. Let them have the distraction of their ignorance. You may even be amused by it. You will appreciate how much you really do know by how much your friends cannot even fathom. In any case, they cannot appreciate that you are right."

Irena spoke for the first time in Tedic's oration. "Now," she said. "*Now* you have me scared."

"Of dying? Who isn't?"

"Oh, shit no," Irena said. She added very simply, "Of living like this."

Tedic stopped at that. He wasn't reaching for punctuation or drama, or to reposition his argument. His face took on something mournful. "Remember," he said, "all we wanted in Sarajevo was to be left alone. Left alone to smoke and drink, stay up late and listen to jazz, ski and screw, and otherwise pursue this brilliantly irrelevant mixed culture we have built over five centuries. Then one weekend that changed. They knocked down our doors. They dragged us out of the cafés in which we used to so wisely declaim about Kafka, Sidney Bechet, and Michael Jordan. They raped us, dear. Now they're starving and shooting us. The mandarins in Washington and London, the café crowd in Paris and New York, wring their hands over our fate. They wail against war. But they don't undo their fingers from their prayers or their espresso cups to help. Right now, five seconds only, the window is closing; we have at least the brief hope of a choice. We can stay with our frivolous, peaceful ways and die silently, leaving the world our names for another memorial. Or we can use every wicked trick they have used on us, and a few more we can think up, to strike back. And buy an extra day of life."

...

THE MORTAR FIRE and sniping were especially intense that night. Aleksandra came up from her apartment to sleep with the Zarics in their living room—that was what they now called Grandma's apartment.

Irena found it comic and uncomfortable to sleep in the same room as her parents. When she shifted or flinched—or, as she did a couple of times, screamed in her sleep—her mother would roll over and take her flailing arms into her own hands. She thought Irena looked like a kitten twitching in her sleep.

Irena cried out that night. Mrs. Zaric awoke first, but she couldn't make out the words. She crawled over and held Irena, who was trembling.

"What's wrong?" she asked. "What's wrong?"

Irena stirred. Then she began to laugh. She thrummed her fists against her chest.

"You're laughing," said Mrs. Zaric. "What's wrong?"

"What's wrong?" said Irena. "Say that again, Mother."

"What's wrong?"

Mr. Zaric had pulled himself up on his elbows and he, too, began to laugh. "Again, Dalila dear," he said. "Listen to yourself. Think about each word. What's. Wrong. What's. Wrong. *What's wrong?*"

Aleksandra, Irena, and her father laughed harder.

Mrs. Zaric suddenly raised a hand to her forehead. "Oh, I understand now," she said. "Yes, that's pretty funny. What's wrong? *Oh, nothing special.*" She was finally laughing. She laughed so much that she decided she needed a cigarette to settle her breathing, and fumbled around on the floor for anyone's pack of Drinas.

"What's wrong? What's wrong? What's wrong?" Irena repeated the words drowsily, as if they were the refrain of a favorite song. She could see the orange veins of mortar rounds scoring the sky as she laughed herself to sleep like a child.

IN THE MORNING she found a small blue envelope folded into the right pocket of the jeans she had left beside her on the floor, in case she had to dress quickly. Aleksandra's handwriting looped across one side. "Shh," she had written. "For Your Eyes Only. A."

When Irena turned the envelope around, she recognized Tomaslav's handwriting:

TO IRENA ZARIC PERSONAL PLEASE
FOR HER ONLY

Aleksandra must have retrieved it from the synagogue. Irena's new duties did not always permit her to make that run for the building, and Aleksandra enjoyed arranging her route to run into French soldiers and their chivalrous donations of cigarettes to old ladies. Irena crawled below the living-room window in her panties, her jeans with the note slung over her shoulders, to slip into the bathroom and close the door. Her brother's note was written on a British Museum greeting card that showed an eighteenth-century Wenceslaus Hollar engraving of a cat receiving a deputation of mice. Tomaslav's handwriting looked plain and firm.

Dearest sister:

On my way to Chicago. Man at Bosnian office here got me student visa. Now, I must find something to study. You will hear from me. Will make your case to Toni Kukoc. Will write another note to Milan and Dalila from there c/o synagogue. Don't tell them about this—please—I want no one to worry. You are the ones who are bearing the worst. I hope to begin to pay you back soon. Those who love Sarajevo should not stay away. Funny—but Chicago may be a step closer.

With love always,
Tomaslav

And on the back of the card, above "The rights to this image reserved by the British Museum," Tomaslav had added:

PS: Pretty Bird would join up, too! *Chirrrp!* Pretty Bird!

I'm not going to tell him about Pretty Bird, Irena thought, at least not yet. Then she realized: I don't know how to reach him. I don't know where he is. I don't know where he's going. And I don't like the way he suddenly says "With love always," like the note some people leave on a pillow before they steal away in the dark and you never see them again.

19.

TEDIC HAD DRAGAN'S GRAY SMOCK UNROLLED LIKE A FAIRY-TALE cloak and waiting for Irena in the storeroom the next morning. "Something for you and Molly this morning," he told her. "The first time, he will go with you."

"I AM HAPPY to announce," Tedic began, speaking to both Irena and Molly now, over some flour sacks, "that today's target of opportunity—like so much else in life, I have lately been convinced—begins with beer."

A couple of "higher minds," as Tedic called them, whose job was to stay tuned to the radio chitchat of Serb artillery teams, had heard a supply unit assure one of the firing squads that their promised provisions of piss would be delivered at a guaranteed hour. The higher minds interpreted "piss" as beer.

"You do not always have to be MI-5," Tedic explained, "to crack these codes." The artillery team, he said, had installed themselves in the basement of a mental-health clinic in Jagomir. "Where, no doubt," he went on, "the ka-thump ka-thumps are so very therapeutic for their patients. Where, no doubt, the patients enlisted because of all the beer the Serb units are drinking."

"Excuse me, sir," said Molly with a show of timidity. "But all we know for sure is that it's piss."

Tedic explained that they would not want to fire shots into a mental-health clinic, even if all the patients had been trucked out to make room for gun crews; the publicity would be ruinous. But a truck delivering all of that piss, plus, the higher minds assumed, cans of ham, beef, cabbage, and coffee, bullets, shells, and rubbers, would need to make a turn on one of two streets that lead into Nahorevska Street. They should be able to see the truck coming. They should be able to get it in their sights. They should be able to get off a shot that might shatter the windshield, or blast out a tire.

"At least when they pop open their bottles of piss," said Tedic, "it will spray in their faces. They will know we can catch up with them."

"Do we know what kind of piss, sir?" asked Molly, and Tedic smiled.

"In fact," he told them, "the higher minds say they have reason to believe it's Tuborg."

"Perhaps, sir, it would be equally effective," ventured Molly, "just to deliver a case of ours."

TEDIC HAD SELECTED an old apartment building in Breka as their perch. It was abandoned, but there were squatters. He told them to take care to fire from the ninth floor, because people had moved in below. He was counting on the Serbs to know this—and think that they would not fire any shots from that site.

"Ninth floor, kids. In the stairwell off the elevator shaft. There is a hole about nine inches across, no more than two inches tall, from what we can tell. Right near the floor, so you can lie down. Molly will spot the target. He'll show you how. You, Ingrid, take care of actual delivery. Up, out, back."

The building was one of the standard brown-and-gray blocks that had been built in time for the Olympics. Irena couldn't remember what the city's landscape had been without them, but she also couldn't tell the difference between that apartment house and half a dozen others nearby.

Molly and Irena trudged up the building's unlit staircase, which had mostly been spared the damage of mortars and bullets that had so effectively razed the rest of the structure. It was too dark to see, too dark even to speak. They had to feel with their toes for the next step up, and use their footfalls to gauge the nearness of walls and corners. Even in daylight, their orders were not to carry electric torches. Lights playing across darkened interiors could attract attention, although the instruction seemed particularly pointless in the stairwell, which was completely hidden from view. It seemed to take five minutes to feel their way past each floor.

Now and then they could hear sounds of habitation through the cinder-block walls: the whispers of squatters trying to stay quiet, radios turned on low for just a few minutes to save batteries. The squatters may have heard them, too, and feared that they were Bosnian police intent on clearing the building—or stealthy Serb paramilitaries there to steal and slaughter. Quiet, then, was in everybody's interest.

A strong smell of turds and urine hovered on each floor. There was no running water in this building, either. But the squatters, afraid of losing their places to other squatters, were even more reluctant than other Sarajevans to venture out to water lines.

"Better we can't see so well," Molly called back to Irena softly. "Some of the things . . . Dogs and cats crawl in for food, and curl up to die. They become meals, bones. I had a great dog back home." He cut his speech short, as he felt for the next step.

Molly stayed half a floor ahead of Irena. When they reached the eighth-floor landing, he turned around so that Irena could hear him. "We stop here, Ingrid."

"A floor short?"

"Your last lesson," he explained.

There were streaks of light when they exited the stairwell from a small industrial window just above their heads, and perhaps half a dozen small mortar holes. It made the light slice over their shoulders. Molly pointed at two jagged gashes, no more than four inches wide, about four feet from the floor.

"The space upstairs would be better for surveillance and operation," he said. "That's why Tedic chose it. But these two gashes here will do well enough."

"Shouldn't we follow orders?" asked Irena.

"We will make the delivery," Molly assured her.

"But surely," she said, "we were told to go to the other place for good reason."

"The other place is a better shooting spot."

When Irena stood unblinking and disbelieving before Molly for more than a moment he turned gruff. They were both wearing ski masks. Tuck in his strawberry ponytail, Irena thought, cloak his cottony beard, and Molly turned back into a pig-faced Boer.

"Just get ready here," he said. "I'll explain it later."

"When I'm older?" Her sarcasm was biting.

"Yes," said Molly. "And you'll be a lot older when this is over."

She stood in a small space on the eighth-floor landing. The ski mask prickled with sweat from the long walk up, and now exasperation. "I'm here," she told Molly. "I'm old enough now."

He sighed, rolled his mask up to his forehead, and fluffed out his wispy beard before speaking. "Whenever there is an obvious best spot," he told her, "*don't* take it. Take something less perfect nearby. The best place is always where *they* will be looking for you. When it comes to our own lives, we can only really trust ourselves."

Irena took the opportunity to roll her own ski mask up off her eyes. Wordlessly, she took the M-14 parts out of the pockets and sleeves of Dragan's smock and began to assemble her rifle.

In the clacking and clatter between the spikes of light, Molly added, a little more gently, "You can trust me on this, Ingrid. Because I am alive to tell you."

MOLLY MADE THEM roll their masks back down over their noses, but he said they could get away with leaving their mouths uncovered; he didn't like the feel of wool and nylon threads on his tongue. He also insisted that they observe the mandated silence, after pointing out to Irena that she would need to make a standing shot in which she could at least rest her rifle barrel on a crook in the wall, aiming her shot from a kind of half-squat. She bent her knees to test the position.

"I can do this," she told Molly. "It's a free-throw stance."

Molly raised only his eyes and forehead into a corner of the gash. "Now, we know the truck is supposed to be coming along Nahorevska Street," he whispered. "But you don't stare, remember? Things move. Look all around."

He had a pair of field glasses, the stubby kind that Westerners take to the opera. Every now and then he'd raise them, careful not to bring them forward where they might catch a glint of the sun, squint through the eyepieces, then fold the glasses back into his smock. Once he handed them over to Irena and watched her as she focused them on Potok Street, the small dollhouses in pinks and yellows hugging the hills. It had been a Serb neighborhood since she could remember, and she could not remember ever having been on those streets.

Molly nudged her. "The clinic is in the pale green house, three houses in from that corner," he said. "Do you see it? They take the mortar up to the roof. You see the third-floor window leading out?" Irena did. "They open it up, leap out, fire a few shells into the Kosevo neighborhood, then scramble back in. Two-man teams, boys and girls. In thirty seconds, they fire a shell that can kill twenty."

The two of them stood in position, peering down from the shadows. Out of the corner of her eye, Irena could just see Molly, his half-face of a smile and quarter-face of a beard, and she couldn't help thinking of new parents gazing into a nursery window.

"THERE IS OUR truck," Molly said quietly. He handed the field glasses back to Irena. "Red, military green tarp pulled over the load. Take a quick look, then get it in your sights."

The truck was rusting into orange. Irena took up her rifle. Tedic had been right—few cars moved, few people were ever visible—and in less than a breath she had the rust in her rifle's sights. When it bounced, Irena wondered who was at the wheel, or lashed down under the load.

"How do you know it's the truck we want?" she asked Molly.

"The way it rides," he told her. "It rides heavy."

"Beer is so heavy?"

"Beer, ammunition, and food all together is." Molly nodded. "No one but paramilitaries are getting such big deliveries over there right now."

"Why don't they use army trucks?" Irena could take both her eyes from her sight and still see the rusty truck moving with the slow determination of a ladybug down Potok Street.

"Serb paras stole everybody's trucks for themselves," Molly said. His words had picked up pace. He could see the progress of the truck, too. "You know that," he added. "Don't expect to see a truck with Karadzic's picture on the side."

"I wasn't expecting just a normal truck," said Irena. She put her left eye back on the sight and rested the snout of her rifle in the craggy edge of the mortar hole. The wound, she thought, from which I am preparing another. The truck's windshield had come into plain view. But, even as she squinted, sun and soil kept her from glimpsing who was inside.

Now the truck was close enough for them to hear it, bouncing and rattling toward the turn on Nahorevska Street, clouds of grit coming up from its tires, catching the sun like sneezes.

"It doesn't matter, Ingrid." Molly answered her hesitation. "Anyone delivering anything there, bullets or just beer, is loading the gun pointed down our throats." He swallowed. "If this is a philosophy class, dear," he said finally, "sorry. I didn't come prepared."

Irena let the breath of a laugh escape her mouth. She ran the breath up the barrel, bent her knees to take the charge, and pulled the trigger with the same tender touch that she would use to scratch a dog's ears. *Easy now. Oh, yes. Therrre we go.*

The first shot hit the engine block. Irena was able to keep the sight to her eye as the rifle bucked back into Pretty Bird's spot on her shoulder. The second shot struck the windshield. As she fired the third, she saw the glass swell and break into a thousand pieces, like the glitter of a waterfall. It shone blue and pink before going dark and dry, like the inside of a cave. The truck turned on its wheels, sputtered, foundered, and stopped. Irena waited for people to spring out of the cab. When no one did, she fired her third, fourth, and fifth bullets into the expanse of tarpaulin in the back, and decided that she might be the first Bosnian to know what it was like to shoot at a beached whale.

MOLLY WAS LOOKING through the field glasses with approval.

"One Serb truck down, Ingrid. No brewski tonight. Maybe no mortar shells, either. Okay now, no fuss, keep the barrel down. You've shot your clip, but put on the safety. We pick up our shell casings—we are good guests. Keep the snout pointed at your toes while we walk down the stairs."

When they turned the corner into the dimming light of the stairwell, Molly took a small penlight out of his smock.

"I thought—" Irena began.

"Tedic wanted the full test."

They walked together on the way down, so they could both see into the same spot of light on the stairs. Irena thought that this posture confirmed a partnership.

"Did I pass?" she asked after the first floor.

"No test," said Molly. "That's a joke."

"Still. Did I do well?"

"A few Serbs surely think so."

"I can do even better," she said.

"No one could have done better today," Molly told Irena. "Not even if you had hit with the first shot. The first made them flinch, and hold up for the second. Did you notice? Still, it's good that you know you were also lucky. Otherwise, doing well can shut down your learning."

When they reached the fourth floor, Molly turned and handed the penlight to Irena. She shrank back at first, uncomprehendingly, as if he were giving her the keys to a vehicle she couldn't drive.

"A quick bit of business, dear," was all he explained. "Go down and hang around for two minutes before you leave for the truck. No, three, please. Count to two hundred. I'll be along."

"So I'll just wait for you."

"No. Just wait for a count of two hundred."

"What the hell—" Irena shined the penlight into Molly's wispy beard and saw his mouth curling up.

"When you're older, dear."

Irena continued a slow, careful tread down the staircase. Within half a minute, she heard a burst of five shots behind her. They were outgoing—Molly's. They made the cinder blocks shiver. Irena faltered slightly when her right foot came down in midstep over a stair, but she had made it to the ground floor by the time the echo of the fifth shot was leaking out of the stairwell and into the street.

WHEN TEDIC ZIPPED open the back of the beer truck to receive them, he was stern.

"That last burst back there," he said. "Freelance, I assume? Sudden artistic inspiration?"

Molly did the talking for Irena and himself, and affected deference.

"I assumed, sir, that their mortar team would try to take their toy to the roof."

"And were they there?" asked Tedic. His tone was wintry.

"I didn't see them," said Molly. "Maybe they were getting ready."

"Maybe they were hiding under their beds, or in the showers they still have there. Maybe they were watching TV and eating last night's cold roast chicken. Maybe they didn't notice that you wasted five precious bullets on the ghost of a chance."

"They noticed," Molly asserted. "I put a wreath of bullets around that window."

Tedic put a huge, silly grin of surrender on his face. When he spoke, it was to Irena. "Molly," he said, "I love you. Molly, I truly do. I pretend to be mad, and Molly pretends to be contrite. We are like an old married couple, the Queen of the Veldt and I, aren't we?" he asked Irena. "We will do this all over, many times."

"Her Highness says the first shot hit the engine," said Molly. They were on to Irena's part of the play. "The second went through the windshield and killed the truck."

"That's what Mandy saw," said Tedic. He turned back to Irena.

"Mandy is someone you don't know. She says the truck was killed. Was there mist?" he asked Molly.

"Something in the windshield, I think." Tedic shrugged.

"Mandy thinks she saw that, too. It could be shards causing lots of cuts, nothing serious."

"Bits and pieces, then, not mist," said Molly.

"Our Ingrid here was up to the role."

"A star is born," said Molly. "A star rises in the east. Or whatever Muslims say."

Tedic turned his compact charm on Irena. "Mist has been explained to you?" he asked.

"I think I've figured it out," she told him.

Tedic rolled out a drawer for some phantom consultation, then rolled it back. When he brought his head up, his chin was challenging. "And did Molly here show you any tricks I'm not supposed to know?"

Irena was ready to block his shot. "What could you possibly not know?" she asked.

The three of them laughed. As Tedic laughed, cigarette smoke spurted from his nostrils. "Ingrid, my Ingrid, my great sixteen-point scorer," he said. "You belong in these leagues. The insult that flatters, the compliment that ridicules. *Killer charm*. Praise be that you are on our side."

MOLLY AND IRENA took their leave under the covered section of driveway leading out of the brewery. Mel was driving Irena home. Molly lived God knows where. A few dark, dirt-floored rooms were rumored to exist in the bowels of the brewery, where their dinginess was slightly relieved by bare lightbulbs powered by the springs below. Irena could picture Molly flopping down on a stark cot, eating cold French beans out of a can, and buffing his nails before unscrewing the bulb and sinking into the night.

"Let me guess," she said straightaway. "The business on the fourth floor. You were trying to draw fire to the fourth so they wouldn't know we had been on the eighth. Protecting our spot. But you knew they'd be loaded, so you got me out from under."

"I don't know basketball," said Molly. "But in football we protect the striker."

"So," said Irena. "Is this graduation? Do we wait for the tenth reunion before we see each other again? We could have coffee sometime and catch up. Or do you just go back home and wait for some rich brute to ring you up and send you a ticket?"

Molly fingered a spot on his chin with one of his superb nails. "I can't go back home," he explained. "Or much of anywhere. Change is afoot. Not that we couldn't use it, mind you. The new regime wants me to talk about some ancient history in Natal."

"Tell them what they want," Irena suddenly urged him. "Finger the folks who ordered you to do whatever it was. Old apartheid swine are making deals and getting rich. You make a deal, too."

"I made an offer," said Molly. "They had another. I'd have to give up some mates. Bastards like I am. But still mates."

"Like me," said Irena. "So give me another guess. We here in gallant little Bosnia have given you a home."

Molly hugged himself in imitation of a shivering African caught in a cold clime. In the gloom of a long October shadow, his imitation was convincing.

"Bosnia in winter," Molly shuddered. "Not my dream of paradise. It's here or Tuzla for me. But don't think I'm not grateful. No tears and flowers called for, but I don't have a country."

"Use ours," Irena offered.

WHEN IRENA TRAMPED upstairs into her apartment, her mother brightened at the turn of the latch. She called out from behind the bathroom door, "How did it go today, dear?"

"I can't go into it," said Irena. "National security."

Mr. Zaric was sitting with his legs folded below his mother's old sofa table, rolling over one of his candles to find a seam for the wick. "I understand why you can't tell your mother," he said soberly. "But I dig trenches for the army. I am involved in national security myself. You can tell me about your highly placed exploits and skulduggery."

"Don't force me," said Irena. "If you make me talk, the repercussions could be dire."

Irena and her father shared a peal of laughter. Mrs. Zaric opened the door in time to join them. Aleksandra, who was trying to kindle a fire for hot water in the kitchen, joined in the merriment, too. But Irena saw in a flash—like the sudden chill in summer when rain clouds slide under the sun—that when Aleksandra looked through the doorframe she wasn't laughing in the least.

20.

TEDIC RECEIVED HER IN THE STOREROOM THE NEXT MORNING, DRAgan's smock drooping over a hanger like some headless ghoul behind his shoulder. Irena noticed that he seemed to keep no paperwork outside his pockets, and no implements of his actual daily business in front of him.

"Should the U.N. pay a surprise visit," he explained, "I swear, they'll be disappointed. They'll think they've stormed into a brewery."

He pointedly stood back from Dragan's costume, and away from the doorway. He wanted to give Irena the sensation of more air, more light, and the liberty to make a choice. "You must have questions," he said. "Questions let me know what you're thinking." Tedic was pleased by what he heard first.

"Well, what would I be paid?" asked Irena. She had grasped that her gifts were worth some reward that it was in his power to bestow.

"Believe it or not, money is not such a problem," Tedic said quickly. "We have Muslim friends in Riyadh and Tehran who would like to buy a little bit of Mecca here. We have Jewish friends in New York, London, and Jerusalem who remember who their friends were when the Nazis stormed in."

Tedic lifted a leg up onto one of the overstuffed sacks, as if to take the weight off his vast responsibilities.

"But fistfuls of money," he went on, "only buy all the wrong things here now. Neighbors would suspect that you're selling drugs, or screwing government ministers. Or playing grab-ass with Frenchies in the Protection Force. We can't afford to have you scrutinized. So we give you twenty cans of beer a month. Share them. Let it be known that you can get a little more if friends persist. You work in a brewery. For other duties as specified, you will also get three cartons of cigarettes a month, American. You and your family can smoke what you like, trade what you like. Our own currency is worth less than a product that gives you cancer.

"And every month, like Swiss clockwork, two hundred deutsche marks go into an account in your name in a bank in Bern. A very nice, clean, thrifty, and cheerful city, I'm told, which I hope to see myself after the war."

"Why only five bullets in a clip?" Irena moved on to her next item coolly. "They can take twenty."

"Bullets are expensive," he answered.

"Bullets are *expendable*," she snapped. "That's the idea, right? Expend them."

"Only if we can get them," he told her. "Right now, cocaine comes into this city more easily than bullets. It's easier to put a condom of cocaine into someone's asshole or vagina than a box of bullets. Americans stuff bullets into their guns like cans of Coke in a cooler. They can write the price of war into the cost of Marlboros. But here in Sarajevo five bullets in a clip are what we manage. If we don't get more soon, it could be three.

"Besides," Tedic said, softening, "we can't contact you by radio without signaling where you are. All alone up in the girders, you can feel that nobody cares about you. We don't want you to go for too long without remembering who loves you."

"Can I quit?"

Tedic couldn't suppress a smile. His eyes crinkled, his brows arched, his bald skull wrinkled with the pleasure of having a student who could anticipate his lesson plan.

"Of course. This isn't the Red Army," he said. "We don't have Cossacks to drag you back. But it's not as if we would be content to see you loose on your own. You will have seen and heard things by virtue of our trust, and you will have been recompensed for it. We have an investment in you. It makes us want to protect you. It also makes us keen to keep up our investment. So if you feel tired and lousy we give you time off. Not in Monaco, mind you, much as we'd all like to join you there. We can't even get our cabinet ministers to Antwerp for a conference without having them inspected and certified by the authorities like a fine cheese. But we'll put you in a place here where you can sleep, have a little to drink, and repair your circuits—no questions asked, no mark against you."

Irena persisted. "And if I *still* want to quit?"

"We haven't written that chapter in the handbook," said Tedic. "I suppose we hope this will all be over before we have to."

. . .

"YOU SAID WE killed the truck yesterday," said Irena.

"It's a phrase."

"To avoid saying that we killed someone?"

"We can't tell."

"Someone can," Irena insisted. "What did the Knight say this morning? I took the long way round so I wouldn't hear him."

"Why bother with what he says?" asked Tedic.

"I don't believe him," Irena returned tartly, "any more than I believe everything you say. It just lets me know the lies I have to account for to figure out the truth. What did he say?"

Tedic began to squirm. It was a bit of stage business to encourage Irena to think she had pierced his flesh. Tedic had figured Irena would feel flashes of guilt or disdain for her work; he knew that she might even get frightened. But he calculated that the remorse Irena felt would drive her not away from the work he had set out for her, but closer to someone who exhorted and rewarded her—who coached her.

Tedic paused, to appear trapped and hesitant. "The Knight said two people were shot dead by Muslim fanatics," he said finally. "Two angelic Serbian kids—Boy and Girl Scouts, no doubt—who were delivering medical supplies and food to famished mental patients."

"Is that possible?"

"No."

"They just made it up? If they made it up, they would have said that we shot a busload of legless orphans."

"They just acknowledged what suits their story," he replied. "Medical supplies and food must have been all mixed in with bullets and mortar shells. Believe me, no truck—*no truck*—is going to risk a journey now just to deliver food and medical supplies on that side of the city. Imagine braving bullets only to throw back the tarp and find Tuborg and Spam, but no mortar rounds."

"Maybe the facts are so damning, all they have to do is tell the truth," said Irena.

"If just two was the truth," Tedic avowed, "they'd say that twenty had died. Take it from an accomplished prevaricator. Two means one. Maybe none. Maybe just a couple of Serbs with complexion problems that will heal."

"It's hard to keep score in this twisted little game," Irena said quietly.

...

STILL, IRENA DIDN'T walk out the open door.

"It was them or you," Tedic told her. "If not yesterday, then today. Or a week from today."

"Soldiers are honorable," Irena said. "They face each other, even from a long way away. Soldiers have uniforms and manners. But what's the difference between doing this and being an assassin?"

Tedic paused again. "Perhaps none," he finally offered. "But what's the difference between doing this and doing nothing? You might run that play in your mind, too. In this place, conscience is not a virtue. It is a self-inflicted wound.

"You cannot expect to feel easy about any of it. But how much anguish do you want to expend when each and every day they are coming for us? When they march in to sweep away our bones, I don't want my hands to be empty. I want them to find my fingers clenched around a sword, a slingshot, or at least a rock."

Irena let Tedic's words settle between them. There was no longer any question—really, there never had been—that she would do the job he had set out for her. But she wanted to remind him that she wasn't one of his hired assassins, working for Marlboros, deutsche marks, and beer.

"How are we different from them?" she asked finally.

Tedic seemed to stagger backward. Then he laughed, a sharp, astonished, nearly giggly laugh that both bewildered and elated Irena. Something she said to Tedic had finally pierced his scales. "Kids. *Kids,*" he said, shaking his head. "Bless your heart. Bless my soul."

Irena found his response so out of character that she wondered if he was speaking in a kind of code.

"Of all the times and places to be reminded," he said.

"Of what?" asked Irena.

"Of why I became a teacher." Tedic fished inside his vast leather pockets and pulled out a pack of Marlboros. He stood the box on a flour sack between them.

"Take one," he offered. "Take the pack. Take them all. I could give you lots of reasons," he said. "Maybe we lose a few each day." Tedic had become so utterly still that when he spoke his words seemed to launch from the dead center of his two blistering brown eyes. "In the end, I'll settle for just one. *We* will *survive.*"

21.

"ANY JOB IS LIKE HIGH SCHOOL," ALEKSANDRA JULIANOVIC TOLD Irena. "Hospital, bank, brewery, factory. I imagine a lingerie store, too. From the moment you arrive, you're told—you see for yourself—that some people are pretty, some are smart, some are good at sports. Some people are popular, some are lonely. They might as well loop signs around everyone's neck. Or one of those simple, clever Hindu dots."

"Caste marks," Irena suggested.

"Precisely. High school imprints a mark you bear for life. A few people get put into several groups. I'll bet you did."

"Oh, I don't know about that," said Irena, fidgeting.

"A, pretty; B, good at sports; and C, popular?" asked Aleksandra.

"That may have been the general impression," Irena finally allowed.

"But you don't get equal points in every category," Aleksandra continued. "Pretty tops smart. Pretty tops everything. Girls and boys—there's no use pretending otherwise. If Marie Curie and Princess Diana had gone to the same high school, which one do you think everyone would remember?"

"Marie Curie?" asked Irena with a show of innocence. It took a moment for the joke to impress Aleksandra.

"You are *sooo* shrewd," she crowed. "Smart is next in points. And sometimes there's a special category. The Plain Girl Who Plays Beautiful Piano. The Boy with a Withered Leg Who Still Carries On. Nice is far down on most lists. It's usually 'Nice, but . . .' "

"Nice but dumb, nice but ugly. Nice but dull," Irena said, finishing the thought.

They were sitting on the two bottom stairs of the building, smoking and hunching their shoulders against the cold.

"Can you begin to identify the brewery people that way?" asked Aleksandra.

"It's a little harder," said Irena. "I work such odd hours, I don't see everyone. In our group in school, Amela was the prettiest. I was the best athlete. Nermina was the smartest. But Amela was also smart, for someone so pretty, and a good athlete. I was pretty for someone who was a good athlete, and most people knew I was also pretty smart. Nermina—you know, who died—was so smart, you were surprised she was a good athlete."

Aleksandra detected the omission instantly.

"She had very beautiful eyes," Irena said after a pause. "Brown, with flecks of green."

Aleksandra had spent enough time with the family to tell that Mr. Zaric was vexing Irena. The days he spent out of the apartment, digging trenches and latrines for the army, seemed the most satisfying for him. Irena reasoned that it was because while her father was getting calluses and scrapes on his hands, all that was expected of him was another shovelful of dirt. When he dug in the woods and scrub, he couldn't be held accountable for his own survival, much less anyone else's.

The government gave the diggers a meager food ration. The diggers, who often had to chip and chisel into flinty soil while ducking rifle shots, knew the price of each mouthful. But Mr. Zaric was guilty and embarrassed that his daughter's work alone brought them the food, water, and batteries they had at home. The beer and cigarettes were welcome, but awkward for him to enjoy.

Irena thought that her father was trying to recover a sense of importance with increasingly preposterous contrivances. He spent several days folding the tiny tin wrappers from Marlboro packs into a slide. He then pressed them carefully against the frame of the frosted bathroom window so that they could catch water that would run into a plastic bucket next to the toilet. But the foils were more paper than metal. They fell apart in the first rain and dropped on the floor and into the bucket in small white clumps, like smashed baby ducks.

"Perhaps if I wait until they dry," he told Mrs. Zaric. "This mishap may merely be disguised opportunity. Isn't that how penicillin was invented?"

"I wouldn't count on the same momentous result, dear."

"I will press the unfortunate puffs flat," he rallied. "Squeeze out the water and mold them into a kind of pipeline." Mr. Zaric's amber eyes flickered with wildfire, which amused his wife and appalled his daughter. "Then, the foils will be reconstituted," he concluded, his voice rising.

"They will dry out and possess the pliability of paper and the tensile strength of metal." He acted out a kind of ballet of basic osmosis.

"We can attach them to large horns that will trap snow in the winter," he enthused. "The snows will thaw in direct sunlight. Water will be created! Fresh rainwater that sluices into the pipelines and directly into the bathroom. Water to drink and bathe—nothing makes your hair softer than rainwater. Standing in water lines, begging Frenchies or Ukes for another couple of bottles—all of that will be part of a bygone age when the Zaric pipeline is completed!"

Irena shot out from the hallway behind them. "Those foils will have the tensile strength of toilet paper and the pliability of shit!" she railed. She was becoming accustomed to the grim competence that Molly, Jackie, and even Tedic personified. Her father, absorbed in his nonsensical schemes, seemed ridiculous and useless. Or, as she complained to Aleksandra, "My father is *sooo* boring."

Worse, Irena found herself condescending to be protective of her father. One afternoon she delivered an impassioned and gratuitous speech to Tedic in which she bewailed "this twisted, sick fuck of a world you so-called grown-ups have given us."

Tedic clapped the heel of a hand against his forehead. "Omigod, of course!" he exclaimed. "This war. All wars. Cruelty, hate, and ruin. *It's your parents' fault!* What a totally original idea!"

This wrung an involuntary laugh from Irena. But she went on. "Not my father's fault," she said more quietly. "He spends whole days just sleeping and staring. He has nothing to wear but a tweed jacket he had on the day this all began. So much weight has melted off him—he looks like a bum dressed in a stranger's clothes. He melts down the butts of candles to make more candles so I can read my magazines. Occasionally, he goes off and digs trenches. He comes back filthy and can't even take a bath. I . . . I blame him for nothing."

Tedic looked down.

Irena was encouraged by his deferential silence. "Oh, for fuck's sake!" she cried out. "All my friends and I ever wanted was to smoke, drink, stay up late, listen to the Clash, and screw!"

Tedic kept his head down, like a front-row mourner, but he raised it as he said, in a slow tone of discovery, "So, *that's* our incandescent mixed culture I keep hearing about on the BBC!"

Which won another laugh from Irena. "I'll thank you to respect that" was all she could manage in return.

...

IRENA HAD HAD little time to see Dr. Pekar. Her office hours were shrinking, in any case. Her supplies were running short, and fewer people sought out help for their pets—so many dogs, cats, hamsters, and rabbits had disappeared and died.

Irena would walk over the bridge from the brewery to the veterinarian's office, ring the bell, and shout up her name. Once, Dr. Pekar came down bleary-eyed from sleep, and they made coffee and talked—mostly about how sad and soundless her office had become without the animals. Dr. Pekar said she knew that many people had pets in their homes that they were afraid to bring out. Irena said that she would put up a notice at the synagogue announcing that the doctor was eager to see them.

"In fact," said Dr. Pekar, "I'm willing to go and see them, if the snipers so allow."

"I'll help you," said Irena. "Let me come along someday after work."

But when Irena came by in the gloom of a late afternoon two days later, Dr. Pekar was not to be found in her office or in her home. Irena crept under a tree, now bare-branched and clattering in winter, around to the back, where Cesar had been cremated. A wooden door slapped against its frame. Irena entered the kitchen, saying the doctor's name softly, so as not to startle her. When there was no response, she called out more urgently.

"Kee! Kee! It's Irena! I want to show you the note for the synagogue!"

She walked around quietly. The wind rattled the branches outdoors and whisked in to stir up grains of grit and yellowing papers. Irena reached out to touch a tin oil stove, hammered out of old bean cans, that the doctor had set up in the sink to heat water in a pan. The stove was charred, empty, and cold. Moving to the small adjacent examination room, she could make out a single sheet of Dr. Pekar's stationery on the steel-topped table, weighted down by a Serbo-Croatian-German dictionary. The paper shuddered every few seconds with a draft of wind. Irena drew close enough to read the note, written in thick black pencil in Dr. Pekar's hand.

It said, "Take whatever. Love."

Irena did not explore farther from where she stood. Through a closet door, she saw the flaps of a blue skirt dangling, and she realized that she had never seen Dr. Pekar in a skirt. She would help her choose a top sometimes. On her way out, she stopped to take a small bottle of olive oil that she noticed on the edge of the sink, and slipped it into her coat. She kept the note for the synagogue flattened and warm against her chest. She told herself that Dr. Pekar had ventured elsewhere in the city to look for an apartment that was warmer and not so isolated. She would find Irena when she had the chance.

IRENA HIKED BACK home but stepped off on Aleksandra's floor, where she found her neighbor in the hallway, squishing old, used tea leaves with the bottom of a glass. Aleksandra had decided that shredding tea leaves might expose fresh sides to boiling water—when they had water to boil, that is. It had been nearly a month since they had had any fresh tea.

Aleksandra told Irena that she had heard distressing news about Arnaud, her favorite Frenchie, who slipped her cigarettes and posted her letters. She hadn't seen him for more than a week, and asked another Frenchie at a checkpoint about his whereabouts. The other Frenchie told her that he thought Arnaud had been sent back home. He was happy, said the Frenchie, because he would be home in Marseilles for Christmas.

"Imagine!" Aleksandra exclaimed. "Back home in the bosom, as it were. Roast goose, chestnut pie, local wine, Gitanes spilling from your pockets. There is some willowy, dark-eyed slattern waiting for him. He's known her since grade school. While Arnaud has been off civilizing the masses in Africa and Bosnia, the tart has been cultivating his parents. I don't object to young love. It's as necessary as measles to proper development. But winter is falling like a vase rolling off a table, and I'm left here without Gitanes or Arnaud's wonderfully shy smile. He doesn't want to marry that girl," she added. "He said she was simply the best lover he ever had. Men confide in me. But at the age of twenty his experience could scarcely be profound."

"Even a Frenchman?" Irena teased. Aleksandra wouldn't dignify the jape with more than a nod. "All our relationships these days are intense and ephemeral," she told her. "But that doesn't make them any less worthwhile. Someone who gives you a smile and a cigarette at the right time gives you another day, doesn't he? You don't say that a person who pulled you out of the Miljacka is no longer important to you if you never see him again."

Aleksandra leaned down on the rim of the glass and twisted it, and the water that she squeezed out was as transparent as tears.

22.

IRENA STILL SPENT MANY DAYS SWEEPING FLOORS AND COUNTING crates. Bullets could be scarce. So were targets, Tedic explained. Firing aimlessly into the other side would look inept and desperate. Worse, the shots might go unnoticed, and even the power they had to alarm would be wasted.

One day Irena put three shots into the right fender of a Serb staff car that had been clumsily parked behind a barrier on Dinarska Street. The car was visibly empty. Irena wondered why it was a target even as she leveled her rifle. But Tedic was gratified. He savored the scene of three Serb officers coming out of their meeting at night, fumbling with their keys in the gloom of darkness, bumping and scraping their way into their seats—and discovering that they were sitting against fresh bullet holes. "They will hop up like they'd just sat on a dog turd!" he predicted. "They will crawl out of their car, and creep away on hands and knees in the dark, worrying whether we have them in our sights. 'Dear Mr. Serb,' " Tedic mouthed as he wrote in the air with his finger. " 'While you were gone, Bosnian bullets paid a call. They left a message: *We will find you later.*' "

IRENA BEGAN TO work overnight. Tedic advised her to tell her parents that it was because of increased production at the brewery. Against all expectation, Milan and Dalila were delighted. They reasoned that the basement of the brewery would be safer for their daughter than her place near them on the living-room floor. But once, Irena was rash enough to mention how quiet and still the city seemed at night, with no sounds of traffic, soccer matches on television, loud banter in bars and cafés, pots clanging, or the Clash blaring over the radio.

"Sometimes," said Irena, "I look up into the silent sky and I think I can practically hear the moon move through the clouds."

Her parents were appalled by her poetic reflection. "What in the hell are you doing going outside to look up at the moon?" her father shouted. "*The fucking moon!* Are you some kind of wolf?"

"I go out for a smoke," Irena said quickly, but her improvisation was swiftly found to be foolish.

"You mean you light a *match* and hold it to your *lips*?" Mrs. Zaric shrieked. "Why don't you just train a torch on your skull and shout, '*Shoot here!*' across the bridge."

Irena tried to regain her footing. "I stay kind of in the loading-dock area," she said.

"You can't smoke in the *basement*?" Mr. Zaric asked with growing astonishment. "It's a brewery, not a hospital."

"Doctors smoke in hospitals," Mrs. Zaric asserted. "In surgery! Remember when we were in for your mother, Milan?"

"I don't know about *the old days*," said Irena. "But *these days* there are health codes." She held her gaze steady. "Even in breweries," she added.

Mrs. Zaric glared back at her daughter, and finally turned away. "Well, they should have some small room with a small window that people can crawl into and smoke," she said.

"Does Dr. Tedic know you're going outside?" asked her father. "It's stupid."

"I suppose," said Irena. But she could tell that the topic had been closed.

TEDIC HAD TOLD Irena that she would be fractionally safer climbing up to her roost in the dusk than in daylight, but that staying there until she had an opportunity to fire would be colder and gloomier. He said she must take care not to rush a shot just to get it done.

And there was the fact of the flash to consider, too.

"We tell you to take pains to conceal yourself," Tedic explained. "But you've probably figured out that when you fire at night the flash from your muzzle becomes visible. Positively dazzling, in fact."

"That's why Molly taught me to fire and roll away."

"Fundamental," said Tedic. "But remember, if it's that basic, they know it, too."

...

MOLLY CONSIDERED THE moments just before dawn to be the most opportune. People left in apartments on the Serb side were likely to be tired, twitching, and restless from the sounds of a night of their own shelling. Serb snipers, mortar, and artillery crews were tired, hungover, and reckless. They might dare to stretch their legs, get some air, take their coffee, or find a piece of fruit; that could bring them out of their concealed lairs and into the growing light. The first sparks of sun would help obscure any flash from Irena's gun.

Early one morning Irena was concealed behind a yellow vinyl couch that had been upended over a window in a fourth-floor apartment on Linden Street. She saw three gray figures scurry across a rooftop on Julijo Vares Street, carrying what she thought looked like a long pipe. But after a hard blink in the dim light she decided it must be a mortar tube. She rushed three quick shots into the midst of the shapes—she was surprised at how quickly she had developed reflexes for this new game—which missed and skipped, but scattered them. One of them stumbled. Irena saw a flickering of pink fingers in the dimness. She thought that the tube must have been valuable for the man to try to hold on to it under fire. A mortar must surely be more important than a length of plumbing. But then there were probably more mortar tubes on the Serb side of Sarajevo—they would be easier to replace—than pipes. The man dropped whatever it was and ran out of view before Irena could decide if she wanted to devote her last two shots to stopping him from carrying a mortar—or risk revealing her hiding place just to prevent him from hauling a length of water pipe.

"Don't twist yourself into weaver's knots agonizing," Tedic affected to scold her when they reviewed her night's work. "Life or death, Serb or Muslim, sewage pipe or mortar? Men carrying a pipe tonight can carry a cannon tomorrow. Did you figure that the bastards trying to kill us have stopped eating, drinking, and shitting? 'If you prick them, will they not bleed?' But another shot from that spot would have lit up your hiding place like Hong Kong."

A FEW MORNINGS later, Irena perched on the blackened rim of an old toilet seat and rested her head against the white-tiled wall in a bombed-out third-floor apartment on Drina Street. Tedic had told her that three trucks would be threading over Branka Surbata Road at first light (they, too, wanted to avoid the burst of brightness from their headlights).

Irena could feel the dawn begin to creep up around her shortly after six in the morning. Rooftops and trees began to hum with a mild light. She could see a glimmer around her hands from the chutes of light that seeped in through bullet holes. Molly had shown her how to squeeze her eyes shut, count to ten, and open them wide; this widened her pupils to let in more light. The three trucks were open-backed pickups, probably delivering planks to shore up gun emplacements. Irena had told Tedic that she would wait to see the three in a line before firing.

"I figure that I try to hit the first truck," she told Tedic. "But not until I can see all three in a line. Or at least two. If I hit the first, the other two have to stop. I have a chance at all of them then. Down the line—one, two, three."

Tedic beamed. "From the mouths of babes," he said.

When Irena saw the first truck begin to slip past a building and nose down Drina Street, she stayed still. As the second pulled in slowly behind, she lifted the far end of the rifle barrel into the jagged crook of her chosen mortar hole. She was looking through her sight when the third truck began to pull into view from behind a building, and the first one began to slip behind another building. She fired.

She hit the first truck just behind the driver's cab. The shot fell uselessly somewhere under the brown tenting. But she put her second shot into the driver's window of the cab of the second truck, and she could see the truck begin to veer out of her line of sight. The third truck stopped, like a mouse that has run into a wall and tries to see if it can climb over it. Irena squeezed a third, a fourth, and then her last shot into the cab. She could see the glass smash, hear the horn begin to scream. She kept the gun in her slot for a moment, so that she could look down the sight into the cab of the truck. She saw no one slumped against the seat. They would be down on the floor, she figured, hiding or bleeding. She kept her eye there for just a moment to see if the rising light would show her that a slick of pink mist had painted the seats. She was squeezing her eyes and straining to see when rifle shots began to spray around her like hail.

Two or three bullets whistled through the hole so close to Irena's head that she could feel clapping in her ears. Another shot smacked just below the old mortar hole in which she had rested her rifle, and burst into a powder that dashed into her eyes and nose. Irena fell back, gagging on the grit.

Her eyes burned with gravel. Her gun leaped to the floor. The force of the blast threw her back and head against a wall. She rolled left just to breathe, and saw that she was in the hallway. She ran the back of her hand across her eyes to blot out dust. When she looked at her hand she saw blood.

She crawled onto her elbows and tucked a hand into her chest to feel for a wound; her chest was fine. She could feel bruises squishing on her knees as she scuttled down the dark hallway into a black corridor, rolled onto her back, and rubbed her hands over her head, feeling for a gash. She found nothing, but she began to feel something leaching into her left eye. She had her hands over her eyes when a shell banged into the bathroom she had just left and shook down the wall above her head. The hall got suddenly bright as the wall fell away. A gale of plaster, paper, tile, glass, glue, soot, and shit rolled into her. She made herself lunge through the shit and bright light.

She found the first step and went down, leading with her head until she thought better of that and rose in a crouch to crawl up. She was halfway up the flight to the fourth floor when another shell thudded in a room below. The stairs under her hands and knees shuddered. Irena clambered into the hallway of the fourth floor, and realized it was the top. She couldn't run down, because mortar crews across the way had decided—she would have—that if the sniper whose muzzle flash they had seen was still alive, he would be trying to dash downstairs and out of the building.

"A TRICK MOLLY gave me," Irena told Tedic after she had napped for an hour against the rubble of a door before picking her way down the back of the littered staircase, where Tedic was waiting in his truck. " 'Go up where they won't think you'll be,' he said. 'Take a nap, and go down when they think you're dead.' It's good. Until they figure it out the next time."

Irena had half a dozen small cuts along her eyebrows and forehead, almost like cat's scratches, from the debris that fell from the bathroom. Tedic had Mel heat a tub of water so that she could bathe before he drove her home. He winked at her from the snugness of his vulture's perch at the steel desk near the loading dock. "Tell your parents that you got the scratches from slipping on the stairs when you went outside to smoke," he said. "It will make them feel richly justified. And deeply incurious."

"You don't have to explain to anyone these days why someone dies," Irena reminded him. "Why is anyone still alive? That's tricky."

. . .

TEDIC DECIDED THAT Irena had earned a couple of daytime assignments. She spent the next day firing four shots spaced over six hours at shades in the windows of an apartment building on Avala Street in which mortar teams were trying to obscure themselves, or so Tedic was convinced. If Irena thought she saw a shade sagging against the sill, or pinned against the window, she assumed that someone had tugged it down for extra concealment, or even emotional security.

"Fools," she muttered to herself while aiming and firing. "Bloody, bloody fools."

IT WAS EARLY, not much before ten in the morning. The Knight was signing off with Peter Tosh. *Oh, your majesty, can't you rescue me from war, war, war.* He chuckled there—the very idea seemed made for the Knight's amusement. Irena was looking for sagging shades from a gash in the bricks on the third floor of a flour warehouse that had been looted long ago. A few sacks were still strewn on the floor, deflating more each day as rats darted inside their folds, then out again with whitened snouts. Irena was no longer afraid of rats, at least in daylight, but she wasn't going to compete with them for a sack of flour.

A flash of pink flesh winked at her through a bristle of bare tree branches, from the roof of a garage in an alleyway just beyond Lenin Street in Grbavica. It was six inches of a stomach, a stomach so still that Irena assumed its owner must be dead. Or wounded, she decided when she saw it shudder slightly. Irena raised her rifle carefully and squinted through her sight. It was a girl's stomach, for sure, tapering into a pair of high-boned hips, and now it seemed to jiggle with laughter. A boy's hands, Irena guessed, pushed and patted the hips.

Tedic had said that alleyway was a place where Serbs rolled their field artillery pieces at night. The garages concealed the artillery from the U.N. monitors, who did not, at any rate, seem to be searching for the big guns as if their lives depended on it; and theirs did not.

Irena guessed that the stomach belonged to a girl no older than herself, a sturdy birch of a girl soldier, she imagined, from one of the outlying Serb hamlets, who had taken a joyride into Sarajevo with a soldier boyfriend. Irena pictured them rolling their cannon into the garage to cool it down from the night's firings into Bistrik and Stup, and locking it away for the day. It was a bright day, after a few that had been overcast. The high midmorning sun was warm enough to make you doff your coat, loosen your shirt, or, in the case of this girl, shuck it aside to boast to your friends that although it was December in Sarajevo, you were going to get a tawny Monte Carlo tan.

Irena imagined the boys on the crew clapping as the girl swayed her hips and slipped out of her black sweater, perhaps draping it around the neck and shoulders of a shy lieutenant. She imagined a black brassiere beneath, with a shocking red ribbon. *Oh, you bitch, you.* Perhaps the Knight, if they could hear him, had goaded them along with the Clash: *We're a garage band, we come from garageland, things hotting up. . . .*

Someone placed a beer can over the girl's belly button. She laughed at the cold, laughed at the can, and tried to balance it along the ridges of her muscles without laughing. But she kept laughing, giddy after a night's work sending black steel shells and fire into the pale flesh of hiding people, and drunk after just a sip. The can was the particular leaf-green of a Heineken, with a white medallion declaring it was the official beer of Her Majesty the Queen of the Netherlands, whoever she was, dead center in Irena's sights when she squeezed out her last shot. *For queen and country.* She felt the thump of the shot clap her shoulder like the fist of an old teammate, as if to say, "Way to go."

"Mist and foam" was all Irena told Tedic later.

23.

ONE MORNING IRENA HEARD SOMEONE CALLING HER NAME OUTSIDE on the staircase, and Aleksandra shouting back, "Careful out there, whoever you are! You could get shot looking for her!" Then, after a moment, she shouted again. "Third floor! If she's home, she's heard you. Now, off the damn staircase!"

A man's right to endanger his own life stamping up their building's staircase was circumscribed—Irena and Aleksandra had talked it over, and established the principle firmly—by the fact that his appearance might attract the attention of snipers and mortar crews across the way.

Irena was home; she opened the door speculatively. A short man with an eggshell head and an unclipped mustache that bobbed above his mouth in time with each word walked carefully down the hallway toward her until his words could reach her.

"Scary lady down there," he said.

"You have to know her," said Irena.

"No, I don't," said the man. He had stopped in front of the door and was close enough for Irena to smell the wet dirt on his shoes.

"Are you Irena?" he asked. She nodded.

"Zaric?" Irena nodded again.

"Number Three High School basketball team?"

"Are you scouting for the Bulls?" she asked.

The man hesitated for a moment, then, realizing the joke, slapped a palm against his baggy pants.

"I'm a cabdriver," he said. "A friend wants to talk to you."

"Where?"

The man threw his right hand over his left shoulder, two, then three times.

"Over there somewhere," he said. "Across the way. I'm Zoran Vikic, by the way."

"Who?"

"Zoran Vikic."

"No. Who wants to talk to me?"

"I don't know."

"And you are," asked Irena, "related?"

Mrs. Zaric had been napping against a wall, but by now she had awakened and was standing behind her daughter.

"I told you. I'm a *cabdriver,*" he repeated testily.

Mrs. Zaric stepped in front of her daughter. "I'm afraid I don't quite—" she began.

"Cabdrivers have radios," Zoran said. "It's the only way both sides of Sarajevo can talk. Some friend of yours over there has something to tell you. The friend found a cabdriver over there that radioed your name. Correction: your friend *paid* a cabdriver. That's how we make a living now. That driver put out a call, and I heard it. Your friend said you had probably left Grbavica and that you had a grandmother over here near the synagogue. So I asked at the synagogue."

"Excuse me." Mrs. Zaric stepped in. "He asked for my daughter? I am Dalila. My husband is Milan Zaric. Not us?"

Zoran Vikic shook his head a little too proudly. "First time I heard of you. The Serb driver over there says his guy asked for Irena. Said she is pretty. Come on down now, he's waiting."

Mrs. Zaric turned to murmur something to Irena. "Tomaslav," she said softly. "He got over there somehow, and no one knows who he is."

The driver tapped his wrist impatiently, even though he had no watch. "Come on, he's waiting."

"Tomaslav is in Chicago," Irena finally answered. "Remember Aunt Senada's letter from Cleveland."

"How long do you think you can fool me?" Mrs. Zaric lashed out suddenly. "I know that my son and my sister are keeping something from me. And you, too. Tomaslav couldn't hide his jerking off and he can't hide that he's coming here. Don't think you kids are the only ones with secrets," hissed Mrs. Zaric.

"I'll remember that," Irena shot back. She took heavy, hesitant steps down the staircase, as if she were walking on a sprain. With each step, she wondered what she would say over the cabdriver's radio to Coach Dino.

...

IT WAS A Sarajevo Taxi, a Marlboro-red Lada, practically as small as the flip-top box. Zoran reached in for the radio above the dashboard. "Talk standing," he commanded. "If shooting breaks out, we can run better.

"This is thirty-four over here," he announced. "Eighteen, this is thirty-four, near the synagogue. I found the package, and have it here."

Thirty-four then paused and clicked the microphone twice. "Eighteen, thirty-four, do you read? Over."

Mrs. Zaric had an arm around her daughter. The radio squealed once more before a coarse voice sizzled from the speaker.

"Thirty-four, eighteen here," he said. "Good, good. I have shipper here. Shipper is here and wants to say hello. Over."

Zoran held the microphone out to Irena, like a small revolver. "Squeeze the trigger on the microphone to talk," he explained. "Let it go to listen. When you're done saying something, say 'Over,' so they know you're done, and let up on the trigger."

"Perhaps I should speak first," said Irena.

It was her best hope to alert Coach Dino to her mother's presence. She wanted to stop him from declaring through the fizz and pops that he longed to squeeze her ass in his hands, which is what Irena was expecting—and hoping—to hear.

But when the voice hissed out of the radio, it belonged to a girl.

"HELLO?"

It was a young voice. Maybe Coach Dino had taken the precaution of bringing along a friend. Maybe—the possibility was so likely that Irena was seething as the mere suggestion burned in her brain—Coach Dino had made a new friend. Or perhaps it really was Tomaslav. He might have found an old friend on the other side of town who would do the speaking to protect his identity.

"Hello?" the girl said again. Then, after some audible coaching, she said, "Over?"

"Hello, yes," said Irena. "Over."

"Irena? Hello, Irena? Over."

"Yes, over. I mean, yes, this is me. Who is this, please? Over."

The voice might have said something, but it was blocked. Irena kept forgetting to release the trigger after saying "Over." She held it down and repeated herself.

"This is Irena, yes, Irena. I am Irena. Over, over."

"Irena! Irena, this is Amela. Amela Divacs. Something has happened! Princess Diana and Prince Charles are separated!"

Seconds passed as Irena wheeled around to look at her mother. The muscles in Mrs. Zaric's face had tightened into the look of a frightened cat.

"Over." It was Amela's voice, or someone pretending to be Amela.

The driver dipped his head to signal that Irena should squeeze to respond.

"Princess Diana and Prince Charles are *what*?" And then she remembered: "Over."

"*Separated*," said Amela. "The first step of divorce. It's all in the news here. Over."

"What about her two boys?" asked Irena. "Over."

"They'll live with her and see Prince Charles on weekends," Amela answered. "Over. Wait. But some of her friends worry that the Queen might try to keep them. Over."

"How does she look?" asked Irena.

"Diana? Over."

"Diana." Irena forgot to depress the trigger, but Amela's voice came back regardless. And it *was* Amela, Irena realized; they knew each other's timing.

"She looks very sad. Her picture—you can imagine the news here—is all over. Over."

"Where are you?" asked Irena. "Over."

"We had to move out of Grbavica," said Amela. "Things got rough. We are now on Alexander I Street. Are you at your grandmother's? Over."

Mrs. Zaric had turned her back and was walking in small circles away from the cab to give her daughter at least a semblance of privacy. But Zoran motioned her back.

"Not that far," he said. "Snipers can see over there."

"Yes," said Irena. "Her old apartment. She's dead. Over."

"I'm sorry," Amela said. "Was she old? Over."

"Yes. But she was shot," said Irena. The microphone trigger slipped once under her finger. "Just before we got here. Over."

"Mr. Dragoslav is dead," said Amela. He was a small man with a plum-shaped beard who taught physics. "He was in the army and got shot. Over."

"Nermina is dead," Irena told her softly. "Over." It was a moment before Amela responded, and her voice was so quiet that it threatened to fade out.

"Was she a soldier? Over."

"She was waiting for bread. Over," said Irena. But she went on—that sounded so stupid. "People have to wait outside for bread and water now. We put up a note for her parents, and it's still up. They must be dead, too. Over," she said.

Excitement—unexpected, with a tinge of elation that Irena realized she had not heard for months—came into Amela's voice. "But I'm calling with good news," she said. "Pretty Bird. We have Pretty Bird. Pretty Bird is fine." Her voice disappeared into the static. When it came back, Irena heard trembling. "I'm sorry," said Amela. "I forgot to pass off to you. Penalty, penalty. Pretty Bird is fine. Over."

Irena had to lower the arm with the microphone. She slumped against the taxi.

Mrs. Zaric, arms clasped around her own shoulders, crept back into her daughter's conversation. "Pretty Bird? She said Pretty Bird?"

"That's what I heard."

Mrs. Zaric mouthed to the driver, "Our bird."

Amela came back. "We figured he was gone with everyone else. But a few months ago someone came running. They said Pretty Bird was back at the basketball court. I couldn't believe it. I said, no, couldn't be. But it was. He was perched on the hoop. He must have flown back. Over."

"We tried to keep him," said Irena. "But we ran out of food. We had to let him go." Irena knew that she had let up the trigger of the microphone before finishing that thought. "Is he there now?" she was finally able to ask. "Over."

"At home," said Amela. "Our apartment. We thought—you weren't here—he is safe with us. We will keep him for you. Until all this is over. Over."

"Does he make his sounds? Over."

"For sure," said Amela. "Washing machine, coffeemaker, phone."

All sounds he can't hear here, thought Irena.

"I think—it's sad, but he's so smart—we hear him going *p-kow, p-kow, boom*, like the shells, at night," Amela said. "Over."

That's how they sound going out, Irena thought to herself. "Take care of him" was all she could manage. "Please. Over."

"Until you can," said Amela, and after a couple of clicks and pops she added, "How are you? Over."

"We are"—she clicked the trigger up and down—"fine," Irena said finally. "There are problems."

"Here, too."

"Our team?"

"All gone somewhere."

"Emina? Danica? Miss Ferenc?" Then Irena remembered. "Over."

"Can't find them. Lucky we don't play Number One tonight. Over."

"Coach Dino?" Irena had deliberately saved his name to attach casually after a roster of old teammates.

"You hear about him," said Amela. "He wins rifle matches in the army. Over."

Mrs. Zaric was motioning with her hands.

"Your parents?" asked Irena. "Over."

"Good. Father is in the army, but he doesn't do much. Thank God. Over."

"Mine too! Digs trenches!"

"With those elegant hands!"

Irena didn't know that Amela had noticed her father's hands.

"I have to be in the army, too," Amela added. "Over."

"What do you do? Over."

"Office stuff. Not much. No school. Over."

"I work in a brewery," said Irena. "Office work. The U.N. keeps it open. Over."

"Fantastic! The U.N. Cute French soldiers? Over." Irena and her mother flashed smiles at each other.

"A few."

"Get to drink what you make? Over."

"We're paid in beer and cigarettes," Irena said, laughing. "Over."

"Sounds great! We're paid money. Worth shit. Over."

Mrs. Zaric had to turn away from Irena when she heard her daughter's laugh chiming alongside Amela's from the radio speaker.

"I have to go," said Amela. "Driver has to go. Did you hear? Madonna wrote a book called just *Sex*." She used the English word. "Over."

"She is so wild!"

"She is fantastic!"

"I love her!"

"Fucking incredible!"

"Have a few old *VOX* and *Q*'s here," said Irena, "That's all. Over."

"Me, too," said Amela. "Sometimes old stuff comes in. We will take care of Pretty Bird. Can you talk again?"

"Yes! Yes, over."

"Maybe," said Amela, "I can get him to talk into the microphone! Can you talk Thursday? Same time? Over."

Irena calculated that she would either be home after a night in her roost or waiting to boost herself up in the afternoon.

"Yes," she said, casting a glance at Zoran, who shrugged and nodded. "Yes, fine. Over!"

"Take care, then," Amela said. "Driver says to say 'Over and out.' Pretty Bird makes a refrigerator sound. Over, out!" she shouted through the pops and bubbles.

"Over, out, love to Pretty Bird!" said Irena. She dropped the microphone to her chest and reached for her mother's hands. "Pretty Bird" was all she could say.

Mrs. Zaric just squeezed her daughter's fingers. "Pretty Bird" was all she could manage, too.

ZORAN REMINDED THEM that he was not with one of the humanitarian agencies in town—he had to be paid. He said the price was a carton of cigarettes. Mrs. Zaric said he was being ridiculous. She had heard that some of the French soldiers in town were selling short calls on the satellite telephones some units carried for one hundred U.S. dollars. "To places like London and Chicago," she said. "This was just to the other side of town."

"If you want a bargain, call London and Chicago," Zoran answered. "A call to the other side of Sarajevo costs."

"Five packs, then."

"The carton."

"The carton, then," Mrs. Zaric said with a sigh of annoyance. "But the Thursday phone call, too."

"A carton and five packs."

"The carton," Mrs. Zaric said evenly, and glanced at her daughter. "Did I mention they were Marlboros?"

Zoran began to smile as he scuffed his feet against the taxi's tires.

"A pretty girl has ways to convince me," he said, and Mrs. Zaric stiffened as her hand tightened on her daughter's arm. Before she could shout—or slap—him down, Zoran spoke in the voice of a faded French movie star. "I don't mean your girl, ma'am. I'm a man who values experience."

Irena was dispatched upstairs to bring back half a carton of cigarettes.

AFTERWARD, IRENA AND her mother sat on the stairs and opened a spare pack plucked from their cache of Marlboros.

"I felt safe about him being in London," Mrs. Zaric said of her son. "I even thought he was safe in Chicago."

"Al Capone is dead," Irena pointed out.

"There are *Serbs* in Chicago," Mrs. Zaric reminded her. "Lots. But they're Americans. They all have cars, CD players, computers. Most of them want another Bulls championship, not a Greater Serbia."

"So do I," said Irena.

"It was the rabbi who told me. I wandered in to look at the board while you were at work one day, and he said, 'The girl picked one up. I think she has a boyfriend or something who is going to Chicago to join one of our fighting units. Praise be, they will be here in good time.' Praise be," Mrs. Zaric continued. "Those boys and girls will never get farther than Cleveland. If Tomaslav and the rest manage to sneak into Bosnia, he'll only wind up in the haystacks of Zenica, sharing mud and bugs, and risking his life for peasants."

"Country people in black dresses and plain scarves?" Irena asked. "Not city folks like us?"

Mrs. Zaric's eyes narrowed comically. She tilted her head back, peered down the barrel of her nose, and blew a ring of smoke between them. "I've told Milan a hundred times," she said. "We should have had dim-witted children, like everyone else. They are more grateful. They don't remember everything you ever told them and serve it back to you, cold, in your face."

Mrs. Zaric studied the tip of her cigarette as it darkened and scattered. "We've had our misfortunes," she said carefully. "The first day in Grbavica. Your grandmother. Nermina I count, too. But how remarkable it is that you, your father, and I, even Tommy, are still alive. We've been so lucky. So favored. If I knew whom to thank—if I believed—I'd give them the rest of my life. But your father digging in the dirt—Tomaslav maybe crawling around some bloody wood, for all we know—you going back and forth doing whatever at the brewery . . . Aleksandra sitting on the stoop and signaling snipers with her cigarettes. I worry about our luck lasting. And now we have to be grateful that Pretty Bird has made it so far, too."

The two women sat with their hands knotted in their laps and listened to the winter wind scratch over the empty streets.

"Pretty Bird," said Irena.

"Amazing," said her mother.

"Pretty Bird."

AMELA WAS SAFE, and Pretty Bird had survived—Irena wanted to bring the news to Tedic. But Tedic had been called out to Franko Hospital, where good fortune had just run out.

24.

FRANKO HOSPITAL HAD WINDOWS. AFTER JUST A FEW MONTHS OF war, windowpanes looked like extravagant embellishments in the wracked gray cityscape. It was like finding a teacup intact in the wreckage of a tornado.

The hospital still had whole windows that looked north, into the curve of Mount Zuc, and windows that stared south into the smashed and forsaken towers downtown. Nearly all of the city's other windows had been shattered. Almost every block looked like a gallery of blinded heads.

"We are the only building left that has eyes," said Alma Ademovic, the hospital director.

The hospital had been finished against a deadline in 1984 to welcome the Olympic Games (and thereby named for Jure Franko, the first Yugoslav slalom skier to win an Olympic medal). The new building was meant to impress the West with a show of modernity. It was an Eastern bloc hospital in which the interior walls were not gray concrete blocks but chest-high panels in lemon, mauve, and peach—pastel socialism, topped with transparent plastic leaves that displayed the latest imported medical machinery, like glossy cars in a California parking lot.

Marxism that let the sunshine in.

The windows remained luxuriously whole because there was a whale-backed little flip of the mountain that prevented snipers from firing from the north, and the hospital was too far from the lines to be struck by shots from any snipers roosting in the trees east and west of the city. The south was close, just across the Miljacka River and Serb lines, but the thicket of scarred steel buildings downtown protected that side.

Bosnians were wary about advertising the hospital's seclusion. Officials did not want a community of refugees pitching tents there. But they used the hospital for meetings, battening down participants into the back of ambulances for delivery at the appointed times, and kept the state's reserves of deutsche marks, dollars, and Swiss francs in the basement, as well as rings, necklaces, bracelets, earrings, brooches, and silver coffee servers that several old Sarajevo Serb families had donated, with unwitting generosity, after taking flight across the river. The basement also held boxes of bullets.

Alma Ademovic considered the provisions to be unwarranted incursions into her domain. She complained to the Home Minister as he was conveyed to a conference one afternoon.

"You are violating the Geneva convention," she said, stamping her right foot in her fury. "I'm sure of it."

The Home Minister considered the Geneva convention as unenforceable in Sarajevo—and as unaffordable—as the Ten Commandments. Camouflaged in an ambulance attendant's smock, the Home Minister looked like an especially insolent underling.

But Alma Ademovic was adamant. "Your pirate's booty and bombs are taking space that could store neomycin, lidocaine, or sulfonamide," she said heatedly. "That's what's *supposed* to be in this hospital."

"I was not aware that our shelves are short of space to hold such an excess," the Home Minister called back as he turned. "But if I had to choose between antibiotics and ammunition . . ." He let the thought hang as he stamped away.

RADOVAN KARADZIC, THE Bosnian Serb leader, had once been a consulting psychiatrist at Franko. Staffers asked about their recollections either had to acknowledge that they had no clear memories of him—which awarded them no prestige—or pass on anecdotes that would prompt the question, "Didn't you know he was a lunatic?"

Karadzic would bustle in, the lapels of his Burberry trench coat flapping expensively, great Waikiki swells of silver hair breaking over his forehead. "Close your eyes with me a moment," he would command some dimpled and appealing nurse, and take her hands at the wrists, as if the recitation that followed was a human response test.

"*The gentlefolks' aortas will gush without me,*" he would begin, eyes half closed, like the hired singer at a wedding party.

The last chance to get stained with blood
I let go by.

Ever more often I answer ancient calls
And watch the mountains turn green.

The doctor was moved, manifestly. He usually peeked at his ensnared audience. The nurses tended to be considerate in their reactions. The doctor had them by the wrist. He was also the consulting psychiatrist for Sarajevo's soccer team, and sometimes doled out tickets.

"Those lines are beautiful, are they not? Images mix over centuries. I like to think that I am perhaps the third-best living poet in our language. And I cannot remember the names of the other two!"

The woman he had detained for his recitation would be stuck for an accolade commensurate with Karadzic's.

"It reminds me of that song about what a cat sees at night," said one lab technician. "You know: '*Midnight*, dah-dah-dah-dah-dah-dah-dah, *the moon has no memory*. . . .' You know, that Englishman."

The doctor's eyes bulged at the affront. "Andrew Lloyd Webber writes—*pop tunes*," he sputtered. "Cheap, flimsy"—he was the poet struggling for just the right words here—"*Coca-Cola-flavored* words cannot be compared to my poetry."

Most of the hospital's psychiatric staff had become scarce since the start of the war, feeling useless or absurd. Anxiety, paranoia, and doom are not disorders when snipers are trying to shoot you through your bathroom window. How could a psychiatrist tell any Sarajevan that he was suffering from depression? Feeling safe and free from terror—*that* would be a clinical disturbance.

IN THE FALL, the U.N. officials overseeing the siege of the city permitted the hospital to receive a skin-graft machine donated by the Charles Nicolle Medical Center of Normandy. The equipment had been packed into a grave-looking silvered valise, heavy as a casket, that came attached to a fifty-three-year-old emergency surgeon, Dr. Olivier Despres, a lean, graying man with the agreeably long face of a pedigreed hound. He was wearing smart field khakis that bore the wrinkles of previous deployment.

He was delivered to Franko Hospital in a French Foreign Legion armored personnel carrier that smelled of other men's boots, breath, and sweat. The young Foreign Legion captain overseeing his delivery was Cambodian; he was the one legionnaire who spoke French. The two enlisted men who turned the slings of their rifles around onto their backs in order to haul the doctor's bags and boxes into the carrier were Kazakh—Russian army refugees who had signed on to the Legion because it paid its troops. The driver was an Egyptian army sergeant whose head could not be seen in the roost in which he sat, above their shoulders. He had to call down in English over the toes of his shoes.

"Franko Hospital, yes?"

The legionnaires yelled back up the sergeant's muddy pant legs.

"Franko Hospital, yes!" They clanged the butts of their rifles twice against the muddy floor. "Franko! Franko!"

There were six small open slits on the khaki-painted steel walls of the carrier. Dr. Despres steeled himself over the bumps and tried to steady his head against a window to glimpse something of the wreckage that had moved him to come to the city. But the slits were so small—no larger than the space under a door—that the doctor could see nothing. One of the Kazakh soldiers waved his hand as Dr. Despres tried to peer through one of the minute openings.

"No," the soldier called over. "Dangerous." He held his hands out, as if holding a rifle, and trained his two index fingers toward the doctor's chin. *"P-eee-owww! P-eee-owww!"* he said, then shut his eyes and slumped forward. "Dead, bye-bye. *P-eee-owww!*" Dr. Despres joined in the laughter, and pulled back from the slit with comic haste, as if the wall were electrified. The carrier bounced up and down over rubble and clutter as the soldiers banged their rifle butts against the floor.

"We all live in a yellow submarine!" they sang.

Clang!

"A yellow submarine!"

Clang!

"A yellow submarine!"

Clang!

Dr. Despres offered to take down names and phone numbers of loved ones he could call when he returned to France. But the men said they could think of no one who was eager to hear of them.

"I am gone," said one of the Kazakhs. He laughed joylessly through a three-toothed smile. "Happy here dead."

WHEN DR. DESPRES reached his destination up on a hill in the north of the city, Franko Hospital doctors expressed gratitude, but also bewilderment.

"We haven't had power for several months," they said, shaking their heads.

A German army truck drove a generator at the hospital that could power surgical lights, a sterilizer, and a water pump, but not at the same time. The doctors and nurses had learned how to conduct surgeries by lantern light, sluicing away blood and slime by squeezing clumps of soaked paper towels carefully over the wounds as they probed and stitched. The staff squinted at a large block of type on the underside of Dr. Despres's Swiss skin-shearing machine and deduced that it would draw more power than they could deliver.

"You would need at least the lights and the water pump working at the same time," said Dr. Despres. "This is not a procedure for dim light. Or no water pressure."

The hospital director was more put out than apologetic. "I know it must seem like we are living in caves," Alma Ademovic said. "But, honestly, I don't know why the U.N. sent you here. Our limitations cannot surprise them. Of all people," she added almost into her chin.

Dr. Despres tried to reply lightly. "Oh, that alphabet soup of U.N. agencies often gets things jumbled," he said. "I learned that in Somalia and Ethiopia."

"Well," the hospital director sniffed, "we are surely better off than *that*. We are *Europeans*."

The director clipped away quickly. Dr. Despres was standing rather forlornly in the hall when the hospital's chief surgical nurse introduced herself. "We had a message telling us that you were coming, Doctor," she said in English. "But nothing about preparations for a skin-graft machine. Perhaps we can get in to see the U.N. official who approves our equipment to find about getting another generator. Perhaps *you* can get in to see him."

Zule Rasulavic was fortyish, with a redhead's sprinkling of freckles over her nose. When Dr. Despres took her right hand and unexpectedly brushed it with his lips, she regretted the blue jeans that she had been left with to wear through the war. No matter how much weight had melted away over the months, she was sure that the jeans thickened the look of her hips.

"I am certainly willing," said Dr. Despres. "I didn't come here just for the mountain view. It is lovely," he added quickly, having been alerted to local sensitivities. "But I want to help."

This brought Alma Ademovic back from halfway down the corridor. "What kind of help do you think we need?" she said. "We are taking care of our patients in a modern, educated way. We are *Europeans,*" she fairly hissed at him. "Do you think we are witch doctors?"

The nurses took Dr. Despres by the shoulders and steered him into one of the hospital's waiting rooms, where they told him that he might want to rest and restore himself after a rough journey. After a few minutes, Dr. Despres closed his eyes in the dim midmorning light strained, like weak tea, through the hospital's soiled windows, and fell asleep in a chair that had only one arm.

SHORTLY BEFORE NOON, Dr. Despres towed a heavy brown box that the legionnaires had delivered with him against a wall just across from Alma Ademovic's open office door. The open door did not signal Miss Ademovic's manner of administration. It was an operational necessity, to allow daylight from her window to filter into the murky hallway.

Dr. Despres approached her door cautiously, and pointedly took up a position just outside. "Excuse me, Miss Ademovic," he said. "I wonder if I might ask about lunch."

The hospital director's reply was brisk. "Of course. There are no restaurants to speak of. We will serve you in our kitchen."

"I was advised to provide for myself."

"That is ridiculous," she said. "You are our guest. I am sure that we can find *something.*" In fact, the United Nations administration made certain that the hospital was well provisioned. They did not want any stories arising from Sarajevo that the U.N. had failed to provide food for war victims in their hospital beds. The monotony of rice, beans, saltines, and an occasional frozen cutlet was more of a problem than scarcity. But Alma Ademovic had discovered that giving foreign visitors a few pangs of hunger gratified their guests; it sent them back to the West with a vivid story for after-dinner speeches.

Throughout his years in emergency medicine, Dr. Despres had uncomplainingly consumed rather a lot of relief agency–issue beans and rice. But he had another plan.

"You know we French—we take such pleasure in our own foods," he said. "So I have brought enough for everyone here, if you will permit." He stepped back to pat the big brown box and lug it several inches into view. "I brought a few *saucissons,* some of our flavorful dried sausages. Also some lovely cured ham from Bayonne. It has the most amazing velvet feel as you carve it away from the bone. We are very proud of our patés in Normandy. I have some tins of very nice duck and goose patés. The goose liver is studded with pistachios. I have also added some small rounds of toasts and a jar of cornichons. I thought a good, tangy Gruyère would compliment all. I have included a couple of pounds of ground coffee—I haven't seen the hospital yet that isn't fueled by coffee—and some Côte d'Or chocolate. I also thought that some of our tasty crisp Brittany butter cookies might be welcome, although," he added, "I left several with the Norwegian soldiers at the airport who examined my equipment. I thought it might make them more amenable about weight restrictions."

Alma Ademovic looked up from her desk with unblinking blue eyes, as hard as tile.

"The food is all packaged very soundly," added the doctor. "Anything left will keep."

When the administrator remained expressionless, Dr. Despres made an instant diagnosis: he would have to extract any insinuation of charity.

"When I consult in Paris, I frequently bring a ripe Neufchâtel cheese," he said.

"I'm sure the girls will appreciate your snacks," Alma Ademovic said finally. "I do without lunch. But help yourself."

Dr. Despres pushed the brown box back around the corner of the administrator's office. He thought about the *saucissons* and Gruyère as his stomach growled and churned over the rest of the afternoon. But he left the box, untouched, on the worn green alga carpet just outside Alma Ademovic's office. He hoped the administrator would observe that he had not helped himself to so much as a cornichon.

DR. DESPRES SPENT the first part of the afternoon removing stitches from the wounds of an elderly woman who had been hiding in her bathroom when a bullet pierced her closed wooden door and smashed the mirror over her head. He tried to play a card game with a thin girl who had forgotten her name and had been found sleeping against the steps of an empty housing block. But only the girl knew the rules, and she soon tired of easy triumphs.

A nurse brought the doctor to the bedside of a small boy with a shaved head who said that his name was Zijo. The boy lay on his stomach, a strap cinched over his waist, so that a large bandage plastered over a wound in his left shoulder blade would not be disturbed.

"Shrapnel," the nurse explained in a low voice. "It came through the window. Thank God he was turned away."

Zijo had twisted his head on the pillow to face Dr. Despres, who knelt down beside the boy's left shoulder. "Zijo?" he said gently. "I'm Dr. Despres." A hospital orderly, wearing blue jeans under his white coat, stood over the doctor as he translated. The boy blinked once. Dr. Despres motioned to the orderly to kneel with him on the floor. Years of talking to wounded children in field hospitals had taught him that children usually attended to the translator, not the physician.

"I would like to take a little look at your back," said Dr. Despres.

He waited for the orderly to finish before putting the palm of his right hand lightly on the small of Zijo's back. He then ran his index finger gently below the surgical tape to lift up the bottom edge of the boy's bandage.

Zijo began to twitch and shudder. He squeezed his bony shoulders toward his ears, as if the sting were a sound he could shut out.

"I'm sorry," said the doctor. "I am sorry that it hurts."

The orderly didn't translate; he felt sure that Zijo understood as much from the doctor's tone. A nurse shined a flashlight under the flap of the bandage so that Dr. Despres could see the boy's wound. It was as wide as the doctor's palm and still glistening.

"You are a brave young man," he continued. The orderly translated that. Dr. Despres saw white threads of nerves shimmering in the wound, and red ribbons of ragged, unmended muscle.

"It's been three days since he came, and they cut out the steel," said the orderly quietly.

"Another three hundred before this heals without a skin graft. Don't—there is no need—to tell him that," he added in an even tone. Dr. Despres patted the flap of the dressing in place and rested his hand just above the boy's waist.

"Zijo, I am sorry that it feels the way it does." The doctor looked into the little boy's face. "It itches, yes?"

Zijo shook his head slightly and mumbled into his pillow.

"A little, he says," said the orderly.

Dr. Despres laid the hand that had lifted up the bandage and caused so much hurt on the boy's small, bald, bony head. It was slightly damp, and cold. Above his pillow was a stuffed bear with a stitched smile wearing a worn red T-shirt with gold lettering across the front. It said CONGRATULATIONS!

"The bear was just around here," the orderly explained.

"Maternity ward, I would think," said the doctor with a mild laugh.

"We give it to children."

Dr. Despres kept his manicured right hand on Zijo's back, below the wound, pressing lightly on his spine. "Where was this boy when he was hit?" he asked.

"In an apartment," said the orderly. "Alone."

"Were his parents killed?"

"Or lost. Or he's lost."

"Why would anyone"—Dr. Despres could not prevent his voice from rising—"leave a little boy alone in the middle of a war?"

"Perhaps to save his life," said the orderly.

"His parents could have been running away," a nurse who had come in added. "They could have left him behind and hoped he would be found."

"Or Serbs could have taken his parents and spared the boy," said the orderly. "Even demons make exceptions."

"Paramilitaries sometimes kill little boys but let go of little girls, because they won't grow up to be soldiers," said the nurse. "Sometimes they kill the little girls because they will grow up to bear soldiers. But they pass over the little boys because they remind them of themselves."

"People are killed for no reason and for any reason," the orderly added. "We will be dead before we can figure out the difference."

Dr. Despres rose slightly from his crouch to pick up the CONGRATULATIONS! bear. Then he bent back down to hold the bear in front of Zijo's small, pebble-gray eyes.

"Have you given your friend a name?" asked the doctor.

Zijo nodded once on his pillow.

"Zarko," explained the nurse. "I think it is the name of someone he knows."

"Well, that's great," said Dr. Despres slowly. "Zarko. It is almost like your name."

While the orderly passed on his words, the doctor sat on the edge of Zijo's cot and took a roll of white surgical tape from the nurse's cart. The nurse pulled out sheets of cotton wadding to replace Zijo's bandage. But Dr. Despres took the wadding from her hand and folded it into a small square, which he pressed against the bear's worn back. With the nurse's help, he pulled a length of tape over one side of the bandage, then another.

"Here is what we have done for Zarko," he said, bringing the bear closer for Zijo to see. "You are hurt, Zarko is hurt. We will take care of you both."

The little boy looked on dully as Dr. Despres tucked the bear against his pillow.

THE FIRST WHITE stick candles were being lit in the wards when Dr. Despres excused himself and found Nurse Rasulavic standing in a weak wash of light near a window at the end of a darkened hallway. The doctor's stomach was rumbling, and he thought that his hands were beginning to shake.

"I am sorry to disturb you," he said, "but I'm not used to going so long without a cigarette. Is there somewhere I can smoke?" When Nurse Rasulavic looked up, he could see that her eyes were smoky gray.

"This hospital is a no-smoking zone," she said. "A few years ago, Miss Ademovic came back from a conference in California."

Dr. Despres smiled. "We have a new law in France, too," he said.

Nurse Rasulavic returned the doctor's smile and widened it. "Let me show you a place that is lawless," she said.

NURSE RASULAVIC LED the doctor to a pair of steel doors in a hallway loading dock. The space was far from any windows and darkened quickly in the late afternoon. "There is a small area out here," she said, pressing her shoulder against one of the doors. The door rocked open with an iron groan. The sky was dimming, and the last gold light of the day grazed against their hands as they took them out of the pockets of their white hospital smocks. Dr. Despres shook a pack of Gauloises, and held it out to Nurse Rasulavic.

"How lovely to see that. Thank you. You know, you could get a lot for these here now," she said.

"Money?" The doctor affected an expression of mock surprise.

"Oh, no," she said. "What could you do with money? Sardines, olive paste, beans." In the pause that followed, Dr. Despres counted the sound of three rifle shots popping in the distance. "Drugs. Sex. Anchovy paste. We are fine down here," she added.

"Bullets?"

"Of course. But blocks away."

Dr. Despres produced a black-and-gold enameled Dupont lighter from his right pocket, and flipped the roller three times before he got it to fire. He held the flame under Nurse Rasulavic's cigarette and cupped his left hand just below her chin.

"That lighter would also get you a lot of nice something. Until you ran out of fluid. Then matches would bring more. How long are you staying?"

"It's not determined," said Dr. Despres with a shrug. "I have clothes for a week. I want to get the skin-graft machine running. Then the U.N. is supposed to take me out on a cargo flight back to Zagreb or Italy. I don't want to leave until we know if the machine can be used. Until then, maybe you can use an extra set of hands."

Nurse Rasulavic took a long pull on her cigarette. "We used to come out here for peace and quiet," she said. "Now the quiet is frightening. You used to hear the sizzle and click of streetcars, the clop of feet in the street. That there are still a few of us here worth shooting is almost the only sign of life. Are you from Paris?"

"Actually, a town called Rouen," he said. "In Normandy, along the Seine."

"It is beautiful?"

"It has many beauties. Monet painted the famous cathedral in the center of town. But it got damaged in the war. The Germans rolled in with tanks. When it came time, the Americans and British tried to blast them out, and in spite the Germans burned the heart of town on their way out. The Allies were pink-skinned boys from Texas and Scotland who threw oranges and chocolate bars to children and young girls. I was a child, and my mother was a pretty young girl. Those were some of the best days of my life." Dr. Despres paused and smiled.

Nurse Rasulavic could see a kind of fashion clinging to the doctor, even as his fatigues were rumpled by travel, sweat, and sleep. He still smelled of strong cigarettes and sharp cologne. He was the first man she had seen for months whose face was still softened by cheeks. Sarajevo was beginning to look like a city of hawks.

"Did it take your town long to recover?" she asked.

"It's quite prosperous now," said the doctor. "It drizzles almost every day. That's good for the apples and grows grass for the cows. Tourists come to see where Jeanne d'Arc was burned at the stake. They close the center streets so tourists can walk about, as if they were in the sixteenth century."

"We are rather sixteenth-century ourselves at the moment," said Nurse Rasulavic.

This won a long, low laugh from Dr. Despres. He coughed small clouds of smoke, and Nurse Rasulavic cleared her own throat noisily to put him at ease. It was flattering to make a man laugh until he exploded with smoke.

"Do you have a family?" she asked. She smoothed a thicket of hair that had got bunched behind her right ear.

"Two children," said the doctor. "Teenagers, a girl and a boy. They live with their mother. Our girl wants to be a doctor. But not a surgeon. All her life, she has heard that surgeons are lousy husbands."

Nurse Rasulavic fought back a smile, but not too hard. "I know."

"I'm sure you've heard."

"No," she said. "I *know.* I've married a couple of surgeons."

Their laughter mingled as they leaned back on a parking rail, each waiting for the other to take the next step. It was the doctor. He stepped down delicately onto the butt of his cigarette. Zule Rasulavic saw his soft brown loafer slide away and heard his shin snap like a branch breaking off a tree in an ice storm. When she looked up, bewildered by the sound, she saw Dr. Despres reaching up to try to keep his head from blowing away. She thought she could see the mist around him darken from pink to ruby.

THE SHOOTING OF Dr. Despres at dusk outside the hospital in which he was helping to heal the victims of war was reported as a death that signified the hopelessness of the conflict. The outside world could send some of its most conscientious citizens to try to ease the suffering; they would only die in cross fire. Bosnians, Serbs, Croats—people with a scarcity of vowels in their names, and a surplus of hatred in their hearts.

And centuries of blood on their hands.

The Bosnian security forces, however, did not see the doctor's death as a time for reflection on the futility of war. A good man had died. But, rather more to the point, he had been shot to death in a spot that had been regarded as impenetrable by rifle fire.

Tedic had been alerted to the doctor's shooting when the hospital raised U.N. headquarters over a radio link. Tedic, bent over a street map in the basement of the brewery, dispatched himself to follow. When he arrived in the surgical room, the bright light of a headlight powered by a car battery was trained on a purpling stump. It took Tedic a moment to take in what remained of a man's head after the blood and brains had spilled out.

The presiding physician was a young man named Cibo. He had once been a student in one of Tedic's algebra classes, had gone to medical school in Vienna, and become an orthopedist, whom Tedic would see over the years on habitual trips to the hospital when one of his basketball players cracked a tibia. Cibo's black crow's eyes were the only features by which his old teacher could recognize him; the younger man was shrunken.

"You are looking good," was what Tedic told him.

"The war has been my spa."

"I must ask a few quick questions, Cibo, while we have time. Are there Frenchies around?"

"Out in the 'secured area,'" said the young doctor. "Looking for the bullet. And whatever is left."

"Good. Let Frenchies go out and wave the flashlights just after a sniper shooting."

The bright white light from the lamp curled the hairs on the back of Tedic's hands. Dr. Despres's head had been propped up on a block that was now slick with blood. His shirt had been split and pulled away from his shoulders, where the skin was turning waxy.

"His wounds?"

"One shot," said Cibo. "Near as I can tell."

"Rifle?"

"Not a mortar. But, Mr. Tedic, this is not my line."

"Short range? Long range?"

"Medium."

"From a height?"

"For sure. Look here." Cibo held the eraser end of a pencil above a jagged rim of whitening bone.

"Whatever hit the doctor was tumbling, falling down, and smacked flat. It plunged into the midbrain like"—Cibo wavered; a man's head was still in his hands—"like a hot stone into a pudding. The brain blows up from the pressure. That's why part of the skull comes off"—Cibo paused considerately—"so trimly."

"A tibia mechanic," Tedic said, "figures all that?"

"I've had to branch out," Cibo said.

"As have we all. Can you tell anything about the bullet?"

"Not until someone finds it."

"The radio call mentioned a woman," Tedic noted.

"Zule Rasulavic was having a smoke with the doctor out back."

Tedic didn't know the name.

"You'll recognize her," said Cibo. "A nurse here. Pretty, forty, red-haired most months. The Frenchies asked her some questions and put her in a storeroom."

There was a brief fusillade of cracks and sizzles as hospital attendants began to snap photographs of the doctor's wounds. Tedic thought that he saw only a couple of soldiers in the room jump back, startled. The scent of night and the clang of steel doors reached the room as a half dozen Frenchies stomped in with a bullet in a waxed hospital cup.

"On l'a, on l'a," the apparent captain of the detail sang out. "Right here, my friends, right here." He inclined the cup toward Cibo, who took it between his palms and shook it gently, as if it were brandy.

"More brain than blood," Cibo announced. "Not surprising, given the velocity. It's in and out of the brain before bleeding begins."

Tedic and the French captain drew perceptibly closer to Cibo, though neither man acknowledged the other.

Cibo plunged a pair of forceps into the cup and lifted out the bullet to bring it into the light. "Smashed nose," Cibo announced to the room. "Someone with a microscope will have to make out any other marks. But it's a 7.62 X 39-millimeter. Soviet, with that shorter case. Can we all see that?"

A chorus of murmurs assented. Cibo dropped the flattened gray bullet into a plastic sleeve that the French captain held out before him, between his thumb and forefinger. Tedic stepped out from the circle of shoulders and left to find the storeroom.

TEDIC EXTRACTED ONE of the black wallets he stored in his coat. They afforded him a range of affiliations, and he flashed one at the raw-faced French soldier guarding the room, who had tipped his folding chair back, away from the light, his rifle laid across his knees like an art book.

The room had a fuel lamp that hissed and sputtered and seemed to boil over with light. Nurse Rasulavic was sitting on a blanket on the floor, with her head against her knees. Tedic held a hand in front of his eyes as he sought out her face. He lowered himself to a spot just beyond the blanket.

"Miss Rasulavic, yes?" he said to the dark outline of the woman on the floor. "I am Miro Tedic. Perhaps, if you can glimpse my face, you will find me familiar. I know I recognize you. You are the nurse in the emergency room that all of my high-school basketball players want to hold their hands when I bring them in with injuries."

"I think they prefer some of the young blondes," she said.

"My boys are sophisticated."

He could see Zule Rasulavic's lips part slightly in a smile.

"I think I remember your face."

The last inch of a Marlboro glowed from the hand that grasped her knee. One knee up, one leg down, a shy smile—preposterously, Tedic was reminded of one of the bathing-beauty calendars he used to buy on summer holidays in Dubrovnik. The Frenchies had laid down a beach blanket in the storeroom and lit up a hissing sun.

"I am with the city," Tedic said. "Have the Frenchies had the sense to get you a drink?"

Zule shook her head, shook her hand with the Marlboro, to wave the thought away. Tedic pulled a stainless-steel flask from yet another pocket in his coat, curved to rest against the hip.

"Scotch," he said. "A Canadian mix."

Zule Rasulavic reached over to a small pile of pill cups, curling like a snail from atop a crate. "We have cups," she said. "Not always pills."

Tedic poured carefully in the faint light. He lifted the flask with a grin toward the young soldier, who held up his hand in affable refusal. "Duty, duty," he said in English.

"Let me explain. I am with the Home Ministry," Tedic began.

"Are you some kind of policeman?"

"By no means. But I am concerned with security."

"There's a difference?"

"A policeman investigates crime," said Tedic. Zule had lowered her hand to the floor to snuff out her cigarette, and Tedic spoke low, as she bowed her head to watch the glow smudged against the floor.

"But what would a policeman do here? The world regards shooting down old ladies who are in line for a bag of beans as a blameless tragedy. Not a crime. The ladies were standing in the way of somebody's national destiny."

Tedic took Zule's upturned head as a sign to proceed. "Because of the arms embargo," he said, "in Sarajevo right now, we are afforded only the right to be fatalities. The U.N. sees, hears, and speaks of no evil. They bid us just run back into our holes, and scurry out later for beans. Some of us are refusing to stay in those holes, Miss Rasulavic. Before I crawl back into mine, I need to know what happened here."

...

THEY NODDED AT each other over their pill cups, sipping from their scotches.

"I thought no sniper was supposed to be able to reach here," said Zule.

"There is no isle of refuge here," said Tedic. "Perhaps we should have known that all along. Perhaps something you noticed can help us."

"I was talking to a man," she said, "and then he was shot."

Tedic sat with his shins tucked under his thighs. More out of discomfort than calculation, he shifted, but as he did so he was careful to keep his knees low. He had his own pack of Marlboros in the inexhaustible inventory of his black coat. But he chose not to distract Zule with another cigarette.

"Did you know Dr. Despres?" he asked.

"Barely. Barely an hour."

"You met—was it in the morning? About what time?"

"Eleven or so."

"He was shot close to five."

"I did not see him again until just a few minutes before he was shot."

The French soldier, who gave no indication of being attuned to their Bosnian-language conversation, sat up in his chair and waved his own cigarette pack at Zule. She put her hands before her chest in a shunning motion, mitigated by a smile.

"But thank you," she called over to the soldier in English.

"Yes, thank you," Tedic said, including himself in appreciation of the soldier's generosity. It was a way of conveying to the Frenchie that they had exchanged responsibility for the relief of Zule. Tedic went on, "You were conversing?"

"When he was shot? Yes. He had just finished telling me about his son and daughter. His daughter wants to be a doctor."

"Her name? We might help you get a letter to her."

"I don't remember. He didn't mention it. Really, he didn't have the chance."

Tedic had learned from trying to elicit confessions from students that silence could encourage disclosure. He stared back blankly.

"I mean," Zule continued in the silence, "the shooting came that quickly. Within a few minutes."

"I understand. Would you say two minutes after you started talking?"

"Maybe closer to three or four. He was putting out his cigarette."

"He had smoked down a cigarette. You had already finished yours?"

"I didn't finish mine."

"You lit them at different times, then?"

"In fact, no," said Zule. There was a note of surprise in her voice. "It was off the same flame, in fact. The doctor had a very sweet"—and here she flicked her right thumb—"little Dupont lighter."

Tedic stopped for a moment to squeeze his eyes, as if to visualize some delicacy of which he had only read descriptions. "It is what a man of distinction carries," he said. "He had been all over the world, you know. I would guess that a man so gallant would not light his cigarette before lighting yours."

"I don't believe he did," said Zule. "But more or less at the same time."

"Yours before his?"

She paused, recalled to the last act of a nightmare. "Yes."

"He insisted on this? You did?"

"He didn't insist. It was what he did."

"A gentleman. So, let me understand," said Tedic quietly. "You go out of the loading-dock door at the same time, light up cigarettes at the same time. But he finishes his ahead of you, puts it out, and then is shot. While your cigarette is still dwindling."

"Yes."

Tedic gave Zule another blank look, but she moved no further.

"Yes," she repeated, letting the word hang between them.

"How far from the end?" Tedic asked finally.

"I don't know. Enough so that I didn't look every few seconds."

"Two or three puffs?"

"Probably."

"You each had the same make of cigarette?"

"Gauloises. From the same box."

"Ah. A Gauloise must be nice now."

"It was."

"Perhaps the doctor left the rest of his pack."

Zule scowled at the implication that she would plunder a dead man's pockets for his cigarettes. "Perhaps," she said. "You are welcome to look. I will never smoke one again."

Tedic made sure to cringe. He wanted the nurse to have the satisfaction of winning a point, and play on.

"So," he resumed, "you light up the same make of cigarette at the same time, but he finishes his ahead of you."

"Yes."

"Well, we are not machines. One inhales more than the other. One talks more than the other."

"Maybe having two or three last puffs of a French cigarette meant more to me than it did to him," said Zule.

"For certain. You were talking?"

"For a couple of minutes."

"For three or four minutes."

"Three or four minutes, then."

"Talking, then. About what?"

Zule flailed her hands impatiently. "I told you—his home in France."

"Wife? Kids? Dogs? Horses?"

"Ex-wife, two kids. I don't know the rest."

"And how was it that you opened up this particular avenue for your first conversation and the last two minutes of Dr. Despres's life?"

"There's no mystery."

"Demystify it for me, please."

"I wondered where he was from," said Zule. "I asked him. I asked him if he was from Paris."

"Why Paris?"

"*Everybody* knows Paris."

Tedic consciously leaned back from Zule, affording her enough room to fidget. "Yes, everybody wants to see Paris," he said. "You didn't know he was from the hospital in Rouen?"

"I didn't know *anything*."

"Why was it important to know anything about Dr. Despres?"

"I was being sociable," said Zule.

"Being sociable wouldn't seem to be utterly necessary these days," Tedic said.

"All right, then. Why don't we let the savages take over right now? I was making conversation."

"If I were a doctor," Tedic professed to muse, "and had come into a hell like this, I think I would be the one asking questions. How do you live? Where do you go for fun?"

"Nothing like that."

"He asked you nothing?"

"I don't *remember*," Zule fairly hissed. "I wanted to hear what the real world was like."

"You kept him talking, then."

"He was nice. He talked to me."

"Until he was shot."

"He was not shot because he was talking to me!"

Tedic decided that he and the nurse were beginning to thread themselves into the ground. He sprang to his feet. When Zule looked up in bewilderment, he began to lift her up by the loose white coat around her shoulders, as if he were plucking a disobedient student out of a lunchroom seat. Tedic caught a glimpse of the Frenchie, who was roused by the commotion but didn't interfere or follow. After all, he was under orders not to intervene in assaults.

Tedic took hold of Zule's arm and steered her quickly out of the storeroom and through the groaning steel door. Thin pillars of flashlight slashed the night. French soldiers looked up only briefly from their duties, drawing down tape.

"This is where you were standing?" Tedic demanded with more force than volume.

"Out here, yes."

"Over where? Show me, please."

There was not really a pause between the sentences—and not really a "please." The railing against which the nurse and the doctor had perched was an hour's dark harder to pick out. Zule had to squint, and hold out her hand, as if she were searching for a light switch in a darkened hall. In the days when light switches worked.

"I was like this," she said, turning toward Tedic. "He was standing alongside. Then, to light the cigarette, he stepped *here*." Zule took some satisfaction in taking hold of Tedic's shoulders roughly. "Then, as we talked, he moved to face me."

"As the two of you were talking," said Tedic. "About children, ex-wives, and four hundred cheeses."

"We were talking."

"Replay those moments for me, please."

"I'm not sure I remember."

"It was only two minutes, right?" said Tedic. "Three at the most. You are a woman who has to remember lymphocytes, phagocytes, and thrombocytes." Assistant principals absorb a great deal of extraneous information against that one day when it might become useful. "Please trouble your memory banks to recall a couple of minutes of conversation."

Zule looked over at the soldiers engaged on the floor with rolls of tape, scrawling into field notebooks. They offered no assistance.

"He began," she said. "He asked, 'Where can I smoke?' "

"No one would have prevented the great Dr. Despres from lighting a cigarette anywhere. Surely you told him that?"

"I told him that our hospital administrator does not think smoking is modern. Miss Ademovic scares people."

"Then you led him here?"

"I said, 'We have a place, let me show you.' Something like that."

"You didn't just give him directions?"

"He was a visitor. I didn't want him going down dark halls."

"So your humanitarian instincts induced you to lead him out here."

"Bastard." Zule pronounced the word thoughtfully, as if she were identifying a dark spot on an X-ray.

"I confirm your diagnosis," said Tedic. "And so then, please, what happened?"

Zule paused—to show that she could.

"He lit my cigarette. He lit his."

"Yours first?"

"He was a gentleman, I told you."

"I remember that you mentioned his lighter."

"A Dupont. Black and gold. He flicked it once, twice, then the third produced a flame."

"Where is this lighter now, I wonder?"

"I expect it's still in his pants. Or perhaps in *your* pocket. You may search my belongings. *Bastard!* Do you really think I got a man killed because I wanted his cigarette lighter?"

"Not at all," said Tedic. "But until a few months ago I would not have thought that one of my neighbors would cut the throat of the little girl who lived downstairs because he thought she would grow up to be his enemy. What we used to think . . ." Tedic let the thought trail away.

Zule's face had hardened. The sprinkling of freckles that usually suggested perpetual girlhood now tightened across her face like bolts.

"I told Dr. Despres," she said, "that he could get a lot for such a lighter and his cigarettes."

"Such as?"

"Drugs, sex. Lots of new best friends."

"A curious thing to tell a visitor."

"I was trying to tell him how things are here."

"The humanitarian again."

"You make that sound like an insult."

"I don't find humanitarianism despicable," said Tedic. "Merely useless. Did this advance the conversation as you had hoped?"

"I hoped for nothing," said Zule. "I think I asked him how long he would be here. He said maybe a week. He wanted to get the skin-graft machine working. He said, 'I don't want to leave until it's working. Maybe until then you can use a good pair of hands.' "

"And you took this—may I ask—in what way?"

"In the only way there was." Zule had exploded, if quietly. *"An offer of help from a skilled surgeon."* She spat out the last two words to emphasize the difference between Dr. Despres's proficiency and Tedic's.

"Nothing more?" he asked.

"What more? What madness are you dreaming?"

"Dreaming is enticing," said Tedic. "More seductive than ever, I would say. So here are the two of you, attractive adults, marriage survivors, parents, bright, pleasing in appearance, I would say, thrown together into the fires of hell. It would be only natural, wouldn't it?"

"It was a two- or three-minute conversation."

"Lives pass in seconds these days."

"I asked him about his hometown. He said it was pretty. Tourists come to see where Jeanne d'Arc was burned."

"Jeanne was from Orléans."

"This is crazy," said Zule. "Where she was *burned*." Tedic took a half step backward.

"Where she was *burned*," he agreed, on the strength of her certitude. "And now, let me ask, because it seems to me we are hovering over the defining point in the conversation—three minutes, one, it doesn't matter. You and the doctor are mature people. You know how to sort through the tomato basket. I know, you are about to point out, 'We didn't even have time to smoke a cigarette together.' Rationally, you are right. But we are protons and electrons, not rational elements. Put some people smack up against each other—nothing catches. Others journey from another part of the world and"—Tedic clapped his hands loudly— *"smack!"*

Zule hunched over as Tedic spun out his analysis, like a woman caught in the rain at a bus stop.

Tedic took her acquiescence as encouragement. "I know this state of mind," he continued. "I have spent my professional life trying to fathom adolescents. None of us ever gets beyond, oh, fourteen years old in such matters. You try out the sound of your name beside his. You imagine how your friends will tell your story. A distinguished man of the world, his heart pierced by misery so immense he cannot get his arms around it. So he lifts *you,* the healing angel, into his arms. Some silvery duke to sweep your soiled Cinderella skirts out of the blood and carry you back to the family estate. You can sleep softly there, between linen sheets. You can awaken to see apples blooming, not just stumps of trees that have been cut down for heat. There, you can open the windows and watch cows chewing placidly on grass, and apple-cheeked French children tumbling after soccer balls."

Tedic finally ignited the fireball he had been trying to set off—a detonation of rage in which Nurse Rasulavic burned down to find something unspoken and unsuspected in herself. When she cried this time, the tears spilled quickly down her face.

"I steered him—out here," she began in a gasp, "because *I wanted him for myself*!"

Tedic stood back, as if he had dropped a glass. He waited a minute—he had inflicted the same kind of treatment so many times on fourteen-year-old girls that he impassively counted to sixty in his mind—before speaking, being certain to stay a body length away from Nurse Rasulavic, who had sunk to her knees.

"And so he was yours, in his last few minutes. I am sorry. I *really* am *almost* sorry to put you through this. But we needed to know if you took the doctor out here to see if you two would stick. Or if you brought him outside and got him to stand up and light a cigarette to light a sniper's shot into his head. Nothing else matters quite as much now."

THE HOME MINISTER brought Tedic's finding that a Serb sniper had fired the shot that killed Dr. Despres to the U.N. administration building near the airport. U.N. bureaucrats now sat blandly at steel desks that, only a few months earlier, had been occupied by travel consultants and transport brokers. He was directed into the office of a Mr. Benoît, a Belgian functionary with a broad, red-brown mustache. Mr. Benoît knew what was coming and didn't wait to hear it.

"I cannot accept this finding," he said. His one visible touch of élan was to wear a black turtleneck sweater that slouched down from his throat, almost in frown lines. Like Dr. Despres's khakis, Benoît's sweater bore the folds of prior service in the globe's troubled zones.

"We are conducting our own investigation," he said. "And so far we have found no reason to exclude the prospect that Dr. Despres was shot by someone on this side of the line. He was a world-renowned humanitarian, you know. He closed wounds on the front lines of Ethiopia and Somalia without suffering a scratch. He comes to Sarajevo and gets shot in the head."

The Home Minister had become ashamed of his appearance when meeting foreign officials. Other members of the Bosnian cabinet could travel to conferences in New York or Vienna. The meetings might have done little to secure Bosnia, but those Bosnian politicians in the delegation could at least refresh themselves and repair their wardrobes. When the doors shut on their foreign hotel rooms, most leaped at the chance to punch the numbers of a working phone. They ordered up steak and scotch from room service, telephoned relatives in the West, and called down to have their suits taken away for cleaning. They would travel with half a dozen pairs of shoes, which would hang like white bat's nests from the door handles of their rooms until they were picked up for shining by the valet. They would wrench on the showers and let the hot water gush over their heads until it soaked into their bones.

But the Home Minister was confined to Sarajevo. He was sure he looked dirty and bedraggled to visiting Western Europeans. He could bathe only infrequently. He was lucky to shave every third day. His one London pinstripe was stiffening with sweat and grime. He could feel the trousers stick to his flanks and scuff his backside as he squirmed in his seat, drawing his words out carefully.

"We are saddened and outraged, too," he told Benoît. "Please do not consider our outrage reduced if I note that we—you, none of us—also cannot keep children in this city from getting shot where they sleep on bathroom floors."

But this remark only annoyed Benoît. "We cannot stop a war," he said, "when two peoples are determined to have one."

"We consider this a case in which one people is determined to annihilate the other," said the Home Minister.

"I think we can stop this business far short of that."

"How far?" asked the Home Minister, whose voice now had a slight edge. "Can you share the news? After fifteen thousand lives? Fifty thousand? I would like to be able to tell our citizens how many of our shoes we must burn in order to have heat this winter."

The Home Minister could see a couple of framed citations on the wall behind Benoît's slight shoulders. He couldn't read them; they were probably in Flemish. But between those indecipherable certifications was a portrait-size photograph of Benoît, plumper in a pale gray suit and flapping black tie, shaking hands with a dark-haired woman who was improbably stunning for a bureaucrat's walls. The Home Minister allowed his eyes to linger discreetly for a moment: *Bianca Jagger*. He guessed that Benoît had been mayor of some modest city, lost his office, and enlisted in the U.N.'s bureaucracy. He was sure that the hope of another small chance to meet the likes of Bianca Jagger was what had kept Benoît in public service.

"The knights and dragons in this city are not as easy to distinguish as you insist," Benoît finally said. "This is not always a struggle between good and evil."

"No," said the Home Minister. "Merely between life and death."

Benoît went on placidly. "At that target, at that range, we must begin with the supposition that the shot came from your side."

"Our preliminary evidence suggests otherwise," said the Home Minister. "The ammunition is conclusively a 7.62 X 39-millimeter shell fired from an AK-47. The Yugoslav National Army possesses several million such weapons."

"You don't?"

"Your good offices have imposed an arms embargo that effectively prevents us from possessing anything that can be used to defend ourselves. You will see, in any case." And as Benoît began to fulminate, the Home Minister laid a brown envelope on his desk. "The angle and size of the wound suggest that the shot that struck home could only have been fired from one of the taller buildings almost directly south. From the other side."

Benoît did not reward the envelope with so much as a look. "And why would they shoot a French doctor when they are pleading for Europe to support their Serb state?"

"No Bosnian would shoot a man who had come here to help."

"Oh, come," Benoît said. "Save that line for your suave spokesmen crying on the BBC and CNN. We both know there are Muslims who would shoot a French doctor to make it appear as if Serbs had. 'Oh, those monsters! They rape our women and shoot children. Look—now they have even gunned down a gallant European doctor. Help us, Europe! Save us, America! Rescue us from those swarthy swine!' "

The Home Minister was nearly pleased to see the Belgian show some sign of real indignation. But the Home Minister restrained himself; patting the fingers of his right hand on the envelope helped. "Our preliminary findings are here," he said simply. "I think it is clear which side rules this city with sniper fire."

Both men were glad of the formalities that permitted them to say goodbye quickly and civilly.

BUT BY THE time the Home Minister reviewed the meeting with Tedic, he had begun to have some doubts. "God forbid, maybe it did come from our side," he said. "We have had to pass out so many guns. There are people who will shoot a dog, a doll, a doctor—no difference. At what distance do they say the shot was fired?"

"About six hundred meters south," said Tedic. The Home Minister shook his head.

"Shit—the Bristol Hotel?"

"No. Across the river. Probably an apartment tower in Grbavica."

Neither man needed to remind the other that their security forces had considered that area across from so many shattered buildings inaccessible and unavailing for a sniper's roost.

"All the same," the Home Minister said finally, "I'm glad it was the Frenchies who found the 7.62 X 39-millimeter round. What if your friend Cibo had plucked it out of the cup and announced that it was a round from one of our guns?"

"I was prepared to swallow it on the spot," declared Tedic.

THE HOME MINISTER had several small plastic bottles of drinking water on the edge of his desk, and he handed one to Tedic. They unscrewed the caps and touched the bottles together for a squashy plastic toast.

"To Dr. Despres," intoned the minister. "A good man. God bless him. And please, God, send no more like him." The men clapped their bottles together with vehemence and brittle little laughs.

"Yes," said Tedic. "We don't need Dr. Schweitzers. We need howitzers."

DR. DESPRES'S REMAINS were respectfully repackaged and conveyed to his home in Normandy. The doctor had not been an observant Catholic. He had seen too much mindless, unmerited suffering in the world to believe in a moral puppet master. But his family, friends, and colleagues prepared a huge and affecting memorial for him in the church of the Place du Vieux Marché, where a bishop declared that as Joan had once sacrificed her life for France and God, so Dr. Despres had given his life to uphold France's good name and God's work.

Alma Ademovic could not send a card or make a phone call. But she arranged with the Home Minister to include her name in an official message of condolence approved by the Bosnian cabinet. After she had heard a brief reference to the doctor's funeral on the BBC, she found Zule Rasulavic in the hospital's hallway and motioned to the brown box of delicacies that the doctor had brought along just days earlier.

"Tidbits and luxuries," she told the nurse. "Cheese, coffee, cookies. Give a bit to everyone, patients and staff, as far as it will go. And remind them," she called back as she turned to walk to her office, "that it came from Dr. Despres."

25.

OVER THE NEXT FEW WEEKS, THREE MORE PEOPLE WERE SHOT TO death in places that had been assumed to be inaccessible to snipers.

A man was found early one morning, splayed out beside the parking spots in the enclosed courtyard of the Presidency Building on Marshal Tito Boulevard. He lay face down over a scattering of crushed plastic water bottles, a single 7.62 X 39-millimeter bullet lodged in his right shoulder blade, no identification in his pockets, and a face that no one professed to recognize.

"A drifter, a squatter, a pain in the ass," said Tedic. "But dead he is a marker for dangerous territory."

A Bosnian captain at the scene who had once competed in the biathlon with Coach Dino Cosovic found the shot that felled the man highly improbable. "Not unless they have a balloon they can use to hover above us," he said, pointing to the severe downward trajectory of the bullet. The captain told Tedic that the man must have been shot a block away, on an open section of Marshal Tito Boulevard, and had staggered into the courtyard for help; or just to die.

But no one on duty in the basement of the building recalled hearing a cry or shout. Perhaps they were merely loath to reveal that they had not dashed out of their brick citadel to help a wounded man. Tedic found the theory suspect, in any case. There was no trail of blood leading to the man's body. And, as Molly pointed out, no blood had trickled down from the wound, as would have been the case if the man had staggered upright for a block. The man's slacks were inescapably filthy—stretchy, maroon nylon Tito-era trousers—but there were no fresh tears or abrasions along the knees to suggest that he had crawled before collapsing atop the clutter of squashed bottles.

"If he had crawled," said Molly, "the shooter would have finished him off back in the street."

"Why waste a bullet on a man who's bleeding to death?" asked Tedic.

"Compassion," Molly said with grim humor. "They've got bullets enough to be generous."

Tedic bent over the dead man's body, pinching folds of the shiny maroon fabric in his fingers and stretching it out the way a child might tug on a rubber band. "Imagine," he said, "meeting your Maker wearing"—and here Tedic pulled on the slacks in comic disdain—"these circus pants. Just a lucky shot?" he asked after a pause.

"Fluky. If we're lucky," said Molly, "I'd say someone got up somewhere and arced one lonely, lovely round exactly right."

THE VERY NEXT day, a woman pushing her child in a stroller toward a water line behind the barrier of gutted trucks and buses on Sutjeska Street was shot in the top of the head. She fell forward—Allah be praised, said the Home Minister—onto the stroller and thus protected her two-year-old son.

The citizens standing in line had believed they were sheltered behind the barrier. The woman gasped and blood sputtered out of her mouth while her son screamed. People rolled into gutters and under the bus, a chorus of screams mingling with the scraping and clattering of empty water bottles. The boy shrieked; his mother bled. Voices began to call out from gutters and behind walls.

"We must help her!"

"She's dead!"

"How do you know, Dr. Without Borders?"

"She's not breathing! That's a hint!"

"Her child is screaming!"

"His mother is dead and he's scared. He'll bloody scream for the rest of his life!"

"We should at least lift her body off him."

"Her body shields her child. She wouldn't want to be moved. It's not worth the risk."

"Whoever you are, you're a selfish pig!"

"Run out yourself! We'll bury you with your medal for stupidity!"

It was almost ten minutes before a brewery truck bearing Tedic could pull up to the scene and take the dead mother into their load. She was dark-haired and thin-boned, and felt as light as a sack of dry leaves when Tedic took her shoulders and Mel lifted her feet to place her in the truck. Tedic himself picked up the frightened brown-headed boy, his small legs churning, and tucked him into the arms of a policeman. Tedic then made a point of pacing around the splatter of blood surrounding the empty stroller, while people cautiously began to creep out of their burrows along the street.

"Brave and noble Sarajevans," he intoned. "I hear about you all on the BBC. I must say, you don't look the way you have been described."

But by the time Tedic reported to the Home Minister in the basement of the Presidency Building, his sarcasm was directed at the deceased. "What is a mother doing with her child out on that kind of street, anyway?" he asked.

"Going for water, like everyone else," answered the Home Minister. "There were two empty bottles alongside the boy."

"So!" said Tedic. "If she had left the boy behind, she might have carried back more water."

"Tedic, it is surely best for the world that you have no children," the Home Minister said with a weary shake of his head. "Claimed and acknowledged, in any case. Best for you. Certainly best for the children. Anyone with even a few nieces and nephews will tell you that you can't leave a child cooped up all the time, never breathing fresh air."

But Tedic came back credibly. "I have so many broken windows and mortar holes in my apartment, I gag on the fresh air," he said.

THE HOME MINISTER licked a finger and tried to smooth one of a score of crinkles on his soiled silver London tie. "What do we have here?" he asked finally. "A series of lucky, improbable, unrelated shots, or a pattern?

"Have you heard the Knight?" asked Tedic.

The Home Minister shook his head.

"His words would encourage the latter view." Tedic read some lines from a transcript. "Perhaps they are just words," he said. "Okay. Just yesterday morning our friend begins playing Peter Tosh. *Brothers of scorn in exile for so long, we need majority rule. Early morning dew, fight on,* et cetera." Tedic's Caribbean accent was unconvincing.

"A favorite of my daughter's," said the Home Minister gloomily. "Twisted to become a Serb anthem with steel drums."

Tedic ran his finger over a new paragraph. "Okay. Then he says, 'You know, Muslims, there's something your government won't tell you. They don't think you deserve the truth. You are dolls in a shooting gallery to them. They force you to dodge bullets and go hungry until they can strike their deals and fly into lush exile in the south of France.' "

"If we get to choose," the Home Minister interrupted, "I'd prefer Florida. I find I'm always cold."

"Winter in San Juan, summer in Gstaad is how I've arranged my fantasy life," said Tedic. "Our friend goes on. 'What do you think they're doing,' he asks, 'when they jet off to conferences in Vienna and London? They don't come back waving peace treaties, do they? No gifts for you. What has your mixed-ethnic assembly of Muslim fanatics, Serb stooges, thick-skulled Croats, and anteater-nosed Jews actually done?' "

"Well, this thick-skulled fanatic," observed the Home Minister with an edge, "hasn't been to so much as Zagreb since the start of things."

"He has a phrase coming up," said Tedic, scanning the next section. " 'They have only gotten your friends and family killed. They have only made you starve and freeze. The Americans have a new grinning possum for president. He wouldn't fight for his own country. What makes you think he will risk any precious, pink-assed American boys for your lives?' "

"He's got a point there," said the Home Minister.

" 'Here's what your government won't tell you, Muslims.' " Tedic put the Knight's voice back into his own. " '*We can hit you anywhere*. All those barriers and blind spots? Mere decoration. They are fortifications for fools. Their barricades are as flimsy and worthless as toilet tissue—if you remember toilet tissue. And your leaders know it. Ask around. Every week people are getting shot in what are supposed to be safe zones. The truth? *No place* is safe. We Serbs have a viper here who can thread a bullet into your brain even if you lock yourself inside the basement vault of a bank on Branilaca Sarajeva Street. He is that good. His bite is fatal. He is that poisonous. Where can you turn? How can you breathe? Every step you take—' "

"It should not be difficult to guess the musical accompaniment," the Home Minister interjected, signaling that the point had been made. *"Every breath you take?"* The Home Minister's voice rose in a question. *"Every move you make, step you take, I'll be watching you?"*

"Sting," agreed Tedic. "Like the sting of the viper."

"Let's not get carried away with metaphor," said the Home Minister. He rose from his seat and began to slap his own arms against the gloom and frostiness of the basement.

26.

AMELA AND IRENA WERE ABLE TO TALK THE NEXT WEEK, AND THE week after that. Zoran would stand next to his cab while the girls went back and forth for ten minutes of conversation. Amela had found the *Q* from January 1992. It had pictures of the *Q* Awards ceremonies at Abbey Road Studios.

"There's a picture of a guy named Lou Reed," Amela said. "Short and wrinkled."

"Our parents like him," said Irena. "Over."

"Seal likes him. Seal got best newcomer award. He looks *sooo* damn sexy."

"Tell, tell. Over," said Irena.

"Purple velvet coat, pure white shirt, unbuttoned, diamond necklace, and black leather pants," Amela said, describing it. "Big, big diamond buttons on the crotch. Oh-ver."

"Oh, my," said Irena. "Over." She pretended to fan herself with one of her grandmother's old winter gloves.

"An article on the fifty best albums of last year. Over."

"Who?" asked Irena. "Over."

"Elvis Costello, Billy Bragg, Nirvana, Ice-T." Amela's voice clicked out as she used both hands to turn a page.

"Lenny Kravitz?" asked Irena. "Over."

"For sure. Over."

"Talk about sexy! Over."

"Sean Lennon with him. Do you think he would be famous if he was Sean Jezdic? Sting, of course. *The Soul Cages.* Over."

"Sean grew up quick," said Irena. "So young when his father got shot. Sting is still sexy. But do you remember a single song from that?"

"Neil Young and Crazy Horse—a live tour album." Amela's voice clicked out again for a moment. "Oh, God, he is an old fuck. Why does he drive our mothers wild?"

Zoran turned around and signaled to Irena. "Tell your friend that we old fucks like Neil Young," he said. "There are a lot of old fucks in the world."

"Oh, God!" Amela suddenly exclaimed. "A story. Strange. Group in Nottingham. Carcass. Heard of them? Over."

"Never," Irena said.

"Me neither. Their stuff is *hard-gore* in English. Over."

"Porno? Over."

"No, *gore,*" Amela said. "Like a wound, my driver says. They all hide under long hair and wear black. One guy says, 'No one likes to talk about it, but rotting is a pretty exciting process.' Over."

"Oooh," Irena sneered. "It is not. Over."

"Want to hear their big song?" asked Amela. "Over."

"Sure. Over."

" 'Vomited Anal Track.' Over."

Irena laughed until she began to cough up old cigarette smoke. By the time she had fumbled the microphone back into her hand, Amela's laughing voice had sputtered back on.

"Listen. I'm thinking," she said. "Keep this secret. Can you trust your driver? Over."

"For a carton of cigarettes, sure." Irena glanced over at Zoran and grinned as she used to grin at players she bumped. "I get paid cigarettes," she added.

"There's a spot at the airport," said Amela. "People can wave at each other. Over."

"Of course. I've heard. French soldiers out there. Over."

"Our boys, too. So what if we both showed up sometime?" Amela said. "Over."

"At the airport? Over. To wave? Over."

"To wave," said Amela. "I'd like to show you something, too. Over."

Irena peered at Zoran's face as if he held some answer. She could think of only one thing. "Of course," she said. "We can figure that out. To see you? It's over a hundred yards. Over."

"I guess. Over."

"And you've got to be careful. Everyone has a gun out there. Over."

"We will."

"To see each other? Amazing! Over," said Irena.

Both girls had variable schedules. They could be called in to work for the day or the night. But, as it happened, both could usually figure on being free at six at night, when there should be enough light to get to the airport, and enough to see each other wave. Irena said that the falling darkness would actually help mask their routes to get safely back to their cabs and apartments.

"You are so clever!" Amela enthused. "You should be a general, not a clerk. Over."

"I'm not cut out for brewery work," said Irena. "That's for sure. Seeing you! Amazing. Over." They agreed on a date two weeks from then.

IRENA FIGURED THAT the price of a carton ought to include a brief stop before she was delivered back home, and prevailed upon Zoran to stop first at the central synagogue. There was a room in the basement where old clothes were stored. Clothes were given out freely to anyone who could offer a convincing case for need, but you had to make the case. Synagogues in New York, Paris, and London had collected bales of discarded tweeds, socks, and boots. But the Serb siege stymied delivery. The thin stocks there now were mostly the unintended bequest of dead people. The synagogue sent people in to receive their donation before squatters and scavengers—who, to be sure, also needed clothes—could help themselves.

Irena found an elderly man with an unexpectedly powerful torso sitting on a folding chair, reading a yellowed copy of the *Guardian*. More James Joyce letters had been released in Dublin, but not, Irena gathered from the headline, all that had been promised. Seven-year-olds were being tested in Leeds; their parents were upset. The West, thought Irena, where people fight over a writer's old notes and seven-year-olds don't get tested by gunfire.

"Excuse me," she said.

The man looked up, but barely.

"I have a friend," she said. "He is embarrassed. He needs clothes. He is cold."

The elderly man seemed to welcome the diversion, even as he discouraged expectation. "I just can't give clothes out," he said, rising from his chair. "We have to make sure people really need them. We don't want to give out clothes and see them sold on the black market."

Where they might be exchanged for food, thought Irena, but kept the observation to herself.

"He really needs them. He has just one set of everything, and it's falling apart."

"Who is your friend?" the man asked skeptically. Irena could see that it was not only his broad arms that had gotten him assigned to the storeroom.

"No one special. I mean, quite special, but no relation. He lives in our building."

"Got a name?"

"He is too embarrassed, I told you."

"Why doesn't he have clothes?"

"He was—we all were—driven out of Grbavica with nothing."

"That's what everyone says," the man said.

"I'm telling the truth," said Irena. "I am Irena Zaric. Number Three High School."

The man grunted and brought his thick arms closer to his sides.

"The basketball player." It was a declaration, and Irena returned it simply.

"The same."

"Your friend," he continued. "Perhaps there are other forms of assistance he could use. He is eating?"

"Fairly well, yes. We help out."

"We serve lunch here for elderly people."

"He is not that elderly."

"No one asks for birth certificates," said the man.

"He is embarrassed, I keep telling you."

"What does he eat?" Irena was taken by surprise. It was a case she had not expected to make.

"What we eat. Beans, rice, canned stuff. Grass and leaves, when it was warmer. Powdered cheese and milk. Olives. Whatever."

"Has he ever gone on the black market? You can get clothes for olives."

"He doesn't get out. He is embarrassed, I keep saying."

"You've given him what you can? I think it's a Talmudic saying. We should do all we can to help others before we ask others to help."

"It sounds like the Koran, too," said Irena. "We have given him socks and stuff. But—we took over our grandmother's place. She didn't keep men's clothes."

"Your grandmother—Gita Zaric?"

"Of course."

"I haven't seen her," said the man.

"She is *dead,*" Irena said, and sensed that the game had suddenly turned in her favor.

"I'm sorry," the man said after a pause. "I hadn't heard. There are too many to keep track. This man. How tall?"

"A little taller than me. We can't stand up much in our building."

"How old?"

"Forties, I guess. Like what's-his-name—Brian Wilson. But not as fat."

"Hoo," said the man. Irena thought she could detect a stifled smile. "We have nothing that big. No one here is that big anymore. Your father—can't he help him out?"

"My father—I explained, all of us—left with just the clothes on his back."

"Why didn't he pack a case?"

"We did. All of us. We were robbed, too."

"That's easy to say."

"Because it's true."

"Kids will do anything these days to get money for beer, smokes, rubbers, drugs. If I give you clothes, and you sell them, understand: you can only fuck me over once. Does your father know you're here?"

Irena tried to fight back tears, then realized that she didn't have the strength. The man became fuzzy, and when she finally spoke she had to bite off the words between sobs and sniffles.

"You nasty old son of a bitch!" she yelled. "The clothes are *for* my father! My father is digging *shit holes!* He's wearing shreds, and *they're* falling apart! I see him shivering in the middle of the day, like an embarrassed little boy who has wet his pants. He sleeps all the time, because he's bored! And cold. His mother is dead. My brother is—God knows where by now—wrestling with Serbs in some bloody forest. I'm only trying to get my father a warm shirt and a pair of pants with no holes. And *you*—you, you mean, dumb, overbearing *bully*—guard this pile of old rags like they were the crown jewels!"

Without another word, the old man turned into the storeroom and came back with a heavy dark blue cotton shirt, thick gray cotton pants, and a pair of gray socks. He placed the clothes on his chair and shuffled slowly back into a closet. When he returned, he had a ribbed coffee-colored woolen sweater in his arms, topped by a dark blue ski mask.

"The mask," he said quietly, "may help your father when he digs. The sweater is a little worn, but fine." He pressed his thumbs down into the ribs of the fabric. "Thick. Feel it. Warm. Burberrys', a good name. It belonged to Mr. Levi. He got it on a visit to New Jersey," the man explained as he presented the pile to Irena, but turned away from her. "May your father wear it in good health."

He sent Irena off with the old *Guardian* he had been reading, and a *Jerusalem Post* besides. He told her to come to back if she needed anything, *anything* else.

IT GOT SO cold that the Zarics rarely went anywhere in the apartment but the living room and the bathroom. Mrs. Zaric moved their cookstove under the window, but burned it only at a low temperature. Smoke could draw sniper fire. When Irena returned home, she put the clothes and newspapers into her grandmother's old bedroom, where she sometimes retreated for a few minutes of privacy. Her parents understood; indeed, they welcomed an hour or two to themselves. Irena quietly tucked the shirt, slacks, socks, and ski mask into a drawer and held the sweater under her arm when she rejoined her parents in the living room.

"I found this at the brewery," she announced to her father. "No one minded—they all said I could bring it home for you."

Mr. Zaric rubbed his thumbs over and under the thick shawl collar.

"It's a very good garment," he declared. "Maybe twenty years old. Designed in Britain, made in Hong Kong—the best of both worlds. Are you sure Dr. Tedic said it was all right?"

"He said he wouldn't even know it was gone."

"How did it get there?" Mr. Zaric asked.

"No one seemed to know," said Irena. "Things get left. People don't know where else to bring them. Everyone supposes that whoever owned the sweater is dead. So you may as well wear it. Something so warm shouldn't be wasted."

Mr. Zaric thanked his daughter, and asked her to thank Dr. Tedic. He kept the sweater on his lap as he listened to an afternoon newscast from London and drifted off to sleep in a small pool of winter sunlight.

IRENA WENT TO work early the next morning. She rolled the man's shirt and trousers under her coat and slipped the ski mask into a pocket. She kept the *Guardian* and the *Jerusalem Post*, crumpling and yellowed, under her arm.

She rolled all of her new acquisitions into the sleeves and legs of Dragan's smock as she donned it in the back of the brewery truck. She folded the *Guardian* in half and tucked it into the belt of the smock. Allah be praised, she thought to herself, that Dragan liked his pita and strudel. She slipped the pages of the *Post* behind her, so that it fell over the small of her back.

There were two tall blue modern buildings in Marindvor, just over the river, known as Momo and Uzeir, after two characters in a continuing series of Bosnian jokes. (Momo breaks wind while he's standing in front of Uzeir in a water line. "Pardon the fart," says Momo. "That's all right," answers Uzeir. "Where did you get the beans?") The buildings were referred to as skyscrapers. Indeed, Sarajevans sometimes called them the Twin Towers, although they were a fifth as tall as the towers of New York's World Trade Center. Momo and Uzeir—no one knew which was which, who was Serb and who was Muslim—had been headquarters for an energy company.

The buildings were rigged with sprinklers that were thought to be as sophisticated and effective as any in, say, Toronto. But when they were bombed during the first days of the Serb assault, their water reserves had already been tapped by thirsty citizens. The fires had raged up and down unchecked. The flames burned away all papers, carbon copies, telephone messages, blueprints, schematics, family photos, memorandums, lamp shades, paper plates, manila folders, orange envelopes, and *cevapcici* wrappers. The blaze melted telephones into puddles of ooze, and linoleum-topped steel desks and foam-rubber chairs into scorched skeletons. The heat baked the stain-free nylon carpeting down to a squirrel-gray powder that stank of cold ashes and charred plastic.

Tedic hesitated to send snipers up into Momo and Uzeir. The buildings' floors were mostly bare. Flames, winds, and mortar fire had blown out most of the floor-to-ceiling windowpanes. Effective concealment seemed impossible. And yet both buildings were well situated across from Serb emplacements that had been set up between the airport and Grbavica. Molly and Tedic had worked it out.

When a new snow began to fall that morning, Tedic decided that the storm would drape a veil over the building. He sent Irena up to the sixth floor of the south tower. Irena, per Molly's more persuasive instruction, climbed to the seventh floor. She turned the corner and got thrown back—got frightened, really—by the intense wind and light. The brightness seemed to swell in the snow. But the staircase ran up the center of the tower.

If Irena got down on her knees in the ash and grit, no one across the way would be able to see her. But she might also not be able to find a shot. She needed to inch forward.

Irena took the newspaper pages from under her smock and crumpled the sheets and rolled them over the slick, smoky floor until they looked like game balls. She then slipped out the blue shirt, the gray slacks, and the ski mask, tucking the balls of newspaper into the legs and sleeves. She pressed two broad sheets together and rolled them into the size of a soccer ball, which she stuffed into the ski mask.

"I have kissed worse-looking boys than you," she said to her news-stuffed doll. She began to edge the figure toward the southern edge of the seventh floor. She took the tip of her rifle, poked it into the dummy's back, and pressed the figure forward slowly. Irena had once run a fifty-meter dash in six seconds. She could make that kind of sprint in thirty explosive steps, time after time, in a basketball game. But crawling twenty-five meters across the floor as slowly as a cockroach was harder by miles. Her ankles and toes ached from driving her weight across the floor so slowly. The floor bit into her elbows. Every inch stung her bones and stirred debris into her eyes.

The slow advance was meant to be undetectable to anyone across the way who might be training his field glasses over the vacant windows of the south tower. Irena crept. She slept for several minutes each hour. She wet herself after two hours, as she nosed through the snow that had sluiced in. Three hours of crawling brought her within three feet of the window frames, bordered at the bottom by low-rise platforms, no taller than her old athletic bag, which had covered the grilles of the building's heat and air-conditioning, and had now been rendered so spectacularly superfluous.

When Irena turned her head sideways, she saw a note that Molly had left two days ago, held fast against the grate—it was too good a joke to miss—by a refrigerator magnet from "Adamovic Undertakers. Putting Sarajevo to Rest Since 1955." Molly's writing was small and spidery.

> Long way from the Cape. Look down to yr right and you'll see the holy stones. Call when in the neighbourhood. Cheers.

THE SERBS HAD make a fine shooting perch of the Old Jewish Cemetery, on a hill just above Grbavica. It had location, elevation, and afforded snipers and mortar teams the shelter of scores of stone grave markers, from which they could choose their shots in almost leisurely security. Tedic, who had put the space under observation from Momo and Uzeir, had been told that Serb artillery crews could be seen unrolling blankets behind the stones for winter picnics.

There was a large stone shard directly ahead of Irena, gray like the ash and rubble falling and blowing all around her, although this stone had come from the remains of a mortar blast on Marshal Tito Boulevard and had been hauled up by Molly. Irena pulled the glove off her right hand to feel for the rags, cut from grain sacks, that she knew were wound around the stone.

She tapped the top of the wrapping until she felt something harder, colder than the stone, and more perfect. Oh my, she thought, it's there, and more beautiful than anything any other boyfriend has ever shown me. Master craftsmen at the Sarajevo Brewery had gouged a hole in the stone. They'd cemented an old .38 Browning police revolver—carried by Interpol forces across the continent, and by Serb gangs who needed a light, reliable weapon to shoot people when they rousted them from their homes—into the base of the rock. A chain trailed from the rags and across the stone—the kind of chain you might see rusting inside the flush mechanism of a toilet, which is exactly where Tedic had gotten it.

Irena tucked the paper-muscled shirt into the waist of the trousers and tied it with a rope. She moved the dummy behind the heating grille and balanced the paper-stuffed ski mask atop the torso. When she was certain that her sniper doll would hold his position in the wind and snow, she pushed the snout of her M-14 into the back of the ski mask, gently nudged her gun muzzle from left to right, and back again. The stuffed ski mask turned the way a searching head might turn behind a rifle. She took the end of the chain in her right hand and softly called out to Molly, who should have installed his thin shoulders behind the grille on the floor below by now.

"Our boyfriend is ready, Molls."

There was an anxious moment before she heard his voice chiming back through the ash and snow. "Lovely to hear you, dear," he said softly. "The play begins with you. Take your time."

The cheetah always looks for the abandoned baby wildebeest, Molly had told her the day before. *He doesn't pick on someone his own size.*

For fuck's sake, she had pleaded, *speak a language I understand, Molls. No parables. No tribal elder mumbo jumbo.*

I mean, said Molly, *that when we look weak, they attack. That's the law of this jungle, too.*

Irena took a breath. She counted to three, for no particular reason except that it came up more quickly than five. She feared she might not reach five. One, two, another breath. One, two, and then on this three she jerked on the chain. The chain tugged on the trigger of the gun, which was soldered into the stone. The Browning burst inside the rags. A wild shot went off. The gun muzzle flamed. The rags smoldered.

Across the way, Serb snipers behind the old stones in the cemetery saw Molly's abandoned wildebeest—a lone gunman, a scared kid—fire a wild, foolish shot. They saw their chance to slip their bullets into the shooter's brain while he was still frozen by the shock of the retort.

The first Serb shot clapped the air around Irena's ears. While she rolled over and away from her effigy just behind the heating grate, another bullet bloodlessly clipped the top of the dark blue ski mask she had left behind. It pinged into the ceiling above her, rattling emptily against the concrete like a thunderclap.

"Got them, love," Molly called up softly into the settling ash. "Hold tight."

Molly had seen a slim inch of ski mask and a glint from a glass scope on the other side rise above a stone. Irena tensed her bones, from her toes to her shoulders. She counted one, two, and then the sound of Molly's shot slapped her around the chest and made her ears quiver. By the time the thud died, she could hear Molly cooing from his perch below.

"Got one on the carpet, love."

Irena sprang to her feet. Through her scope she saw a gray shape lying facedown in the snow over a grave. A pink shroud blossomed—a peculiar word, but it's what came to her—around his shoulders. But the Angel of Death had friends. Irena saw another form come into sight against the snow.

Another sniper, she guessed, or a man on a mortar crew, had seen his comrade shot and sprang out to try to save his life. The figure slipped and fell down. He had pluck. He had valor. He groped, got up, and kept running. Irena saw his head and shoulders behind the snowy branches of a tree (she was a city kid, she reminded Tedic later, and didn't know the difference between an oak, a linden, and a palm). As he ran, he shook off snow, and his body stood out against the sprinkling whiteness drifting all around. She raised her rifle and flattened her feet against the floor. She placed her gun sight over the dead center of the broad black back and pulled the trigger against her chin until she felt the smack against her shoulder.

Irena fell to her knees. The shape plunged like a felled bird and flattened against the snow. She crept carefully toward the edge of the floor, and through the soft gauze of fat snowflakes she saw two pink shadows oozing. *Angels in the snow,* she thought.

TEDIC REWARDED MOLLY and Irena with hot baths. He had Mel fill old tin washtubs with scalding water heated in one of the brewing vats. Molly and Irena oohed and inched down into their respective tubs. The floor and walls of the basement were frigid. Steam roiled up from the washtubs, reddening and veiling their chalky bodies.

"The steam is delicious," said Molly. "Rather like hellfire, I imagine." He made a show of patting his cheeks.

Tedic wandered in to apologize. He had no bubble bath, he said. He did have a potent cognac, though, and they toasted the day's work. Irena exulted in feeling her toes again—she had almost given them up for dead—and the cognac braising her brain. But she and Molly didn't tell Tedic about the rag doll she had taken up to the girders. They might find the chance to use the ploy again. And besides—Irena's mother had taught her—it was good to have a few secrets sewn into your pockets, like spare coins.

Tedic said he had gone to see the rabbi at the central synagogue to explain that they had had to fire a few shots into the cemetery. Someone—two people, actually—had been killed, he said. He didn't want the rabbi to hear the news from the Knight, who might say that the snipers had merely been laying wreaths on the graves.

"I said to the rabbi, 'I beg you to understand, Rebbe, that turning the resting place of our ancestors—and for Sarajevans, they are *our* ancestors, too—into a sniper's nest offends all abiding Muslims.' " Tedic made a mock bow of prayer toward Molly and Irena, luxuriating in their tubs.

" 'But murderers are hiding behind those gravestones to rain death upon our city.' And the rabbi," said Tedic, "*the rabbi* shuffles over to a pillow on the floor, reaches behind, and picks up this bottle of cognac. And he thunders at me, like God himself. 'It is better that the stones and bones of our dead be burned to powder,' he says, 'than to see another living child shot down in our streets.' Then the rabbi unplugs the bottle and holds it out to me. He says, 'Give the bastards back *ten times* what they have given us! *Allah be praised*.' Now *there* is a religion *I* can believe in," said Tedic above Molly and Irena's laughter.

Tedic had an old teacher's intuition of when he was being left out, and the sense to accept it. He left the cognac on the brick ledge next to Molly and said hearty, brief goodbyes. The water in their tubs was cooling, the steam falling, flattening. Molly flung water from his fingers to grasp the cognac bottle—something Hungarian and unrecognizable—by the neck and pass it to Irena.

"The two people," she began. "You figure they were anyone you know? Old friends from the bush?"

"Oh, Christ, I never think of that. Vice versa for them, I'm sure. Could have been one of your old mates too, I suppose. Leave it out, love."

Molly splashed as he turned in his tub and peered over the side for the towels they had folded over their shoes.

"Even you, Molls?" said Irena. "There are things even *you* can't bear to wonder about?"

Molly cupped his hands, his exquisite nails steamed and gleaming, to hold some of the last hot water against his face.

"I try to think about what will keep me alive," he said.

"He was running to help his friend, Molls. It's what I'd do for you and the other way round." Irena was beginning to shiver as the sides of the tub cooled. "For fuck's sake, I got him in the back."

"They were trying to shoot us," Molly reminded her. "They would have shot at ten or twenty others who couldn't shoot back. They weren't in the cemetery just for a little groping and dry-humping, love."

"Still, still," said Irena. "Do you think—do you ever wonder—will we go to hell for it?"

"I'll get there way before you," Molly told her.

"Don't fend me off, Molls," said Irena. "We can be girls together. Pour it straight up. Don't save it till I'm older. I may not get much older. Hell may be something I need to know about. Like squeezing your eyes in the dark."

Molly motioned Irena to lift the cognac bottle up from her tub so that he could get hold of it. Her fingers were pink and pretty but trembled slightly in the creeping chill.

Molly sank his bony shoulders into the last layer of heat before popping back up. "When I was a young shoot—Dutch church and all—hell was the place we got sent for being bad," he said. "Now? I think She made hell so that folks in places like Sarajevo would know there's someplace worse."

They reached out for their towels, kidding each other like old teammates about their bruises and scars.

27.

A COUPLE OF WEEKS LATER, WHEN ZORAN DROVE IRENA OUT TO THE airport next to Dobrinja, the snows had hardened and the ice had turned a grimy gray. Zoran parked behind a block of bombed-out apartment buildings and stayed in his cab. Irena walked over the cold courtyards toward a row of hedges that Bosnian smugglers had claimed as a bastion. The Bosnian Army didn't try to displace them. A barrier of hardened professional criminals, ready to die for their plunder, was more dismaying to Serb marauders than Bosnia's army of conscripted clerks and nearsighted students.

A cluster of men in glossy leather jackets stood smoking behind one hedge. They carried their rifles over their shoulders as casually as if they were knapsacks. Irena almost stopped to admonish them: "Don't hold your gun that way if you're serious. You won't be able to find it to point it." But she understood—the roughnecks weren't interested in aiming their rifles.

A man in a smart fur cap snarled at her, "Whore, what are you doing here?"

Irena answered in an even tone. "Meeting a friend."

"Good. We can all use friends. Is your friend as pretty as you?"

"Prettier," Irena answered, with a willing smile.

"Good. We should all have a party." The man wiped the back of his hand against a three-day stubble.

"You don't understand," she said.

"*You* don't understand," he said more harshly.

"My friend," said Irena. "She is not just a friend. We are special friends. We are in love."

The man's gang snickered behind him and stamped their feet as they flicked ashes from their cigarettes.

"That's disgusting," he said. "That is sick." Irena contrived to look earnest.

"Allah made us so," she said.

"Allah has nothing to do with it," said the man. "Allah disapproves. American movies, American music, Sinéad O'Connor, and Elton John have turned you into a bull dyke."

"Then I'll pray for Allah to save me." Irena pressed on around the man and knelt down near the edge of one of the farther hedges to look across the landing strip.

"Allah is far away," he called after her. "I am here and now!" But he stayed on his side of the thicket.

U.N. SOLDIERS PATROLLED the airport. They were Frenchies during most shifts, spelled by Ukrainians and occasional Egyptians, posted to prevent Sarajevans from braving a salvo of Serb bullets to flee a hundred yards across the runway into unbesieged Bosnian territory. The Serbs said the Muslims could slip out from there to take up arms against Serbs. The Bosnians said that anyone who was rash enough to run through gunfire was probably more desperate to eat than to fight, but they had to accept the prohibition. (And, in any case, no one wanted to open a channel for evacuation that could empty the city and drop it, like a deflated football, into Serb hands.)

Smugglers and people wild or desperate enough to try looked forward to Ukrainians or Egyptians relieving the French. A wad of deutsche marks, a plastic flask of Dewar's, or a carton of Camels could induce a Ukrainian or Egyptian soldier to turn his back. Apprehending brave, desperate people gave the best of them no satisfaction anyway. Some Bosnian gangs had successfully bought off Serb units—bribed them to shoot their guns into the sky while gangsters ran across the runway with sacks of cocaine strapped to their waists and saddles of lamb across their backs. But the French didn't lack for money, meat, cigarettes, or alcohol; they were therefore depressingly incorruptible.

As the light flattened into a gold stream that flowed across the landing strip, Irena glimpsed the shoulder patches on three blue-helmeted soldiers: the blue, white, and red of France.

SHE SAW AMELA waving from under a tree that was just above the Serb side of the runway. Blond hair bouncing against her shoulders, still long, slightly curly, like corn silk at the ends, and a fine-boned hand waving at the end of a slender wrist. She wore a dark green coat. She was smiling. Her mouth was open. Irena caught a glimpse of white teeth, a pink flash of tongue, as if Amela were calling to her. Irena called back. "Hello! Hello!" Amela was holding a satchel in her left hand, her ball-handling hand. Perhaps she had been shopping. Irena imagined apples, oranges, walnuts, and bananas. "Hello! Hello!" she called.

Her words seemed to fall halfway across the field before her voice was swallowed by a larger sound. An aircraft had just landed on the western end of the runway, a dark gray-green transport, probably the last flight in the last light of the day. The whine of its engines overwhelmed Irena. It rolled slowly in between the two sides of the runway—snub nose, vast belly, beady windows, obese, dawdling wheels, and finally the stout tail with the yellow, red, and black patch of the German Air Force.

Craning around a wheel, Irena saw Amela galloping across the runway. Her blond curls, which she always wore pinned up in a game, flounced like a horse's mane with each stride. With no Frenchie to stop her on the Serb side of the field—why would any Serb risk a bullet to escape into beleaguered Sarajevo?—Amela was drawing near to the plane's rear wheels. Irena leaped into her own run. She had taken three, four strides when she saw that Amela's satchel had a mesh screen. A gray bird with a black beak and a sweet red feather-fluff of a tail was inside.

THE GIRLS RAN into each other's arms under the back end of the aircraft. They swung each other around in a dance step, locking arms, skipping, giggling, laughing, and crying too much to draw enough breath to speak. A Blue Helmet surprised them. He had the stock of his rifle against his chin, and was shouting in English into the scream of the engines.

"Get down!" he yelled.

They did.

"Go back!" he added. "Don't make me shoot!"

"We are friends!" yelled Amela.

"I'm not your friend," the soldier shouted. "My orders—keep people away."

Amela was on her knees, right hand stretched out to hold her up in the blast blowing back over their shoulders, left hand still locked onto the handle of Pretty Bird's case. Irena rolled over onto her stomach to see his pearly crown and black pebbly eyes, set in yellow, blinking back.

"This bird belongs to my friend," Amela shouted. "I must give him to her."

The soldier hesitated. He could embarrass himself trying to round up two teenage girls who were determined to outrun him. He could shoot them, of course. His standing orders were to open fire on anyone who refused to stop and return. But shoot two young girls for laughing and dancing in tearful reunion over a parrot? That could put his service photo into *Paris Match*. It could get him permanently posted to Chad.

"Give her the bird," he ordered. "Then both run back."

The German plane had pulled farther away, and the whimper of its engines trailed off. Amela pleaded from her knees. "*S'il vous plaît, mon capitaine*. Let us talk."

"This is not a café," said the soldier.

"It's been almost a year," said Irena. "We are sisters."

"Merde," he replied. *"Merde."*

"We are *like* sisters."

Irena heard the field boots of two more Blue Helmets stamping across the tarmac. But she didn't break away from the Frenchman's gaze. He looked from girl to girl, then held up his right arm to wave the other soldiers away. Cradling his rifle in the crook of his other arm, he flashed two fingers—pointedly, thought Irena—across the trigger guard.

"Two minutes. Two minutes. Then, run."

IRENA AND AMELA stayed on their knees, their fingers plaited together.

"We've packed his cage with seed," said Amela. "Enough for four months. This will all be over by then. If not, we'll get more."

"I can't—I can't think of the words to thank you," said Irena, squeezing Amela's hand until her fingertips were reddened like rows of candles.

"Don't. It will waste our two minutes. Pretty Bird has missed you."

"There's been a hollow space on my shoulder," said Irena. "That's for sure."

Amela took back a hand to draw two magazines from her right pocket. She had the April 1992 *VOX*, with Bruce Springsteen and Tina Turner sharing the cover in separate squares.

"Look at these," said Amela. "Bruce is back. Tina says she never wants to be young again."

"Me too," said Irena.

Amela tapped a British *Vogue*—from just last August. Geena Davis was on the cover in something black, lacy, and flimsy.

"Oooh, she is so long and beautiful," said Irena.

"It is a wonderful magazine," said Amela. "Tom and Nicole's new movie. A study says smoking gives you cancer but keeps you from losing your mind. There's a picture story on women shooters."

Irena hesitated, hoping to appear confused.

"Women *photographers*," Amela went on, unconcerned. "Fashion, war. They can do anything as well as any man. Better."

"They sure can. We can."

"Nermina," said Amela, shaking her head. "I can't get over it."

"Me neither."

"It's too much," she said. "Too many people. It is good to see you. Your brother?"

"We don't know," said Irena. "He went to London, he went to Chicago."

"Chicago!" Amela practically sang. "Michael Jordan and Toni Kukoc!"

"Tomaslav said he would tie up Toni for me," said Irena.

"I want Scottie Pippen."

"I'll tell him."

"How?"

"I'll tell Toni to tell Scottie."

The girls laughed, and rubbed their hands over each other's shoulders as they talked.

"Have you seen Jagoda?" asked Irena.

"No. I don't know what side of the city she's on."

"Coach Dino?"

"No. You hear of him," Amela explained. "He's a champion shooter."

"He's the best," Irena said with unconvincing disinterest. Then she slumped back to the ground and squeezed her eyes shut. When she spoke, her words came in little rushes of breath. "There's something. I haven't been able to tell anyone. Coach Dino. We had—something."

Irena heard Amela exclaim something in a small voice before she had the nerve to open her eyes.

"Oh, God," Amela repeated.

"It doesn't seem shocking now. So much else has happened."

"I mean, *I'm down on my knees, I want to take you there.*"

Irena used up two seconds of their two minutes just looking into Amela's mild and amused blue eyes.

"Coach was screwing you?" Amela asked.

"Yes." Irena felt Amela's hands reach back for her own and wind even deeper around her fingers.

"Me, too," said Amela. The German plane had rolled to a stop and cut its engines to a low whistle.

All Irena could say was, "The Magic Johnson jersey?"

"He gave it to me."

"He gave me a Michael Jordan."

The girls laughed and rocked back and forth on their knees in each other's arms on the cold field as the French soldier looked on from a distance.

"Do you remember Anica?" asked Amela.

"The center from Veterans. Dark hair, blue eyes. Snow White."

"*Snow White.*" Amela snickered. "She's in the army, too. Not long ago, I saw her at a fruit stand. She was wearing a Patrick Ewing jersey."

"I guess Coach Dino is doing okay," said Irena.

The soldier had clomped back above them. His rifle was slung down, but he waved two fingers into their faces. "Two minutes gone," he said. "Get going. Get out."

AMELA TURNED AS she ran back into the Serb woods.

"Tell your brother hello," she called out. "He's cute."

Irena looked around from her own sprint toward the hedges on the Bosnian side of the field. "I didn't know you'd noticed," she said.

Amela turned around and gripped her hands to her chest, as if she were launching a last shot from half-court. "Maybe there's one boy I can screw that you won't!" she yelled across the runway.

THE ZARICS OPENED a can of small German frankfurters in celebration of Pretty Bird's return. They wiped down his cage with a discarded sock and installed him in the living-room corner near where Irena bedded down. He was quiet through the preparations for dinner—no fizzes or whirrs—but apparently unperturbed at his relocation. Irena abandoned herself to the feeling that Pretty Bird was at ease and happy.

Mrs. Zaric brought Pretty Bird up to her mouth and kissed his black beak. She let him press his pearly crown into her chin. "Pretty Bird," she cooed with deliberate elegance. "Pret-tee Bird, we are glad to see you."

Mr. Zaric seemed to be revived by Pretty Bird's return. He shaved, brushed his teeth, and clipped back the dead skin on his toes. "It is so amazing," he told Irena. "All that has happened, and he is back with us. So amazing what Amela risked to bring him."

The account of the reunion that Irena had given her parents had been thoughtfully incomplete.

"When you speak to Amela again," he said, "as I hope you will—"

"I will."

"—tell her we are grateful. And that she is so brave," her father said, putting his hand out so that Pretty Bird could nip it with his beak. "As we are thankful to you." Irena's silence—she had absorbed the tactic from Tedic—forced her father to go on. "The way you go back and forth—I know, it's dangerous. Sweeping mud floors at the brewery so we can have a little more."

"The drudgery must be killing," said her mother.

Aleksandra interrupted by holding a *Vogue* up to the light of Mrs. Zaric's cooking fire. "There are beautiful models in here who look like frogs because they cover themselves with sludge from seaweed," she announced.

Irena turned to her with an air of authority. "It draws out the toxins," she explained.

"*Vogue* models are so toxic? Look," she said, nudging Irena.

It was a recruitment ad for the Royal Navy. There were small, full-color murals of thatched beach huts in some unspecified West Indian port, sapphire blue waves lapping the beaches of Rio, and the gull wings of the Opera House against the glitter of Sydney's skyline.

"Look at this," Alexandra said again, tracing over the words with the burning end of her cigarette. " 'The sport, the social life, the comradeship, the travel.' I think I've figured out why the West won't help us," she said. "War is messy. The beaches close. How do we get help when all we can advertise is 'The snipers. The cold. Getting shot in a place you don't know or care about.' Why should we expect anyone in the world to come and save us?"

The small gray franks began to sputter and pop in the pan.

28.

TEDIC RELIEVED THE DRUDGERY OF IRENA'S DAILY DUTIES BY ASKing her to assist the crew from an Arabic-language television service that had been slipped into Sarajevo to interview the Home Minister. Some delicacy was involved. Arab groups had been generous in their support for Bosnia's besieged Muslims. Bosnians were grateful. And yet many Arabs sensed something chilly in their expressions of appreciation—the cold, merely correct formality of a printed thank-you card.

Bosnian officials eloquently told the world that they were European and ecumenical. Some Arabs heard a sniff of disdain in these boasts of secularism.

"As if," the Home Minister had explained to Tedic, "we do not see ourselves as Muslims. As if Bosnians do not see our plight as being at one with the beleaguered Palestinians."

"And *you* have been selected to reassure Arab viewers otherwise?" Tedic inquired with comically arched brows.

The Home Minister was married to a woman who had been educated in convent schools. Their religious life was nominal, sundry, and ceremonial. They observed Ramadan by attending parties to break the fast, and offered similar devotions on Yom Kippur. When their children were growing up, the Home Minister and his wife decorated Easter eggs and opened presents on Christmas morning. They did not want their children to feel as if Islam had cheated them of some seasonal reward. But the Home Minister tended to venture into actual houses of worship only for funerals and weddings. He shifted from foot to foot during the most solemn intonations, rushing through the text of a prayer as if it were the fine print on a car-rental contract.

"I hope to God, Kemal, they don't ask you when you were last in a mosque," said Tedic.

"I can answer that," replied the Home Minister smoothly. "Eid ul-Adha."

"Nineteen seventy-five?"

"The year escapes me. Yoko Ono had just broken up the Beatles. I was bereft. But I will assure our guests from the Kingdom of Saud that I look forward to making my pilgrimage someday."

"To the four-star restaurants of Rome," said Tedic.

Yet the Home Minister was a faithful man. He believed in Sarajevo.

TEDIC TOLD IRENA that she should accompany the television crew to their interview in the Home Minister's basement office in the Presidency Building.

"Smile. Laugh at their sly witticisms and marvel at the brilliance of their Muhammadan parables. Lug their equipment, flatter them, make them at home," he told her. "Then, listen carefully to what they say and repeat it to me, word for word."

"And if they don't say a thing?"

"They will," Tedic asserted. "*They will.* To a young Muslim girl they are trying to impress."

"These people are trying to help us," said Irena. "Why don't you trust them?"

"I'll need a better reason than that," Tedic told her. "In the country—some of the villages—they sneak in guns and fighters to save the place for Islam. Which means they drive out everyone else. Officially, we don't notice. Moral reservations are an expensive indulgence. As long as Uncle Sam stays away, we need the ayatollahs. That's why the Home Minister is participating in such a farce. But we watch the bastards," said Tedic. "Just as closely as they watch us."

The delegation from the television syndicate consisted of four men, all dangling U.N. media credentials stamped the day before in Zagreb. The Home Ministry had given them rooms at a former Holiday Inn along the front lines in which certain diplomats, soldiers, U.N. officials, and Bosnian functionaries were staying, as well as most of the international press covering the siege. The hotel was no safer than the rest of the city, and only marginally more comfortable. The water pipes were dry. The rooms were dark and powerless. Some groups brought in generators. But because of the lack of gas they were useful only for the sporadic operation of computers and satellite television and telephones.

Freebooters in the employ of the hotel brought in black-market food and old Slovenian wines, which they sold at the hotel at magnified prices. The Americans, British, and Canadians bought and enjoyed the wines, which the French and Italians pronounced "Barely drinkable" before draining their glasses.

The hotel's mountain-side rooms had once been the most prestigious. But now direct views onto snow-clad peaks were dangerous, as so many shattered windows attested. Tedic had dispatched Jackie, rosy Jackie, to be his liaison for the Arab delegation, and to explain why they had to be housed in such dark, grim, common quarters. Irena did not see any of the Arabs in the hotel's dining area—they may have felt uncomfortable around such public drinking—and so walked up seven flights to find their fleet of rooms. She was pleased not to feel winded; the coil in her legs was still tight and strong.

A man named Charif answered the door of Room 706. He wore a white shirt, buttoned to the neck, and smooth black pants. He had a black beard and small, dark, merry eyes.

"Hi, Ingrid, yes. Tedic said you would be making contact. We have some other guests here, too."

The visitors had opened the door between two adjoining rooms and had arrayed small plastic drums of raisins and nuts on one of the beds. There were easily twenty people between the two rooms, standing and talking. But it was the first time in months that Irena had been in a room with more than two people that wasn't suffused with smoke. Some of the men wore black or white turbans, which Irena had not seen outside of textbooks or movies, or variations in Western women's fashion magazines. Many also wore expensive-looking woolen winter coats over black vests and high-collared white shirts.

Jackie stood near the curtained windows, caught in conversation, and met Irena's eye with a wink. Jackie had a soft black silk head scarf with gold embroidery clasped at her coltish throat. Irena flushed with embarrassment and thrust a hand up to her own head.

"I'm sorry," she told Charif. "No one warned me."

"No problem, Ingrid," he said. "We know most women here want to look European."

He led her toward the nuts and raisins, and offered her tea and coffee from brass pots they had set over a small camp stove in another corner of the room.

"Are you a Muslim, Ingrid?" he asked in English as he handed her a small glass of dark coffee.

"Yes."

"Aha," said Charif, as if he had just removed the wrapping of an unexpected present. "You say 'Yes,' not 'Of course.' "

Irena hesitated but smiled. "I say 'Yes' because we can be a great many things here in Sarajevo."

"I understand," said Charif. "I am Egyptian. Those who say 'Yes, I am a Muslim' leave open the chance of other choices. But those of us who know the word of God and His Prophet say 'Of course.' Once we have heard His word, there is no other choice to make."

Charif delivered his speech with utter cheerfulness. If he admitted of no other spiritual choice, his graciousness seemed to invite Irena to respond with a question, or perhaps even a contrary opinion. Instead, she said, "I see."

"You will see more," said Charif. "You have come at just the right moment. The Prince is visiting. We are going to hear from the Prince."

"I was not told about any prince," Irena said carefully. "Only about you and your crew."

"The Prince is amazing," Charif said in a quieter voice. "The Prince carries the message of the Prophet. He wanted no official notice of his visit. He did not want to inconvenience anyone. He is that modest. A prince, truly, a man of great wealth. A prominent Saudi family that built the great modern structures of Mecca. But the Prince lives among refugees and outcasts. His presence will be an immense gift to all he meets here. You do not know who I mean?"

Irena shook her head.

"Take my hand here, Ingrid," Charif said. "Let's see if we can get across this busy room before he begins."

Charif took Irena's hand and she clasped her glass of coffee to her chest as he led her to the far side of the room. The men in turbans and high-collared shirts had turned toward a tall man with a long beard, who was wearing an immaculate long white gown underneath a soiled green American army-surplus jacket. At last, Irena thought to herself, the U.S. Army comes to Sarajevo. Charif lifted Irena's free hand as he held both of his palms up humbly to the Prince. It took a moment for the Prince to see this.

"May I present a new friend," said Charif with his head bowed. Irena reflexively turned her face down toward the floor in time to hear the Prince respond simply, "If it pleases you."

"This is Ingrid, my Prince. Ingrid, who lives here. Ingrid, who is helping us."

Irena lifted her head in time to see the Prince raise a hand to his heart. His fingers were long and lean, his nails so polished and glassy that his hands reminded Irena of long branches on a tree, glistening with ice.

Irena opened her mouth. But she had nothing—she found it hard to know what—to say. She picked up Jackie in the corner of her eye, and noticed that she had tugged her head scarf more tightly over the crown of her head as the Prince faced the room to speak.

HE DID NOT need to clear his throat, tap a glass, clap his hands, or shout. The din of the room just stopped, as if someone had clicked off a switch. When the quiet was complete, the Prince received it with a small smile.

"Allah Akhbar, God is great," he said quietly. And then he took a long, jaguar stride toward the windows. With wiry arms he took hold of the curtains and yanked them open. Somebody's coffee cup was knocked to the floor. Somebody's pad of paper sailed a few inches across the ledge. Twenty cries of surprise sprang up around the room. Two men sank onto the bed, eyes brimming. The malevolent mountains, cloaked by snow and swarming with unseen snipers, looked grim and gray in the top of the window frame. The Prince turned his back to them and faced the room.

"God will protect us," he announced softly. "There is no God but Allah. In the name of God the most merciful, I bring you greetings."

"Allah Akhbar! Allah Akhbar!" Shouts and cries moved over the room.

THE PRINCE BEGAN in a low, slow tone.

"You here in Sarajevo live on the edge of the West," he told them. "You live within the hot breath of the beast. In fact"—and here the Prince leveled one of his lean, elegant fingers at the blank screen of the mute television—"the beast has revealed himself to you. Now that the lack of electricity has blinded him, your own eyes can open. You can see how this beast was filling your lives with vile and useless images. Sex without love. Flesh without humanity. Bloodshed without consequence. Prosperity without spirituality. Nike, Marlboro, Rolex, Coca-Cola, Heineken, Air Jordan. You know those names, don't you?"

The men around the room gave amused and knowing murmurs of assent.

"They mock us with things that adorn or invade our bodies. But these things do nothing to nourish our souls. What you have seen should not make you envious. The beast is rich but empty. Violent but cowardly. He is surrounded by things, but lonely inside without our real God."

Heads nodded. People murmured low, involuntary sounds of enchantment as the Prince continued in a voice as soft as spun wool.

"We can see now, as we approach the end of the twentieth century, how much of history has been manipulated by Jews. I don't say this as an anti-Semite. Whenever the West hears some truth it would rather conceal, they dismiss it as anti-Semitic. We Muslims cannot be anti-Semitic. It would be against ourselves. *We are Semites.* When it comes to Semites, we Muslims are far more numerous than Jews.

"The people of the East are Muslims. The people of the West are the Crusaders. They may call themselves Christians, Jews, British, French, Italians, or Americans. These days, even Russians. But those are different brand names for the same lethal cigarette. They are the Crusaders. They are the infidels. They defile our faith. They rape our sisters, mothers, and daughters. God says, 'Never will the Jews or the Christians be satisfied with thee unless thou follow their form of religion.' "

The Prince stopped for a moment to peer above the heads of the men and women in the room. "World War I began here. Just steps away, right? Were it possible for me to walk around outside, like a simple visitor, I would see the plaque on that spot where it began. Someday we must chisel in the truth. With that war, which the Serbs began, the whole Islamic world fell under the Crusaders' banner. The British, French, and Italian governments divided the world. Britain got Palestine, our Holy Land. Who divided Palestine, our lands and families? The British Lord Arthur Balfour, servant of the Jews Weizmann and Rothschild. How many hundreds of thousands of Muslims have since been killed, imprisoned, or maimed?"

"Millions," a voice called out.

"This war in Bosnia is a continuation of this genocide," said the Prince. "This battle is part of a chain of the long, fierce, and ugly Crusader war."

Irena finally noticed his eyes. They were milky brown, warm, and light. The Prince pitched his voice even lower, but the silence of the room seemed to deepen as people stood on their toes and drew in their breath to hear him.

"In the twentieth century, whenever a nation tries to protect itself against craven Jews, the Jews cry genocide. The vast armies of the Crusaders march to save Jews. Jews like Weizmann and Einstein invent the most terrible weapons and use them against those who do not accept the god of the Crusaders.

"But when Muslims are killed those vast armies stay home. They play games. This war here is practically within the Crusaders' breast. It is on television all over America. Our Muslim brothers are being killed, our women raped, our children massacred—all under the watch of the United Nations. And the Blue Helmets sit idly by. And should we be so surprised?"

Several men had to pinch tears from their eyes as the Prince permitted his voice to rise.

"No. *No! God* cannot be deceived. The United Nations partitioned Palestine at the command of the British and turned Muslim land into a Jewish nation. A Jew can be British or French prime minister or the richest man in America. Who owns the great newspapers of London, New York, Paris, and Toronto? Who controls the eyes of the beast?"

Here the Prince slapped the tip of his finger against the television screen.

"Who controls the movie studios in Hollywood, and even in India? And yet it is the Jew who screams genocide. The Jew who says he needs a homeland and steals our land. Those who cannot see this disavow the Holy Book and the Prophet Muhammad, God's peace and blessings be upon him."

"Allah Akhbar! Allah Akhbar!" Calls went up again.

"I will warn you," the Prince continued. "When the Muslim begins to strike back, the Crusaders call us terrorists. If a terrorist is a man who fights for freedom with the rocks God has placed in front of him, then I am a terrorist. But how can we be terrorists? The West has atom bombs, smart bombs, and rocket ships. We have only a few rocks, a few bullets, and bombs made from gas poured into their filthy Coke bottles."

Laughter flickered around the room. Irena heard her own laugh mingling in.

"History keeps count," said the Prince. "If you take all of the victims of the Crusades, all who were slaughtered by imperialists, all of the Palestinian mothers and children slaughtered in the name of Israel, they would not add up to our small bombs and satchels of dynamite. The United Nations, which created Israel, will not let Muslims defend themselves here in Bosnia. They permit us to be only fatalities. But when the victim starts to take revenge for those innocent children—in Palestine, Iraq, Sudan, Somalia, Lebanon, the Philippines, and now Bosnia—the Crusaders defend this blasphemy by calling us terrorists."

By now the laughter of the men was rolling and boiling in their throats. The Prince widened his eyes, as if he had just heard something bizarre and confounding.

"Now there are Muslims in Sarajevo who say—perhaps some of you have said it yourself—'But, Prince, we are Europeans.' I say, you are mocking God and fooling yourself. The Crusader does not call you European. Ask the Muslims of Brixton in London. Or Saint-Denis in Paris. Or Brooklyn, New York. Ask the Muslims in Haifa if they are treated as European. The Crusaders drove you here, five centuries ago, with the sword, the lash, and the word of their depraved Jew god, who feasts on the blood of children, even his own son."

"Jews were driven here, too!" a voice rang out, a woman's voice. Irena snapped around to see that it was Jackie, and the men around her seemed to be stepping back slightly.

"Who is that, please?" asked the Prince in a mild voice. "No, please," he said when a moment passed with no response. "Let her be heard."

Jackie raised her hand, and lowered it quickly to tug her head scarf forward. "I spoke, Your Highness," she called out.

"I am glad," said the Prince. "I congratulate you. I would rather hear the voice of a brave person challenge me than a thousand cowards shower me with compliments. May I ask, are you Jewish?"

"I am *Muslim*," Jackie called back in a rising voice. "I may have a touch of Jew. I know I have a touch of Serb. I also refuse to eat animal flesh—a touch of Hindu. You will find, Prince, that here in Sarajevo we all have a touch of something."

Jackie's performance sent a hissing spark of laughter around the room. The Prince smiled and seemed to cough out a laugh himself.

"We seek only the pure of heart. Not purity of race. Muslims come in all stripes and colors. I admire Jews greatly. We Muslims can—we have to—learn from the Jews. They are not just smart. *They fight*. They scheme and succeed. Small in number, yet they control great nations."

"Muslims, Serbs, Christians, and Jews have gotten along here for five centuries," said Jackie. Irena thought that she had permitted her black head scarf to slip to the back of her head. She could see more glints of shiny chestnut hair and creamy cheeks.

"Five centuries?" asked the Prince. *"Is that all?"*

The laughter in the room surged back decisively toward the tall Prince standing so boldly against the view of the mountains.

"Certainly the Serbs," he continued, "who say you have deprived them of their kingdom, believe that five centuries is the blink of an eye."

"I don't want to live in Iran," Jackie shot back. "I don't want to go through life in a black sack. I don't want women to be locked away in closets, like vacuum cleaners that get rolled out for occasional service."

Jackie won a round of snorts. She was still standing, nearly as tall as the Prince, shoulders back, hands strapped against her incomparable hips. The Prince was in no peril of losing the encounter in front of his court, and so he relaxed to enjoy a smart and pretty challenge.

"We haven't built our kingdom yet," he told her.

Irena wondered how many times he had spoken directly, even as he made love, into a woman's face.

"Saudi Arabia, Pakistan—they are sham Islamic states. They mock Islam to flatter the Crusader. They let him roll his armies across our holy places. They think they can adorn themselves with his things but not catch his diseases. When we get the chance to create our own Islamic state—here, elsewhere, or everywhere—you will see how glorious it will be."

"Will the mullahs let me drive?" Jackie persisted. "Will they let me get rid of a bastard husband? Will they stone me for showing my elbows, telling a dirty joke, or listening to Madonna? Would the mullahs let girls like me go to school if they knew what kind of pains in the ass we could all become? Will they let me be a Jew, a Christian, an atheist, a vegetarian, or whatever else we risk our lives here for?"

"Surely you can be a vegetarian," the Prince countered with more laughter. Jackie refused to concede the round.

"Jews die for Bosnia, Mr. Bin Laden," she said evenly. "So do Serbs. So do Crusaders. You shouldn't mock them."

"Don't mock yourself," the Prince said. He was not ruffled by the unexpected mention of his name. "Use the Jews, if you think you can. Use the Crusader. But know that they bring themselves close only to use you. There is a *holy war* going on here," the Prince continued as he took a pointed step away from Jackie and gathered the room in his mild brown eyes. "A *genocide* that we fight with *jihad*. The West sends Blue Helmets and dried beans. We bring you guns and men. It is our faith. It is our duty. When our enemies lie slain before us, Sarajevo will become a monument to God and his Prophet. Sarajevo will be Mecca."

The Prince pressed his back against the precarious, tempting pane of cracked glass behind him, squared his shoulders, and raised his voice until it sounded like the urgent call of a lover. "You are not alone," he declared. "Every Muslim suffers with you. The tears you shed scour our hearts. Your blood gives us life. Let the faith of hundreds of millions of Muslim men, women, and children, from the camps of Palestine to the golden holy spires of Mecca, offer you strength. We stand with you! We bleed with you! Every Muslim stands under your banner. There is no God but Allah! There is no faith but his! We have heard you! *Islam calls you!* I pray I have conveyed God's message. His peace and blessings be upon you."

The hand clapping gathered under the Prince's last words. He tipped his chin into his chest and bent his head in the swelling thunder of exaltation and tears. The clapping and crying seemed to gust through the room. Irena was raised to her toes. The pealing rang in her ears like the retort of a shot. Her eyes shone red, and wet with awe and dread. Irena didn't like the talk of Jews, blood, and jihad. But something in the room had shot electricity into her veins. She could no more keep tears from her eyes in the rush of clapping, cries, prayers, and shouts than she could keep herself dry in a rainstorm.

Jackie was still on the other side of the room, and more than ever the center of attention. She twitched her hips, flicked a cigarette, and flipped the ends of her hair like a chestnut switch from beneath her head scarf. She leaned toward Irena.

"Ingrid, darling, hi."

They brushed each other's cheeks with their lips. They took one another into their arms.

"You were quite magnificent," Irena told her.

Jackie squeezed Irena's elbow tightly and switched to the Bosnian language.

"I was scared."

"The Prince loved it," said Irena. "He is in love with you. I could tell. You brought out the best."

"Not of him," said Jackie. "*Them.* The crew we are supposed to work with. One of the reasons I spoke up is they were getting a little too attentive to me."

"Why not?" Irena said. "I love you, too. You are so amazing and beautiful."

"I'm not wearing a black potato sack," said Jackie. "They hear that Bosnian women are like Western ones—we drink, smoke, and fuck. We're crazy for it in all ways." Jackie revised her vocabulary to avoid offending—

or alerting—Bosnian speakers standing nearby. "To them, it's like romancing a sheep. Allah is not offended if you screw Bosnians. Lipstick, tight pants, Madonna—we are not women. We are another species."

Irena laughed and leaned over Jackie's shoulder to breathe a question into her ear.

"Did you scare them away?"

Jackie laughed so powerfully that her head scarf began to slip to her shoulders. Irena caught it and held it against her ears.

"Now they say, 'Jackie, you are so brave. We must keep you very close to us.' "

IRENA AND JACKIE joined Charif and his three colleagues the next morning in a van that Tedic had provided. Molly met them, his pale skin whiter than the winter sun, wearing an AK-47 slung across his shoulders the way a long-haired German college student might carry a guitar while hitchhiking. Molly wordlessly took the passenger seat of the van and Jackie did the driving. The Arab men rather quickly got the point of that.

"We know women can drive," Charif said gently. "We are sure that women can drive moon rockets, if they have to."

"Not much to show you on the way over," Jackie said as they made their way along Marshal Tito Boulevard. Charif and his crew were quiet and, Irena thought, alert and anxious in their seats.

"This used to be a leafy street, like the Champs-Élysées," Jackie called back to the men in the van. When she heard Irena stifle a small laugh from the back, she chuckled aloud. "All right, not quite. But leafy."

"There is not much traffic," observed one of the men in the crew, Heydar. Nervous talk, thought Irena; it was like driving around Rome and saying, "A lot of history here."

"Fuel is impossible," Jackie explained. "Serbs took the best cars anyway. And there's the snipers."

"Snipers knocked down all these trees?" asked Heydar. She could hear apprehension tightening his voice.

"People here," Irena said. "To get wood for heat and fuel."

"Burning your furniture might be better," observed Charif, "than giving snipers an easier shot."

"Furniture is going up now," Jackie said. "Doors, chairs. Even clothes and shoes. A worn-out old shirt can make a small pot of tea if you have the water."

Irena thought the men took a moment to puzzle over the sense of her remark, and look down at their own clothes and shoes.

Jackie steered the van into the courtyard of the Presidency Building and pulled it alongside the upturned undersides of an old delivery truck that formed part of a barrier. Irena threw open the doors in the back of the van and helped the men put down battered black and silver cases. She helped a short man they called Abdullah sling a band of silvery lights over his shoulders.

"Everything will have to be checked," Molly admonished them; it was the first time Irena had heard him speak that morning.

Charif cast a glance at his watch. "We are even a little early," he observed.

"No traffic jams," Jackie said. "We'll go inside."

"So early? I don't want to inconvenience anyone," said Charif.

Irena was taken by his consideration.

"Better inside than out here," Jackie said simply, and cast a glance at the overturned carriage of the delivery truck that now rose above their heads. "Even so."

But the Home Minister had sent a functionary to wait for their arrival. Gerry heard the van pull up to the building. Irena remembered him from the basement in Dobrinja, all bluff and roly-poly. He stepped out from behind a scarred steel door in a thick blue jacket and began to fill his hands and arms with some of the crew's cases. His words burst into puffs in the cold.

"We have some coffee inside, good and hot," he told them. "German. The Home Minister gets nothing on the black market, of course. But friends give him some for honored guests."

Irena took up a small silver case that was studded with travel stickers: Lufthansa, Royal Jordanian, Air Pakistan. First class all the way, she noted. Two police officers, a man and a woman, kept the steel door open while they all stamped in heftily, boots and latches clattering. The crew snapped opened their cases. The police picked up their lenses and lights and looked them over, tapping, peering, occasionally unclasping.

"I'm sure everything is in order," Gerry said with apology coating his voice.

"And we understand you must be certain," Charif said.

The police bowed slightly and stood back as Gerry steered the crew down a half flight of stairs and into the Home Minister's spare office. It was unpainted, undecorated, and pale, almost like the inside of an eggshell.

"Hello, hello, Allah Akhbar," the Home Minister said as they came through the door. "God is great."

Charif bowed his head slightly and took the Home Minister's hands into his own. "May the peace of the Prophet be upon you," he replied.

The Home Minister had received a briefing only that morning, but Irena thought he was still mixing a bit of Christianity into his Muslim lexicon.

"And also upon you," he said. "I am but a poor messenger of the Messenger," the Home Minister continued as he showed the crew into a sitting area.

Irena made a mental note to report the Home Minister's virtuosity to Tedic. I wonder, she asked herself, how long he can keep this up.

COFFEE CUPS APPEARED. Tired, scuffed plastic cafeteria cups, but indeed they were steaming. Irena accepted one and sipped eagerly. She was about to apologize for slurping when she saw Charif smiling fondly at the sound to save her the embarrassment. It had been months since she'd had coffee this dark. The intensity prickled her tongue, and seemed to give her eyes sharper focus.

"Your people have been most hospitable," Charif told the Home Minister.

"A small repayment for the generosity of so many of your viewers," the Home Minister replied warmly. "I am glad of the chance to tell them myself."

Irena was given a pair of lights to hold at her waist while Abdullah unfolded the legs of a tripod.

"I am sorry I did not have the chance to meet the Prince," the Home Minister said while slipping back casually into his office chair. It was not an observation, Irena sensed, so much as a cast into rippled waters.

"He departed early this morning," Charif offered cheerfully, but no more than that. "I am told. I am sure he would have welcomed the opportunity to meet your good self, too."

Abdullah had the camera up on the tripod and was running his hand over some cables that hung down from the rear like rats' tails.

"We will be ready momentarily," Charif assured the Home Minister.

The Home Minister shifted in his graying pinstripes. "I would have welcomed the occasion to speak with the Prince," he said. "I am eager to have my own faith enriched by his wisdom."

Abdullah took the two lamps from Irena and clipped them above the glassy blank eye of his camera.

"He impresses everyone," Charif assured them. Abdullah made a kind of winding signal with his right hand, and Charif turned to Irena sheepishly. "This is," he said quietly, "too embarrassing. Could I—do you mind—if I ask you for a favor?"

Irena stepped to his side as the Home Minister pretended to turn away, and Jackie moved close to Abdullah, who was crouching behind the stork legs of the camera.

"We have only a twenty-minute tape," Charif whispered. "We need another. I am so forgetful. It must be nerves. All the talk of snipers and burning my shoes." He laughed under his breath. "The man with the rifle—"

"I saw him," was all Irena said.

"He has been with the car?"

"I assume."

"Do you think he would let you back in?"

"If I asked him. If I told him that it is your instruction," Irena corrected herself.

"There should be three or four tapes in black cases on the backseat. We have enough to begin."

"Bring them all?"

"Why not?" said Charif. "I am sure the Home Minister will be most eloquent." Charif raised his voice to draw the rest of the room into the conversation. "Our audience will be most eager to hear him."

Irena glanced over her shoulder as she scurried out. Charif and the Home Minister clasped hands, closed their eyes, and bent their heads together. Jackie, Gerry, Abdullah, and Heydar stood by silently as Charif said, "Praise to those who hear and heed the words of his Prophet. May the peace of the world be upon them."

"Allah Akhbar," agreed the Home Minister quietly. "The peace of the world upon us all."

TEDIC WAS ON his knees inside the van, lifting up a panel of black vinyl flooring and running his hand over the underside while Molly stood watch in front of the windshield. The sling of his gun had been turned around to cross his chest.

"Good Christ," Tedic said without looking up when Irena unlatched the door. "What did our friends forget?"

"Tapes," said Irena. "Somewhere on the backseat."

At this, Tedic lifted his head and widened his eyes. "Not there," he said.

"Black cases, like small books," Irena persisted.

"I know what they look like. They're not here," said Tedic. "Anyone say anything about how the Prince got out of town?"

"Not that I heard," said Irena. "Maybe the man named Charif mentioned it to the Home Minister."

"Or how he got *in* town?"

"Nothing," Irena repeated.

"He somehow bought his way over. We'd like to know his travel agent."

Molly had crooked his chin over his shoulder and was calling Irena through the windshield. "Better find those tapes or scurry back, love, and say you can't."

"Maybe they're back at the hotel," Irena told him, and then asked Tedic, "You're sure—no tapes?"

"I would have stolen them by now," he said sternly. "I'm not down here looking for cigarette butts. Wait another minute, so you can say you've been thorough."

"Two," suggested Molly. "I gave you a hard time about opening the car. Tell them you found nothing in the back but decided to check everything, including the glove box. Wait—check that there is a glove box."

"And *maybe*," Irena suggested with an edge of irritation, "they are *just* a television crew that forgot their tapes."

"Too embarrassing," said Tedic. "They wouldn't send you."

"They have one," she told him. "To start. They didn't want to keep the Home Minister waiting."

"A test for sure," Molly said. "Shit. They probably have someone watching us right now."

Irena began to clamber ostentatiously over the backseat to convince anyone watching of the sincerity of her search for the small black cases.

"Impossible," said Tedic. "They wouldn't know where they were going to park."

"It shouldn't be too hard to guess," Molly said, shrugging.

"You'd have to be inside the building to see the car," said Tedic.

"You think they don't have someone inside?"

Irena was sitting on her haunches on the floor just in front of the backseat. She could feel muddy footprints beginning to seep, tread by tread, through her blue jeans.

"Can I have a Marlboro?" she asked. "If I have two minutes left. I'm getting footprints stained onto my ass. I can't smoke in front of our visitors."

"They'll smell it on your breath and wonder," Tedic said.

"They'll smell it on your breath and think they are James Bond for figuring out what took you so long to find nothing," cut in Molly.

Tedic's right hand was beginning to dive deep into his pocket, keys jangling and cellophane cigarette wrappers crinkling, when a thud in front of them popped their ears. The glass in the van quivered. Molly and Tedic felt a shudder in their heels and toes. When they tried to run, the ground trembled and sent sparks into their knees. Irena, Tedic, and Molly turned their heads back toward the building in time to see a couple of small basement windows hiccup clouds of dust that burst open with the shower of glass that gouged the pavement in front of them with screams.

MOLLY, HIS RIFLE borne like a spear, ran into the last clatter of glass and slid, feet first, into the hole of one of the smashed windows. Tedic had reached into his pocket and come up with a black-nosed gun. He waved it unconvincingly as he stumbled after Molly, like a child running after a lost kite waving a candy stick. By the time Irena had gotten unstuck from the floor, the steel door that Gerry had wrenched open for them had been thrown open for people trying to escape the smoke and fire. They were coughing and crying. When they hit the cold air, they remembered that they were under the eyes of snipers. They stumbled onto their knees and began to crawl.

Irena high-stepped over them. She hurtled down the half flight with a single step and ran flat-out, head up, shoulders back, into a stinging fog of plaster dust, brick dust, and mud in the Home Minister's office. Jackie, beautiful Jackie, was on the floor, her brown eyes twitching like hummingbirds. Her right hand reached out for reassurance, but her right arm was rolling over and away from her, like a sausage that had fallen out of a truck. Irena ran after Jackie's arm. She stepped on Gerry's dead, bleeding boulder of a chest. Abdullah waved at her in the storm of smoke. But his head had blown back into Charif's stomach. Irena saw Jackie's arm, still clad in its stretchy red sleeve. She picked it up for safekeeping, and as the blood gushed out, Irena was appalled to find herself warmed. She put Jackie's arm behind her back, as if she were hiding a bouquet of flowers. Molly had the snout of his rifle thrust into Charif's mild, unmoving smile. But the Home Minister stalked over on his one whole leg, stretching a flap of his suit coat over his mouth so that he could breathe.

"We can't spare the bullet," he commanded Molly. "Someone in pain might need it."

ABDULLAH, CHARIF, HEYDAR, and the other man in their crew had died in the blast, which had apparently been set off by their camera. Tedic and Molly guessed that plastic explosives had been packed into the casing panels of the camera.

They dismissed the possibility that the crew had been the unwitting agents for someone else's bomb. Molly concluded that a real television crew, innocent and unsuspecting men, would have noticed the difference in weight after their equipment had been altered. They would have been alarmed.

Gerry was dead. His death was despicable, terrible, and a crime. But, Tedic reminded them, it was also a remarkably modest showing for a bomb that four people had journeyed thousands of miles to blow up in the world's most dangerous city, for some purpose they could not yet fathom.

Jackie lost her right arm. The Home Minister had stripped off his suit coat, leaned down into the sickening clouds, and pressed his jacket against her spurting wound. She was still lovely, as Tedic had assured her at the scene, ever so much more.

"You are even more like Venus," he'd told her, clasping her surviving hand to his cheek.

The dead men had a collection of driver's licenses and citizenship cards in their pockets, a dozen names and identities by which they could become Lebanese, Egyptian, British, German, or French. Days later, Tedic passed some of their names along to certain contacts in Zagreb, London, and Jerusalem. They said the names were unconnected and clean. They might as well have been—they might well have been—from the New York City phone book.

The television syndicate for which the men ostensibly worked was real. It was based in London and beamed to cable systems in Europe and Arabia. Tedic offered the men's conjured names to company managers, who reported that none of them appeared in their payroll records. An executive explained that freelancers often exaggerated their connections to secure an interview. They suggested that Tedic deliver to the men a stern sermon about misrepresenting their credentials. Tedic assured them blandly that he would.

The Home Minister was presumed to be the principal target of the bomb (Jackie may have been an improvised addition). Some of the people who were steering aid into Bosnia held the Home Minister's pronounced ecumenical Islam in contempt. Tedic asked him—in a frank, just-guys-together tone—to appraise his life and consider whether someone had a more personal motive for his assassination.

"Like a jealous husband?" he barked from his hospital bed. "A scorned lover?"

"A former business associate who may feel cheated," Tedic suggested carefully. "An old employee who was fired. A black-market gangster," he added more quietly.

The Home Minister didn't fly into a rage or even protest. Instead, he took a long draw on his cigarette and appraised Tedic through the smoke. "You must belong to all of those categories," he told him. "Unless it was you, Miro, I can think of no one."

But Tedic was mostly trying to snip off loose ends. The expensive preparations that the plot involved didn't support a personal motive. Four men were not likely to sacrifice their lives to avenge an affronted husband, a foiled lover, or a thwarted gangster. And it certainly didn't explain the Prince's proximity to the crime. He seemed to have appeared mysteriously, and to have departed without a trace that would lead to the detonation.

Some of Tedic's recruits went over the rooms that the men had slept in at the Holiday Inn. They found soiled clothes of no particular significance left behind the sliding doors of the closets; they would be checked for traces of explosives. More interesting was a smattering of small bills of different denominations and nationalities in the room of the man who had posed as Charif. But an accountant in the hotel's office who worked with foreign currencies quickly calculated that the bills amounted to no more than one hundred U.S. dollars. That was scarcely enough to buy a bottle of scotch in Sarajevo, much less finance an uprising. She ventured a sensible guess that the bills were merely the accumulation of constant travelers.

The men left behind nail clippers, lilac and sandalwood soaps, combs and brushes, toothpaste, and, in one room, contact-lens solution. None of them left notes for family, friends, survivors, adversaries, or posterity, although, as Tedic thought it through, such letters could have been thoughtfully drafted and dispatched from Vienna, Rome, or some other stopover before the men made the journey into Sarajevo.

There was a single sentence written in Arabic on the back of the plastic card in the bathroom that invited people to ring 777 to have ice delivered to their room. The card was from the time of the Olympics. But the thick black letters seemed fresher: THOSE WHO MOCK ALLAH ARE THE ENEMIES OF ISLAM.

"I cannot believe that they would inscribe their motto—if that was their motto—in a place so easily overlooked," the Home Minister told Tedic.

"Unless they knew that *no place* would be overlooked," Tedic suggested.

"Besides," said the Home Minister, flicking a sheet from his shin, "who is mocking Allah? An imperfect Muslim like me? Or sick bastards who use Allah's name like some kind of bath soap to rinse blood from their knuckles?"

"An excellent speech," Tedic told him. "Let's win the war before you start campaigning."

The Home Minister drew the gray sheet back over his legs with a sigh.

Tedic reached over to tuck the rough fabric around the Home Minister's waist. "The note was probably written years ago by a carpet salesman from Istanbul," Tedic assured him. "He was distressed because the hotel ran out of ice. Allah was mocked."

The Home Minister flung the sheet off again and smacked the heels of both hands against his pillow. "They are using *our war* to start *their own*," he said, punching at the pillow behind him, while Tedic fumbled in the pockets of his vast black coat for his gunmetal flask of scotch.

THE HOME MINISTRY made no announcement about the death of the men in the television crew. No news service working in the city knew anything about the explosion; nothing was reported. Assistance to Bosnia from sources in the Arab world continued with no evident decline. Tedic received occasional reports that the Prince had been glimpsed in various localities in Bosnia's interior. But he discounted most of the reports as wishful. Besides, Tedic knew that the inspirational appearance of a rich, outcast Arab prince was scarcely necessary for Arab irregulars who had managed to steal into the country to incite thuggish local Muslim and Croat militia to drive Serb families into the forest. And it was scarcely possible for Tedic, the Home Minister, or President Izetbegovic himself to stop them. Even if they had so desired.

Tedic did have one last conversation on the incident with Irena. He didn't summon her to his office, but found her absently flipping through the pages of an old *VOX* in a stairwell lit by a splinter of daylight.

"You can say anything," he began without introduction. "Any answer will do. There is nothing you can say that will bring any penalty, disfavor, or reprimand. Is there any reason—*any reason you can fathom*—why they would send you out to the van?"

"Why did they spare my life?" she asked back.

"Or why they would want you alive and Jackie, Gerry, the Home Minister, and anyone else who happened along dead?"

Irena closed the magazine and rolled it up in her hands.

"I don't know," she said. "Why did they blow themselves up, too?"

"That I know," said Tedic. "They recognized the likes of Molly. They knew they weren't about to set a bomb and sneak out of town with their lives. Killing themselves was their exclamation point. Blood—the universal language. It was a way of proclaiming that they can kill anyone they want because they're not afraid to die."

Irena shook her whole body *no* over and over. "Well, I'm afraid to die," she said finally. "Maybe they sent me back because they knew my courage is lacking."

"There is no courage," said Tedic, "like that of some of the ten-year-old boys they have sent to die in Iraq, Iran, Gaza. *Allah be praised.*" He spat out the phrase as if it had been made from sour milk.

"The Crusaders had their ten-year-olds," Irena answered.

"The Prince has made his mark." Tedic met her slow smile. "If there was something else—a tender moment, a rambunctious romp—that made any one of them send you away . . ." Tedic allowed his sentence to run out of fuel. He took a step back down the stairwell to let the light fall back into Irena's lap.

"I suppose we will just have to consider it a last act of benevolence," he said, "bestowed by men who didn't want to be remembered just for the blood they shed." The heavy sound of Tedic's footsteps seemed to pursue him as he continued down the staircase and returned to his perch by the loading dock.

29.

AS THE BOASTS ABOUT A VIPER SEEMED TO INCREASE OVER THE weeks that followed, Irena saw Tedic showing a visitor through the brewery. She caught sight of Tedic gesturing and speaking to the man as they stood on a catwalk above the brewing floor. ("As if," she told Tedic later, "you know something about making beer.") She even heard Tedic raising his voice over the rumpus of churning and sloshing in a brewing vat to recite statistics to the poor man about drainage capacity. ("As if," she added later, "you know anything about drainage capacity.")

Mel volunteered to Irena that the visitor ran a brewery in Mexico. The United Nations had permitted him passage on a supply flight so that he could advise the Sarajevo Brewery on how certain aspects of production might be streamlined to compensate for the inevitable demands and shortages caused by war. (Especially, Irena thought, when half the cans in the production line are used to make hand grenades.)

Irena had never seen a Mexican. She had a vague impression of sun, prickly plants, and fiery spices. The Mexican visitor seemed to carry the sun with him. It had seeped into his smile, blackened his hair, and crisped his skin. He seemed to dispense winks when he knew that eyes were upon him.

On the second afternoon of his round of inspections and appraisals, Tedic took the visitor into one of the dirt-floored basement rooms and unrolled a map under a bright, buzzing light. He took care to secure each corner against the floor with a full can from the production line.

"I think I understand your drainage problems," said the visitor in English with a tight smile. "Please show me what you're talking about here."

Tedic crushed the end of a Marlboro into the dirt and pointed into nine circles on the map, from Mount Hum in the north to Novo Sarajevo in the south.

...

THE VISITOR WAS Jacobo Leyva, who had a family-run brewery in Guadalajara, in the Mexican state of Jalisco, producing Cerveza Moctezuma, which was popularized on billboards throughout west-central Mexico as "the beer of emperors." In fact, it was a brew of refugees. Jacob Levy had created Der Schwarzwald beer just after the Great War in the Black Forest town of Baden. It was considered to have a distinctive taste of caramel. The beer won a widening following through the 1920s and '30s, and Jacob Levy grew prosperous (though German Jews, eager to avoid the taint of ostentation, preferred to say "comfortable").

But the Nuremberg Laws, known explicitly at the time as the Law for the Protection of German Blood and Honor, were handed down in 1935. Jacob Levy had married a young Catholic woman, Maria Fenzel. They had two children, whom the new laws deemed as outlaw as their Jewish father and crossbreeding mother.

A committee of brown shirts in hobnailed boots strutted noisily into Jacob Levy's brewery to announce that they were taking over his business and home for the state. Jacob Levy himself took a prideful stride outside and wrenched down the German flag that had flapped over the brewery's entrance.

While many other German Jews debated how long the hopelessly hooligan Nazis could keep a grip on power, Jacob Levy and his family booked passage on a ship from Bremerhaven to Havana.

"We got out," he told his grandson years later, "just before they would have measured our noses and pinned yellow stars on our breasts."

In Havana, the Levys hired a boat to Veracruz. They purchased Mexican citizenship there with the last scraps of cash with which they had escaped. The family brew was lightened to tempt the local tastes of Jalisco, where the Levys settled, and renamed for the Aztec emperor who died defending his city from conquistadores in hobnailed boots.

Jacob Levy's grandson inherited his name, which was also modified to fit the local culture. Jacobo Leyva was resigned to finding a place in the family business. But first he spent a summer on the Kibbutz Gvulot in Israel's Negev, digging up peanuts, potatoes, and carrots. It was the early 1970s. Eight Arab armies encircled Israel and threatened to storm over the border on any given dawn.

Jacobo Leyva dug up legumes and tubers in the hot, dry daylight. He could see his smooth student's hands toughening and the muscles in his arms tightening into lean cords. At nightfall, he applied those same muscles in the embrace of willing young kibbutznik daughters who considered him exotic. "A jolt of tequila for little girls raised on dairy milk," said one.

But shortly before midnight Jacobo would slip back into his American blue jeans and substitute an Uzi in his arms. Until dawn, he and other slightly spoiled sons and daughters from Westchester and Winnetka would stand guard along Gvulot's barbed fences, scouring the dark-violet desert horizon.

Jacobo Leyva thought about staying. He had found a fresh and precious sense of identity away from Mexico and his family's business. His grandfather had been stripped of citizenship and sent into exile. The grandson could help build a national homeland for the children of the Holocaust.

One day three visitors drove down from Tel Aviv to explore geological sites nearby and stopped for lunch in the flowery garden restaurant that the kibbutz stocked from its own farms. Jacobo Leyva had finished that morning's excavation of carrots. He was hurrying back to his communal quarters for a scrub and a nap when he heard visitors calling his name.

"*Jacobo?*"

Small world, small world, imagine that, the guests said in confident European Spanish. "You must be Jacobo." They had met his mother and father in Athens on vacation. Mrs. Leyva had gushed, "You are Israelis. My son is in Israel, discovering his roots—digging potatoes like an Irishman." The visitors recalled that she had trawled through the deep of her vast tooled Oaxacan purse and dredged up recent photographs. "See here? *My Jacobo* holding up an enormous potato like an Olympic trophy. *My Jacobo* holding another potato with Mickey Mouse ears. *Jacobo* holding an Uzi in one arm, a fawn-haired girl from West Los Angeles in the other. My son, the warrior-lover," said Eva Leyva.

"Why not join us for lunch, *Jacobo*?" said the visitors.

Jacobo was intrigued. He had learned that intrigue sprinkled savor into the everyday anxieties of Israelis. The breadth of particular detail the visitors possessed about him was striking. They knew the specific poses of people in the pictures he had sent back home. They deftly mimicked the way his mother, a Mexican Catholic, seemed to italicize her son's name each time she spoke it.

A falcon-faced man named Avi made conversation while his two companions, a man and a woman, moved their eyes back and forth over the six spare selections on the menu. Chicken, beef, or lamb, baked or broiled. Hummus all around.

"Your mother says—she says a mother can tell—that you might want to make a life here in Eretz Yisroel."

"The thought occurs," Jacobo answered without expression. He had confided no such thought to his mother.

"Would you take up the beer business?" asked Avi. "Most beers have to be imported. Even now, sometimes there is no escape from German technology."

"I'm content here in these fields," Jacobo Leyva assured them. If they were intelligence agents, he wanted to see how they worked for their points. "Digging root vegetables here—it's blissful." He took a sip of the kibbutz's ice tea, sweetened with the kibbutz's own beet sugar. "Deli*th*-ee-oso," Jacobo enthused, slyly stressing a Castilian *c*, which his generation of Mexicans found pretentious. "We build a homeland with a hoe in one hand and an Uzi in the other. I wouldn't recommend the chicken here," he advised the men. "I know them personally."

Avi beamed so widely that he had to push himself back slightly from the table. His companions slapped down their menus as if they were the last cards in a hand. "There are many ways you might be able to assist Israel in her many trials," Avi said finally when he had wrestled down his smile. "And many places in which you might assist her. Because those who would destroy us are spread all over the world."

TWENTY YEARS LATER, Jacobo Leyva, thickened, wizened, with wrinkles in the corners of his black eyes, had come to Sarajevo to counsel the city's brewery on techniques for emergency operations, as he had previously advised beer makers in war-ravaged El Salvador, Guatemala, and Eritrea. Jacobo told Tedic that the firm he represented believed they owed a debt to the Muslims, Serbs, and Croats of his city. Their forebears had hidden two thousand of Sarajevo's Jews in pantries, attics, and drainpipes in 1941, as the thugs of Prime Minister Milan Nedic tried to appease their Nazi overseers by storming up the stairs of apartment blocks—"in hobnailed boots, you can be sure"—to drag out Jews, faggots, and Gypsies.

"Eight thousand died in the camps," Jacobo told Tedic. "It might have been ten thousand. Sometimes that's the math of salvation."

If Sarajevo should fall now, said Jacobo Levya, Jews would be extinguished from one more place on earth. His firm could not permit that. Nor could they allow the only volunteers to be armed gangs from the Arab world, or else there would be no place for Jews in any Sarajevo that survived.

"Our friends," he told Tedic, "must be as sure of us as our enemies."

"Your firm?" Tedic said simply. But Jacobo went on blandly. He trained his gaze over Tedic's map before lowering himself back onto the hard floor. Jacobo was a fastidious man. He slipped a palm beneath his worsted buttocks to avoid sitting on muck in his Swiss slacks.

"It doesn't matter if these are all the work of one man or several," he said heavily. "One viper or a whole nest of vipers. They have at least one superlative shooter over there. If you can find him—or one of them—stop him."

It was the answer Tedic expected, if not the one that he had hoped to hear.

"Let's suppose we can find him," he suggested. "Or, at least, *one* such him."

"Bait a trap. But that would be taking a chance. He might slip the trap and leave you nothing. A better plan is to figure out who he is, then find out where he sleeps. Kill him," Jacobo said softly, "between breaths."

The barefaced gravity of the phrase made Tedic squirm and smile. "*If* we can find out who he is," he said finally. "But Sarajevo is not Gaza. Unlike your firm, we hardly have the means to go house to house on the other side of the river."

"You have no one over there?"

"A few people passing information. *Selling it*, I should say. No one to send on that kind of operation."

Jacobo shifted to slide his left hand beneath his backside. With his right hand, he rubbed a thumbnail over a stray thread creeping out of a buttonhole of his soft blue shirt. "It doesn't take a team of commandos," he said. "A pretty girl with a rope or a razor. Or a pretty boy. A grandmother who can tuck a bomb under a pillow could get the job done."

Tedic lifted the beer can that held down the north of Sarajevo and let the map snap back between them over the line of the Miljacka.

Jacobo offered his next question as quietly as if there were a stranger in the room. "What about the Prince?" he asked.

Tedic lifted the eastward can. Most of Sarajevo rolled up beneath them. Only the streets and lots south and west of the river, marked by thick red pen strokes showing artillery emplacements and snipers roosts, were visible. "We don't do business with him," he answered. He thought a moment before adding, "His firm. Not anymore."

"Sometimes," Jacobo admonished, "you have to go to the one man who sells just the right nail you need to finish the whole barn. What you think of him doesn't matter."

"Arabs playing *Day of the Jackal* on the Serb side of Sarajevo? Arabs swinging through the evergreens on Mount Igman?" said Tedic. "That's too hilarious. They'd have no chance."

Jacobo Leyva was no longer a lion-legged young kibbutznik. His knees ached like an old dog's. He had to stand before he fell over. Tedic noticed caramel-brown Italian loafers, their prosciutto-thin soles squishing in the muck, as Jacobo's knees snapped back into place. "You mean it could be a suicide mission?" he asked.

Whatever else Jacobo knew, he left unsaid, on the floor. His hands smacked as he rubbed flecks of dirt from his palms and discreetly tapped the tips of his fingers against his worsted thighs.

Tedic stood up, too. He was a head shorter than the Mexican, and had some trouble catching his eye. "You'd be amazed," he told Jacobo, "at some of the people we have to work with."

"I wouldn't be," said Jacobo.

TEDIC TOOK JACOBO upstairs, where he had another room prepared for a further conference. But first, near the loading dock Mel had heated some water on one of the small wood cookstoves that leather and silver craftsmen in the Old City hammered out for two hundred deutsche marks. He poured the water over the grounds of some dark Italian coffee their visitor had brought along in a waxed bag.

Tedic smelled the fresh coffee brewing. His nose flared with the quivering alertness of a foxhound. Jacobo had also brought along Perugina candies, chocolate-coated hazelnuts in shiny blue wrappers. Mel plopped them into a small pile next to three ironstone brewery mugs. Jacobo gratefully sipped the coffee. He left his candies on the plate, respectful of the difference between the midday craving of an overstuffed middle-aged man for something sweet and the relentless ache and faintness that was real hunger, diverted only by lethargy and cigarettes.

With the brewery's supply of electricity, Mel was able to keep a radio buzzing in the loading dock for most of the day. The Knight was on—an extra shift—and he was reciting poetry.

"You might find this worth hearing," Tedic told Jacobo.

...

THE KNIGHT WAS rolling into his full cadence. Jacobo couldn't understand the national language. But he could hear phrases rising and falling, flaring and cracking, like the fire in a forge.

"What is it?" asked Jacobo.

"A long story," said Tedic, staring up at the radio's speaker. "An old one, at any rate. Serb Genesis."

Jacobo inclined his head with curiosity.

"The Battle of Kosovo," Tedic told him. "In *1389*," he emphasized. "In the Field of Blackbirds. It's read every week here. The story of the great Serb nation strangled in its womb. *By Muslims*, it may be gratuitous to add."

Tedic lowered his head to listen for a point at which to latch onto the narrative for his guest. After half a minute, he raised a hand next to his mouth, as if he were announcing a basketball game. "Here. Sultan Murad is preparing to lead his hairy Muslim hordes against the noble Tsar Lazar."

"A poem?" asked Jacobo.

"An epic," Tedic assured him. "Nothing less than *The Rape of Lucrece*. Here." He motioned Jacobo to stand closer while he interpreted from Serbo-Croatian into English:

From Jerusalem, O from that holy place
A great gray bird, a falcon flew!
And in his beak he held a swallow
With a letter
Lazar! Lazar! Tsar of noble family
Which Kingdom is it that you long for most?
Will you choose a heavenly crown today?
Or will you choose an earthly crown?
For all shall perish utterly,
And you, O Tsar, shall perish with them.

"This is not headed for a happy ending," Jacobo observed.

Tedic held back further comment with his hand. "Please. One of my favorite parts." He recited:

Though the Turkish army is not small,
We can easily battle them

And defeat them. . . . They are
Not an army of knights and warriors
But of weary pilgrims, the old and crippled,
Artisans and skinny adolescents
Who have never tasted blood. . . .
They shit upon the earth
In fear of us.

"No knights or warriors," said Tedic when he finally turned back to his guest. "That's us. An army of artisans and skinny adolescents. Serb Shakespeare got that right."

"What year?" asked Jacobo.

"It was 1389. Well before Shakespeare."

"The emperor Montezuma was killed in 1520," said Jacobo. "Probably stoned to death by his own people."

"Practically last week," said Tedic.

The men turned their heads back up toward the radio's speaker. The Knight had rolled in Peter Tosh just as he had the Turkish army shitting in fear: *Dem mus get a beaten, dem ha fe get a beaten, Lord, and dem can't get away.*

The Knight returned, husky, heartsick, and unswerving, with a verse that rang bones and roused blood over six centuries. Tedic thundered in imitation:

Whoever is a Serb,
Whoever shares this heritage,
And does not come to fight,
May he never have the sons
His heart desires;
Let nothing decent grow beneath his hand—
Neither purple grapes nor healthy wheat;
Let him rust away like dripping iron
Until his name shall be extinguished!

Tedic thrust his hands back into the pockets of his black leather coat to grip his cigarettes and quiet his trembling. He lifted an eye to Jacobo. "Makes all that Shakespearean *For he today that sheds his blood with me shall be my brother* sound rather fainthearted, doesn't it?"

. . .

IRENA HAD ARRIVED after Tedic's last meeting with Jacobo. Tedic took a couple of the Peruginas from the pile next to the emptied coffee cups and placed them beside her as she sat in a basement room, zipping herself into her gray jumpsuit.

"Your personal business is your own," he said when she looked over. "This is not personal. Have you heard from Coach Dino?"

"Of course not," she said instantly. "Have you?"

"I'm not trying to fence with you." Tedic sounded weary.

"No," Irena said decisively. "No letters, no phone calls, no roses. How would we talk anyway?"

"People get messages through. Do you ever talk to someone who's heard from Coach Dino?"

"Who would that be?" Irena sat back on her stool and thumped her fists on her knees. "You? My mother? Molly? Ratfucker Mladic?"

"Maybe without even realizing it. Do you have any friends on the other side?"

"Of course!" Irena exploded. "Who doesn't? If *you* had *any* friends, you'd have some there, too." It was an insult to make Tedic smile and retreat, and it allowed Irena to sit back more easily. "He would only try to reach me," she said more softly, "if he could reach me with his dick. He's on to new conquests, I'm sure."

Tedic handed Irena another Italian candy and made certain to take the crackling blue wrapper from her hand, so that she wouldn't let it flutter down from the perch on Omer Maslic Street, where she would spend the next few hours of the night, and shoot a man's shoulder while he was pumping fuel into a truck off Duro Salaj Street.

IRENA'S PARENTS HAD the BBC playing at low volume, like a sauce simmering, when she arrived home in the early morning. She got batteries easily at the brewery. Tedic had them pitched out of flashlights and radios before they could run out in the course of duty. Mel kept the discards in a box near his desk for the taking. Irena would bring them home, where they would work for a few hours—give voice to the radio, or light to a torch—then flicker and die.

Mrs. Zaric had put a fistful of twigs into the tin cookstove to try to heat water for tea while Peter Gabriel sang over the night's disheveled sheets on the floor.

Mr. Zaric was indisposed. Aleksandra Julianovic was rolling and pressing tea leaves out on a cloth.

"Busy night, dear?" Mrs. Zaric asked.

"Dreary and cold." She brought her lips against her mother's cheek.

"It's getting warmer," her mother observed, as she had for more than a week.

"Not fast enough," said Irena.

She could hear the water trill inside the kettle. Pretty Bird joined along. Irena reached for an opened pack of Marlboros and thumped it against her forearm to release a cigarette. She had matches in her shirt, and drew one out. She watched the flame plume before she spoke. "I was screwing Coach Dino," she announced. "Before all this."

Mrs. Zaric turned around from the kettle on the cookstove and knelt down across from her daughter.

"Screwing. *Screwing.*" Mrs. Zaric kept her voice quiet, but it betrayed a quaver. "Screwing. How do you mean?"

"All ways," said Irena.

"I don't mean all the ways. I mean—*you* mean—*sex?*"

"Of course."

Aleksandra crawled over on her knees to take the kettle down from the cookstove.

Mrs. Zaric picked up the cigarette that Irena had put down on a plate. "Of course," she said. Then, more sharply, "Of course, most of us get through school without screwing our teachers."

"He was my basketball coach."

"He was a *teacher,*" Mrs. Zaric repeated. "*An adult.* Twice your age."

"Seventeen plus seventeen," said Irena. "That's just a math problem."

"I'm glad he helped you with your homework."

"It was a joke between us. Seventeen years—almost the same as Charles and Diana."

"You see how that worked out," said Mrs. Zaric.

"She was inexperienced," Irena retorted. "She needed to be—the royal family insisted that she be—a virgin."

Aleksandra Julianovic turned around from the cookstove, holding the kettle delicately by its handle.

"She even had to have a doctor's exam," Aleksandra attested. "To certify that she was virtuous."

Mrs. Zaric looked over at her daughter and aimed the shot she knew would close the argument with no retort, and no victor. "That's not one of *your* problems, is it?"

Mr. Zaric pushed against the bathroom door and shuffled out in his mother's old pale jade robe, waving a *Q* magazine with a cherry-haired Cher on the cover. "Give it some time in there," he announced. He joined them, sitting cross-legged on the tangle of blankets.

Pretty Bird waddled over to the cigarette that Mrs. Zaric had dropped into the crags of a sheet, rolling it over like a log with his beak.

"Our daughter was having sex with Coach Dino," Mrs. Zaric announced. "She just revealed it. Like Kissinger going to China."

"Her basketball coach?" asked Mr. Zaric.

Irena watched her father incline his head with interest, but saw that he had his eyes on the cup of tea that Aleksandra had poured out.

"He's very hairy," said Mr. Zaric.

Aleksandra had reached out with one of the brownstone cups.

"I used to see him," Mr. Zaric recalled. "At the games. Wearing those shirts with no sleeves. To show off his muscles and that mermaid tattoo." He blew across the surface of his tea, then drew back. "I thought he was very hairy," he said. He then slipped the tip of his tongue out speculatively into the tea. "Whooo," he said. "That must have been interesting."

Mum and Dad . . . you know I'm growing up sad, Irena could pick out from Peter Gabriel through the clatter of the kettle and the tapping of Pretty Bird's claws. *I shoot into the light.*

Mrs. Zaric took two more cups from Aleksandra and handed one to Irena, who held it against her cheek. Then she broke into slow laughter. "Your father doesn't know what he's saying," she said. Her laughter clanged and roiled like the kettle. "All the trauma has made him forget that he agrees with me."

ON THE NIGHTS when Irena wasn't working, she had little difficulty falling asleep at home. She was tired and often hungry. The snap and pop of gunfire—even whimpers and screams—were like snores and stomach growls to her now. But almost every night she would awake in the middle of the night—two, three, who could say?—and drag herself over to Pretty Bird's cage. Usually his gray head was cocked slightly to the left. His eyes would be shut, baring small, pearly lids, his small clawed toes, pink and precious as veins, clasping his perch. His red-fringed tail would droop and rustle slightly, lightly, breezily. Irena would marvel. Such a small, soft thing to survive bombs and vipers' bullets. He was just breath, blood, matchstick bones, and feathers. She would put her right hand up to Pretty Bird's tender black beak and wait a second or more until she felt a small puff of his breath brush against her knuckles, then creep back under her blankets and fall asleep.

30.

IRENA AND AMELA HATCHED A PLAN—THE WAY, THEY TOLD EACH other, they did every spring, when they would devise some new feat or trick as the play-offs began and they prepared to play Number One High School. Amela was going to come over for a party.

A British comedian, Sasha Marx (no relation to Karl, Groucho, or Chico, though he encouraged all such speculation; Sanford Moore was his birth name), received U.N. authorization to mount a production of *Hair* in Sarajevo. Much of *Hair*'s music was already familiar to Bosnians of a certain age. The story—peace, free love, and long-haired outcasts who find community—was considered newly pertinent and appealing to younger Sarajevans. The play was a piece of nostalgia that managed to maintain, in a recovering old socialist society, a more intriguing reputation for being slightly naughty.

"How can we not wish to 'let the sun shine' on Sarajevo?" the Home Minister responded even as he was having shrapnel picked out of his leg in the hospital. "How can Sarajevans not wish for the Age of Aquarius to reign?"

But the Home Minister's functionaries immediately tamped his enthusiasm with practical considerations. They said it would not be possible for Sir Sasha (for Marx had recently received the Order of the British Empire) to present the play in any of the city's theaters. The danger of drawing a crowd to a prominent location was too great. Serb gunners could pick off playgoers as they arrived—or wait until they were seated to obliterate the audience with a mortar shell. Stage lights were also out of the question. Moore had offered to bring them in on a U.N. relief flight, along with generators to power them. But such prominent generators would set off a hum that would illuminate the stage—and guide snipers to their targets.

The Home Minister's subordinates informed him that the play was a significant cultural opportunity. But it would have to be presented in secret, they said. No advance notice. Only a small, incidental audience. And in the dark.

"At least costumes aren't a problem," the Home Minister advised Tedic. "As I recall, much of *Hair* is done nude."

Tedic regarded each caution as an opportunity to outwit the mentality of the old socialist bureaucracy. He suggested that the ministry appropriate one of the ample basement conference centers of one of the bank buildings on Branilaca Sarajeva Street, which was lined with a long and apparently effective sniper barrier. The building was secure enough to keep deutsche marks, dollars, and diamond brooches safe from attack. People should have the same benefit. They could sit on the floor of the conference center, to maximize seating. Tickets could be handed out at water and food lines—arrival times staggered—to deliver a wide and delighted audience for, say, three performances. Sir Sasha and his fellow actors, both Bosnians and West Enders, could meanwhile rehearse in a subterranean room of the brewery, where comings and goings could be efficiently disguised.

Tedic had even heard of a simple trick to compensate for the loss of stage lights. A couple of satirical troupes that performed from time to time in basements around town had devised the idea of using electric torches. Half a dozen would be set up on the floor, and each actor issued one to shine a light on his or her face.

"Or elsewhere, I suppose," Tedic said drolly.

"As the play dictates," the Home Minister agreed. He had seen a production of *Hair* years ago, when he'd attended a transportation conference in Stockholm. He raised his eyebrows in recollection of pink flesh and lank, pale hair. "That is an artistic decision that under this free government is left solely to the discretion of the director."

Tedic suggested to the Home Minister that a few Western news organizations be cautiously apprised of the production and invited to report on it. The world seemed to turn away from stories about massacres and mortar shells. But a story about *Hair* playing besieged Sarajevo offered more enthralling elements: music, danger, Western movie stars, and sensitively illuminated nudity.

TEDIC ALSO PROPOSED that the Home Minister put on a small party for Sasha Marx and his company the evening before the play. The Home Minister instantly agreed. Everyone could use a party. Bosnians were famously hospitable. A troupe of British actors might not be as useful to Sarajevo's survival as, say, a company of British paratroopers. But the graciousness and even the nerve of the artists were appreciated.

Irena, Sigourney, Arnold, Jean-Claude, Nicki, Kevin, Ken, Emma, and other attractive young people whom Tedic employed would be included in the party. The visitors would be charmed; they would want to identify with their hosts, and their real-life roles.

And Jackie should be sufficiently healed to attend. Jackie would astound them even more than usual. "Imagine," said Tedic. "The most alluring woman in the room will be a russet-haired, snake-hipped Sarajevan whom the war has visibly robbed of the means to give each visitor a full embrace."

"But she cannot tell them how she came to lose her arm," the Home Minister interjected. "She has to say, 'I'd rather not elaborate. I am but one of so many who have suffered.' "

"Show people will find such modesty incomprehensible," Tedic assured him. "They will be overwhelmed."

Obviously beer would be on tap. Other traditional party victuals could be brought in with the visitors—the Home Minister moistened his lips on remembering the tin of smoked oysters that had come with a recent U.N. guest.

But Tedic suggested that it would more neatly serve their interests to have the folks at the brewery prepare a repast of humanitarian relief delicacies. "Beans and rice, replete with the occasional worm," he said. "Peanut butter and Spam, with toenail curls of neon cheese food sprinkled over all. Our guests have grown up hearing heroic tales from their parents about plucky Londoners eating cold beans in Tube tunnels while the Luftwaffe booms overhead. They feel they have missed out on their own heroic period. They will feel privileged to eat cold beans in a darkened brewery with plucky Sarajevans shaking their fists under the guns of the Serbs."

The Home Minister sat back for a moment before a smile broke slowly across his face and he shook his head. "And if any press coverage resulting should venture the same plucky comparison?"

"As you say, it's a free country."

"Just prompt me when to start humming 'White Cliffs of Dover,' " the Home Minister said.

THE GIRLS HAD arranged their rendezvous for five, when the bronze light of early spring that still flowed across the field might make a crossing unexpected. They enlisted Zoran and his taxi, with an up-front payment of two cartons of Marlboros from Irena and two pouches of Balkan Sobranie tobacco on promise from Amela; she would bring them across under her blouse.

For almost an hour, the girls discreetly waved across the field every four or five minutes, Irena flashing a hand from the hedges on her side, Amela replying with a hand peeking out of the trees on hers. Shortly after six, the whine of a transport plane began to whir in their ears. Irena and Amela had guessed correctly; at least one flight would come in just before dusk. They saw soldiers tramp away from the center of the runway. The hedges around Irena began to clatter slightly from the breeze of the plane's props. Irena could see the red leaf of Canada on the front of the plane's gray whale of a belly, and the horizontal blue and yellow bars on the soldiers' right shoulders. Skies of blue, fields of grain, the flag of Ukraine.

Amela darted out. Three, five seconds passed with no soldier taking notice; they tended to watch the Bosnian side of the runway more closely, in any case. She had her hair down, long and full. How shrewd, Irena thought with admiration. How cunning of her to recall that referees overlook the penalties of curly-haired blondes. Irena heard Russian-accented shouts under the blast of the plane. But Amela ducked to run in the shadow of the plane's wheels. No soldier would chance a shot that might strike a tire on the transport plane—it could disable the aircraft and close the airport for days.

Just as Amela reached the hedges, two soldiers caught her by the shoulders. They turned her around and stood back, their guns pressed tactfully against their chests.

"You go back!" shouted one in English. "Please! Now!"

Irena and Zoran stood back, hoping to leave an impression of deference.

"Run back there?" said Amela, throwing a thumb across to the Serb side of the runway. "That's *dangerous*!"

"You not supposed to be here," said the other, breathing heavily; he had chased her most of the way.

"I'm not supposed to run across," Amela pointed out. "I could get shot."

Irena stepped forward. "You're here to keep people from running across the runway," she reminded them. "Not order them to run across. What if she got run over? Or, God forbid, shot."

One of the soldiers put a hand on his comrade's arm before speaking. The two young Ukrainians were confused and a little afraid. No smuggler would run across the field carrying nothing. No husband, father, or romantic love would expose a girl to so much danger. So the soldiers conferred in Russian and decided that she must be a rich man's mistress or, anyhow, a trifle that might have a price.

One turned to Amela and said in English, "We take you back. We walk with you. No worry. We protect you." He flashed his finger back and forth between his chest and her shoulders. "No one will shoot. We go now."

Zoran inched into view, waving a hand like a small boy at a parade. "Excuse me, sirs," he said with elaborate deference. Zoran patted the edge of something inside his jacket. Irena heard a small, hollow thump at which the soldiers tightened their fingers around the stocks of their rifles and ground their boots into the gravel.

"I am sure this is the kind of situation," Zoran said, "that can be resolved to everyone's satisfaction."

"We get cigarettes," one soldier said with a sly smile. "No problem."

"American?" asked Zoran.

The soldiers waited while Zoran unzipped his jacket.

TWO CARTONS OF Marlboros—one for each girl, or one for each Ukrainian soldier—put Irena and Amela in the back of Zoran's taxicab. With the back windows rolled down, their cries and giggles echoed in the cracked, abandoned streets and the prickled ears of lost, wandering dogs.

"You owe me *five* cartons for that one," Zoran called back to them. "And an invitation to that party besides."

THEY TURNED DOWN May 1st Street. Amela squirmed around in the backseat, looking from side to side, and reached over for Irena's hand. She counted shattered windows as they sped past the smashed housing blocks of Dobrinja. She stopped after reaching twelve. "The people who lived there," she asked quietly. "Where did they go?"

"Look closely," Zoran advised her.

Then Amela saw gray shapes shivering, rags moving, and even the flames of cooking fires. Hands flickered in the overcast licks of gray smoke.

In silence, they crossed over the Otoka Bridge and turned right to face

Grbavica. Night was falling, and lights in the hills and towers on the Serb side of town blinked out as shades were drawn, doors shut, and switches turned down.

"So close," was all Amela said.

"Very," was all Irena could manage in return. Their fingers tightened against each other's palms.

"Over there," said Zoran, inclining his head to the right. "Your school."

The cab clipped over the bare, darkening streets, howling when Zoran ground it into another gear. Amela was surprised that she could see stars in the sky as they pulled onto Marshal Tito Boulevard. Most of the trees had been pruned by shells or felled where they stood. "I have heard about this," she said.

"People had to chop them down for heat," Irena explained. "To cook food, make tea, keep out the cold. Soon we'll have to burn one book to have enough light to read another."

Amela craned out the window for a better look.

"That's not smart," Zoran told her.

"I will be okay," she said. "It's too dark to see your car, or my head. I know the missing trees make it easier for snipers. That's what we've been told across the way."

"Over here, snipers may or may not hit us," Irena reasoned. They could have been discussing Descartes, the Chaldean Empire, or any number of half-remembered things from their classes. "Cold hits us all. So we play our chance of getting shot against the certainty of getting cold."

Amela settled back in the seat and rolled the window up halfway. "We've been getting a little cold, too," she said softly. "There's an embargo. Fuel can be hard to come by."

Irena squeezed her friend's hand more tightly. They waved their fused fists back and forth playfully, from their chests to their chins.

"I'm sorry, I didn't know," said Irena.

"Hard to come by," said Amela. "Not impossible. We're fine."

Zoran turned the taxi into Sarajevska Pivo Street, along the west side of the brewery. Every few weeks, the brewery set out bins of all the trash that couldn't be burned. Trash collection in Sarajevo had become as unthinkable as postal delivery. Swarms of rats had taken over entire buildings for the spreading empire they now claimed along with flies, worms, moths, and fleas.

A small boy scuttled over a mound of cans. There were bean cans, cooking-oil cans, powdered-milk cans, Spam cans, and yeast cans, their lids curled back, gasping.

"Even the cans look hungry," Irena joked.

The boy was five or six years old, discernibly sandy-haired even in the dying light, wearing grubby green pants cinched around the waist with somebody's old burgundy tie, and a man's blue nylon shirt wound around him like a sheet. He picked up a can and peered through it as if it were field glasses, looking for bits of beans or Spam crusting along the seams. He was young enough to fit his whole hand into the can and, every few cans, he brought out his hand with great excitement, and licked oil or powder off his wrist, knuckles, and fingers.

"Oh," was all Amela said.

"He's hungry, that's all," said Irena. "Bless him. We see him from time to time."

"His mother lets him out?"

"He lives in a basement on the next block with a few other people," Irena explained. "His mother? Who knows where."

"That happens a lot," Zoran volunteered.

Amela watched the boy scamper down one mound and up another.

"I don't have a thing to give him," she said. "Not even a candy or a stick of gum."

"He's having his fun," Irena assured her. "He will get more out of the garbage than he could from your pockets. As long as the snipers leave him alone."

They got out of the car on the back side of the building, which was blocked to snipers. Irena took Amela by her wrists and looked at her. She was beautiful. But Irena had always known that. What made her wince was that Amela still looked lovely. Her face was full, soft, almost blushing. It had the pink flush of hope. Irena felt that her own skin was tight and white, like a corpse's. Creases now slashed the skin around her eyes and pulled tight across her forehead. Sometimes Irena could feel her skin squeezing against her bones.

"I hadn't noticed before," she told Amela.

"What?"

"Wearing the winter coat, I couldn't see. But you look so much"—Irena hesitated for a moment—"rounder and healthier than we do on this side."

"I haven't been hungry," said Amela.

"I haven't either," said Irena. "Only a few nights. But I see now, I am like a bird. And not Pretty Bird," she added with a smile. "He eats fine, thanks to you."

Amela slipped her right hand into the pocket of her jeans and brought out a small, glossy bronze tube. She pulled off the top and gave a half turn to the base until a sculpted tip emerged, a glistening candy red. Irena was reminded of the bullets in her clip.

"A dash on each cheek," Amela suggested. "We smear it in."

Irena was touched.

"But let me show you the latest advance in women's beauty," she told Amela. "You won't find it in *Vogue*." Irena rolled her fingers against her chin. She asked Zoran for a pin.

At first the driver turned up the empty palms of his hands. Then he turned his thumbs down at his belt. "One keeps my pants together," he said. "That's kind of necessary."

"I'll just borrow it," said Irena.

Zoran turned, his back to the girls, and fiddled with the flaps on his pants. "I've lost so much," he said simply, reaching back with a safety pin pinched between his thumb and his forefinger.

Irena took the pin and unclasped it. She held up her left thumb and pricked it with the pin. A drop of blood gleamed. She blotted it against her left cheek, gave her thumb three or four shakes, then pressed it lightly against her right cheek and turned to Amela.

Amela's eyes shone as she smudged the red into the flesh below Irena's eyes. "Lasts longer than Revlon, I'm sure," she said, as Irena solemnly pressed her thumb into Amela's left cheek, then right, as if she were lighting candles in church. Zoran looked away. With both her thumbs, Irena rubbed the blood over her friend's plump cheekbones until the color seemed to match her pink skin.

"Ready to meet Prince Charles," Amela said quietly.

"Maybe Scottie Pippen," said Irena. They took each other's hands, clasped their arms around Zoran, and walked down the ramp into the brewery.

TEDIC HAD TURNED the ground floor of the brewery into a beguiling party space. Stubby white candles had been melted on the bottoms and stuck to odd-sized wooden tables. The flames spit and sparkled off the sides of the copper brewing vats. Brewery personnel had laid out slices of Spam, sectioned so thin that they clapped tight around the rim of the serving plate, which was secured at the center by old soda crackers turning as soft as dampened cardboard.

Tedic was beaming. He had showered, shaved, and was strutting like the lord of the manor welcoming his minions. He had kept his shiny black leather coat spread authoritatively across his shoulders, but put on a white shirt underneath, soft and unblemished as fresh cream. He smelled of someone else's Givenchy. He was standing with a red-haired woman of a certain age, whom he introduced as Zule.

Irena had a hand on Amela's arm as she presented her. "My old teammate," she said. "You said I could bring a friend."

"Of course!" Tedic's enthusiasm was genuine and detailed. "The great Divacs. The best passer on the team. The whole league, I might say."

"Dr. Tedic was the assistant principal at Number Four," Irena explained. "Also the assistant basketball coach."

"You would not remember me," Tedic assured her. Amela smiled shyly.

But Zoran shook Tedic's hand without introduction. "We are old friends," he said.

"I am an old customer," Tedic clarified, with no apparent chagrin. "More than once, Zoran has picked me up in my stocking feet when I was turned out of a girlfriend's place in the middle of the night."

The Mexican brewer who Irena had seen around the ground floor and basement now edged into their circle, wearing a square-cut English blazer with gleaming brass buttons imprinted with some borrowed coat of arms. The metal in the buttons alone—Irena had developed something of her father's eye for such appraisals—could have given her bullets for a month.

"Jacobo," Tedic said simply. "He has come from a long ways away to help us improve our production."

Jacobo shook hands all around.

"I have never met a Mexican," said Irena. "What do I say?"

"Hello does fine."

"Is that what Mexicans say to each other?" she asked.

"Hola."

Irena tried out the word.

"Hola. Hola. Ho-la."

"Like a native," said Jacobo, and Irena thought that she and Amela had both blushed slightly, even through their rouge.

"Where are you living?" Tedic asked Amela. The question was expected for anyone who had been in Grbavica, and Irena and Amela had prepared an answer.

"A few blocks away."

Don't lie, Tedic had once advised Irena. *I mean this tactically, not morally. You can go crazy trying to keep lies from getting crossed. Find the kernel of truth you can say. Then you will at least be sincere and believable.*

"How are you getting by?"

"Fine. There are moments."

"Of course," said Tedic, who had turned back to Zule. Irena hoped Tedic would conclude that it would not be gallant to ask her guest anything further.

Tedic asked Zule, "Ever had these girls as your guests?"

She smiled and shook her head.

"Superb basketballers. Irena works here in the brewery, and we are lucky to have her. Amela?" Tedic inclined his head so that Amela might choose to complete his sentence.

"I help out where I can," she said. "You know how it is."

IRENA'S EYES HAD already alighted on serried ranks of wine bottles. The reds seemed to gleam like rubies—or as Irena imagined rubies—and the whites had the glow of yellow gold.

"From our guests. You should try it," Tedic encouraged. With a wave of his hand, he invited Irena and Amela to help themselves. The girls lifted the bottles as if they were dolls, examining them for different features.

"Oh God, they're *French,*" gushed Amela. The light inside the bottle dimmed when she lifted it; the wine seemed to darken to the color of blood.

"Beau*jjj*o*lll*ais," she announced, trying to soften the *j* and trill the *l* for authenticity.

"I've got a Côtes d*uuu Rrr*hône here," said Irena.

"Is it like the difference between red and green Smarties?" asked Amela.

"That's no difference," Irena pointed out. "This is different grapes, not just colors."

"More like the difference between Marlboro and Camel?"

Irena had already scooped up a small stack of waxed paper cups. "No reason not to conduct our own investigation," she declared. She poured a splash of the Côtes du Rhône into two cups, which the girls tapped together.

"It is so amazing that you're here," said Irena.

"Amazing."

They swallowed together.

"Smoother than Slovenian," Amela said. She took another sip thoughtfully. "I don't think the Slovenes have Côtes d*uuu Rrr*hône."

"I could like this," said Irena.

"White wine is what athletes are supposed to drink after they stop working out," said Amela. "It doesn't put on weight the way beer does."

"I'll never stop working out," said Irena. "When this is over, I'm back to my routine."

"Me too," said Amela.

The girls drained their cups of Côtes du Rhône at the same time.

"I'd like to invite you over, you know," said Amela, staring ahead into the flicker of candles against one of the brass cauldrons. "It's just difficult. Even if you could sneak across."

"I understand. I've figured that out, too."

"My parents love you. No one we know has a problem with Muslims."

"A lot of people we both know have a problem with Muslims," Irena pointed out. "I guess that's why I'm here." She could feel the wine redden her face, and she laughed to release the tautness in her voice.

Amela had been running her fingers along the neck of a bottle of white wine when a large man startled both girls by stopping on his heels and turning back to them. "If you're going to drink piss, dear," he admonished Amela, "at least make it Sancerre."

Their host was huge. Sir Sasha Marx wore a black suit over a black turtleneck sweater. The slimming effect of black was overmatched. His belly proceeded past the flaps of his jacket like the prow of a ship pulling against its anchorage. His red jowls engulfed the ribbed collar of his turtleneck like a lava flow. When he took up the bottle of white wine, it looked like something from a child's tea set in his stout fingers.

"Muscadet is a drink for grandmothers having a Christmas lunch at Fortnum's," he declared. "Not young starlets."

Irena was quite sure that she and Amela were blushing now. "Actually, we're not actresses," she said.

"Ah, real people," remarked Sir Sasha. "I'm Sasha Marx."

"We know," said Amela.

"You didn't expect me to be so portly. I can tell."

"Yes, we did," Amela answered, then reddened deeply. "I mean, *Giancarlo's Full House* used to be on here." Sir Sasha had played a widowed opera tenor who marries a Manchester policewoman with seven children and a sheepdog named Dr. Watson. They open a restaurant and much warm hilarity ensues.

"Oh, Christ. Off for years, but that show follows me around the globe. Checks do, too, thank God. Remember, ducks. The camera always adds ten pounds."

Amela and Irena were taken aback just long enough for Sir Sasha to laugh and splash out big-handed portions of his recommended wine into their cups.

"You may recognize some other faces around here, then," he explained. "I keep telling the young folks, 'Your careers are pitiably dependent on your pathetic beauty. Whereas mine can withstand the depredations of time, drink, and lack of talent. As long as there is so much as a single production of *Henry IV*,' I tell them, 'on some backwater provincial stage, this fat fuck of a Falstaff has employment!' "

He used the girls' agreeable laughter as a kind of exit theme.

"Sasha Marx!" said Amela. She squeezed Irena's hands again.

"Not quite Toni Kukoc," said Irena. "But my mother loves him."

There were three small, sweating grayish bricks on plates on the table, embellished with limp green strands of parsley.

"All we can't get here," said Irena. "Food, medicine. And someone finds parsley."

"People are taking bites from the brick," Amela noticed.

"It's Olga Finci cheese," Irena explained.

Amela eyed the brick with amusement.

"Cheese?"

"Condensed milk, garlic powder, salt," Irena explained. "Onions, when possible. Heat it, cool it, let it sit out for three, four days."

"Olga what's-it's-name is a Dutch recipe?"

"I doubt it," said Irena. "One hears she was some kind of chemistry teacher."

The girls stood facing the block of cheese as if it were a dead rat that one of them would have to find the nerve to tap with a stick.

"You get first pick," Amela suggested.

"You're the guest," Irena countered. She shaved a half inch of the springy mass onto one of the soft crackers and held it out to Amela.

Amela took it into her mouth in a single bite, and followed with a quick jolt of Sasha Marx's Sancerre. "Definitely a chemistry experiment," she said through painfully parted lips.

THERE WAS A rapping of knuckles against tables, and taps against beer bottles. The Home Minister wanted to make a few remarks. He was wearing his one set of graying London pinstripes, further frayed by grime and the tug of the crutches he now needed to walk. But tonight he wore no tie against his cheerless white shirt, and let the collar fall open so that a small portion of his collarbone was nearly visible.

Tedic had been merciless. "Oh, my word," he had exclaimed, slapping a hand against his head. "Have you become a reggae singer?"

"Our guests are artists and bon vivants," the Home Minister had said stiffly. "I'm hoping to blend in."

Irena and Amela could make out only every few words. There was still much scuffling of chairs and shushing of conversation by the time the Home Minister began. He said he was deeply grateful that Sir Sasha and his players were joining with Sarajevo actors to present a play that was so poignant and important all over the world. And then he stood aside so that Sasha Marx's immense black-suited shoulders and Volkswagen stomach filled the space.

"I want to thank the United Nations," Sir Sasha began, and silenced a ripple of snickers with a sharp glance from his great rubber ball of a face.

"The United Nations," he repeated slowly. "For letting us in to this besieged city. The United Nations is only as staunch as the spines of its membership. Which seem to be made of that very same thin shitty gruel of a cheese which has been laid out for our delectation," he said with a smart flick of his hand.

There were laughs and claps all around.

"The U.N. has assigned French soldiers as the protection force here in Sarajevo." He paused, and jutted out his chin. "Protection," he mused, and took another, longer pause. "Odd word. Don't seem to have protected much, do they?"

The tinkling of laughter was like the thrum of a motor for Sasha Marx. He shifted forward onto his right foot. "They seem first-rate lads. Taut and disciplined. I'm sure much like our British boys and girls assigned elsewhere in Bosnia. They haven't protected very much, either. We have our own experience with French soldiers, after all. Let me ask our Bosnian friends. Would you know why there are so many trees along the Champs-Élysées?"

There was a pause as small, speculative mutterings made their way around the room.

"Because the French Army is so very fond of retreating in the shade," Sir Sasha declared.

Hoots and applause broke over the room as Sasha Marx made a show of trying to outshout them. "Oh, I'm so very sorry! There goes my chance for the Légion d'Honneur! Wait—what's that? *I already have one!* But I am not a political man," he said sorrowfully. "It is not the world I know best. There was once a production in the provinces."

Sir Sasha's associates rocked back in expectation of a story.

Amela leaned in toward Irena, her eyes glimmering. "I cannot believe," she said, "that we are lucky enough to be here."

"Macbeth," Sir Sasha went on. "Portrayed by a saturated old stage star. When the King was informed, 'The Queen, milord, is dead,' our star knew that the time for his turn had struck. He came downstage to deliver—can we call it the best-known monologue in theater? I think so. But he was terrible. *Awful.*"

Sir Sasha paused for a moment, and went on, "He intoned, 'Tomorrow, and tomorrow, and tomorrow creeps in this petty pace from day to day, to the last syllable of recorded time.' And the audience booed. He proceeded. 'And all our yesterdays have lighted fools the way to dusty death.' The booing crashed across the stage in bloody waves. Yet our star went ahead.

" 'Out, out, brief candle!' he flashed. 'Life's but a walking shadow, a poor player that struts and frets his hour upon the stage. . . .' But he had to halt. The booing was so bad, he couldn't be heard. The star crossed to the footlights. 'Ladies and gentlemen,' he said, 'I don't know why you're booing me. *I didn't write this shit!*' "

The new wave of applause made the candle flames flicker. Sir Sasha put a beery arm around Ken and Emma, whom Irena recognized as members of Tedic's troupe, and explained that they wanted to sing a couple of songs inspired by the production the visitors were about to mount.

Emma was slender, with hair the color of amber honey. Ken had a thin bristle of a mustache that curled around his mouth, musketeer style. Emma patted her hand over her throat, as if stifling a cough.

"I will try to make our song heard," she said daintily. "Sir Sasha is so hard to follow. We have reworked some lyrics for your consideration." Ken and Emma softly began:

When the Serbs take over your house
And Boris aligns with Uncle Sam
Then Slobo will guide the planet
And they won't give a damn!
This is the dawning of the Age of Hilarious
Isn't it precarious?
Precarious? Hilarious!

Sasha Marx had been standing at a distance from Ken and Emma. But as their song took hold he came closer, so that the look of marvel on his face became visible as they moved into the chorus:

Serbia is expanding
Sniper shots and bombs abounding
No more food, lights, or water
Just hunger, blood, and slaughter
Chaos and dissolution
Fear and destitution
Hilarious!
Hilarious!

The applause that broke in was dense as a drum roll. Sasha Marx stepped forward to press his lips with suction force against both performers. Emma said they had one more song. Sigourney and Jean-Claude were waved up to join them. Emma, who seemed to own the sweetest voice, struck up the first notes:

Good morning snipers
Your shots say hello
Serbs shoot above us
We huddle below
Good morning snipers
You lead us along
My love and me as we sing
Our early morning running song.

All the singers joined in, and motioned for the audience to do the same. Irena looked over at Amela, and saw that she was singing:

Doo-bee-doo-wee-doo-doo
Doo-bee-doo-wee-doo-doo
Doo-bee-doo-doo-waa
Doo-bee-doo-wee-doo-doo
Doo-bee-doo-wee-doo-doo
Doo-bee-doo-doo-waa

Ken and Emma rang out the last stanza:

Run along
Don't guess wrong
Run and hide the whole day long.

By the time the ovation had died down, Tedic had sent Kevin before the crowd. He was a thin man with a mortician's neat mustache and slender, expressive wrists. "A man goes to confession," he said. "He hems and haws—he is embarrassed. Finally, he says through the small screen, 'Father, forgive me. But I fucked a chicken.'

" 'Fuck whatever you want,' says the priest. 'Just tell me. Where did you get the chicken?' "

Ken returned, sandy-haired and blue-eyed, blinking a smile like the keys of a small spinet. "I, too, have a religious experience," he declared. "Just yesterday I was walking along Vase Miskina to the water line when I saw"—he allowed his voice to dip here—*"Jesus Christ."*

Low hoots and whoops whistled around the room.

"*Un*mistakably Jesus," Ken asserted. "*Himself*. He looks just like his pictures. Long, sandy hair. Thin, scraggly beard. But if that wasn't enough, he was carrying a cross. Now, I don't believe in messiahs. Any more than I believe in Blue Helmets. But to be gracious I said, 'Welcome to Sarajevo, my Lord Jesus. May I ask a question?'

" 'Of course,' Jesus said. 'The loaves and fishes? Sleight of hand.'

" 'No, my Lord.'

" 'Water into wine?' he asked. 'Basic chemistry.'

" 'No, my Lord,' I said.

" 'Rising from the dead?'

" 'No, my Lord.'

"Then I tapped the cross he bore on his back and asked, 'Where did you get all of this wood? I'd like to heat a cup of coffee.' "

Laughter scuffed across the sharp cement floor and rubbed against Irena's ears. Emma returned, eggshell blue eyes shining under her straw-blond hair. Her voice got soft as the flutter of a bird's wings. The room was rapt. "You have all been here for a day or two," she said. "Let me ask, have you noticed? What is the difference between Auschwitz and Sarajevo?

There was an uncomfortable stirring. No one in the room wanted to hazard an answer.

Emma ducked her head against her chest. "Auschwitz," she avowed simply, "had gas."

Groans and guffaws took over the room.

JACKIE WAS MAKING her way to Sir Sasha's impromptu stage. She wore a clinging sleeveless black dress that made a slinky, sliding sound brushing against her backside, audible in the immaculate silence of people watching a woman with no right arm advance into their gaze. Sir Sasha Marx received her with a delicate bow. He touched his hand to her remaining forearm and brought her head against his shoulder for an intimate whisper. Jackie turned around and whisked a wisp of russet hair from over her arresting chestnut-velvet eyes; it fell back. She smoothed it in place with her one thumb.

"The first thing that I want to say," said Jackie, "is—sorry if I didn't get a chance to shake your hand."

SHRIEKS PIERCED THE room. Sasha Marx's great rump roast of a face opened with a roar. Jackie's face held, grave, tender, and benignly bemused. People were appalled and enthralled—Jackie held them rapt.

"Our visitors say, 'You folks are so plucky,' she went on. "Isn't that how you put it? '*Plucky.*' Speaking for myself, I don't know how to be plucky. We have just done what we have had to do. All of this hiding, running, scrounging. All of this bleeding and dying—we don't come by it naturally. What's natural for us is a cigarette in one hand, an espresso in the other. A beer on the café table, some leftist rags at our elbow, and the whole afternoon to argue about captivating inconsequentialities. Michael Jordan. The Princess of Wales. Madonna. Sir Sasha Marx. The Pet Shop Boys.

"Well," Jackie went on quietly in a hush so deep that Irena thought she could hear the sputter of candle flames. "It's been about a year now. The way we add up our lives has changed. It's not 'Do you have a job? Do you have money?' No one does. Cigarettes are more precious than money, anyway, because we live in three-minute scenes—that's as much life as we can count on. A night like this—we should look around. Next year, next week, tomorrow—faces will be gone."

Irena felt Amela's hand settle softly around her waist. She reached over with her own hand and rested it on Amela's forearm.

"Something called Sarajevo will survive. It will never be the city we knew. But there is still a chance for it to be open-minded, curious, frivolous, and free. Not a smelly, vanquished little capital for strutting bullies, bigots, and thugs."

There was flesh-colored gauze freshly wrapped where Jackie's arm had been. Carefully, she twisted her right hip forward and stamped her foot slightly, so that the stump of her arm was visible throughout the room. "Just let us use our *own arms* to fight," she declared, "and we will save our own city."

Those who were sitting on their haunches in the front of the room began to rise. Those who had been standing behind them, including Irena and Amela, sank to their knees under the weight of emotion. Sir Sasha gathered Jackie into his embrace, lifting her high against his chest. Then, sobbing, he took another step back so that Jackie could stand alone in the ringing adoration.

At last Sir Sasha stepped up and slid his arm around her shoulders. In his free hand was a handkerchief, which he made a show of wringing out. "You know," he said as the room began to settle, "we like to think that when barbarians storm the gates, and lesser peoples fall back from the fray, a distinctly British voice will ring out above the battle: 'I say, old chap. You don't really believe that we will permit this, do you?'

"But we have nothing to teach Sarajevo about holding back barbarians. We have nothing to teach you about blood, toil, tears, and sweat. We poor players, strutting and fretting upon your stage, are ennobled to stand alongside you for a few minutes. When we return to our slumbering, green island, we will grab every passerby we can find. We will peal from every stage on which we appear, that the people of Sarajevo"—he offered a polite, beautifully restrained bow in Jackie's direction—"have single-handedly held back the fist of tyranny. It is time to lend *our hands!*"

...

THE HOME MINISTER searched the assembled, shining faces and found Tedic. He was standing darkly next to one of the brewing vats, and had just taken a long draw of his Marlboro. The Home Minister followed the glow up to Tedic's eyes. When he was sure that Tedic had caught his gaze, the Minister nodded his head ever so slightly.

TEDIC HAD A tape player plugged in, and soon Peter Gabriel, Madonna, Joni Mitchell, the Clash, Peter Tosh, and Sting joined the festivities.

Irena took Amela over to meet Jackie. Jackie swirled smoke out of her lips and leaned in to throw her arm around Irena (who was reasonably sure that Amela didn't hear her greeted as "Ingrid") and kiss her, and then, because she was Irena's friend, brush a more than reflexive kiss against Amela's cheek, too.

Molly seemed to have had a better briefing, and merely put his head against Irena's and called her "little sister." "I'm not sure Irena has told me about you," he shouted down to Amela from his streetlight height.

"I'm not sure she has mentioned *you,*" Amela returned.

"Bitch," Molly hissed. "She's been saving you!"

Molly was childless, womanless, and friendless. Yet somewhere along his surreptitious journey he had learned that teenage girls could be diverted and amused whenever a grown-up stooped to share a profanity. It was as if someone had leaked a code.

Jean-Claude, whom Irena had barely met, made a point of meeting Amela. "Irena did not tell me she had such wonderful friends," he shouted.

"It should be assumed," Amela answered with a smile.

Sir Sasha had one of the few voices that could pierce the din. He upbraided one of his players with Falstaffian ferocity when he thought the man had poured himself too large a cup of a Bourgogne Hautes Côtes de Nuits.

"Drink bloody *beer,* bloody wanker!" he sang out. "Not the bloody fifteen quid Burgundy! As if you had discriminating tastes. Leave the wine for our hosts!"

ZORAN FOUND THEM shortly after midnight. The actors had slipped back to Mel's loading dock to light fat, ashy joints rolled in newspapers as Tedic and Zule helped them onto brewery trucks for the ride back to the Holiday Inn.

Zoran was holding his stomach and joggling his head. "In ordinary times," he told the girls, "I would say I'm too fucking drunk to drive."

"What do you say now?" asked Irena.

"I hope we don't hit a fucking tank."

31.

THE GIRLS HAD A FEW HOURS BEFORE DAWN SEEPED ACROSS THE city and Amela would have to make her way back home. Zoran drove them to Irena's building and said he would sleep off the party in his taxi, below the windows, until Amela was ready to leave. There was moonlight enough to see their way up the outdoor staircase to the Zarics' apartment on the third floor. Their rubber-soled shoes squished softly on the worn wooden stairs.

"It's nice out after all the smoke," Amela said in a whisper. "It's fresh and warm. Can we sit out here?"

"Bad idea," Irena said. "Just about here is where we found my grandmother."

"They can hit people here?"

"Anywhere. Haven't you heard of the Viper?"

"Everyone has," said Amela. *"Every move you make, every step you take . . ."*

"He's not just a song."

"I wonder," said Amela.

THE THIRD-FLOOR HALLWAY was dark. Irena patted a wall so that Amela could hear it and position herself against it to slip down to the floor.

"Besides," said Irena, "we can smoke in this hallway. Give me a second."

Amela heard the sound of a lock turning, and quiet shuffling. When Irena returned, she had two cans of Sarajevo Beer under an arm, and her head was cocked to the side so that she could balance something on her shoulder.

"Pretty Bird," said Amela.

"He was so eager to see you."

Irena leaned forward for Pretty Bird to bump his beak against Amela's nose. He was sleepy, and made only a slight burbling.

Amela put his head into the well of her shoulder and blew gently across the top of his head. "I've missed him," she said.

"He gets that Amela look," said Irena. "I can see it." The hall blushed with light briefly as she lit their Marlboros off a single match.

Amela lifted the tab on each beer with a *pffft* and handed one to Irena. "What is this shit?" she asked. "No Sancerre?"

"I'll check the cellar," said Irena. *"Madame."*

They clanged beer cans together softly.

"Amazing."

"Fucking amazing."

Pretty Bird was coming to. He took a stutter step and began to waddle in a small circle between them.

"Living like this. Day to day. All day. I don't know how you do it." Amela had locked her arms around her knees and sat back against the wall.

"You get used to it," said Irena. "I suppose you can get used to anything. I bet people in Paris ride the bus past the Eiffel Tower twice a day and never look up from their crossword puzzles."

"Those jokes," said Amela. "I couldn't believe those jokes."

"We laugh at strange things now," Irena explained. "Or else we wouldn't laugh at all."

"Do the Blue Helmets help?"

"Tedic—the bald guy. The old assistant coach. Tedic says that hell is a place where French and Egyptian soldiers are the army, the British are in charge of food, the Ukrainians are the police, and the United Nations is the government."

Amela tapped a gray ash into the palm of her left hand.

Irena told her, "Flick it on the floor if you like. We're the only ones on this floor, and it just blends in with the rest of the rubble."

Amela delicately overturned her palm full of ashes next to her on the floor. "I'll get them later," she said. "How do you—do you mind—get by?"

"We're fine," said Irena. "Hardest on my father. Nothing to do, and everything to feel bad about. I guess my brother feels that way, too. My mother and I—we have a lot to do."

"Anything from your brother?" asked Amela. Irena drew on her cigarette as she smiled.

"I thought you'd ask. Not for a while."

"Chicago still?"

"Maybe," said Irena. "Maybe Zagreb," she added softly. "Some people are trying to get to Bihac, one hears."

"I have," said Amela, and settled her eyes on the charred cameo of flame on the wall behind Irena's head. "We have our complaints, but I would feel cloddish to say anything here. We eat, we work."

"Snipers a problem?" Irena asked carefully.

"A little. People living along the front lines can get a bullet up their ass while they're taking a shower."

"We don't take showers," Irena told her.

"You see why I don't complain," said Amela. "You can always come up with something better."

"Something worse?"

"That's what I mean."

They mashed their cigarettes into the floor as they laughed, and lit up new ones.

"Have any fun?" asked Irena.

"The usual, I guess. Listen to music. Watch videos. I'm actually reading. Snipers aren't such a problem where we live. People tend to stay in, anyway. There are a few clubs. Mobster hangouts, really. They have money, they get things. But their acquaintance can be dangerous. Besides, I don't drink well when I'm not playing basketball and working it off."

"Ever see anyone?"

"Our old friends?" Amela asked. She blew out a cloud of smoke—like a distress signal, Irena thought—before answering. "People have scattered."

Irena put her chin over her knees and made her voice breathless and husky. "I . . . meant . . . *some-one.*"

"Oh. Boys," said Amela shyly.

"Or men."

"I haven't seen Dino."

"Oh, shit," said Irena. "Don't fuck with me. I didn't mean him. We're both too old for him now."

Amela palmed down another load of ashes and ran her hand absently through her hair.

"No," she said quietly. "No one regular. You?"

A speckling of bullet holes in the far end of the hallway was beginning to spark with morning light. Irena repositioned herself against the wall and crooked her legs to one side. "It's difficult. It's not like meeting boys on a spring holiday in Dubrovnik over here," she said. "You must see plenty of boys in the army."

"Not my part of it," said Amela. "You see almost no one. Some of the officers are slobs. They tell me that if I go off with them I can earn extra money, extra food. American cigarettes."

Irena shook out a fresh Marlboro. "What do you tell them?" she asked.

"No!" said Amela, drawing in the first breath from Irena's match. "And that if they ask me again I'll shoot off their balls."

Irena rocked back and forth and slapped her hand with her cigarette against her knee. "You can do that?"

"I get a gun in the army, yes. I wouldn't miss at that distance, I'm sure."

"Sweet little Amela!" said Irena.

"Hairy bastards, sometimes," Amela said, laughing.

Irena joined in when she grasped that they were remembering the same hairy bastard. "My mother threatened to cut someone's balls off," she said. "One of the bastards who dragged us out of Grbavica. She swore at him and stabbed him in the nuts with her house keys."

"Dalila?" said Amela, expecting a funny story to follow.

"I'd already kicked him in the nuts," Irena explained. She looked down at her Air Jordans and jiggled their black toes up and down. "Fabulous shoes," she added.

"You must meet soldiers," said Amela.

"All the boys are headed to the front," said Irena. "Except for people like my father."

"Mild Milan, always singing 'All You Need Is Love'?"

"A regular Marshal Tito," teased Irena. "He digs trenches and shit holes. The U.N. soldiers are around, of course. They're not hard to run into."

"We can see a few sometimes," said Amela. "Hard bodies."

"They wear armored vests."

"I didn't mean their chests," said Amela with an impish grin.

"You can tell?"

"Don't you think every girl can?"

Irena's voice softened. As the little spokes of sunrise licked in from the end of the hallway, she remembered that her parents were behind the door. "There was this one French soldier—I've told this to no one." She looked up at the apartment door, then at Pretty Bird, and rolled over a Marlboro for the bird to nose and clutch.

"He did me a favor. Then he—we—went around a corner. He unzipped his pants. Didn't even unhitch his belt. Didn't even drop his pants. Just popped it out. As if he were taking a piss. That's all it meant. It meant nothing. He was as scared as I was. I might as well have been milking a cow. He might as well have been licked by a dog. I scarcely touched him. It was like a sneeze."

Amela fumbled in her pockets for her own pack of Camels. She had to dig her fingers under the cellophane wrap for matches. "Sometimes that's the way to do it. Sometimes it can take forever." She handed a cigarette to Irena, and waited until she had taken the light from her match. "Did you see him again?" she asked.

"Just to nod in the street. I don't think he was—neither of us was—pleased with himself. He was Senegalese, I think."

Amela let a haze of smoke fill the space between them before she asked, "What they say—is it true?"

Irena smiled as demurely as an old Dutch portrait. "In this respect, he was a loyal Frenchman," she said.

The cigarette smoke floated away.

"One more illusion," said Amela. "I haven't touched anyone for a favor. Yet. Who knows? I've blown boys just for fun. Usually it wasn't—just something to do."

"That's a favor," Irena pointed out, and as the girls began to snigger and gasp, she motioned her arms, as if trying to tamp down a fire. "A *big* favor."

They paused to catch their breath. Amela leaned over to lend a hand to Pretty Bird, who had inadvertently skewered the Marlboro onto the end of a claw. She gently removed the impaled cigarette and rubbed a finger over his claw.

"Girls?" asked Irena softly.

Amela raised her head slowly. "That may be another matter."

The girls glanced at each other, taking care to keep their faces blank.

"You're quite safe," Amela said finally.

"So are you," Irena said after a hush.

Pretty Bird had the Marlboro back in his beak, and waddled toward the wall like a robed emperor carrying a declaration.

"War is so stupid, isn't it?" asked Amela. But she wasn't really asking.

"Two friends have to brave bullets just to have a little fun and a talk. People call war brutal. Sure, it is. That doesn't scare anyone away, does it? It becomes some kind of spell. Utterly *stupid.* Brainless as a fire. It makes trees into torches, scalds little dogs and children, turns cathedrals into cigarette ash. How many centuries has it been since the dinosaurs? Such small brains, but they still left behind bones. After us, they'll find only cinders."

Irena shifted her weight once more and felt her voice rising higher, but she didn't know at first whether it was anger or irritation. "And who do you think lights those fires?" she asked. "Do you remember that blizzard last summer? The strange moths that melted in our hands? Those were the ashes of the National Library. Your Serbs must have feared that we would take all those books, in so many languages, into our hands and hurl them against your tanks. Fat gray flakes of novels, poems, and plays floated down on our heads while corpses floated in the river."

"There are victims on both sides," Amela said quietly and considerately.

"That's not how *we* add it up," Irena shot back. "The piles of the dead can be just as high—they're not equal. We were hiding in our beds and basements when your brutes in black sweaters came in, swinging their cocks and declaring that Grbavica would be 'cleansed.' As if Muslims had become pests in your drainpipes. Which they purified by ramming their dicks into Muslim girls."

Amela stretched her legs and leaned back on her arms. But she was not at rest. In the spokes of light, Irena could see her face quivering like an exposed muscle. She opened her mouth once; nothing came of it. Her chin snapped back soundlessly. Finally she said, "No one I know has done that."

"Are you *sure*?" Irena challenged her. "Are you quite, quite bloody sure? Where were you that weekend last spring when we had to run for our lives?"

"I would have come running if I had known."

"How could you *not* know?" Irena throttled her own cry in the darkness. "All the gunfire and shelling. All the *screaming.*" She clapped her hands over her ears. "How could you sleep through that?"

Amela rolled onto her knees. She brought her head closer to Irena's shoulders, but turned her face away.

"We weren't sleeping," she said. "We were hiding. Same as you. We were scared."

"I was scared." Irena bit off the affirmation so she could spit it back. "I

still kicked a bully in his balls. My father still went out to try to talk the monsters out of killing us. They dragged his face over the parking lot and jammed a rifle in his ass. They laughed at us and picked us clean, like chickens, fucked and plucked. *My mother* was scared. But she still made that brute bleed. You'd be surprised—amazed, *terrified*—at what you can do when you're scared."

"I am," said Amela.

AMELA'S PACK OF Camels lay between them, but with the faint, unfussy motion of old teammates, she signaled Irena for a Marlboro. When Irena lit it, she kept her right hand softly on the back of Amela's. Irena turned around until they were sitting side by side in the same screen of smoke.

"I don't know if you remember the Zajkos," said Amela.

"Maybe if I saw them," Irena said wearily.

"They lived across the way," Amela explained. "One day—I think that Saturday of the march—Mr. Zajko comes to my father and says, 'Mr. Divacs, we are going through terrifying times. Who can say what will happen? I have a proposal.'

"He said, 'If Muslim bands come here, we will let you into our place. We will protect you as we would our family. If Serb bands come here, you let us hide in your closets or bathroom. No food, no water—we will be fine. Just let us hide until the madness passes. What do you say? Whatever happens, we both live.' "

Pretty Bird had lost interest in his cigarette and had wobbled onto Irena's right foot.

"What did your father say?" she asked.

"That his scheme wasn't real. It sounded nice. It would make a fine fairy tale for the BBC. But it wasn't real. My father told him that Serbs were going to take over our building—rough boys from the country. They would hurt any Serbs who harbored Muslims. So what Mr. Zajko proposed wasn't a fair offer. It couldn't save them, and it could get us killed. My father said that in these times he could only worry about us."

"Do you know what happened to the Zajkos?"

Amela shrugged. She put her Marlboro to her lips, flipped her fingers over her eyes like a bird's claw, and shrugged again. "They got out. Of the building, at least. We're keeping their television and microwave oven for them until the madness passes."

Irena rolled forward slightly and stretched her arms out to her toes. When she felt a muscle snag in her ribs, she began to laugh. "I guess if you can't save their lives," she said, "save their microwave."

Amela, who was uncertain whether Irena was being kind or snide, smiled faintly.

"It's something," she said.

Irena herself wasn't certain if she was being considerate or scornful. "I'm sure if they survive," she told Amela, "those are the first things they'll look for."

GIRLISH GIGGLING IN the hallway had seeped into Mr. Zaric's mind. When he opened his eyes, he heard it distinctly outside the door. He looked over at Dalila. She was still sleeping; sleep and grime had mussed her hair into playful platinum thorns. He didn't see Irena, and her blankets hadn't been unrolled. He didn't see Pretty Bird snoozing in his cage, or shuffling across the sheets. Fighting down alarm, Mr. Zaric reached for his mother's old pale jade robe and had opened the apartment door before he could quite close the flaps over his grimy gray boxer shorts.

"Omigod," said Mr. Zaric when he saw Amela, and he fell almost to his knees, as if he'd seen an apparition in a cave. Amela crawled forward to reach for his hand.

"What the hell . . . what the devil . . ." he stammered.

"Just a visit. A quick visit. I'm going back now."

"Are you . . . on this side now?"

"Just visiting."

"Of course," said Mr. Zaric. His voice seemed to roll through the hallway as he knotted his robe. "*Of course.* Has Irena offered you coffee? Tea? I think we have a little orange marmalade. This is amazing. The marmalade is good in tea when you don't have bread. *Anything* is yours."

"I'm fine, Mr. Zaric."

"I didn't know visits were possible."

"I snuck over."

It was gracious and good—Irena was glad—that Amela had been oblique in describing that course of action.

"Snuck over. *Snuck* over." Mr. Zaric kept pacing and shaking his head, as if it might put something new into place. Amela had gotten up off the floor and was shaking her feet, as if she were about to begin stretching for a game.

"I'm fine. I've got to go. Irena and I . . . I think we both have work today. I have to slip back before it gets too light. We've had a fine time. I've gotten to see Pretty Bird. I've gotten to see my friend. And now I've gotten to see you."

Irena could tell that her father wondered if he were still asleep. He held up one of his hands and brushed it through the spears of light that had begun to seep in from the window at the end of the hallway. He looked down at Pretty Bird, who was now doing a stutter-step back into the apartment. He looked over at his daughter, who had risen to stand beside Amela as they looked down at their strutting bird.

"The little emperor," said Irena.

Mr. Zaric took hold of Amela's arms gently. "I'm sorry. No man looks good in his mother's robe."

"You look fine," she assured him.

"It's been—maybe Irena has told you—hard to keep up appearances."

"You are all still handsome and lovely," said Amela. "I don't know how . . . you're all amazing."

"You are welcome anytime," said Mr. Zaric. "I would say, 'No call is necessary,' except no call is possible. What you have done . . . Pretty Bird," he said. His voice seemed to be smothered someplace in the bottom of his throat. "The seed. Not just that. I just want you to know. So much can't be known these days. Always—you are family."

Amela's eyes shone, and Irena thought she could see her wrists quavering slightly after the long night of little food and strong cigarettes. She could see her own fingers trembling faintly, like branches in a breeze. "Pretty Bird's family," she added.

32.

IRENA WASN'T DRUNK. BUT SHE WAS SLEEPY, FUZZY, AND HAD A QUEASY stomach from socializing with good wine, weak beer, Amela Divacs, Sir Sasha Marx, and Olga Finci cheese. She told her parents that she needed to sleep because she had to work that night. Mr. Zaric would tell her mother about Amela. Irena would go to bed. For the first time in months, she took her sheets into her grandmother's old bedroom and spread them on the floor. She did not bring Pretty Bird with her, because there were gashes and breaks in the windows. She worried that a wind might take him away, back into the street.

It was nearly three in the afternoon when Irena awoke. The sun had gotten bright, and the bedroom was almost stuffy. She twitched in the sheets for a few minutes, then got up to see if there was any water. Pretty Bird had been sleeping, too, and flapped his head, as if he were shucking water. But when he shook his head he made a sound like the opening of the Zarics' old refrigerator door.

"Phhhffft!" Pretty Bird said, and wagged his wings. *"Phhhffft!"*

Mrs. Zaric was reading a book about Panama. Mr. Zaric was dozing. Irena saw the edge of a small blue envelope under the door and went over to pick it up.

"What is that?" called her mother.

"It says *Irena* on the front," she told Mrs. Zaric. "Looks like Aleksandra's handwriting."

The letter was written in a crabbed hand, on old blue-ruled school paper:

> My dear young friend:
>
> When the sun broke through today, I decided—damn it all—to venture out of this block that has become my small shrunken

universe. I walked down Saloma Albaharija Street. People would tell me to get down, to crawl, to turn back. But I needed to see.

I walked by my old tea shop, my old *cevapcici* shop, the old magazine shop on Marshal Tito. All gone, as your father told me, just rats and rubble. I looked for my old friend Azra in the green-and-yellow building—an old art teacher, too. She is dead, many months. Muris, too, an old admirer, a civil engineer, lived on the floor below. He was in line on Vase Miskina Street. Rats and rubble happen to us, too.

The library, the theater, this whole side of the city now—it's like being on the moon. I have lived too long. I was never meant to see this.

Irena could feel a stinging on the very top of her head. As she flipped the sheet of paper over, the words seemed to slide away. She had to reach out with her hands to keep them close. Aleksandra's lettering seemed to grow lighter with each line. The last few letters fairly floated out of their lines and off the page:

We call this *madness*, to make it seem like a mirage. Just hold on, our heads will clear, everything will be back. The world I saw today—it's not worth waking up for.

Please do not be hurt by this! It is just not right that you—your mother, your father—should put yourselves in peril to bring a little food, water, or cigarettes to a feeble old bird like me.

It was not for me to know what you do—*really*—at the brewery. The long hours—so few particulars. I assume it has been secret, scary. We were lazy, sweet-natured children here who lived by our wits. We had to drive steel into our veins. But Sarajevo has a chance to live.

I am not religious (even now, when I should try). But if devout people are right, know that I will reach down whenever I can to try to make life kind for you. My impression of heaven is a place where I can see you. I am not sad. I am going on a voyage. The thought of you is my companion. Like Pretty Bird, I soar.

Aleksandra

Irena said nothing. She leaped from the room—she thought she had been sitting; she couldn't remember getting up—and raced through the Zarics' door, leaving it to whack against the wall like a clap of thunder. She took the interior staircase three steps at a time, and when she reached Aleksandra's door it wrenched open without resistance.

Aleksandra lay across a mossy green sofa trimmed with shriveling brown fringe. Her eyes were closed. Her hands were folded over her waist, as she might hold them in a reception line. She was wearing one of Irena's grandmother's old flowered blouses, her own long black skirt, and, Irena noticed, black nylon stockings and white men's socks for her voyage. Irena drew in her breath. She walked to the sofa to put her hand softly against Aleksandra's forehead. She smelled the drugstore vetiver splash-on that Aleksandra had found last year in Mr. Kovac's bathroom cabinet.

"Oh shit, dear, I'm fine."

Irena leaped back. She dug her thumb into her thigh and quite literally pinched herself.

"I left the door open, so I didn't hear you come in," said Aleksandra. "I was just stretched out here, dreaming of Eduard Shevardnadze."

Irena heard her parents stamp anxiously into the apartment, but she laughed so hard that her head lit up with tears, like a blaze at the end of a match. Mr. Zaric waved Aleksandra's letter as if it were a visa that could get his family into Switzerland.

"*That*," said Aleksandra with a frown. "I was going to come up and get it from under the door, but I was embarrassed. I got up to the roof and decided it was a long way down. The soaring part would be nice. The crashing part—ugh! It would only make more work for you. Pick up the pieces, dig a hole. Besides, you wouldn't like any of my clothes."

The Zarics surrounded Aleksandra on the sofa. Mr. Zaric kissed the top of her head. Mrs. Zaric put her head across her bosom. Irena took hold of her left foot and began to pull on it.

"I worked so hard on that note," Aleksandra protested. "I can see you didn't find it convincing."

IRENA REPORTED FOR work at the brewery and Tedic had her driven to sit behind a trash bin on Ilija Engel Street to look for flares of muzzle fire should they sprout from any of the small hills overlooking Otoka. She saw none. She was deeply tired and dulled. "Life and death," she mumbled. "And I can't keep my eyes open." She was exhausted, emotional, and sure that Tedic had deliberately stored her away for a night—out of sight, and in no position to harm herself, if also no Serb.

She heard the brewery truck pull up a block away shortly after five in the morning. She heard some unzipping and zipping at the back by the rear flap, and stifled the urge to shout out, "If you think you're hiding, you're not!" She waited until the preassigned hour of six before getting up from her post behind the trash bin and scratching on the back flap of the beer truck. There was a small delay. She imagined Tedic inside, pulling threads from around tacks he had stuck on his maps to plot the line of shots.

Irena was booting a rear tire with the toe of her shoe when she finally heard a rustling in the back. Jackie, Venus de Jackie, unexpectedly lifted the flap. Jacobo, the Mexican, reached down with two long cream sleeves to help lift Irena into the back of the truck.

"Ingrid, hi," Jackie said, smiling. "I'm making the run this morning."

She had on another winning black dress, clinging around her waist, a short sleeve pinned over her stump.

"Jacks, great, good to see you," said Irena. "Slow night. No flashes, nothing shot, no report. To what do I owe the honor of not finding Tedic behind this flap?"

"We'll explain." She looked over at Jacobo. "In fact, we need your help."

By now Irena was standing securely in the truck, but it hadn't moved. The motor wasn't running on idle. Jackie didn't rap her fist against the ceiling or call to the driver to pull away. When Irena took down the zipper on her gray smock, she heard it grate with unaccustomed volume.

"There's been a shooting into the Central Bank," Jackie explained. "That's where they put on the play. People were just filing in."

"There's a barrier there," said Irena.

"Yes. Well, they shot through the blue curtain."

Workers had stretched a large blue curtain between two buildings along Branilaca Sarajeva Street. The cloth had once hung in the sports plaza during the Olympic Games and it now flapped over the street like a mainsail in spring winds. The curtain couldn't stop bullets, of course, but it prevented Serb snipers from taking aim.

"Three people are dead," said Jackie. "Two wounded."

Irena sat down heavily on a bag of Swedish-aid wheat.

"One of the Brit actors, Rob. You may have met him."

Irena shook her head. "The Viper?" she asked. "What does Tedic say?"

"To hear them tell it, yes." Jackie replied. She inclined a shoulder toward some imagined speaker. "More important, the Viper must have had a partner. Someone who told him where the play was and when people would be there."

"I didn't know that," said Irena.

"I know. Few people did."

"Tedic saw to that," Irena added. "He knows how people talk. Tedic lives on loose talk."

Jackie fought down a smile. The Mexican may have held Tedic in some deference and dread, which it might be valuable to maintain.

"I know."

"Who knew?" asked Irena.

"We're trying to figure," Jackie explained. "Two wounded, three dead. We have to ask about your friend."

"Fucking Miro Tedic," said Irena. She began to squirm around to slip her arms out of her smock. "Horny Tedic. Ogles a girl and then suspects her. The only person I saw talk to her who knew any particulars about the play was Tedic himself. What does he say to that?"

Jackie tugged on Irena's left sleeve to help her slide it off. Jacobo apparently didn't smoke; he unwrapped a half-inch ash of tinfoil from a roll of mints. Jackie caught Irena's arm gently as she slipped it from her smock.

"Miro," she said, "was one of the three."

33.

"I DON'T WANT YOU TO THINK YOU'RE BEING KEPT PRISONER," Jackie told her.

They had taken her to the brewery, into a small basement room that had no discernible purpose. The floor was black, hard-packed earth. The walls were jagged gray brick. A single bare lightbulb burned overhead. There was no visible chain, switch, or even a string to turn it on or off. There was no table, no chair, no crate, no cot, no cups, no Coca-Cola can, no Marlboro pack, no trash, and no calendar. It could have been seven at night or seven in the morning in the room. It could have been May or December, Uzbekistan or Majorca, 1903, 1930, or 1993.

Jacobo had brought in three empty green plastic pails that had once held cleaning solvent. But they had been washed out long ago, and brought only a thin synthetic scent into the room. Jacobo overturned the pails and they each took a seat. The hard earthen floor seemed to soak up their voices.

"I feel like a prisoner," said Irena, turning around in her seat to take in the cold walls.

"Don't be ridiculous," said Jackie, tossing back a whiplash of her hair. "We need you, that's all."

"I can leave whenever I want?" asked Irena.

Jackie answered with another toss of her head and smiled. "Don't be ridiculous."

"I'VE WORKED MY SHIFT," Irena reminded them. "My parents will wonder."

"Zoran has gone to see them," said Jackie. "Zoran is telling your parents you're fine, you had to work. Which is true."

Irena kept turning to look at the walls, and saw that Jacobo had quietly shut a gray sheet-metal door behind them. The door looked brighter and newer than the bricks or the floor.

Jackie saw Irena looking past her, and leaned over to place her hand on Irena's knees. "I know. It's still a shock," she said.

"Tedic wasn't what you would call a sweetheart," said Irena. "I just always figured he would be the last man standing."

Jackie lightly touched Irena's hands as they lay in her lap. "He thought two steps ahead," she agreed. "While everyone else around here was still staggering back. I used to say, 'Miro, you little gnome. You could never make it with the likes of the girls you order around now, could you? Now, you command us. Jump! Run! Hide! Shoot! You even bestow our names. We have gone way beyond simple boyish fantasies here.' "

For the first time since she had been picked up in the early darkness, Irena managed a smile.

"He gave us a chance to do something useful," Jackie went on softly. "Not just cringe under the windows and wait to see who dies next. You should have seen him last night," she continued. "Someone fell over bleeding. There were screams. Ripping sounds from the curtain. Miro realized before anyone. 'Get down, get down!' he shouted, flapping his arms like an angry bird. Sir Sasha came charging out of the building. Tedic, our small, bald, twisted Tedic, threw himself over the great Sir Sasha Marx's vast Falstaff profile."

"Like a smelt trying to protect a whale," Irena said.

"Conflict reveals," said Jackie. "The one thing I learned in drama school that might hold for real life. Neighbors turn into monsters, and Miro Tedic turns into a hero."

"OKAY NOW," SAID JACKIE. She had taken to lacing shawls across her shoulders—they seemed to restore the symmetry of two arms—and had developed a gesture in which she absently tugged on an end of red fringe as she spoke.

"We are pretty sure we know how your friend got word about the play. The person who told her didn't know who she was, and just wanted to make a little time with her."

But Irena had to take a step back. She hugged her elbows close to her chest, as if she were trying to fit into a small, narrow space. "My friend," she asked. "What is she?"

Jackie inclined her head toward Jacobo.

The Mexican had folded his softly flanneled legs over the edge of the pail. "Your friend is a member of a group"—Irena thought that he hesitated at the next phrase—"called the Hornet's Nest." He sat back so that Jackie could add her corroboration.

"Hornets, the Viper, the Knight. Such nicknames. I swear, military men are only as clever as adolescent boys." Jackie's smile invited Irena to do the same.

Jacobo leaned in toward Irena. It was the first time she could recall looking into his dark eyes. "It was someone in the Hornet's Nest who fired the shot that killed the French doctor at Franko Hospital," he explained. "Someone in the Hornet's Nest fired the shot that killed the man—who knows his name?—in the courtyard of the Presidency Building. That unit got off the shot that killed the mother on Sutjeska Street. We know her name. . . ." Jacobo's voice trailed away into the earthen floor. "At least, Jackie knows it," he said, waving a hand in her direction as if acknowledging a region on a map. Jackie gave a slight nod back.

"From what we overhear," said Jacobo, "and from what the Knight so conscientiously passes on, it was someone from the Hornet's Nest who shot playgoers last night. 'Every step you take, every move you make . . .' however it goes."

"Coach Dino?" Irena asked softly.

Jackie flashed a quiet grin over at Jacobo, and tried to obscure it with the end of her shawl. "The basketball coach? The biathlon champ?"

Irena nodded once.

"Dino Cosovic has been in Belgrade. He shoots targets in tournaments. For him, the front lines might as well be in Tasmania. The only wounds he risks are from jealous husbands."

Irena's head had dropped between her shoulders, and she cast her eyes down along the floor. "Is Amela the Viper?" she finally asked.

Jacobo let out a breath as Jackie tucked a small cough into the red-fringed edge of her shawl. Jacobo leaned forward again, so close that his face almost touched the side of Irena's head.

"Time for a state secret," Jackie said softly from behind them.

"There is no Viper," said Jacobo. "The Viper is their artistic creation. He cannot miss. You cannot kill him. They assign him credit for their most extraordinary shots. He becomes more renowned with each one. Better—he becomes *real*. Everyone in that unit thinks that he or she is the Viper. But no one is. No *one* is. Like most art, he is a collaboration between truth, fraud, and imagination. The Serbs fool us so they can fool their own people. They make everyone scared of the sting of the Viper. The reflection of our fear makes them look larger to themselves."

JACKIE HAD LEANED back on her seat during Jacobo's speech, as if she wanted to observe them from some distance. She settled the rim of the green pail back onto the earthen floor, and kept her tone conversational. "Now here is the hardest part, dear," she said. "It is also the most necessary. Your friend is the enemy. She is *your* enemy. No poetic euphemisms are permissible. She is not just another sniper on the other side. She does not just wear another uniform. She is your predator. If you showed up in her sights, she would shoot you in the back. She has *our blood* on her hands."

Irena raised her own hands over her eyes and tugged at their corners. When she drew back her fingers, she saw that they were wet.

"Whatever kind of friend she ever was," said Jackie, still speaking gently, "she now shares a bed with the men who mistreated you in Grbavica."

JACOBO HELD OUT a pack of Marlboros to Irena. The top was still sealed and shiny.

"I thought you didn't," Irena told him.

"I don't. I just thought—" The pack crackled as he tapped it against his knee. Irena shook her head and smiled faintly. But as Jacobo went on, he slipped a finger through the creases of the cellophane wrap around the cigarettes. "We knew about her when she came over the other night," he said. "She was not supposed to get back. Zoran was supposed to surprise her, when she was all drunk and tired and you two had had your talk, and bring her here. So we could have our own talk."

"Zoran?"

"Zoran has worked for Tedic longer than any of us," Jackie explained. "Miro always had an eye for finding the overlooked man. Two steps ahead," she reminded Irena.

Something tougher entered Jacobo's tone. "If she resisted," he said, "Zoran was supposed to shoot her. If he had, we would have taken his word, no questions asked. And we might not be here now."

"Why not just . . ." Irena began to search for words. "I don't know . . . take her somewhere . . . lock her up . . . arrest her?"

"For what?" asked Jackie. "She is an enemy soldier. The best we can do—the duty we owe the people she killed—is to keep her from shooting anyone else. That duty we can deal with a bullet."

"How do you know what she has done? Like the Viper—there are a thousand boasts for every truth."

"She is helping to slaughter this city," said Jackie evenly. "What more do we need to know?"

JACOBO AND JACKIE exchanged glances again. They both pulled their pails imperceptibly forward toward Irena.

"What changed this beautifully conceived plan," Jacobo began, "was your crafty friend."

"She started begging Zoran for help," said Jackie.

"To stay alive?"

"To come over. *To switch sides.* She said she was on the wrong one."

"They were pulling away from your building when she started in," Jacobo explained. "She said, 'I've got to quit, I can't do this, I have to change. I know you can help me.' "

Jackie tossed an edge of her shawl over her right shoulder and snorted a burst of air that brushed back the ends of her hair. "You know. What hookers usually say."

JACOBO CURLED BACK the tinfoil on the Marlboros and plucked at one for Jackie.

"Zoran said he was glad to hear it. Zoran—a classic case of a compromised asset." Jacobo shook his head like an indulgent older brother. "Zoran knows you, he knows her. He likes you both. He likes your *parrot.* His pretty birds, he calls you all.

"Zoran told her there was a place he could take her where they would be glad to see her. She'd be cooped up and questioned. But she'd be safe. And if what she said checked out, she could be a very valuable teammate.

"But your friend said that if she didn't show up for work her parents would be killed. She said her managers had always made that clear. She said she had been plotting for some time, and that what she had to do was go home and tell her parents something so they could get away."

It was Jackie who finally extracted a cigarette from the pack and flourished it.

"Zoran said—he didn't know what to say," Jacobo went on. "He told her—he actually told her!—that if she didn't come back to the brewery with him his orders were to stop the car and kill her."

Jackie added a kindly, incredulous comic snort. "Zoran. *Secret Agent Man.*"

Irena could think of nothing more resourceful to ask than, "What happened?"

"ZORAN IS NO James Bond," Jackie continued. "Your friend reached around his belly and yanked the wheel to turn the car into a mortar hole along Lukavicka Cesta. She wrenched Zoran's arms behind his back and tied them with his own belt. Zoran is no Schwarzenegger. She tied his feet with her belt. Trussed him like a rabbit. She took his gun out of the glove box and made Zoran bunny-hop to the back of his taxi and forced him into the trunk. His own fucking trunk. The rabbit hopped into the pot."

Jacobo had a gentleman's habit of keeping a brass lighter in his slacks, which he now fired up below Jackie's cigarette. He spoke as he flicked the flint wheel. "Your friend kept saying, 'I'm sorry. I am so sorry.' This girl expects a lot for being sorry. 'It has to be.' She rapped Zoran's own gun against the trunk and said, 'I'm taking this in case I need it. I'm leaving your keys in the glove box. I'll send someone to get you.' Then she said, 'I'm going to come back at six tomorrow night. It's all planned. Tell your people. Tell Irena. If I see Irena from the other side, I'll follow through.' "

Jacobo laughed—despite his vexation, Irena was inclined to think, until she realized that it was because of it.

"The audacity! She asks for help, then gives us orders."

Jackie blew her first puff of smoke, and crossed her legs at her ankles. "She got to the airport, picked one of the thieves in the hedges—the most honest-looking one, I'm sure—and said, 'I've locked a man in the trunk of his taxi back on Lukavicka. His keys are in the glove box. Go back. Let him out, and he'll give you beer, cigarettes, whatever you want.' "

Jacobo was genuinely chuckling by now. "Zoran had to promise the bandit cartons of cigarettes and cases of beer," he said. "He was choking to death in that trunk, he was laughing so hard. Miro made good on the spot. He sent the smuggler away with so much loot, we had to have a truck deliver him back to his hedges."

"I told Miro that the whole play sounded like a ploy," said Jackie.

"Feminine wiles. An athlete's wiliness. She figured out what Zoran was, and shrewdly said the one thing that could buy her the chance to save herself."

"I told Miro that I didn't know why she was coming back," said Jacobo. "But—what did we have? Eighteen hours? As much as a day? Not nearly time enough to certify her story. I said, 'Let her get a few steps across the runway and have Molly bring her down. Blame it on the Frenchies. If the death of one more girl at the airport even makes a story.' "

"I asked Miro not to get dazzled and distracted by dreams of luring defectors and cracking secret cells," said Jackie. "I said, 'This is not one of your foggy British spy stories, full of mist and gray. This is Sarajevo. This girl has killed a lot of us already. You don't have to certify that. Let Molly bring down this spotted leopard and mark one up for our side.' "

Irena leaned over to Jacobo, who understood that she wanted a conspiratorial cigarette. "Tedic disagreed?" she asked, and Jackie smiled as she waited for Irena to draw her first breath from the Marlboro.

"You know Miro," she said into the haze of the cigarette smoke. "Miro was captivated. Miro was in love. Miro said she could have put five bullets into Zoran, emptied his pockets, and we would have blamed it on bandits. Miro thought she might give us something vital. Or that she had spectacular nerve. Either way, he wanted to take a chance on her."

"And so I'm here?"

"If she shows up at the airport," said Jacobo, "we show you."

"And then?"

Jackie tugged on her scarf. "Up to higher minds, dear."

"Molly in the hedges?"

"A possibility, I suppose. Let her get twenty yards across and make her a nice little news story. The Serb girl who dies running toward the outstretched arms of her old Muslim teammate."

Jackie flicked a last ash onto the floor and leaned down to squish out her cigarette. When she sat up, she held the smashed butt daintily in the palm of her hand, like a dried rose. "But Jacobo here reminded me: the airport is not some windblown West Bank settlement," she went on. "Anybody shot crossing the runway comes into the hands of the U.N. A lone girl running across to join a siege who gets brought down by a shot from the Bosnian side? I'm not sure we could explain that. Or blame it on the Frenchies. Of course, they might oblige us. That's how the Blue Helmets get their target practice—plinking desperate people trying to dash across the runway. But I'd say that if your friend makes it across—this yellow jacket in the Hornet's Nest—she's part of this family. Until higher minds decide we have to put her in our own trunk."

...

MEL BROUGHT IRENA a coarse old U.S. Army blanket and a pack of Marlboros to make her time in the room more comfortable. "What the fuck," he said. "Sit, lie down. Ashes on the floor, fine, what the fuck."

He closed the door. Irena declined to try to open it—she didn't want to learn if it had been locked. But when Mel returned within ten minutes, she looked up as she heard a bolt thrown from the other side. Mel was bearing a plate with four American soda crackers, four packets of grape jelly, a plastic bottle of water, and an ironstone mug of tea, the bag trailing a string that he had looped around the handle.

"You get hungry, you want more, what the fuck, let me know," he said.

"And how would I do that, Mel? Dial room service? Can't seem to find the phone. Stroll on down to the café? I seem to be rather sealed off from the world in here."

"Knock, what the fuck, I'll hear you," he said.

Irena had her snack and had stretched back on the blanket, rolling half of it around her, when she heard the lock slid back and looked up to see the door open on a man with an orange horse's tail of hair hanging over his shoulder.

"Molls!"

He had a magazine rolled in his meticulously kept right hand, and a fresh cup of tea in his left. "Sorry it's not something stronger, love. Later. Got to stay alert, both of us, for whatever."

Irena sat up against the wall and Molly sat just across from her, lotus style, pushing his knees into place. He had brought along *The Face* from November 1992, with Marky Mark on the cover.

"Don't know him," Molly said. "But a well-cut piece of stone, as we say."

"Rap star, Molls. Rock is a setting sun. Get with it."

Molly rocked forward slightly and seemed to keep his voice trained on the earthen floor.

"This ground will chill your gonads," he said. "Robben Island style."

"Just to keep an eye on me, they say," said Irena. "Until."

"Until. Say the word, love," Molly said quietly into the dirt. "I'll take you out of here. I protect the striker."

"I should stay. I did nothing wrong."

"Neither did Socrates. He could have used a mate like me."

"How long did Mandela stick it out on Robben Island?"

"About as long as you've been on the planet, I think. But you're supposed to be sprung as soon as your pal shows at the airport."

"And if she doesn't?"

Molly could only shrug. A shrug from a man sitting in the lotus position makes him rock slightly, like a duck waddling ashore.

"I've been running the play through my mind, Molls," Irena said. "If she doesn't show, it looks like I was used all along."

"It might."

"Jackie. The Mexican—whatever he is. They must worry if I'm a dupe—just a dupe—or a viper in our breasts. So to speak."

"They have to worry about everything."

"The locked but unguarded door. Mel coming in, playing housemaid. This could all be a setup, to see if I run. You, too, Molls."

"They only rent me, love. They haven't bought me."

Molly got to his feet, taking care not to step on Irena's blanket or, Irena convinced herself, stand and speak too close to the incessantly burning bulb.

"If you want a deck of cards, let Mel know," he said. "I have one. I'll be over. They've taught me some grand games here, where you can win points by bluffing."

IRENA HELD OUT *The Face* after Molly departed and unseen hands threw the bolt back into place. She looked over the cover photo of Marky Mark. It was black and white. Marky Mark was stripped to his waist and crouching into a sprinter's stance, which emphasized his shoulders nicely. The cover asked, "Is He the New Madonna?"

Omigosh, Irena thought, I was never meant to see this. There's already a new Madonna and I've scarcely heard of him.

IRENA WAS SLEEPING lightly when the door bolt came undone in her head. She looked up as she awakened. Jackie was in the doorway, tapping the right toe of her flats into the hard dirt floor, clasping both ends of her shawl against her throat, smoke snaking through her fingers and shimmering like a lace veil over her face.

"Sorry to disturb your slumber," she announced. "Your friend has just shown. At the airport. Informed sources—which is to say, the Norwegian Air Force mechanic we supply with magic mushrooms—say that a U.N. food plane is landing in thirty-two minutes. We expect her to try to cross behind it. I expect *you* do, too. Take a pee and rinse your hands, dear. The play has begun."

34.

WITHIN FIVE MINUTES, IRENA, JACKIE, JACOBO, AND MOLLY HAD jammed themselves into the congested confines of an old white brewery Lada, with the idea that any vehicle marked with the brewery's emblem was familiar to the Blue Helmets stationed near the airport and would draw no suspicion.

Molly drove with deliberate but unremarkable speed. Irena sat next to him. She was the tallest; the group had an investment in the soundness of her legs. Jackie squeezed herself into half of the small backseat. Jacobo, despite his status as guest and the group's elder eminence, had to put his head between his knees in the other half of the seat. Irena offered to hold his blazer on her lap, carefully folded and preserved from stress. Most of the ride was spent in apprehensive silence, until Irena noticed the deep green silk lining of Jacobo's blazer and ran her fingers over its smoothness.

"This is really lovely," she turned back to tell Jacobo.

"Thank you."

"British?"

"Italian."

"Show me, show me," Jackie demanded.

Irena turned up one of the lapels, lined in the same sumptuous green.

"That's really beautiful," said Jackie. "I wish I could have a dress in that material."

"I'll see to it myself," said Jacobo. "When all of this is over."

"Men make so many promises like that these days," Jackie sighed.

"Am I free or condemned?" Irena asked.

"Neither," Molly and Jacobo rushed to assure her in patently shocked tones.

"Both, of course," Jackie amended.

By the time Molly had steered the Lada to a halt outside the runway hedges, the group was fighting to subdue their laughter.

IRENA MADE A point of falling into step beside Molly and his rangy, veldt-stalking strides.

"You on your own here, Molls? I mean, utterly?"

Molly was already scouring the runway. With his slender neck rising and his red tail hanging, there was something as isolated and elegant as a giraffe in his impassiveness. "There's a lad inside the bushes, if that's what you mean," he said. "He has an M-14 oiled and ready. If that's what you mean."

"Just because?"

"Because we can never tell what may transpire," said Molly, finally turning around but speaking into Irena's shoulder. "We don't want to be caught without—whatever."

Irena brought her mouth over Molly's left shoulder. His horse's tail was freshly gathered into place with the red band from a beer-packing crate.

"Does she even get a chance, Molls?" she asked. "Or am I just the cube of cheese in your trap? Do you just wait until you can see her blond curls dancing and bring her down like the abandoned baby wildebeest—is *that* what you mean?"

"No such orders, love," he said evenly. "No such intentions."

"But then—" said Irena, "would you even tell me?"

Irena could hear Jacobo's extravagantly soled shoes grinding into the gravel and twigs just outside the hedges, and Jackie's voice going on about his silken green blazer lining as she parted a bough of branches to look out on the field.

"I don't know," said Molly. "It's just a suppose. As I say, no such orders."

JACKIE HAD IRENA step through a section of the hedges like a curtain. She had on her old gray West German army jacket from Grbavica, and her Air Jordans. When she heard Jackie's beautifully modulated urgings from behind—"Unzip it now, dear. Just give a tug"—she gave the zipper a yank and the jacket billowed and parted. Her red basketball jersey flapped below, snapping like a signal flag in the wind along the runway.

"I have a fix on your friend," Molly called out from the hedges. "*Our* friend."

Irena paced out steps, five to the right, five to the left, taking care that her red jersey was visible with each turn.

"Hair down. As you prophesied," Jackie called out next. "Damn blondes usually do."

Irena began to pace a longer tread, ten steps right, ten steps left, turning her trunk so that her red jersey shone from her knees to her neck.

"Bird to the east," Molly called out from his hedge after Irena had taken half a dozen such tours.

"What the hell does that mean?" she barked back. "Don't speak in song lyrics."

Molly's voice came through the branches and flutter of leaves with a laugh. "Plane coming in, love. To your right."

IT WAS A white-winged U.N. plane with a black beak and a silver belly, its whine rising as it rolled closer, almost sluggishly, on fat black wheels. Four or five Blue Helmets bobbed against the flat slice of orange sun sliding down toward the far end of the field. Irena could begin to make out the blue emblem on the tail of the plane, abstract fingers stretched across wreaths and stalks.

Amela had leaped out early. Irena, Jackie, Molly—they had all missed it. Irena saw her corn-silk curls flouncing above one of the tires; she seemed to be running in a crouch, with the same strolling pace as the plane.

Irena didn't shout out to Molly, Jackie, or the lad who had brought the rifle into the hedges. But when she froze in her treads, it was as good as painting an arrow from her gaze onto the field. To her left, Irena heard the heels of Blue Helmets begin to stamp and crackle across the runway. She saw Amela hunched behind the nearest tire. As the tire turned, Amela set herself into a fast-break crouch, and took a step to her left, then a quick, compact stride forward. She sprang up to run, and sawed off two, three strong steps and then fell forward. The plane rolled on. Amela lay still.

Irena could see a pale spill of curls sprawled across the ground. She shouted, "Bastards! Bastards!" into the hedges behind her and shot forward onto the field, her black-and-red shoes scoring and grazing the gravel, her shoulders floating and blood boiling in her ears.

...

IRENA FELL ONTO her knees above Amela. The left shoulder of Amela's jacket bulged with blood, dark as plum jam. Amela's head had come down on her chin—Irena could see the scraping—but she had turned her head to the side and was blinking dirt from her blue eyes to look up at Irena.

"Bastards! Bastards!" Irena hissed. She put a hand lightly over Amela's enormous wet blue eyes.

"It came from behind," said Amela. "My bastards."

Amela twisted around to look up at Irena, who had brought her hand gently against the curls cushioning her right cheek.

"They've been watching me," said Amela. "Yesterday, they captured me as soon as I crossed back. They said they already had my parents."

Amela gasped and squeezed her eyes shut, then seemed to will them open again. "I bargained. I told them what I knew about the play. I'm sorry. I figured what I was told must be wrong anyway. The man who whispered it to me—he was only trying to impress me. They said, 'Okay, Amela, if you're so sure, we'll put your own pretty little ass on that perch tonight.' "

Irena put her hand lightly against Amela's chin, as if she were touching a wound.

"They have been waiting. For a year." Amela blinked and took in a breath. "For an excuse. They forced themselves on me. Two at a time. They kept saying, 'So you want to be a Muslim girl.' "

Irena held Amela's face with both hands now, carefully, as if she were picking up a fragile old flower bowl. "Last night," she asked. "You were one of the shooters?"

"Three of us. Two to watch me. But I didn't shoot at anyone. You aim at a spot."

"I know."

"A spot, a target. I shot into a blue curtain."

"Three people died," said Irena.

"I'm sorry. So have my parents—I'm sure."

"So you made a bargain with those bastards for nothing."

Amela's legs twitched slightly. She looked down, startled to see her legs move without her so willing them. She clenched her eyes shut again. "Got me here," she said.

Irena rolled onto her knees and put one hand under Amela's chest, the other below her hips. She had just leaned back to lift Amela into her arms when a flat, sick thud struck her chest and began to soak her red jersey.

...

THE BLUE HELMETS, having overseen the safe passage of the U.N. plane from one end of the runway to the other, were fifty yards away and clomping quickly over the fine-gauge grit and gravel. But Jackie had leaped out first. She had kicked off her shoes and was tearing holes into her black hose and pulling her black jersey dress above her knees with her one good hand to race across the flat, scratchy field to beat the Frenchies to where the girls lay. Molly had thrown down his gun. He had vaulted through a break in the hedges and run over a bristly bush, and his knees were speckled with small green needles as he pumped his arms and legs across the field.

Two Frenchies, red-faced and huffing, faced Jackie across the girls' still bodies.

"Let us have them," she said in English—sharply, like a command.

"One is still breathing," said a pink young face from under a blue helmet. "We have to bring her to the hospital."

"*We'll* bring them to *our* hospital," said Jackie. "You have to pass through a Serb checkpoint. They will make you wait until she bleeds to death. You know that."

The young soldier looked down at the girls. Irena had fallen back with her right arm still under Amela's chest. They must have reminded the boy of two children scrambling in a sandbox.

"We didn't shoot them," he said.

"I know."

"We have orders."

Jacobo, his feathery shoes scuffing in the dust and grit, pulled up, puffing, just behind Jackie, who held the Frenchies back with a snap in her voice.

"They have died to be together. *Let them.*" The young soldier who had spoken turned around to look back at the rest of the runway. Five or six Blue Helmets were lashing down the wheels of the U.N. plane, and a couple had their rifles raised on alert while the plane's silver tail yawned open and bodies clambered on board for boxes and sacks. The young Frenchman turned back to Jackie, waggling the black snout of his rifle under her chin.

"Quick as you can," he said quietly. "Get them out of here."

The two soldiers turned their backs and brought their rifles up into their arms. Molly bent down and carefully unstuck Irena from her embrace and held her against his chest, trying to stanch the bleeding by clinching her body close. Jacobo put his arms under Amela from the other side and brought her body across his shoulders, her face slumbering on a soft blue Italian lapel. The men began to run off the field, Jackie trailing in her stocking feet. She heard a young voice behind her, one of the Blue Helmets calling over her quick, sharp footsteps.

"God give them peace," he said.

35.

SHE DROWSED AND DRIFTED IN AND OUT OF AWARENESS. SHE COULD remember people turning her onto her belly, finding veins in her arms, putting tubes inside her. She remembered the hot, sour breath of people speaking in hushed voices close to her head, lights blaring, lights doused, a night or more passing. She came around gradually. She began to feel itching just below the skin of her chest and shoulders. When she moved her head from side to side against a pillow, it felt as if sharp glass were being jostled inside. She finally raised herself onto her elbows.

She remembered that her clothes had been rolled off or cut away, and finally saw the scratchy, thin white smock that had been stretched over her front. She felt the urge to pee, and just feeling the urge sent her pee down a tube and gurgling into a red rubber bag. She swung her feet over the edge of the bed. She saw that the walls of the room were a stale yellow, like old butter. There was sun sieving in through a single small window to the left of the bed. She settled her bare toes onto the frayed orange carpet. She reached out to take hold of the piss tube as she lowered her feet. She thought she could feel the grit of cigarette ash and food crumbs. She felt suddenly thirsty. Her stomach cringed and yelped. She craved a cigarette. She bent over to look through the window to see the time of day, the street she was on, and whether there were clouds, and saw her face, with short, blunt brown hair, looking back.

She took halting, scuttling steps over to a door and pushed it open onto a blue hallway. There was a man in a white T-shirt and blue jeans drowsing in the flicker of a candlelight, a copy of *The Face* with Marky Mark crouching on the cover overturned on his knee.

"Hello. Excuse me" was all she could think to say. A strawberry-haired woman in blue jeans sprang down the hallway and into the small puddle of light.

"Hi," she announced. "I'm Zule Rasulavic. We've met. With your friend. I'm sure you don't remember."

"Sort of."

"Let's slip back inside." The woman draped her arm around the girl's waist.

"Why?"

"You've had an injury. You'll be fine, but we can't rush."

"Is this a hospital?"

"Yes."

"Can I go outside?"

"It's not safe."

"Nowhere is."

"You're sick."

"I have to throw up," she said. "I can feel it."

The woman held the girl's head against her hip as she emptied her stomach onto the floor—of blood, phlegm, and, she was certain, unsuccessfully digested little brown clumps of Olga Finci cheese.

ZULE RASULAVIC BLOTTED the girl's mouth and stretched a cool cloth across her forehead when she helped her back into bed. She brought her a small carton of apple juice—her first in more than a year; it tasted luxurious—a small stack of McVitie's biscuits, softening with age, and three foil packets of German peanut butter. Zule showed her how to squeeze the packet to expel the peanut butter into small, sticky logs across the biscuit.

There was the muffled rap of a knuckle against the door before it opened. A russet-haired woman in a trim black dress pushed in with her right shoulder, which was swathed in a bright red shawl.

"Hi," she said softly. "You may not remember me."

She paused. "Of course. Jackie."

Jackie smiled and flicked her shawl with her left arm until it reached her chin. She sat down on the edge of the bed.

"Beautiful Jackie," she added after a pause and the phrase had snapped back into her mind.

"Good as new," Jackie said with a smile, and placed her hand gently on her blanketed knees.

"Let me try to tell you what's happened," she said. She paused before going on, like the false start of a race. "Damn," she said, "but I promised not to smoke in here." She let the edge of the shawl slip back from her shoulder.

"THE FRENCHIES STOOD back and let us take you both away," she said at last. "We got you here to Franko Hospital. Your wound was not so great, but you had lost a lot of blood. The surgeons and nurses worked hard. They were moved—two young girls shot trying to save each other. For Irena—it was already too late. We never told them that you were a girl who might have used a surgeon for target practice in their parking lot. While you were drugged out, we clipped your hair and dyed it. If someone thought they saw the blonde—this ridiculousness about the Viper—you might not be safe. I didn't care. But we needed to speak with you."

"I'll tell you anything," said Amela after a while. She spoke in a small voice that was strained through her fingers, which were splayed like bony branches over her eyes. With the tube in her groin, she couldn't turn her back to Jackie. But she also didn't want to give Jackie's blunt, cold, large-caliber brown eyes a chance to bore into her.

"What secrets could you possibly reveal?" Through the thicket of her fingers, Amela could see Jackie's face hardening. "That people are trying to kill us? That there is some confidential plan to encircle and destroy us? Thanks, but we figured that out on our own. Your bullets were—most expressive."

"I want to be useful," said Amela. She was just beginning to grasp that she was still alive.

"You have been. To all the worst people."

"I can change that."

"By running across a field? We had to carry you for the last half, anyway. Don't think we all didn't feel that we should have just—"

Jackie had to stop and turn her face away. Amela sank back against the pillow. But, carefully, she moved her left hand over Jackie's, close enough to touch, but not touching.

JACKIE GAVE THREE short raps with her knuckles over her mouth, into the place where a cigarette might be. "Not that anything you say could impress me," she said. "But just for the exercise—why did you do it?"

"Come over?"

"No. Some of us have always thought this is the right side to put our asses, win or lose. Life or death. Muslim and Serb. Why were you on the other one?"

Amela's voice suddenly toughened. "I'm an athlete," she said simply, even strongly. "I play for whom I'm told."

Jackie turned her face toward one of the butter-colored walls. "And your conscience—" She threw the words at Amela.

"My *stomach,*" said Amela. "Conscience, principles, politics—not my game. But after a while my insides couldn't play along."

Jackie let Amela's hand linger above hers. She rearranged her knees to draw herself another inch away from her. "Tell me," she said. "Was it the tenth or the twentieth massacre that rumbled your intestines? Or did you just begin to miss all of your old Muslim pals whose cries you affected not to hear when they were being rousted and robbed in the apartments next door?"

Jackie smiled—she could feel her mouth widening, and made no effort to call it back—as Amela turned her face away and couldn't turn quite enough to submerge it in her pillow.

"DO YOU KNOW anything about my parents?" she asked after a silence.

Jackie's tone softened. "Zoran tried," she said. "He radioed someone. They tried. Your parents are probably—we cannot be fools about this—gone."

"The Zarics?"

"I spoke with them myself," said Jackie. "I—I loved her too, remember. They have always suspected more than they let on. I told them that if Sarajevo survives, their daughter's name will be inscribed in plaques, stones, and folk songs."

"That must have been a comfort," said Amela, who had turned her face around.

"Of course not. But they seemed . . . touched."

"God, I hate war," Amela declared. She put her hands below her shoulders and brought herself up against her pillow. "Hate it, hate it, *hate it.* What a waste of lives. A waste of the world. The West can afford war. They add it to the cost of gas. But for us—it's throwing diamonds into a ditch. It's throwing *babies* into a ditch, for all the good it's ever done."

"That's a good way of putting it," said Jackie slowly. She plainly missed her cigarettes. She cinched the ends of her shawl around her neck again, and let them drop back. She drummed her fingers discordantly against one thigh.

"That's the poet's way," she added, with apparent admiration. Then her voice hardened. *"The poet's way out."*

Jackie flicked her legs and stood up from the edge of bed, as if it had been suddenly electrified. "War is savage—say that. You'll always have a poem. Say it's repulsive. You'll never be wrong. But do you really think the world would be sweeter today if the Greeks had decided that their civilization was too refined to defend by blood and had surrendered Athens? Do you figure the world would be more just if Joan had stayed in her father's fields and never drawn her sword at Orléans? Maybe Tito should have let Hitler's gray wolves feast on Yugoslavia—instead of fighting them cave by cave. Maybe the British should have said, 'Sorry, our pluck's run out,' and lain back to let Hitler dance his giggling little goose step round Piccadilly. That's how the Frenchies spared their lovely Paris, you know. They gave storm troopers the keys to the city, then served up their Jews."

Jackie bent down until the splayed ends of her hair almost lashed against Amela's cheeks, and her whisper blew fiercely across her eyes. "And do you really think," she asked, "that Eichmann wouldn't have made room for *our kind* in Auschwitz after he had swept aside the ashes of all the kikes, Polacks, cripples, and fairies?"

Jackie stood back on her heels. But for the first time she let her hand stray over Amela's knees, and pressed down lightly. "You and I have grown up free to try on any idea we please," she said in a level tone. "Like hats in a store mirror. Ban the bomb! Viva Che! Smash the state! Save the planet! Peace, love, rock, rasta, techno, macro, Jimi Hendrix, and rap. But don't think our freedom wasn't bought by bloodshed. Ask the people of Prijedor or Vukovar about the kind of peace they parleyed with bullies. Or can you hear them from under the dirt of their mass graves? War is no good. Of course. War is cruel and wasteful. But sometimes—it's better than letting brutes keep their grip on the world."

Jackie turned around so that—quite deliberately and dramatically, Amela was sure—her stump showed when she tugged her shawl back around her shoulders.

"Your war is over," she announced. "We will let you heal. We'll give you the chance to make a confession, if that's what you want, and hear out your self-pity. Maybe there's some small something that you can tell us that we don't already know. After you've unburdened yourself, we'll keep you in the brewery. Under our eyes. Under our thumbs. Cloistered as a nun. These days, more cloistered than most nuns. Days might come when we need to ask you this and that. But not many. The kind of information you have has a short life. Our only desire—our plan—is that you be forgotten."

Amela felt Jackie's hand press more conspicuously down on her knee. She wondered—she couldn't tell from the force of her fingers—if she meant to reassure or warn her.

"You will become the one person in Sarajevo," she said finally, "with the chance to die from boredom."

When Jackie lifted up her hand, Amela risked a smile. "Isn't that a waste of my talent?" she asked.

"War is," Jackie answered.

36.

AMELA LAY AROUND THE HOSPITAL FOR ABOUT SIX WEEKS. BUT IT was hard to figure the toll of time. Entire days were spent drowsing, between painkillers and the tedium that Jackie had prescribed. She read old magazines. She had no radio. She played cards, both solitaire and hands of rummy with Nurse Rasulavic and the tall, horse-maned man she had met at the brewery. On orders, they spoke only of cards. Amela found their determination odd, and a little hard to accept. But Jackie had instructed Irena's old friends that this hornet from the nest was not to be confronted until her head, heart, bones, bowels, and guts had been squeezed of every iota and grain of knowledge she might ever have possessed.

The man named Jacobo came by almost every day. Nurse Rasulavic had told her that he was the one who had carried her away from the runway, and that some of her blood had dripped over his hands and onto the buttery leather of his shoes. She told him what she could recall of the Hornet's Nest. He cast questions casually back, as if he were encouraging her to recollect an old basketball game, which Amela knew she was good at doing. Jacobo's questions grew detailed and precise. But Jackie was right. With each week—probably each day—whatever information Amela possessed became dated, difficult to recognize, much less apply.

One day Amela took pains to stop him as he left the room.

"I have to thank you," she said.

Jacobo made a show of ignorance.

"You carried me," she explained. "They told me. I ruined your shoes."

Jacobo smiled, and ran a smooth thumb over one of his blazer's lustrous brass buttons. "Oh, that. Well. Blood wipes away," he said, and let the door close behind him. Amela crawled from her bed and sat with her back in the corner by the small window. She hugged her knees to her face and cried herself out in about half an hour. (All the crying left a dampness in the knee of her jeans. She thought to herself, *And tears dry, too.*)

JACKIE CAME BY three times. She brought magazines, she brought beer and cigarettes, and she brought clothes. Amela thought there were times when Jackie seemed almost to like her, and times when she seemed to just barely abide her. It was Jackie who told Amela that Michael Jordan's father had been killed, slain somewhere in the southern United States in the expensive car that his son had bought for him.

"It doesn't matter if you have all the money in the world," Amela observed. "And *he* does. You can't buy your way out of death." Amela beamed the kind of mild, wistful smile over at Jackie that invited her to join in.

But Jackie—Jackie snapped back, "Don't be ridiculous. People buy lives all the time. Someone like you should know that."

"I was just . . ." Amela let her thought die.

Her door was not locked. She couldn't see any locks on the front and side doors. One afternoon she carefully tried to extract a sign from Jackie to see if they had counted on her to stay without defiance—or hoped that she would try to break away.

"Some people thought you should be locked in," Jackie told her. "Even chained to this bed. But men with guns—we can't spare them just to sit around. Besides, where would you go? What would you do? The whole city is a jail cell. Run, if you like. It doesn't matter. Really, how long would you last?"

EARLY ONE EVENING Jackie came bustling into Amela's room unexpectedly—silent and unsmiling but bearing a roll of clothing under her arm. Amela sat up. Jackie shook out her bundle. Blue jeans rolled out. A roll of dark blue socks bounced to the floor. Atop all was a yellow T-shirt, streaked with violet. Jackie lifted the shirt by the collar and turned it toward Amela.

"Omigod," she said, recognizing the number on the back: "Vlade Divac."

"Amazing, isn't it?" said Jackie. "A Los Angeles Lakers shirt you could probably sell on the black market here for a month of razor blades or toothpaste. It arrived as a rag in a charity bundle from someplace like Pasadena or Brooklyn. As you said, the West's rubbish becomes spoils of our war. I have appropriated this item in the larger interests of the state."

Amela and Jackie smiled at the same time, and laughed as they realized it.

"We have a bag packed and waiting for you, dear. Have a pee and put on your new shirt. We have places to go."

ZORAN WAS WAITING with his taxi in the parking lot. Amela held back a bit—Jackie could see her cringing—at seeing Zoran in the lot that was customarily kept empty since Dr. Despres's death.

"The last time I saw you," Zoran said with theatrical, great-uncle grouchiness, "you had a gun at my head and were stuffing me into the trunk of my car. My own fucking car."

"I'm so sorry," Amela said softly.

"So you said. And so I believed. Once I got out and could fucking breathe."

Amela had a pack slung over her left shoulder. It hung over the wound in her back, which was no longer dressed and bandaged. She rapped the trunk with her right hand. "In here with me, then?" she said. "I have it coming."

She sat in the front with Zoran. He told her how Tedic had paid the thieves who rescued him from his own trunk with cases of beer and cartons of cigarettes. "Six cases of Sarajevo Beer," he said wonderingly. "Twenty cartons of Drina cigarettes. Old ones, even. Not the new ones they fill with stinkweed they were going to foist off on the Bulgarians and roll up in pages from our old phone books, which are fit only to be toilet paper, anyway. And ten cartons of Marlboros. I said, 'Miro, you must value me, to let go of ten cartons of Marlboros in exchange for my life.' And Tedic said, 'We need your car.' "

They came to a flat stretch along the hedges near the runway, and then Zoran drove on another minute and pulled up to what looked like an old airport equipment shed. The walls were made of thin tin, and were stippled with holes. Rifle shots and mortar spatters, to be sure, but also age and rust.

They went into the shed. Half a dozen soldiers in authentic Bosnian Army–issue moss-green uniforms were smoking, standing at ease but alert, around a hole in the ground. A single gas lantern hissed in the corner, spilling light over the hole. The room smelled of coffee, sweat, earth, rain, cigarettes, and grease.

Jackie took Amela's hand into her own and led her into a corner with three overturned washtubs. They sat on two of them. Jackie kept a grip on

Amela's hand. "Jacobo has given you a name," she began. "Personally. For our purposes. *Amie.* It means "friend" in French. You were a friend—a good friend, if I never said that. But Jacobo says it also means something in his language. *Ami* means "our people." He says—and I think he is right—that this is a good name for you."

Amela heard the lantern popping and sizzling. She had to blink a mist of smoke and cinders from her eyes. Jackie relaxed her hand on Amela's, then laced her fingers through the girl's.

"Perhaps you heard rumors," Jackie said. "Well, it's true. We have built a tunnel under the airport. From besieged Sarajevo into a small speck of free Bosnian territory. That's the tunnel right in front of us. It took miners, plumbers, and engineering professors six months to claw it out of the ground with shovels, kitchen spoons, and hand axes—and their bare hands. People digging toward us from the forests used planks and tree branches to hold back the earth. People digging from the city had to use old car doors and hoods because we've chopped down all the trees here. I don't think anyone has ever had to build a tunnel quite like this: blind, in the dark, two ends scratching and bumbling toward each other. Men and women died running across the runway to tell the other team that they had dug a few more inches. Sometimes two, three people died just to say, 'Another two feet today—here's where we stopped.' I can't tell you how many times the tunnel flooded . . . the oil lights went out . . . people . . ."

Jackie's voice ran out. She had to turn away.

"But today," she went on, "it's the London Underground down there. We run a twenty-four-hour transport service. We bring out some of the sick and wounded in small wooden carts on narrow steel rails. We bring in bandages, bullets, onions, and antibiotics. Smugglers bring in meat, cheese, rubbers, hash—God knows, we don't ask. We're all happy capitalists now."

Jackie sat up on the washtub and held Amela's hand between them, against their chests.

"Amie, we have opened a vein into the heart of the city. The Serbs can't bomb it, and the Blue Helmets can't shut it down. Many more people will suffer and die here, I'm sure. But, for the first time, I think Sarajevo has a chance to live. *To live.*"

Amela dropped her forehead against her and Jackie's entwined hands and fingers.

"We can bring you out through this tunnel," said Jackie, just above the hiss of the light. "It's eight hundred yards long, and you'll have to crawl for every inch of it—it's not even four feet high. But we can bring you out, put you on a truck, and get you near Bihac."

Bihac, Amela remembered. Where Irena's brother and other Bosnians were trying to get to from London, Chicago, Manchester, Cleveland, Detroit, and Toronto.

"A girl as good as you," said Jackie softly into her shoulder, "can do a lot of damage—a lot of good—in a place like that."

THEY STOOD IN the lantern light just in front of the tunnel. Amela had her pack over her left shoulder, puffy with a spare set of blue jeans, socks, panties, and a black T-shirt, three packs of tampons, a box of bullets, a toothbrush, and a small, round bar of French carnation-scented soap that Jackie said Jacobo had sent along personally. Zoran settled a rifle over the shoulder of her right arm.

Jackie took hold of Amela's right shoulder and left a light kiss on her neck, just above the leather gun strap. "Amie," she said softly. "I promise you, Amie, at the end there is a sign that would make you and your friend smile."

Two soldiers lifted her by the arms, like a child being swung between her parents, into the top hole of the tunnel.

AMELA BLINKED. HER first impression was that the underworld blazed with light. Every few feet a small oil fire flickered and flared from inside a tin can. The throttled smoke left black ghosts scorched on the top of the tunnel. The smoldering oil singed Amela's nostrils.

She began to crawl. Water covered her feet and knees, her wrists and hands. After about a hundred yards, the tunnel deepened inexplicably—one of the diggers must have hit an electric cable, a pipe, or a pocket of water—and when Amela unsuspectingly crawled forward she lurched into a swell of cold brown water that rose over her elbows and splashed against her chin. It tasted of rust and worms. Occasionally, a shell crashed overhead and shook the tunnel. The walls shivered and the earth bled more water over the tunnel floor.

She crawled into the wall at the end. Fresh red bricks and a large, silvery electric bulb, blaring light. A couple of spikes of torchlight played over her eyes and chin.

"Amie?" A young man's voice called out.

"I am. I'm here," Amela called up into the lights.

"Reach for the sky, darling, and we'll bring you up."

Four arms reached down and waggled like spider's legs. She handed up her rifle. Then the pack on her back, sodden with water and heavy as a bag of nails. Amela finally held up her own arms and was hoisted up into a dark room by two curly-haired men wearing blue jeans and red T-shirts under unzipped light black jackets. One man's shirt said MANCHESTER UNITED, the other CHICAGO BULLS.

"Nice shirt, Amie," said one. "Vlade, he is the greatest. You are an athlete, too, Amie?"

"I was."

"Slithering through that tunnel is not for grandmas," he said. "You are still a great player."

"We have been waiting for you," said the other man. "You do not need two more made-up names to remember for people you will never see again. We will walk with you up into the mountains tonight, and meet a truck that will take you—wherever."

When Amela could look around, she saw that she had climbed up into a small room of a private home. The men led her into the next room, where three men were sprawled on a brown sofa. A television had been wired into a car battery, and they were watching a football match between Milan AC and Ajax Amsterdam. One of Amela's escorts shined his light on an old woman with a black scarf folded over her head. She was sitting on a stool, and holding out a glass of water.

"Hey, Amie, this is Grandma Sida," he explained. "It is her home. She is the grandmother here. She greets everyone, and goes back to her television."

Amela nodded and wordlessly took the glass from Grandma Sida's hand. She took one gulp, then another, a deeper swallow. She tasted mud in her mouth, then gulped twice more to try to wash away the taste of the tunnel. She handed the glass back to the old woman and leaned down to kiss the back of her hand.

Amela and the men walked out of the house and into a field. The runway lights had been turned out hours ago, before starlight lifted up the overgrown green and yellow grasses that rustled lightly, like soft, sleeping breaths.

"Hey, Amie," said one of her companions. "Jackie said to show you this."

He shined a light onto a small white sign that had been nailed on a stick and planted in Grandma Sida's backyard. The sign read:

PARIS 3765 KM

Amela laughed out loud for the first time, her first girlish giggle since Irena had last made her laugh.

"Jackie said she wanted to make you laugh," said the man with the light. He began to shake with laughter himself, so that the sign seemed to blink off and on.

"Hey, Amie. Are you going to Paris? Take me with you."

Amela looked across the swells of grass and into the stony blue shoulders of Mount Igman. She would walk over the fields and the hills to the other side of the mountain, and find the ride that would take her to Bihac, and the place in which, she was suddenly quite certain, she was going to give her life.

You may keep Sarajevo. You have earned it.

—SLOBODAN MILOSEVIC, PRESIDENT OF SERBIA,
TO ALIJA IZETBEGOVIC, PRESIDENT OF BOSNIA,
AT THE 1995 TALKS IN DAYTON, OHIO, THAT DIVIDED BOSNIA.

Milosevic is now on trial for war crimes.

ACKNOWLEDGMENTS

I am grateful to so many who offered their counsel, cautions, and recollections:

Dr. Wesley Bayles of the Georgetown Veterinary Hospital; Peter Breslow of NPR News; the staff of the Periodical Research Centre of the British Museum; Hamo Cimic of Sarajevo; Chief Terrance W. Gainer of the U.S. Capitol Police; Tom Gjelten of NPR News; Laura Hillenbrand; the staff of the photo archives of London's Imperial War Museum; Lika Job; Avi Kotkowsky of El Paso, Texas; the Lincoln Park Zoo; Elvis Mitchell; Julia Mitric, now of Sacramento; Lawrence K. Morgan of the U.S. Capitol Police; Dr. Lee Morgan of the Georgetown Veterinary Hospital; Jim Naydar; Dika Redzic of Sarajevo; Edouard Richard (my father-in-law); Dr. Pam Schraeger of the Friendship Hospital for Animals; Matthew Scully; Jerry Smith of the U.S. Capitol Police; Dr. Stanley Tempchin; Alphonse Vinh of NPR; Dr. Ronald Warren of Massachusetts General Hospital; Rabbi Daniel Zemel of Temple Micah; and Fahrudin Zilkic, who will one day write his own book about the years he devoted to defending his remarkable city.

Any mistakes are mine alone.

Lily Linton made it possible for much of this volume to be written under the gaze of Picasso's goat. This is the third book I have produced under the watchful goad of Kee Malesky, who could improve the text on a cereal box.

I have tried to contain this story within the timeline and confines of real-life events. But this is a novel, not a history or journalism. I have invented a few streets and buildings. I have also permitted myself to put words in the mouths of a few real personages, including Radovan Karadzic and Osama Bin Laden. However, their remarks are based on statements they made before much of the world paid notice.

Suada Kapic presides over a remarkable enterprise in Sarajevo called FAMA, which works to preserve the history of the longest siege of the twentieth century and keep those lessons vital. In a world beset by urgent causes, I hope that at least some readers might be moved to offer FAMA support to continue its work.

My time as a reporter in Sarajevo was spent in partnership with my longtime recording engineer and friend Manoli Wetherell. Sarajevo deepened our friendship. No doubt many of the feelings that I brought to this book began in her durable heart.

The Millic and Tedic families of Sarajevo took us into their homes and hearts in 1993 and 1994. This book, whatever else it might be, is a small repayment for their kindness and courage.

I talked over many of the themes in this story in the spring of 2003 with my friend Elizabeth Neufer of the *Boston Globe,* on a long, daunting ride from Amman to Baghdad. Elizabeth did not make it home. The human-rights reporting she helped to advance lives on in her influence as a journalist and friend to so many.

I owe Jonathan Lazear abiding thanks for believing in this book and bringing it to the best publisher in America, Dan Menaker at Random House. Stephanie Higgs put extraordinary work and care into the manuscript.

Many of the characters in this story voice contempt for the role of the United Nations in Bosnia. I share that disdain. But I do not forget (and Sarajevans don't) that 166 French, British, Canadian, and other U.N. soldiers lost their lives in Bosnia between 1992 and 1996. Their sacrifice is also part of Sarajevo's legacy.

I had intended that the thanks I owe my wife, Caroline Richard Simon, be embodied in the book's dedication (we had missed meeting in 1993—it's a long story—because I was in Sarajevo). But Caroline came to feel so deeply about the city and its people that she insisted the dedication be to them—a request that bears out her brilliant sensitivity in all things. Caroline named almost every character in this story. I cannot put an adequate name on the love I hold for her.

We pray that our new daughter, Elise Sylvie Simon, will grow up in a world swept clean of the menace that destroyed so many in Bosnia. But we would feel blessed to have a child who faces up to his or her human responsibilities with the courage and poise of Sarajevans.

The city is smaller and grimmer today. The wounds of war are raw.

But, despite its losses, Sarajevo remains an outpost of diversity, civility, culture, and even joy. Its struggle was costly, valuable, brave, and just.

SSS
London
October 2004

PHOTO: © WILL O'LEARY

SCOTT SIMON is the host of NPR's *Weekend Edition with Scott Simon*. He has covered ten wars, from El Salvador to Iraq, and has won every major award in broadcasting, including the Peabody and the Emmy. He has hosted many public television programs, and is a frequent essayist for newspapers and television. His memoir, *Home and Away*, rose to the top of the *Los Angeles Times* nonfiction bestseller list. His following book, *Jackie Robinson and the Integration of Baseball*, was named a Barnes & Noble Sports Book of the Year. He lives with his wife, Caroline, and their daughter, Elise.

ABOUT THE TYPE

This book is set in Fournier, a typeface named for Pierre Simon Fournier, the youngest son of a French printing family. He started out engraving woodblocks and large capitals, then moved on to fonts of type. In 1736 he began his own foundry and made several important contributions in the field of type design; he is said to have cut 147 alphabets of his own creation. Fournier is probably best remembered as the designer of St. Augustine Ordinaire, a face that served as the model for Monotype's Fournier, which was released in 1925.

[illegible]

[illegible]
[illegible]
[illegible]
[illegible]
[illegible]
[illegible]
[illegible]
[illegible]